Reese Ryan wr... ...with captivating family ...osse ...omplex charac...

Midwesterner with deep Southern roots, Reese ...rently resides in semi-small-town North Carolina, ...ere she's an avid reader, a music junkie and a self-...clared connoisseur of cheesy grits. Reese is the author ...the Bourbon Brothers and Pleasure Cove series.

...nnect with her via Instagram, Facebook, Twitter or at ...seryan.com

...n her VIP Readers Lounge at bit.ly/VIPReadersLounge.

...anne Rock credits her decision to write romance ...er a book she picked up during a flight delay ...rossed her so thoroughly that she didn't mind at all ...en her flight was delayed two more times. Giving her ...ders the chance to escape into another world has ...tivated her to write over eighty books for a variety of ...lls & Boon series.

SECRET HEIR SEDUCTION

REESE RYAN

HEARTBREAKER

JOANNE ROCK

This book is produced from independently certified
paper to ensure responsible forest management.

For more information visit: www.harpercollins.co.uk/green

Printed and bound in Spain
by CPI, Barcelona

MILLS & BOON

First Published in Great Britain 2020
by Mills & Boon, an imprint of HarperCollinsPublishers,
1 London Bridge Street, London, SE1 9GF

Secret Heir Seduction © 2020 Harlequin Books S.A.
Heartbreaker © 2020 Joanne Rock

Special thanks and acknowledgement are given to Reese Ryan for her contribution to the *Texas Cattleman's Club: Inheritance* series.

ISBN: 978-0-263-27916-0

0320

MIX

SECRET HEIR
SEDUCTION

REESE RYAN

To the amazing readers who read and recommend my books, especially the members of the Reese Ryan VIP Readers Lounge, y'all rock. I'm grateful you've chosen to come along for the ride.

To Kristan Higgins, LaQuette, Megan Frampton, Robin Covington, Lauren Dane, Cheris Hodges, Michelle Styles, Piper Huguley, Patricia W. Fischer, Naima Simone, HelenKay Dimon and all of my fellow authors who've read and shared my books… thank you from the bottom of my heart for your kindness and generosity.

One

Darius Taylor-Pratt sat in front of a heavy mahogany desk and surveyed the space around him.

The room's dark decor seemed better suited to an older man than to upbeat lifestyle guru and reality TV star Miranda Dupree.

Miranda, founder of the Goddess health and lifestyle brand, had invited him to Royal, Texas, for a meeting. She'd proposed a collaboration with Thr3d, his quickly growing performance wear company, to create a Goddess-branded line of athletic wear.

The timing was terrible.

His team was preparing for their first LA Fashion Week runway show. Still, this deal could catapult Thr3d to the next level. So he hadn't been able to board the plane she'd sent for him quickly enough.

Heavy footsteps approached. Too heavy to be the five-foot-three, redheaded sprite. Miranda probably weighed less than a buck twenty-five.

A man with a messy shock of brown hair, brown eyes and a five o'clock shadow entered the room.

"Hello, Darius. I'm Kace LeBlanc." The man extended his hand. "Attorney."

Darius regarded him warily as he stood to shake his hand. "Don't lawyers typically get involved *after* an agreement has been reached?"

Kace thumbed through papers in a folder already on the desk. "In a business deal, yes. But I'm not Miranda's lawyer."

"Then whose attorney are you, Mr. LeBlanc?" Darius's shoulders tensed.

"I represent the estate of Mr. Buckley Blackwood, recently deceased. The estate which he left to his ex-wife, Miranda Dupree Blackwood."

"How nice for her."

That explains the furniture, but not why he's here.

Darius returned to his seat and glanced at his black-and-gold Tissot chronograph watch before meeting the man's gaze again. "Will it be much longer before Miranda joins us?"

"I apologize for the subterfuge in bringing you here. But you've been summoned to meet with me about a completely different matter."

"Miranda has no interest in partnering with my company?" When the man didn't respond, Darius shot to his feet. "Look, I don't know what this is about, but I'm a busy man. I don't have time for your little shell game."

"I assure you, you'll want to hear what I have to say," the man said calmly. "I only need ten minutes of your time. When I'm done, if you'd still like to head straight back to LA, the driver will take you to a fueled and ready plane."

Darius set his stopwatch. "You've got exactly ten minutes." He sank onto the chair. "Why am I here?"

"Does the name Buckley Blackwood mean anything to you?"

Darius shrugged. "I know he's Miranda's ex-husband, and that he owned a bank."

"Plus this six-hundred-acre ranch, homes around the globe and investments in a variety of other business interests, like Thr3d."

"You're saying he invested in my company?" *Impossible.* He knew the names of every investor. Buckley Blackwood wasn't one of them.

"He invested in Thr3d using a shell company."

"That still doesn't explain why I'm here." Darius's patience was wearing thin.

"You're here for a private reading of Buck's will." The man tapped the document in front of him.

"Why would an investor include me in his will?"

"Buck was more than just an investor, Darius. He was… your father."

The room became eerily quiet. The only sound was the ticking of the grandfather clock on the wall behind him.

Darius stared at the man a few moments longer, sure someone would pop through the door and declare that this was a prank.

"Look, Mr. LeBlanc—"

"Kace."

"Kace…there must be some mix-up. You've got the wrong guy."

"You're Darius Taylor-Pratt, son of former actress Liberty Taylor. Adopted by your stepfather, William Pratt, at the age of two. You're thirty years old, and you received your undergrad at—"

"All right." Darius held up a hand. He wanted Kace to stop talking long enough for him to wrap his head around what was happening. He sucked in a deep breath and tried to slow his rocketing heart rate. "You're saying that this guy, this…"

"Buckley Blackwood."

"…and my mother…they were *together* at some point."

"Yes."

"He knew I was his son. Yet, he never so much as called or dropped a birthday card in the mail in thirty years." Anger slowly crept up his spine. "Why? Was he ashamed that he'd fathered a son by a black woman?"

"No," Kace responded emphatically. "That wasn't it at all."

"Then what was it *exactly*?" Darius seethed, unconvinced.

"You were the product of an affair during his first marriage. That's why he thought it best to care for you from a distance. When you were two, and your mother married Mr. Pratt, Buck agreed to allow him to adopt you and raise you as his son. You were to be informed of the adoption once you turned eighteen, which I assume you were."

Darius gripped the armrest without response, his head pounding and his muscles tense.

He'd been told that Will wasn't his biological father. But his mother wouldn't reveal his father's identity beyond saying he was a wealthy man who didn't want to "complicate" his life.

"Darius," the man said, "I realize this must come as a shock to you, but—"

"That's the understatement of the year, Mr. LeBlanc." He gritted the words through clenched teeth.

"Just Kace is fine," the man insisted.

Darius was beginning to hate Kace's sympathetic expression. It felt a lot like condescension and pity.

"The old man is dead, so I'm obviously not here for a father-son reunion." The declaration made him sound like a heartless ass, but Buckley Blackwood had shown him the same callous disregard. "And you could've conducted the reading of the will via video conference. So why the hell am I really here?"

"I'll allow Buck to explain for himself." Kace read the final will and testament of Buckley Blackwood. The more he read, the more agitated Darius became.

Buckley Blackwood was a coward and an asshole.

Too cowardly to claim him as his son while he was alive. And the kind of jerk who left everything to his pretty, young ex-wife while leaving nothing to his children. And just for shits and giggles, Darius was being asked to take a DNA test to prove he was Buck's son.

"Any questions?" Kace put down the will and clasped

his hands on the desk. The man seemed braced for a verbal assault.

"What's the point of a DNA test? The man's dead, and it's not as if I'm in line to inherit anything."

"You have three siblings." Kace laid out the photos individually. "Kellan, Vaughn and Sophie."

Darius's mouth went dry, and he couldn't speak. He wanted to shove the photos onto the floor and call bullshit on this entire charade.

But he couldn't.

Darius picked up each photo and studied it.

His brown skin was darker than theirs, but they shared many facial features.

His nose, chin and cheekbones were similar to theirs, and he and Sophie had the same rich brown eyes.

An unexpected sense of belonging washed over him, like a wave at high tide, with the power to knock him off his feet. He swallowed hard, returning each photo to the mahogany desk.

"Do they know about me?"

"They learned of you after their father's death."

"Does anyone else know?"

"So far, just the family," Kace said.

"Good. Let's keep it that way." A knot tightened in his gut. The same one he'd developed when he'd gone to school with wealthy kids who'd treated him like an undeserving outsider.

He'd learned to relish that status. Had incorporated it into the Thr3d brand. But he wasn't keen on experiencing that kind of painful rejection again. Especially not from people with whom he shared DNA.

Darius wanted to walk out. Refuse to play along with the old man's sick game. But a part of him *needed* answers. And this was the only way he'd finally get them.

"I'll take the test."

"They're expecting you at Royal Memorial Hospital." Kace slid a sheet of paper across the desk, then closed the folder. "As for the estate…from what I've learned about you, you've always been a fighter. Two of your siblings are contesting the will. I'm certainly not encouraging you to do so, but—"

"It is an option." Darius rubbed his jaw.

Kace gave him a subtle nod. "I'll be in touch when I get the DNA results. In the meantime, someone else would like to speak with you. Should I send her in?"

Darius nodded absently, not really listening. He pulled his phone from his pocket once the door clicked shut behind Kace. He needed to tell his mother and stepfather he finally knew the truth about his paternity. But they were on vacation. And this wasn't the kind of conversation they should have over the phone while they were an ocean away. He'd wait until they returned from Europe and talk to them in person.

His relationship with them had been strained since he'd learned that Will wasn't his biological father. He could've forgiven that lie. Maybe even understood it. But when his mother refused to reveal the identity of his father, Darius had been furious.

Now he knew the truth.

He was the son of some rich asshole who hadn't wanted him when he was alive but felt the need to alleviate his conscience on his deathbed.

The door opened suddenly, startling him.

"Hello, Darius. It's a pleasure to finally meet you." Miranda Dupree extended a hand.

He scrambled to his feet and shook her hand. She was nearly a foot shorter than him. "Pleasure to meet you, Ms. Dupree."

"Call me Miranda, and please, have a seat." She settled onto the chair beside him. "I apologize for not being direct about why I invited you here." She sifted her fingers through her wavy red hair. Her sparkling, deep blue eyes seemed sincere. "But I didn't think you'd come if I'd told you the truth."

True.

But that didn't earn her a pass for lying to him.

"So the collaboration was just a ruse?"

"I prefer to think of it as bait." Miranda smiled sweetly. "What I said about wanting to create a signature clothing line…that's absolutely true. I'd like to revisit the topic once all of this is sorted out."

He acknowledged her statement with a slight nod. But his head still swirled with the news of his paternity.

So much for those fantasies of a reunion with my long-lost father.

"Darius…" Miranda placed a gentle hand on his forearm. "I can only imagine what you must be feeling."

"Then I'll tell you." He glared at her. "I feel like I'm being manipulated. By you. By that lawyer. And by a gutless old man who never gave a damn about me when he was alive but wants to play God with my life now that he's dead."

Miranda seemed willing to absorb his anger, her gaze still warm and sincere. "If I was in your shoes, I'd probably feel the same. But there's something you need to see."

Miranda retrieved a thick envelope from the desk and sat beside him again.

"Buck and I hadn't spoken much since our divorce. So I was as shocked as anyone that he charged me with handling some very sensitive matters after his death. I've received more instructions via letters over the past few months. Yes, the man could be an asshole." She laughed bitterly. "But one of his deepest regrets was never getting to know you. He implored me to bring you here, so you'd have the opportunity to get to know your brothers and sister. And he

wanted you to know that, regardless of what you might believe, you were never far from his thoughts."

"He had a damn funny way of showing it."

"Buck struggled to show affection with everyone. It destroyed both of his marriages. And it's the reason his relationships with his children were strained. The reason he
died alone." She frowned. "But it doesn't mean he didn't
care about you."

Miranda handed him the envelope. "Buck wanted you
to have this…to know that even though you were apart, he
always held you in his heart."

She stood. "I'll leave you alone with it. You can review it
here for now. Once the DNA results have been confirmed,
it's yours to keep. When you're ready, my driver will take
you anywhere you'd like to go. I've reserved a furnished
rental home in town for you. It's yours for as long as you
need it."

Miranda handed him two business cards. "If you need
me or Kace, just give us a call. I'll be in touch."

Once Miranda was gone, he opened the envelope. It
held a scrapbook overflowing with photos and newspaper
articles. On the first page, there was a photo of a newborn
he recognized as himself. A duplicate was in his mother's
prized photo album.

Darius made his way through the scrapbook one aged
photo, yellowed newspaper clipping and dog-eared magazine article at a time.

The man had been following his childhood, his academic
career and his business triumphs. Yet, he hadn't reached
out to him once in thirty years.

What am I supposed to feel for a man like that?

Darius dropped the scrapbook onto the desk, slipped
his Prada shades back on and met Miranda's driver, Leslie, at the car.

"Where shall I take you, sir?" She opened the door. "Back to the airport or to your rental home?"

Darius slid into the back seat. "Neither. Take me someplace I can get a decent hamburger, fries and shake, please."

He wasn't sure what he'd do next. He only knew that he thought better on a full stomach, and he longed for the comfort of carbs while he plotted his next move.

Two

Darius stepped inside the quaint little Royal Diner. The place looked like a throwback from the fifties, with its red faux-leather booths and black-and-white checkerboard linoleum tile floor.

He ordered a mile-high bacon cheeseburger, wedge fries and a thick, handmade strawberry shake. The same meal he'd ordered when his mother and Will would take him out to eat after a big win or a devastating loss.

It was still his go-to meal for either.

And today he found himself thinking of his mother and stepfather more than he had in months.

He was furious that his mother hadn't told him Buckley Blackwood was his biological father. But part of him missed the great hugs his mom gave whenever he'd had a bad day. And the corny jokes Will would tell to lift his spirits.

But then, they hadn't distanced themselves from him. He'd pulled away from them because they'd been lying to him his entire life.

Buckley Blackwood was just another lying parent who only revealed the truth when it was convenient. Darius already had a bookend set of those.

He should feel badly that he'd never meet his biological father. But the only thing he felt toward Blackwood was resentment. The man could've picked up the telephone or flown his private plane to reach him at any point in the past thirty years.

He'd *chosen* not to. Not even when he was dying and knew he had only weeks to live. Instead, he'd apparently spent the end of his life concocting this manipulative scheme.

But to what end?

Amanda Battle, the woman who'd introduced herself as the owner of the little diner, brought him his meal and shake. He nibbled on one of the fries, dipping it into the ketchup he'd poured on his plate.

Darius had spent the past twelve years musing about his mysterious biological father. Right now, he wanted to hate the man. But the scrapbook Miranda had given him didn't correspond with the heartless man he'd imagined.

It wasn't just that the old man had been collecting photos, news clippings and such about Darius his entire life. The photos showed signs of frequent handling. The dog-eared magazine articles appeared to have been read repeatedly. It was the kind of scrapbook he'd expect from a parent who actually gave a damn about his kid.

He sighed, nibbling on more fries. The two sides of the man who was likely his father were incongruent, at best. But clipping out a few magazine articles didn't excuse Blackwood for being a shitty, absent father.

For that, he would never forgive him.

Darius took another of the wedge fries, swiped it in the milkshake and popped it in his mouth.

It was something people over the age of twelve usually found repulsive. But today, he deserved to indulge himself.

"A bacon cheeseburger, fries and a strawberry shake. I was going to ask if it was a really good day or a really bad one, but then you dipped your fry into your shake, so I guess that answers that."

Darius froze, then turned toward the familiar voice. His eyes widened.

"Audra Lee Covington?"

No, it isn't possible.

What would his grad school girlfriend be doing in Royal, Texas?

"So you do remember me." She folded her arms. "I wasn't sure you would. After all, you never returned my calls."

Remember? He couldn't forget her if he tried. She'd been his biggest regret. The woman who still haunted his dreams.

He stared at her, blinking. Still not sure he could believe his eyes.

She was stunning, as always. Her dark wavy hair was tucked behind her ears and fell to her shoulders. Gold-and-diamond starburst ear climbers decorated the outer curve of each ear. She wore a cream-colored, chunky-knit sweater and distressed skinny jeans that hugged every curve. And there was a small, star-shaped diamond stud in one nostril.

"Audra." He stood, wiping his hands on a napkin. He inhaled her sweet scent as they shared an awkward hug. "What on earth are you doing here?"

"Good to see you, too," she said sarcastically as she stepped away, folding her arms again. Her lips pressed into a harsh line as she narrowed her gaze at him.

If looks could kill, he'd be laid out on the black-and-white tile floor with a chalk line around him.

"It's good to see you, Audra, of course. I should've said I'm stunned to see you here in Royal, Texas." He gestured toward the opposite side of the booth. "You look…amazing." It was an egregious understatement. She was drop-dead gorgeous. "Join me?"

Audra's sensual lips, shiny with lip gloss, quirked in a semi-frown as she studied him. Finally, she nodded and slid across from him in the booth.

"The new look—" she indicated his bald head, a look he'd transitioned to nearly three years ago "—I like it. It suits you."

"Thanks." He cleared his throat. "What did you order?"

"They make an incredible Cobb salad. It probably has as many calories as your burger and fries, but at least I feel like I'm making an effort."

He'd always loved her refreshing honesty. Too bad he hadn't afforded her the same. Their story still would've ended. But if he'd been honest with her then, at least he'd have no regrets where Audra was concerned.

"LA Fashion Week is just a few weeks away. I'd expect the great Audra Lee Covington to be in the design studio right now."

Audra was a diamond heiress. She'd broken rank with her very traditional family and formed her own company that catered to a younger, trendier clientele. Her name got frequent mentions in fashion magazines when A-list actors, musicians and social influencers bragged that they were iced in Audra Lee Covington diamond earrings, necklaces, bracelets and tiaras.

"Royal isn't my usual hangout. That's for sure." A deep smile lit Audra's rich espresso-brown eyes, the same color as her shoulder-length hair. "I got an early start on the season this year. So when I received a lucrative request from a wealthy bride-to-be here in Royal, I couldn't resist. I'm creating custom wedding jewelry for the couple and gifts for their bridal party. So I'm staying in town for a bit. Getting to know the area and the bride, who will be returning from New York tomorrow with her fiancé. I'd hardly expect to run into you here, either." She clasped her hands on the table. "I hear Thr3d will be doing a runway show this year."

"We are. My team is back in LA working tirelessly to prepare for it."

She produced a gum-filled lollipop from her pocket, opened the wrapper and popped it in her mouth.

Was that a fucking tongue ring?

Darius was pretty sure his jaw hit the ground and another part of his body reached for the sky.

Good thing he'd returned to his seat.

Audra propped her elbows on the table and tilted her head as she studied him. "What brings you to Royal?"

"A business opportunity." It wasn't a lie. The opportunity to collaborate with Miranda had brought him to town.

She sucked on that damn lollipop, which had already stained her tongue red, and awaited further explanation.

"It's too early to share details." He picked up his burger. "But I'm hoping to create a clothing line for a major fitness brand."

"Ah." When she said it, he couldn't help staring at her candy-red, pierced tongue. "Miranda Dupree. Scoring the clothing line for her Goddess brand would be a major coup."

"How'd you—"

"It's a small world, I guess." She shrugged. "Miranda is my client's ex-stepmother. My client is Sophie Blackwood. Do you know her?"

His half sister. Damn. It *was* a small world.

"Never met her." He shrugged. "But I've heard the name."

Less than an hour ago, in fact.

Audra's mouth made a popping sound when she yanked the lollipop from between her lips. She stared at him, her brown eyes narrowed. Judging him. As if she didn't believe him.

Darius bit a mouthful of the bacon cheeseburger.

He hadn't seen Audra in five years. They weren't together, and she had no right to know his personal business.

So why did he feel as guilty now for telling her a half-truth as he had when they were together?

Audra returned the sucker to her mouth and rose from the table. She didn't believe him, but she obviously didn't deem pursuing the truth worth her time.

Knowing she found him unworthy made his chest ache. Her wordless condemnation was exactly what he deserved.

"Looks like they're done with my order." Audra nodded toward where Amanda was packing a to-go bag. "Nice seeing you again, Darius. Good luck with Fashion Week."

Darius groaned quietly as he swiped another French fry into his milkshake and took a bite.

Audra made a hasty escape, and he couldn't blame her. He was a liar. Apparently, it was hereditary.

Three

Audra slid into the driver's seat of the Bentley Continental GT convertible her parents had gifted her four years ago, after her business cleared a million dollars in profits in its first year.

She glanced back at the diner. Darius sat motionless in the booth where she'd left him.

Of all the people in the world that she could run into, she had to run into Darius Freaking Taylor-Pratt. The man who'd broken her heart five years ago.

She'd been madly in love with him, and she'd believed he loved her, too. Right up to the moment he'd said things had gotten too serious between them, and he needed space.

There had been no discussion. No evidence he'd fallen for someone else. And no real explanation.

She'd been devastated.

They'd met at a party during grad school at Harvard. The attraction between them had almost been instant. She'd told her friend that she was pretty sure she'd met the man she was going to marry.

Sure, she'd been a little buzzed when she said it. But every day they were together made her believe those words to be true.

Darius suddenly ending things had come of out nowhere. It had left her reeling, wondering what she'd done wrong.

But that was the past. It'd taken some time, but she'd gotten over it and moved on.

Or at least she'd always believed she had. But seeing Darius today made her feel as if things between them weren't finished at all.

He was more handsome than ever in his navy Tom Ford

suit, a white shirt and a navy print tie. His story about being in Royal on business was undoubtedly true. Never a fan of suits, Darius would require a damn good reason to wear one.

And the bald head he was rocking…on him it was sexy as sin. Her fingers had itched with the desire to run her palm over the smooth, brown skin on his clean-shaven head. She'd balled her hands into fists, her fingernails leaving marks on her palms.

Darius's dark brown eyes registered a mix of emotions she couldn't quite read.

Sadness. Anger? Maybe even regret.

The only thing she knew for sure was that she'd desperately wanted to lean in and kiss him. If only to remind him of what he'd walked away from five years ago.

Her cell phone rang.

Sophie Blackwood.

Audra smiled, thankful for the distraction. She hit the call button and pulled out of her parking space, heading back toward the house she was renting while she stayed in Royal.

"Hello, Sophie. Back in town yet?"

"We arrived a couple of hours ago. Nigel, my fiancé, needed to stay a couple more days to take care of a staffing issue with the show."

Audra couldn't help smiling. Sophie was doing that thing that many newly engaged women did where they referred to their intended as their *fiancé*, as frequently as possible. It was adorable. And everything about Sophie's bubbly excitement and the warmth with which she talked about him spoke to just how in love they were.

For Sophie's sake, Audra truly hoped that their love would last.

"No worries. I've been keeping myself occupied. I sketched out a few designs. I'll show them to you when we get together."

"Are you busy now? We're going to grab a bite with friends over at the Glass House in an hour or so. You should join us."

"Thanks, but I just picked up a salad." Hopefully, Sophie didn't think her rude for turning down her offer.

"Is everything all right?" Sophie's voice was laced with concern.

"Yes. I'm just a bit stunned. I ran into my grad school ex just now."

"A local?" Sophie asked.

"No, in fact, I got the impression this is his first time here, too. So it was weird to run into him." Audra bit into the sucker she'd teased Darius with.

She was pretty sure he'd nearly fainted when he caught a glimpse of her pierced tongue.

Good.

She might be over Darius, but she wasn't above reminding him that he should be sorry he'd walked out on her.

"Oh? Who is he?" Sophie's voice sounded less jovial.

"Darius Taylor-Pratt. He runs the athletic performance clothing company Thr3d."

"That must've been quite a surprise." Sophie laughed nervously, then quickly changed the subject. "So the venue where I'd like to have my wedding got damaged during the recent wildfires. The damaged portions have been rebuilt, but there's still a lot of work to do. If you could spare the time this Saturday, we could definitely use the help. Besides, it would be a chance for you to get to know some of the folks you're creating custom jewelry pieces for."

"Sure." Audra shrugged. "And maybe we can meet tomorrow afternoon to discuss your custom designs?"

"Come to my place tomorrow afternoon at one. We'll have a late lunch and go over everything." Full-blown giddiness had returned to Sophie's voice. "See you then!"

God, I remember what it felt like to be that in love.

Seeing Darius and talking to Sophie made her even more certain she'd done the right thing when she'd broken it off with her most recent ex a few months ago.

Cassius "Cash" Johannsson was *exactly* the man her mother and United States senator father wanted her to marry. A perfectly nice gentleman from the right family with ambitions to one day sit in the Oval Office. But she wanted more than just "perfectly nice."

She wanted a man who made her laugh. Who was her friend as well as her lover. A man who understood the manic craziness that often accompanied a creative mind. A man who made her body burn for his.

Cash had never engendered that kind of spark in her. Nor had she ever gushed over Cash the way Sophie did over Nigel. The way she once had over Darius.

In the end, she'd broken it off with Cash because she was just settling. He deserved someone who would feel like the luckiest girl in the world to be on his arm.

Audra entered the beautiful gated community where her rental house was located. She was traveling with sample jewelry pieces and loose diamonds, the value of which easily topped two million dollars. So she required the additional security afforded by this gated community and the safety measures of the home she was renting from the Blackwoods' family friend—Dixie Musgraves.

She grabbed her meal, courtesy of the Royal Diner, and headed inside, determined to banish all thoughts of Darius.

Four

It already felt like the longest day of Darius's life, and he still had a few hours of work ahead of him. He settled behind the glass-and-steel desk in the office of his rental home and prepared for yet another conference call. This one with his production manager and a few key members of the production staff.

The preparations for LA Fashion Week had to go off without a hitch. This would be Thr3d's first runway show at the event. And he was determined it wouldn't be the last.

It was an honor to get a runway show for his athletic gear. One he wouldn't squander. And if everything went as expected, buyers in untapped markets would order the Thr3d fall line for their stores. So despite the issues with his paternity and his biological father's estate, he wouldn't allow himself to be distracted.

Fifteen minutes into the conversation with his team, he heard water splash.

Darius walked over to the bank of windows along the back wall of the office and stared down. There was a woman swimming in his pool.

"Boss? Boss?" His production manager Leeson Brown was saying.

"Oh… I…uh…" He cleared his throat. "Sorry. Didn't catch that last part."

"I said unless you have something else for us, that pretty much covers everything," Lee repeated. "Don't worry. The entire team understands the importance of this show. We won't let you down."

"I know you won't." Darius watched the woman's movements. There was something oddly familiar about her strong, elegant strokes.

Who is she and what the hell is she doing here?

"The team is doing a great job," Darius assured Lee. "I'll touch base soon. But if you run into any problems…"

"We won't hesitate to call," Lee assured him.

"Day or night," Darius told the man as his gaze followed the woman swimming laps in his pool.

"I promise. In the meantime, I know it's a tall order for you, but try to relax."

Darius promised he would try. Then he slipped the phone into his pocket and headed down to the pool to find out who was trespassing on the Blackwoods' property and distracting him from his work.

As he made his way across the patio, the woman climbed out of the pool in a tiny bikini that showed off her delicious curves. She tugged the cap off her head and tossed it on a lounge chair and bent over to grab her beach towel.

Good. God. Almighty.

This woman's behind was a museum-worthy work of art.

"Excuse me," he said, finally.

Startled, the woman dropped her towel and whipped around, her eyes widening.

"Darius?"

"Audra?"

They spoke simultaneously. Then Darius added, "Did you follow me back here?"

She propped a fist on one generous hip, drawing his attention to her belly button piercing and the connected gold chain looped around her waist. "Do you honestly believe I need to resort to following random dudes home?"

Ouch.

She'd just called him a *random dude*. As if he didn't matter to her and never really had.

Audra didn't wait for his response. She snatched the

towel off the lounge chair and dried herself. Doubtless, the pool was heated, but the temperature outside had cooled considerably. She was shivering.

He couldn't help thinking of the last time he'd seen her shivering. She'd been lying beneath him, gloriously naked. He swallowed hard. Heat crawled up his neck and face.

"Does that mean you're renting this house now?" She pulled a short, black cover-up over her head and slipped her arms inside before plopping down on the end of the lounger to dry her hair. "Because it was empty when I went for a swim this morning."

"My business will keep me here a few more days." He shoved a hand in his pocket. "Miranda offered me this place for as long as I need it."

Darius surveyed the well-manicured patio with its lovely landscaping and the pool complete with a hot tub and water feature. He'd paid little attention to the backyard during the cursory tour Leslie had given him when she'd deposited him here a couple of hours ago.

He'd been in the office, sifting through emails or on one call after another, ever since. Starting with the call he'd placed to his attorney, apprising him of the situation and charging the man with exploring his options.

Darius didn't need Buckley Blackwood's money. His athletic clothing line was one of the fastest-growing companies of its kind in the US, and it was already making millions each year. If Thr3d maintained its current trajectory, it was positioned to climb its way to being one of the top ten athletic wear companies in the country within ten years.

Still, Darius felt compelled to fight for some portion of the estate—to demand acknowledgment as a Blackwood heir. Even if he simply donated the money to a worthy cause. But he wasn't prepared to tell Audra any of that. There was no reason for him to tell his pedigreed ex that he was a bastard child. The product of an illicit affair between an asshole banker and a failed actress. An inconvenience neither of them had planned for or wanted.

"How long will you be in Royal?" Audra stood, her towel folded over her arm. She didn't sound happy about him staying in town.

"It's hard to say right now." He shoved his hands in his pockets and leaned against the edge of the hot tub. "You?"

"Same." Audra slipped her feet into her bejeweled flip-flops. "But my client Sophie and her fiancé are back in town. I should be able to make some serious progress in the next week or two."

He sucked in a deep breath at the mention of his half sister's name. After lying to Audra about his family in the past, he hated the idea of keeping this secret from her, even if they weren't together. But he wasn't prepared to air his family's dirty laundry. Especially when his paternity had yet to be definitively proven.

"Great," he said. "But that doesn't explain why you're in my pool. You aren't staying here, too, are you?"

"Heaven forbid." Audra pressed an open hand to her chest in feigned outrage. She nodded toward the house on the other side of the brick wall. "I'm renting the darling house next door. It has a proper workshop, great office space and plenty of security. But it doesn't have a pool, and back home in Dallas I swim nearly every day."

"You're in Dallas now?"

"I moved there after grad school." She shrugged. "I needed a fresh start and Dallas felt right."

Guilt churned in his gut. *Did she need a fresh start because of our breakup?*

"Anyway, Sophie gave me permission to use this pool since her family owns the house and it's empty. At least it *was* empty. In light of everything that's been going on with her father's death and the estate going to her stepmother... I'm sure Sophie had no idea you were staying here."

"Makes sense." He stared at her, unable to tear his gaze from her expressive eyes. He wanted to take her in his arms and get reacquainted with every one of her sensual curves.

"Sorry I disturbed you." She broke their gaze. "I'm sure there's another pool in town I could use."

"No. You don't need to do that." He objected far too quickly, and he couldn't help but notice she was restraining a smile. "You aren't bothering me. I only came out because I thought you were a trespasser." He folded his arms. "Come over whenever you want. I doubt I'll be using the pool while I'm here."

"That's a shame." She shrugged. "My time in the pool relaxes me and sparks my creativity. You should try it."

"You're shivering. Can I make you some coffee or tea? Hot cocoa, maybe?" He gestured toward the house.

What the hell was he thinking?

The last thing he needed was to spend *more* time with Audra. Yet, he wanted her to stay a little while longer. Even if it meant he'd lie awake all night, revisiting his regrets.

But he could never go back. There were no do-overs in romantic or family relationships. He'd burned that bridge when he'd walked away from her.

"That's kind of you." She managed a polite smile. "But I'll be plenty warm between the hot bubble bath with my name on it and the Sex on the Beach I plan to have…the drink, not the actual—"

"Of course." He ran a hand over his clean-shaven head.

But all he could think about was that time they'd gone to Martha's Vineyard and ended up having sex on the beach.

It wasn't nearly as glamorous as people made it out to be. They'd both gotten sand in places sand should never, *ever* be. But they'd had fun that night. A night he'd never forget.

Audra began ordering Sex on the Beach cocktails after that. Initially, as a private joke between them which ignited that passionate memory. But then she'd actually started to like them, and it became her signature drink.

As they stood awkwardly staring at one another, he wondered if she still regarded the memory fondly. Or was every memory of what they once shared now tainted?

"Thank you for letting me use the pool. I'll try not to disturb you. Good night."

"Good night," he called to her retreating back.

Audra disappeared through the iron gate that connected the two backyards.

Darius rubbed a hand over his head and groaned. The universe had it in for him. He was sure of it.

The collaboration project with Goddess had turned out to be a ruse to get him to Royal. He'd finally—*probably*—discovered who his father was, but the selfish bastard had gone and died before Darius had a chance to tell him to go to hell. The man was richer than God but hadn't left any of his children a dime. Darius had siblings, but with them already fighting Miranda on the will, he doubted they would appreciate a surprise heir popping up out of the woodwork.

And then there's Audra.

Not only was she right here in Royal, but she was staying next door and using his pool wearing a scrap of fabric masquerading as a bikini.

Yep. Either he was being punked or the universe was having a nice laugh at his expense.

His eyes were drawn to the light that suddenly went on upstairs in the house next door.

Audra.

Probably drawing a bubble bath with her Sex on the Beach in hand.

He shut his eyes against the erotic images that flooded his brain, his body stiffening in response.

There would be a lot of cold showers and sleepless nights in his future.

* * *

Audra dropped her damp towel in the laundry bin and went to the kitchen to retrieve the pitcher of cocktails she'd made earlier and put in the fridge.

She'd mixed her favorite drink the moment she'd returned home after seeing Darius. It was bad enough he was in the same Texas town where she was. Did he have to be staying next door, too?

Audra pulled out a glass and filled it, the liquid sloshing onto the counter.

Her hands were shaking.

She sucked in a deep breath, her eyes drifting closed.

"Of all the goddamn places in the world he could possibly be," she muttered under her breath as she wiped up the mess.

Not that it mattered.

She was over Darius. So it didn't matter how good he looked in those black basketball pants and a heather-gray performance shirt emblazoned with the Thr3d logo. A shirt that clung to the muscles of his chest and biceps.

He was her past. A mistake she'd never repeat.

But God, parts of her wanted to. And right now, those parts were drowning out her common sense, which reminded her that she should know better.

She went upstairs and turned on the warm water, adding some of the decadent bath foam with a heavenly crème brûlée scent. It was pricey, but it left her skin incredibly soft and smelling sweet. And the luxurious bubbles it created were perfect for a day like this.

Audra stripped out of her wet bikini and removed the belly chain before slipping beneath the scented bubbles.

Her phone rang. Because…of course it would. She sat up and peeked at the caller ID.

Cash.

She groaned as she slipped beneath the water again.

Some much-needed distance from her ex, who still didn't seem to understand it was over, was the real reason she'd found Sophie Blackwood's project so intriguing. Audra looked forward to immersing herself completely in the project without the possibility of running into her ex or seeing the local politician's face splashed across television commercials and on the side of buses.

The chorus of the old George Strait song, "All My Ex's Live in Texas," a favorite of her grandfather's, suddenly came to her and she couldn't help laughing.

Cash was a good guy. She honestly felt badly about ignoring his call. But she simply didn't have the energy to deal with another ex tonight.

Besides, how many more ways can I explain that it's over?

Audra wouldn't change her mind. She didn't care that their mothers had been hoping for a match between them since she and Cash were teens, and their fathers had served together as senators.

Their relationship seemed picture-perfect from the outside—like the chocolate shell on the outside of a cherry cordial. But on the inside, there were no cherries and there was no cream filling. There was nothing at all beyond the surface, leaving her with a hollow, empty feeling.

She needed something more.

Something like what she and Darius had shared. But this time, with someone who *wanted* to be with her. Always.

The way she'd once felt about Darius.

Her phone signaled that she had a new voice mail and she sighed quietly. For the first time, she understood why Darius hadn't returned her calls five years ago.

When it's really over, what else is there to discuss?

The realization made her heart ache. No matter how much she tried to deny it, a part of her heart still harbored the small hope that she and Darius could one day get it right.

That was why she'd turned down his invitation to join him for coffee. She needed to protect the fragile part of her heart that held on to that hope.

She gave her phone the voice command to play the eighties and nineties soft rock music playlist that always relaxed her.

Steve Perry sang the opening lines of "Foolish Heart."

It was just the reminder she needed.

You're here for one reason and one reason only. Stay focused.

Anything else was a foolish distraction that would only lead to a broken heart.

She'd had enough of those to last a lifetime.

Five

It was his second day in Royal. Despite barely sleeping four hours last night, he'd risen early this morning to the sound of Audra diving into the pool. He'd gotten up, taken a quick shower, dressed, grabbed a cup of coffee and then watched her graceful movements as she finished her laps.

When she was done, she toweled off and made her way back to her yard without casting so much as a glance toward the house.

Not that he wanted or expected her to look for him. But he certainly hadn't been able to take his eyes off of her.

The swimsuit she'd worn that morning was a one-piece, long-sleeve suit with a zipper down the front. Suitable for the chillier early-morning temperature. But he couldn't help thinking of how amazing she'd looked in the two-piece she'd worn last night.

He was groggy and jetlagged. Restless, because it was still too early to call any of his team back home in LA. But watching Audra for the past two days had given him an idea. Swimwear for both men and women.

When he'd originally started the line five years ago, it had consisted of a handful of men's sportswear pieces. Little by little, he'd expanded the collection. Two years ago, they'd tested their first women's collection. It had been a resounding success. But neither line included swimwear.

It was risky to throw something else into the mix so close to their first LA Fashion Week runway show. But if they could pull it off, the swimwear pieces might even become the centerpiece of the show.

Darius pulled out his sketchpad and the wooden case that contained his watercolor pencils. He drafted a rough outline of a woman's suit adorning the shapely curves that had inspired the idea. The same ones that haunted his sleep.

Audra couldn't help smiling as she sat across the table from Sophie Blackwood and her fiancé, Nigel Townshend. They made a handsome couple.

Sophie had long, glossy auburn hair, warm brown eyes and killer curves, highlighted by the peplum blouse she wore coupled with a maxi skirt.

Nigel's stunning, baby blue eyes practically danced as he watched Sophie. He sat with an arm wrapped around his fiancée's waist. His mouth curved in a contented smile.

The two of them were beyond adorable.

And as if the man wasn't handsome enough with his good looks and his short, tousled brown hair, he spoke with a thick British accent. Audra could happily listen to Nigel Townshend recite the periodic table.

After lunch, they'd moved to a sun-filled room just off the patio. Where Sophie and Nigel shared their vision for their wedding rings and the custom jewelry pieces they wanted to give each member of their bridal party. Audra took notes and sketched in her notebook as the couple talked. She loved hearing the funny, sweet and moving stories about the friends and family they'd selected to stand beside them on their wedding day.

This was why she loved working with engaged couples. It reminded her true love really existed.

She'd thought she'd found the love of her life the night she met Darius. But she'd been wrong. Then she'd taken the expected path by getting into a relationship with Cash. But getting involved with her longtime family friend had been a mistake, too.

Working with couples like Sophie and Nigel revived her belief that, regardless of her failures and false starts, she'd eventually find the man she'd want to be with forever.

Someone who'd feel the same about her.

As they chatted, Audra made a few amendments to the three concepts she'd developed for Sophie's and Nigel's rings.

"Okay," Audra said finally, her heart beating a mile a minute. "Here are a few options for your engagement and wedding rings. They're just preliminary sketches that'll give me a better sense of the right design for you." She turned the sketchpad toward the couple and pushed it across the table tentatively. "What do you think? Am I on the right track?"

Audra was good at what she did, and she'd designed hundreds of pieces over the past five years. But it always made her incredibly nervous to show clients her first draft. This moment could make or break the rest of the design experience.

"Oh my God." Sophie pressed a trembling hand to her lips. Her eyes filled with tears as she traced the sketch of the vintage-inspired, floral-themed engagement ring. "It's stunning. I love it." She gripped Nigel's forearm and gazed up at him. "What do you think?"

"I couldn't possibly imagine a better reaction." He beamed, wiping tears from her cheek with his thumb. "So I'm happy if you're happy, love."

It was sweet of Nigel, but it wasn't the enthusiastic re-action Audra was hoping for. He obviously didn't care for the corresponding design for his ring. Instead, his eye was drawn to the sketch of a set of sleek, modern wedding bands.

They were a stark contrast to the engagement ring Sophie adored.

"I realize that tradition dictates matching wedding bands, but this is *your* life and *your* marriage," Audra said. "Who says you have to be bound by tradition?"

"You're suggesting we have different styles of wedding bands?" Sophie asked.

"Why not?" Audra shrugged. "Your differences are part of what attracted you two, right? Why not celebrate them by selecting individual ring styles connected by the same metals?"

"Bloody brilliant, Audra." Nigel grinned. He turned back to Sophie. "What do you think, love?"

"I love the symbolism of it." Sophie sounded unconvinced as she pressed a hand to her cheek.

Translation: she hates the idea.

"It would be better if I showed you." Audra smiled confidently. "I'll have new sketches ready for you tomorrow afternoon. And I'll bring samples so you can get a better sense of how the finished design will look."

"Thank you." The joy returned to Sophie's eyes.

Audra gathered her sketchbook and pencils. "I'd better get back to my office and get started."

Nigel excused himself to take a call, and Sophie walked her toward the door.

"So that was crazy, you running into your ex here, huh?" Sophie said.

Audra halted at the mention of Darius, but feigned indifference. "It was, but what was even more bizarre is that when I went for a swim last night, I discovered he's staying at the house next door while he's in town."

"Wait…why is he staying there?"

"He's in Royal on business with your former stepmother. She owns the property now, right? I guess she's putting him up there while he's in town."

"I see." Sophie frowned. "I wonder what kind of business they have together."

Audra didn't answer. It wasn't her place to reveal what Darius had shared with her about his potential deal with Miranda.

"What was it like seeing him again after all these years?" Sophie asked.

"Weird, I guess, is the best way to describe it." Audra shrugged, though emotion welled in her chest. "He broke my heart, but we didn't part on bad terms. He simply made the choice to walk away."

"Did he leave you for someone else?"

"That's just it, I don't believe he did." Audra lifted the strap of her bag higher on her shoulder. "He just didn't want to be with me anymore. Honestly? It hurt like hell, but I get it. It's the same reason I broke it off with my recent ex. He's a perfectly good guy. He just isn't the one I want to spend a lifetime with."

"But Darius was. Wasn't he?" Sophie placed a comforting hand on Audra's arm.

Something about the younger woman's offer of comfort moved Audra. Tears welled in her eyes. She blinked them away. "I thought so at the time, but later I learned that he hadn't been honest with me about something important."

"Like?" Sophie asked tentatively.

They weren't friends. Sophie was her client. But Audra had a compelling need to talk to *someone* about this.

"He told me his parents were dead. A few years later, I read a magazine article where he said he had an estranged relationship with his mother and stepfather. But they were very much alive." Audra dragged her fingers through her hair and sighed. "What kind of man would lie about something like that?"

"That is curious." Sophie frowned. "But perhaps he had a good reason. Did you confront him about it?"

"It was over between us, and I hadn't seen him in years by then." Audra shrugged. "What would be the point?"

"He obviously meant a lot to you," Sophie said in a hushed tone as Nigel approached. "Now that you've reconnected—"

"We *haven't* reconnected," Audra corrected her.

"Okay. Now that you two are neighbors and on friendly terms…" Sophie shrugged. "If it was me, I'd want to know."

Of course I want to know why Darius lied to me about his parents.

But demanding an explanation from him now would only make him believe she still cared. Which she didn't. Because she was definitely over him.

"I'd better be going. Thank you both for a lovely lunch." Audra smiled politely but didn't acknowledge Sophie's comment.

Audra focused on the short drive back to her rental house in the same community of Pine Valley. A small part of her was envious of Sophie and Nigel. She didn't begrudge them their happiness. She just wanted a little of that bliss for herself.

Six

Darius had been so busy working on the swimwear designs that he'd lost track of time. He didn't realize how late it was until the setting of the sun forced him to turn on the lights.

He left his makeshift drafting table and sat at his computer to catch up on an email chain circulating between members of his team.

They'd been stunned during a video conference that morning when he'd announced the addition of swimwear to the runway show collection. First there was silence, except for his production chief Leeson. The man laughed, thinking Darius must be joking.

When he realized Darius was serious, Lee's chuckles gave way to full-blown panic.

"So much for that relaxing we talked about," Lee muttered.

"This *is* me relaxing." Darius's response prompted the entire team's laughter, easing their tension.

After the initial shock, he was able to get everyone focused.

The team had discussed the designs, agreed on a few changes, debated the correct ratio of nylon and spandex for the fabric, and identified sources for all of the materials.

In a few days he'd have prototypes for each swimsuit.

The doorbell rang and he checked his watch. Nearly six thirty. Was it that lawyer with the paternity test results?

Darius made his way toward the front door, with its large central glass pane. He'd only seen the face of the man standing on the other side of the door once before, but he'd never forget it.

He hesitated a moment. His steps suddenly felt leaden, and his heart pounded inside his chest.

For the past two days, he'd kept himself preoccupied with work. He hadn't allowed himself to wonder about the man who'd been his biological father or his newly discovered half siblings. But staring at the man in front of him, bearing features similar to his own, he was no longer able to avoid his new reality.

Darius exhaled slowly, as he unlocked the door.

How am I supposed to greet a possible sibling I didn't know I had until two days ago?

"Yes?" Lame, but the best he could do on short notice.

The man stared at him, wide-eyed, for a beat without response. Perhaps he was silently cataloguing Darius's features, too. The man withdrew a hand from his pocket and extended it. "Hello, Darius. I'm Kellan Blackwood." They shook hands. "It would appear that we're brothers."

They were complete strangers. Yet, they shared DNA. Their handshake was awkward. Too much and not enough, all at once.

"It seems so." Darius slid his hands into his pockets and leaned against the doorframe. "But I guess the paternity test will tell the final story."

"True." Kellan nodded. "My father and I weren't close. Mostly because we agreed on very little, and the man could be an asshole," he said without apology. "But I knew him well enough to know he'd never have gone to the trouble of bringing you here if he wasn't already dead sure you were his son. I get the feeling that the paternity test was requested to erase any doubt in our minds."

An uncomfortable silence settled over them.

Finally, Darius spoke. "Would you like to come in for a minute? I haven't had a chance to order groceries, but a fruit basket came with the place."

"No worries." Kellan pulled a bottle of premium Scotch

from the inside of his denim jacket. He handed it to Darius. "Brought you a housewarming gift."

Darius thanked the man with a wary smile.

Is Kellan simply being hospitable? Does he want to get to know his newfound brother? Or is he here to dissuade me from sticking around and staking a claim on the estate?

"Come in." He led Kellan to the sitting room that overlooked the patio and pool. Darius grabbed two tumblers and set one in front of each of them, pouring them each two fingers of Scotch.

He was more of an imported beer guy, but he had the feeling this was some kind of test. One he didn't plan to fail.

Once they were both seated with glasses in hand, the awkward silence settled over them again.

Kellan took a deep sip of his Scotch, then set his glass down. "Darius, my brother, sister and I wanted you to know that we have no plans to dispute your right to a share of the estate."

"Good to know." Darius set his glass down, too. "Though it doesn't much matter since the old man cut all of us out of the estate."

"Straightforward and to the point. I like you already." Kellan chuckled and took another sip from his glass. "Guess we both got that trait honest."

Darius chuckled, too, sipping a bit of his Scotch. He resisted the urge to cough. Instead, he cleared his throat and met his brother's gaze. "Our father… What was he like?"

Kellan frowned. There was anger in his expression, but also pain. Maybe even a hint of guilt.

"A few months ago, I would've simply described him as an asshole. That's how I saw him most of my life."

"And now?"

"I still say he was an asshole, but he was a complicated one. He apparently had more depth than any of us gave him credit for. Too bad he didn't show any of us that side of him—

self while he was alive." Kellan drained the remainder of his glass. "Maybe then the old man wouldn't have died alone."

Kellan blamed their father's sad demise on the old man's gruff disposition. Still, there was the clear ring of guilt in his brother's tone and tortured expression. Darius didn't need to know the man well to recognize it.

It was the same guilt he felt regarding his mother and stepfather. They'd kept the truth from him, and he had every right to be angry. Yet, he'd begun to feel a deep sense of guilt about the distance he'd created between them.

"What shifted your opinion about him?" Darius needed to know there had been some good in the man who'd given him life.

Kellan's frown deepened. "I'm hungry," he declared suddenly. "Have you eaten yet?"

He'd evidently touched a nerve. So he wouldn't press the man.

"No." Darius shook his head. "Now that you mention it, I'm starving."

"There's this great little diner in town." Kellan stood.

"Royal Diner." Darius nodded. "Do they deliver? This isn't a conversation I'd like to have in public. In fact, I'm not ready to talk about any of this outside of…" The word caught in his throat.

"The family?" One edge of Kellan's mouth curved. "I should've considered that. I'll request delivery."

Kellan ordered himself a steak, though he confessed to having already eaten a light dinner earlier with Irina, his new bride. Darius requested the same meal he'd had the day before.

"Anything else?" Kellan asked. "Dinner's on me."

A light went on in the house next door and Audra walked past one of the downstairs windows.

Darius sighed, turning to Kellan. "I hear they make a really good Cobb salad."

* * *

Despite the initial awkwardness, Darius enjoyed getting to know Kellan, and through him, the rest of his newfound family. He couldn't help laughing at Kellan's tales of his and Vaughn's misadventures as boys. And he'd been moved by sweet stories about Sophie who'd been precocious, but sheltered, as a child.

"She's getting married." Kellan smiled fondly as he stared into his glass of Scotch after he'd finished his meal. "I'm nine years older than Sophie, so I took the job of looking out for her seriously. Sometimes I feel more like her father than her brother." Lines around his eyes crinkled. "I can't believe she's getting married. Then again, I can't believe I'm married again and that we're expecting a baby."

Darius had met this man a few hours ago. Had learned of his existence just yesterday. Yet, he was genuinely happy for him.

There was a natural kinship between them. A connection he hadn't felt with anyone else.

It was comforting, yet unnerving.

A splash in the pool snagged both men's attention.

Kellan stood abruptly. "Sorry. Didn't realize you had company."

Darius stood, too. "That's my neighbor. She's working on a project for your… I mean, *our* sister. The house next door doesn't have a pool, so Sophie told her she could use this one." He shrugged. "Didn't see the harm in allowing her to continue."

Kellan's mouth curved in a sly grin. "Must be quite a hardship to have a beautiful woman traipsing through your backyard in a swimsuit."

"How'd you know she's beautiful?" Darius eyed his brother suspiciously.

"The expression on your face said it all." Kellan chuckled. "You've got a thing for this woman."

"She also happens to be my ex," Darius confessed. "You can't imagine how shocked I was to see her here."

"Hmm… Is that right?" Kellan furrowed his brows. He picked up his empty to-go containers and cleaned his space. "Well, I've kept you long enough. I'd better check on my wife. She's been exhausted and sleeping a lot the past few weeks."

"I imagine it's tough work growing a human being." Darius walked Kellan to the front door. He extended a hand to his half brother. "Thank you for coming by, Kellan. It was good to meet you."

"Same." Kellan grinned as he shook Darius's hand. "This Saturday, we're volunteering at the Texas Cattleman's Club after the recent wildfires. The organization is important to our family, and we're all members. Sophie's a designer, so fixing the clubhouse back up has become her special project. Vaughn, Sophie and her fiancé, Nigel, will all be there. If you have the time, you should join us. We could use the help, and you'll be able to meet the rest of the family."

"Won't it be awkward if I'm there with all of you, since I'm not ready to make our relationship public?"

"You're a stranger here on business. That's all anyone needs to know." Kellan shrugged. "I'll make sure Sophie and Vaughn know you want to keep this under wraps for now. We've had longer to sit with the idea than you have. I'm sure you must be overwhelmed by all of this."

He was.

"Thanks for understanding. And, if I can manage it, I'll help out on Saturday."

Kellan clapped a hand on his shoulder. "Great. Hope to see you then. If you need anything in the meantime…" He retrieved his wallet from his back pocket and handed Darius a business card. "Call my cell number anytime, day or night."

"Will do." Darius studied the card. Kellan was a Nashville-based real estate developer.

He gave Kellan one of his business cards, then cleared his throat. The words he'd needed to say all night lay at the back of his tongue, like heavy, immovable stones.

"About this whole thing... I'm sorry. I realize how hard it must be to learn that your father was unfaithful to your mother. I wouldn't blame any of you for being upset by me being here."

"I appreciate the thought." Kellan winced, almost imperceptibly. "But you're not to blame. We knew who our father was. Unfortunately, my mother did, too." He flashed a pained smile. "None of that matters anymore. You're family now."

Darius wished his brother a good night and closed the door behind him. A deep sense of relief alleviated the heaviness in his chest.

He returned to the darkened room overlooking the pool and stood quietly, watching Audra's arms slice through the water as she swam laps.

Seeing Audra again, after all of these years, had brought all those feelings to the surface that he'd buried so deeply when he'd walked away from her.

It'd been the right decision, but one he'd often regretted.

Audra was an amazing woman. Devastatingly sexy, stunningly beautiful and smart as a whip. She had a goofy sense of humor most people wouldn't expect of the product of two legendary families, deeply entrenched in business and politics. Regardless of what was happening in his life, she'd always been able to make him laugh.

She was a fellow creative who understood the mania of needing to work through the night on a project. Or the need to wake up at three in the morning to sketch out a design that came to him in his sleep.

Despite her family's wealth, Audra never came off as

spoiled or pampered. She was the quintessential girl next door. Her house just happened to be a sprawling, multimillion-dollar mansion.

Go back to the office. You've got a ton of work to do.

He hadn't been honest with Audra back then, nor was he prepared to tell her everything now. He'd hurt her when he'd ended their relationship. He wouldn't hurt her again.

But Audra was like the sun. Her gravitational pull hauled him into her orbit. He was inescapably drawn to her then and now. And with everything else going on in his life, he didn't have the strength to resist her pull.

He grabbed the Cobb salad he'd put in the fridge and made his way to the backyard.

Audra was in the middle of her tenth lap when she noticed Darius approaching.

She gripped the edge of the pool and slid her goggles on top of her head. "Hi."

He sat on the edge of the lounge chair beside the one that held her things. "Hey."

She made her way to the stainless steel ladder, and Darius extended his open palm, pulling her up. Then he handed her one of her towels.

"Thanks." Audra dried her face and dripping wet hair before wrapping the other towel around her body. His expression was largely unreadable, but there was clearly *something* he wanted to say. "Have you changed your mind about me using the pool?"

"No, of course not. It's just that it's late and—"

"Sorry, I don't usually swim this late, but I've been reworking a client design and I got so absorbed in the project that time got away from me."

"Audra." Darius placed a hand on her arm. "You're fine. Stay out here all night, if you'd like. I don't care. I just… I had dinner delivered from the Royal Diner. I thought I'd try the Cobb salad you recommended, but I honestly couldn't eat another bite. I thought you might like it."

He nodded toward the bag he'd set on a small table between the lounge chairs. "Have you eaten?"

"No. I planned to throw something together after my laps."

"Well, now you won't have to. If you want it, that is." Darius shoved his hands in his pockets.

"Sure." She shrugged. "Thanks."

Silence, as thick and heavy as the brick wall that separated their yards, hung between them in the chilly night air. The weight of their unspoken words sent a shiver down her spine and made her belly tense.

Darius's cell phone rang, and she could swear he sighed in relief. He pulled it from his pocket and checked the caller ID. Darius groaned, then flashed an apologetic smile.

"I'd better take this." He stared at her a moment longer. "Good night, Audra."

He strode away, answering the call.

Audra released a long, slow breath as Darius walked away.

There were a million reasons she shouldn't be eyeing his perfect ass and broad shoulders, remembering how it felt to lie in his arms.

Audra tightened the towel wrapped around her to ward off the chilly, night air. But the shiver running up her spine stemmed from the vivid, visceral memories of how amazing it had felt when Darius kissed her. Made love to her.

She'd never been with anyone like him. The sex had been incredible, yes. But it had been so much more than that. No one had ever made her feel the way Darius had. Like she was the center of his universe. Not her famous family or her bank account. Just her.

She hadn't had that feeling before or since. Sometimes, she wondered if she'd ever feel that way again.

But clearly, it had all been an act. If she'd meant half as much to him as he had to her, he'd never have walked away. And he wouldn't have lied to her about something as important as his family.

Audra nibbled on her lower lip. Her heart felt heavy and her gut twisted in a knot. She should be glad Darius hadn't invited her inside.

So why do I wish he had?

She grabbed her things, slipped on her sandals and picked up the bag from the Royal Diner. Then she headed toward the iron gate that separated the properties.

Audra couldn't help glancing at the office window where Darius was on the phone, pacing.

Two days ago, she was sure she was over Darius. Now she couldn't help wondering if she would ever *truly* be over him.

Seven

It was just after nine on Saturday morning and Darius had already been up for a couple of hours. He stared at the magnetic whiteboard he'd purchased the previous day.

He'd printed out sketches of the garments in Thr3d's fall collection and secured them to the whiteboard with colorful magnets. Darius moved the pieces around several times, pairing items that could be worn together. He rearranged the order of the runway lineup to best convey his vision of Thr3d to the fashion buyers and the audience.

Thr3d produced functional, high-performance, technology-friendly athletic wear. The hip, colorful vibe allowed wearers to express themselves. The range of sizes were inclusive. The basic collection was priced to be accessible, while the premier collection offered high-end sportswear.

He'd been so intent on the task that he'd only been minimally distracted by Audra's morning swim.

A runway show at LA Fashion Week was huge for Thr3d. This show could get Thr3d into more retail spaces and raise brand awareness among consumers and social influencers around the world. The pressure to put on a perfect show weighed on his shoulders like a boulder.

He couldn't get this wrong. Too much was riding on it. So he wouldn't allow deceased, absentee fathers, newfound siblings or resurfacing exes to divert him from the vision he'd been working toward for the past five years. The success he'd craved his entire life.

He needed to keep his mind in motion and thoughts of Audra out of his head.

The doorbell rang. Part of him hoped it was Audra dropping by. But she'd obviously moved on, as he'd hoped she would. Still, after seeing her the past few days, he couldn't help reminiscing about their past.

He cared for Audra. Wanted her to be happy. But the thought of her being happy with some other guy killed him inside.

The bell rang again, shaking him from his daze. He approached the door and saw a familiar figure on the other side.

Kace LeBlanc. The lawyer.

The man was dressed in jeans and a T-shirt, rather than his expensive suit.

Darius opened the door. "Mr. LeBlanc. I assume you're here with news for me."

"Kace will do just fine." The man looked beyond him. "Would it be all right if I stepped inside to update you on the latest development?"

Darius gestured for the man to come inside. "Are you here to toss me out as an imposter?"

"Not at all." Kace handed Darius two envelopes. The larger one contained the scrapbook Buck had compiled with all of his accomplishments. The one Miranda had promised him once the DNA test proved that he was Buckley Blackwood's son. "You are indeed a legal heir of Buckley Blackwood, entitled to the same rights as his legitimate children."

The man's use of the word *legitimate* reignited the ugly feelings he'd struggled with for more than a decade. The feeling of not belonging anywhere. Not being wanted by his own father.

"And that entitles me to what, exactly?" Darius shrugged, setting both the envelopes on a nearby table without opening them. "A general 'fuck-you, son'? Blackwood has given me that my entire life. But at least he's been consistent. Seems the man treated all his children that way—*legitimate* or otherwise."

"I can understand why you'd see things that way." Kace

folded his arms. "But your father cared for you—all of you—more than you know. Coming here wasn't a waste of your time, Darius. You've discovered that you have siblings, whom you seem to have a lot in common with."

"Such as?" Darius stared at the man.

"You're all good people and successful entrepreneurs. And you're all working through your grief over the loss of your father." The man's expression was kind.

"How could I possibly grieve for a man I never knew?" Darius's voice was strangled. His neck and shoulders tensed as he clenched his fists at his sides.

"I suppose you've been grieving, in a way, from the moment you learned Will Pratt wasn't your biological father."

Heat flared in Darius's face. He was still angry with his mother and Will, but he wouldn't allow anyone else to disparage them.

"You don't know anything about my relationship with Will Pratt," he said, quietly seething beneath his calm facade. "He's ten times the father Buckley Blackwood ever was."

The truth of that statement struck him like an aluminum bat to the back of his head.

William Pratt had been a father to him by choice—in name and deed. The man deserved credit for that. Credit Darius hadn't given him.

"I'm sure, and I didn't mean to offend you." The two men stood in momentary silence before Kace spoke again. "Now that you know the truth, what's next for you, Darius?"

"Getting to know my brothers and sister, I suppose." Darius shrugged. "Then I'll decide whether or not to contest the will."

"Then I guess we'll be seeing you around town," Kace said. "In fact, several of us are volunteering at the Texas Cattleman's Club today. The clubhouse means a lot to folks in Royal, and your siblings will be there. This project is Sophie's baby."

"Shit," Darius muttered, checking his watch. "That's today? Kellan asked if I'd help."

"Royal Diner is providing breakfast. I'm headed to the TCC clubhouse now, if you need a lift into town."

Darius turned the idea over in his head.

Now that he was officially a Blackwood, he felt a pressing need to get to know his siblings. His meeting with Kellan had gone well. But that didn't guarantee things would go as smoothly with Sophie and Vaughn.

Hell, for all he knew, the meeting with Kellan was just a pretense to make him let down his guard. Maybe Kellan just wanted to gain his trust so he could convince him to pack his things and leave town.

"Darius." Kace sounded apologetic as he broke into his thoughts. "Can I give you a ride to the clubhouse?" He patted his belly. "I don't mind telling you I'm starving."

"Give me five minutes?"

Kace nodded. "I'll give you ten."

Darius went to the master bedroom and changed into a Thr3d T-shirt, cargo pants and sneakers. Then he inhaled a deep breath, mentally preparing himself to spend the day getting to know his half siblings without revealing his parentage to anyone else in town.

"Darius." Kellan approached him with a wide smile. "Glad you made it."

Darius shook his brother's hand. "Kace came over earlier with some news. He reminded me about volunteering today."

"So your paternity has been confirmed?" Kellan lowered his voice.

"I'm definitely a Blackwood."

"It was pretty clear to me the moment I met you. You've got a lot of the family features."

Darius scanned the room. *Will anyone else notice our physical similarities?*

"I talked to Sophie and Vaughn. We respect your decision to keep the news quiet while you process all of this," Kellan assured him.

"I appreciate that. I'd like to talk to my mother and stepfather before the news goes public. My relationship with them hasn't been the best these past few years." He felt the need to justify his decision. "But they deserve a conversation in person before word gets out."

"Of course." Kellan nodded. "Let me show you around and introduce you to some of the folks in—"

"Oh my God. Darius, you came."

They both turned to the sweet voice that trembled with emotion. He recognized his half sister, Sophie, from the picture Kace had shown him and the two hours of her lifestyle show webisodes he'd watched after Googling her. She was a gorgeous, full-figured woman with a smile as bright as the sun. Her brown eyes shone with tears.

She wiped at them and forced a laugh. "I mean, it's kind of you to volunteer this morning. For the club and for me. This is where I hope to have my wedding." She paused, studying his face. She lowered her voice to just above a whisper. "Is it all right if I hug you?"

His mouth spread in an involuntary grin and his eyes burned with emotion. Darius nodded. "I'd like that."

Sophie wrapped her arms around him and squeezed tight. She held on to him, and he let her. Her response was so sincere. He forced himself not to obsess over the conclusions other people might jump to about them.

Instead, he was grateful for her warm reception.

He was an older brother now. His sister seemed to need

this moment of connection, and he already felt an instinctive protectiveness toward her.

He'd been an only child, so this was a new experience for him. But he enjoyed this unfamiliar sense of belonging.

He was lucky. Things could've gone much differently. He was keenly aware of that.

"I'm sorry." Sophie released him, dabbing at her eyes. "I know we're keeping this on the low for now."

"It's okay." Darius smiled. "Congratulations on your engagement."

"Thank you." She beamed, then lowered her voice. "Please tell me you'll come to the wedding. No one has to know you're my brother, if that's what you'd prefer. But it would mean a lot to me if you came."

"If there are no conflicts with my schedule, I promise I'll be there."

"Good." Sophie seemed satisfied with his response. "Have you eaten? If not, you have to grab a breakfast sandwich and some coffee or juice. Then I'll introduce you to some of the folks in town. Let me go find Nigel. He's probably on the phone somewhere." Sophie wandered off to locate her fiancé.

"Welcome to the family." Kellan chuckled, his voice low.

"Is Vaughn here?" Darius asked.

Kellan frowned and sipped his coffee. "He sent a couple of his ranch hands instead." Kellan nodded toward two men standing in the corner nibbling on breakfast sandwiches.

"Maybe he wasn't up for meeting me," Darius said without resentment. It made sense that at least one of the three wouldn't be eager to welcome him to the family.

"Vaughn lives in Fort Worth, and he doesn't darken the town's doorstep, if he can avoid it. He wants nothing to do with our father, dead or alive."

Perhaps that was why Vaughn wasn't contesting the estate. He didn't want any part of the painful memories that went along with it.

Seems he was the lucky one to never have known Buckley Blackwood.

"I get it." Darius shrugged as they walked toward the breakfast buffet setup. "I didn't take the revelation that Will wasn't my biological father very well. I didn't feel I could trust them anymore. Our relationship hasn't been the same since."

"I can appreciate how difficult that must've been for you. But I wouldn't be surprised if your parents were obligated to keep your paternity to themselves. That's the way my father operated. So I wouldn't be too hard on them. Maybe they didn't have much choice." Kellan patted his shoulder. "I see someone I need to speak with, but I'll be back in a minute."

Darius stood there as Kellan walked away. He hadn't considered the possibility that there was a viable reason his mother hadn't disclosed his bio father's name.

Had Buck forced his parents to keep his secret in exchange for the financial support that had made it possible for him to attend schools like Harvard?

It was a secret the old man probably would've done just about anything to keep.

Maybe Kellan was right. Maybe he'd been too hard on them.

"Darius. What are you doing here?" Audra stared at him, her eyes wide.

She looked adorable in a pair of gray, cropped cargo pants and a long-sleeve white T-shirt. A heart-shaped gold locket, which matched the color and shape of her nose ring, dragged his attention to the deep vee of her shirt.

"A few of the locals invited me to volunteer. I decided I could use the mental break." His gaze shifted from hers.

A deep ache in his gut nagged at him for hiding his

connection to the Blackwoods from Audra. But the run-way show was just a few weeks away. He wouldn't risk the story about the CEO of Thr3d being the "bastard child" of the late Buckley Blackwood getting out and overshadowing the show. He didn't believe Audra would intentionally sabotage him. But what if someone overheard them or she told the wrong person?

Everything has to be perfect for this show.

It wasn't a chance he could afford to take. "I figured I'd help out for a few hours. How about you?"

"Sophie…my client—" Audra nodded in Sophie's direction "—asked me to help. Besides, several members of the bridal party are here. This gives me the chance to get to know them as I try to finalize the designs for their custom jewelry gifts."

"Makes perfect sense." He nodded.

They stood together in awkward silence. Close enough that he could feel the heat radiating from her smooth, toasted-brown skin and smell the sweet citrus scent wafting from her hair. Finally, Darius couldn't take the vivid images of them together—him touching her, kissing her, making love to her—that his brain conjured in the absence of words.

"Have you eaten breakfast yet?" he asked, abruptly. "I haven't, and I'm starving. I was about to grab a sandwich, if you'd care to join me."

"Sure." Audra followed him toward the bar where the food was set up. "And thank you for the salad the other night. It was thoughtful of you."

"For you, Audra? Anything."

Eight

Resentment bubbled up in Audra's chest and her hands clenched at her side.

Liar.

How dare he utter those words to her? If he'd truly do anything for her, he wouldn't have lied about his parents who were still very much alive. And he would've been honest about whatever it was that had prompted him to end their relationship.

"Darius, I want you to meet my fiancé, Nigel Townshend," Sophie was saying as she approached him. When Sophie caught sight of her behind Darius, her eyes widened. "Audra, I didn't realize you were here."

"I arrived five minutes ago." Audra folded her arms. "I thought you didn't know Darius."

"We met this morning," Sophie said quickly. "I wanted him to meet Nigel."

"Hello, Darius." Nigel extended his hand. "I'm Nigel Townshend, Sophie's fiancé. I run the *Secret Lives of NYC Ex-Wives*."

"Good to meet you." Darius shook Nigel's hand.

"Coffee?" Audra grabbed a mug and pulled the lever on the stainless steel coffee urn, dispensing the hot, black, aromatic liquid.

"Please," Darius said. "Black with—"

"Two sugars," she completed his sentence without thought.

They'd studied together over coffee. First at a coffee shop on campus. Eventually at her apartment the morning after he'd stayed over for breakfast…and more.

"Yes. Thank you." There was something warm and familiar in Darius's gaze that filled her chest with heat and made her belly flutter.

Audra returned her attention to the coffee station where she made his cup, then her own. By the time she'd grabbed a Danish for herself and rejoined the conversation, Sophie was asking Darius about his upcoming runway show at LA Fashion Week.

"I try to get out to the show whenever I can," Sophie said. "But with all of the preparations still to be made for the wedding... I don't know if I'll make it this year."

"If you can swing it, I hope you'll come. Just let me know and I'll reserve VIP passes for both of you." Darius sipped his coffee.

A generous offer to make to strangers.

But then, Sophie was a social influencer with an ever-popular lifestyle channel on YouTube and Nigel was a powerful television exec. It paid to have high-powered friends like that.

"You'll be attending the event, too, won't you, Audra?" Sophie asked excitedly.

"I'm supplying the jewelry for a couple of the designers," Audra confirmed.

It was a lucrative partnership. The design houses didn't purchase her jewelry for their runway shows. She loaned them the pieces. But she cleared millions of dollars in jewelry sales based on the free publicity.

"Great. Maybe we can get together in LA after your shows and celebrate." Sophie's gaze went from Darius's face to hers.

Neither of them responded right away.

"That would be great," Darius said, finally, then added, "If that's something Audra would want."

"Sure. If I can fit it into my schedule." Audra shrugged, then nibbled on the last of her Danish. "Now, who is it that I'm supposed to see about a volunteer assignment?"

"Ah...fresh blood." A strikingly handsome man with intense green eyes joined them.

"Ryan Bateman, meet Audra Lee Covington. She's in town to design some custom jewelry pieces for my wedding. And this is Darius Taylor-Pratt, who is here on business with Miranda Dupree. He's the founder and CEO of the athletic wear company, Thr3d." Sophie almost sounded proud of Darius.

"I'm a fan of your men's sportswear." Ryan tugged on the black shirt he was wearing. "And the Neapolitan engagement ring I got my wife was one of your limited edition pieces." He nodded toward Audra. "It's a stunning ring."

"Where is Tessa?" Sophie asked.

"Sophie! How are you?" A beautiful, brown-skinned woman with long, curly hair approached them. Her generous hips and full figure reminded Audra a lot of Sophie's as the two women hugged.

"Congratulations on your engagement. This must be your fiancé." Tessa shook Nigel's hand. "I've seen your crew around town."

"I trust that they aren't causing you too much trouble." Nigel's eyes sparkled.

Sophie introduced Tessa to Darius and then to her. Tessa was delighted to meet the designer of her engagement ring, and Audra was touched by the woman's heartfelt appreciation.

After five years of designing her own jewelry collections, it still moved her when a client gushed over one of her creations.

"I'm honored that you love it so much," Audra said.

"And I'm honored to meet you." A handsome man with the same nearly glowing, light brown eyes as Tessa's suddenly appeared. He shook her hand, staring at her as if he were mesmerized. "I'm Tessa's brother, Tripp Noble."

I bet you are a trip.

"Audra Lee Covington." She tugged her hand from his. "Good to meet you, Tripp."

She glanced over at Darius. His nostrils flared, and he looked like he wanted to toss Tripp outside, Jazzy Jeff style.

"Looks like we'll be teamed up." Tripp smirked.

"Darius and Audra are already teamed up," Sophie pinned Tripp with a narrowed gaze. "They dated back in grad school."

Tripp gave Sophie a subtle shrug.

"Milan!" Sophie waved another woman over. "You're just in time. Tripp needs a partner."

"Wait…what?" Milan narrowed her gaze at Tripp. He smiled sheepishly.

There was a story there if ever Audra had seen one.

Sophie introduced Milan Valez, a professional makeup artist who worked at the local salon and spa PURE.

"Our assignment is to replant the vegetation and to clean up the outdoor furniture that was salvaged by moving it offsite." Sophie reviewed a clipboard. "We'll be working throughout the outdoor space in teams of two, so…" She surveyed everyone gathered. "That's Ryan and Tess, Tripp and Milan, Darius and Audra, me and Nigel, Kace and…"

"Good morning, Lulu," Nigel greeted a woman Audra recognized as Lulu Shepard, one of the stars of the *Secret Lives of NYC Ex-Wives* show.

"Good morning, everyone." The woman raked her fingernails through her glossy black hair. Her gorgeous, dark brown skin practically glowed. She wore moto-style Balmain skinny jeans in a gray wash, a high-end, celebrity-brand graphic T-shirt that proclaimed *I'm Not Bossy, I'm a Boss* and a pair of black Prada riding boots. Not the kind of gear one typically wore for a dirty job like gardening or cleaning. But still, she looked amazing.

When Lulu's eyes met Kace's, there was a definite spark between the two. The man shifted his gaze.

Another man being mysterious about his feelings.

"I'm not sure where I should be right now." Lulu shrugged.

"Perfect. Because Kace needs a partner," Sophie said. "And Kellan, would you float between projects and give folks a hand wherever needed?"

"Sure, sis." Kellan held up his cup of coffee.

"I'm surprised you didn't object to Sophie teaming us up." Darius spoke in a hushed tone as they trailed Ryan and Tessa to the outdoor space.

"You did buy me dinner last night." She shrugged. "Wait… Did you ask Sophie to team us up?"

"Me?" His dark eyes went wide. There was definitely something up with him today. Not that he owed her an explanation. "No, I thought maybe you did. You obviously told her about our history."

"I wasn't gossiping about us, if that's what you're thinking." Audra's cheeks heated and her heart beat faster. "I mentioned that I'd run into my ex in town. Sophie asked who, and I told her. End of story. Maybe she thought we'd be comfortable working together because we already know each other."

"Well, I'm glad we're working together," he said. "It'll be nice to catch up."

Audra wasn't sure she agreed.

But she could do this. She could let go of her resentment and work with Darius. All she had to do was pretend her heart wasn't still tender over their breakup. And ignore the attraction that made her belly do flips whenever his gaze met hers.

Lulu stood on the TCC pool deck where she and Kace had been assigned to clean all of the furniture that had been stored offsite, beyond the fire's reach, but had still sustained some smoke damage.

She realized that most folks there probably believed she was volunteering simply to get prime footage for their reality show. But she'd asked the camera crew—currently following Rafaela and a few of the other women from the show who were there volunteering, too—to leave her out of any footage filmed that day. She'd come here for one reason: she wanted to help.

The devastation she'd seen, caused by the wildfires, had broken her heart. And despite what some people might think, she did in fact have a heart. A huge one she worked hard to hide behind her bubbly, playful, nothing-gets-to-me persona.

A woman in television had to be tough. A woman of color doubly so.

It was the façade she'd needed to adopt to protect her heart from the humiliation of her former football player ex-husband, Roderick Evans, replacing her with a pop star who'd had her own show on a kids' television network just a few years earlier.

And it was that bubbly, playful persona that garnered the attention of Nigel Townshend and the other execs when they were putting together their new reality show. The show was looking for a funny, wise-cracking character who never let anything faze her. Lulu's painstakingly procured persona fit the bill.

Her vulnerabilities she kept carefully tucked away.

"Everything okay?" Kace touched her arm, startling her. She could feel his warm, sweet breath on her ear.

Did anyone else notice the intimate gesture?

"I'm fine." Lulu withdrew her arm and stepped backward, nearly tripping over a small table.

Kace steadied her. His warm brown eyes glinted in the sunlight as they focused on hers, hidden behind a pair of Dolce & Gabbana sunglasses.

"Lu, are you sure you're okay?" he whispered.

"Of course." Lulu looked around. Fortunately, the camera crew was following Rafaela.

She stepped away from him, carefully this time, and picked up the two aprons, handing one to Kace.

"Why are we the only ones wearing aprons?" he asked, one brow raised. "Are they afraid you'll ruin your designer jeans and T-shirt?" His voice had a light, teasing tone, rather than the harsh one they'd used with each other when they'd met a few months ago.

"I suspect it's because we're the only ones working with bleach." She sniffed the scent rising from one of the buckets to confirm her suspicions.

"Noted." Kace was a man of few words when he wasn't being paid by the hour as a lawyer for his wealthy clientele. Clients like the obscenely rich, dead ex-husband of Lulu's costar Miranda Dupree.

Lulu looped the apron over her head and reached behind her to tie the strings.

"Let me get that," Kace offered, dropping his apron back onto the nearby chair. He took the apron strings from her hand and tied them at her back before her brain could register any objection.

"There." Kace secured the strings and stepped back, his eyes slowly gliding over her.

She was fully dressed. So why did she feel so naked beneath his gaze?

It was as if Kace could see to the very core of her being. Beyond the fronting, assumed persona, and any of the other bullshit she employed that served as a moat, drawbridge and flaming arrows to protect the one thing she was determined never to expose again: her heart.

Then, of course, there was the fact that he had, in reality, seen her naked.

Geez. What was with her? And why couldn't she resist this man?

Kace LeBlanc projected a "Just the facts, ma'am," by-the-book, stick-up-his-ass image to the world. But beneath that rigid exterior lay sensitivity and insight. Compassion. And an extremely passionate lover. All of which made her want him even more. But they were so different. Any attempt at a real relationship between them would surely end in disaster.

Yet, they had failed spectacularly at staying away from each other.

Did Sophie pick up on that vibe? Is that why she assigned us to work together?

They were getting sloppy with this whole undercover hookup thing. And the longer this went on, the more inconspicuous they were becoming.

"You're staring again." A barely perceptible smile turned up one edge of his sensual mouth.

"You've got soot on your cheek," she said, reaching up to wipe it away with her thumb.

"Must've transferred from the furniture when I picked up this apron." He positioned the garment over his clothing.

"Here, I've got it." Lulu stepped behind him and returned the favor by tying his apron. Then she slipped gloves on over her short but manicured fingernails. "Ready to get started?"

"You bet." Kace picked up a pair of gloves and put them on, too. "The quicker we get this done, the sooner I can get you back to my place." He leaned closer, whispering that last part in her ear.

A shiver ran down her spine.

"And just what makes you think I have any intention of going to your place?" She propped a hand on her hip. "I'm going to be grimy and dirty, and I'll need a shower and a change of clothes."

"I just happen to have a shower at my place," he said with a sarcastic grin. "And as for clothing, you're not going to need those for what I've got planned."

Damn.

Kace LeBlanc was getting more comfortable revealing glimpses of his softer, more relaxed self to her. The side of himself he didn't seem comfortable showing the rest of the world. Even in a white apron, scruffy casual clothing and a pair of rubber gloves, she couldn't help being attracted to him.

Her nipples grew taut and there was a steady pulse between her thighs, just thinking of all the ways he'd sated her body. Even just his kiss possessed the power to set her entire body on fire and leave her stunned, babbling nonsense.

It felt good to have a man so damn willing to satisfy her every need. But it was terrifying, too.

Mediocre lovers were easy to walk away from.

But a man who had brains, an incredible body and a sense of compassion... That combination was damned hard to leave behind.

"To be determined" was the only comeback she could manage.

Yep, he was definitely fucking with her head. She was the Queen of Quips. When had she ever been speechless?

"I'll take this bucket with the bleach solution." Kace stooped to pick up the bucket. "Wouldn't want you to get bleach spots on all that fancy gear you're wearing."

"These were supplied by the show's wardrobe department," she replied, picking up her bucket and sitting it beside a chair. "Besides, if I get bleach spots on these jeans, it'll make them look distressed, which is totally on trend this season."

Kace narrowed his gaze at her, shook his head and chuckled. He pulled out the scrub brush and went to work.

Lulu couldn't help smiling to herself as she picked up her soft brush and started to scrub a chair nearby.

Nine

After a grueling day working in the gardens at the Texas Cattleman's Club, Audra was tired and dirty, and her muscles ached.

She wanted nothing more than a long, hot, relaxing bubble bath with the jets turned up to full blast.

Despite the exhaustion and soreness, she'd enjoyed the day immensely. It'd been fun getting to know Sophie and her friends. And as much as she hated to admit it, she'd enjoyed working with Darius.

He'd been thoughtful—making sure she had water, coffee and snacks throughout the day. He'd been fiercely protective—worrying that she'd hurt herself using some of the equipment. And he'd been sweet and supportive when she'd chattered on, bouncing ideas off of him about a new limited edition collection of jewelry she was putting together.

It reminded her of how well matched they'd always been. Like two pieces of a puzzle. Which only made it more painful that he'd lied to her and then given up on their relationship without the decency of leveling with her about why.

She'd been determined to keep their interactions friendly and platonic. But she couldn't help that her wandering eyes were repeatedly drawn to the curve of his ass and the way his broad chest and shoulders expanded the material of his fitted shirt.

Nor could she help the naughty thoughts that ran rampant through her head as she remembered the feel of his body and wondered how much it had changed.

"Thanks for coming, Audra." Sophie squeezed her hand. "You, too, Darius."

"Of course." He nodded. "It was a pleasure to meet you all." He surveyed the main room of the clubhouse where people laughed and talked after a hard day's work. "I can see why everyone seems to love this town so much."

"Then maybe you'll stick around after your business with Miranda is done." Sophie grinned. "By the way, Kace had to leave, and he mentioned that he gave you a ride here. I imagine you'll need a ride back."

"I'm calling a car service." He held up his phone, the app already open.

"That's silly," Audra objected. "You're staying right next door to me. I'll give you a ride."

"Perfect." Sophie beamed. "Audra, I'll call you later. And Darius, I guess I'll be seeing you around town."

They said their good-nights to Sophie and then headed toward the parking lot.

"I didn't want to assume you were going straight home. Nor do I want to impose on you," Darius said.

"Where else would I possibly go looking like I've been making mud pies all day?" She stopped and turned toward him.

He broke into laughter, a sound she realized she'd missed. The corner of his mouth curved in a slow smile. "You might be a little dirty, Audra. That doesn't change the fact that you're a head turner. It certainly didn't keep your new friend Tripp from buzzing around you all day."

"Jealous?" She folded her arms, enjoying the tortured look on Darius's face.

"Of course not." His cheeks turned bright red and he cleared his throat. "What right do I have to be jealous of Tripp or any other man who takes an interest in you?"

Not the response she was hoping for—especially since it was complete bullshit. He'd practically stumbled over a garden hoe earlier, trying to get close enough to hear the conversation she'd been having with Tripp, an unabashed flirt.

"It was just an observation." Darius glanced at her convertible, quickly changing the subject. "Nice ride, but we're going to get your leather seats dirty."

"I've got it covered."

She popped the trunk and took out an old blanket she kept in the car, just in case.

"I should've known you would've come prepared." He chuckled.

Audra opened the door and started spreading the blanket on her side. It was long enough to cover Darius's seat, too, while leaving their seat belts and the central panel with the gearshift exposed.

They got buckled in and she headed toward their rental homes, riding mostly in silence.

"You're not actually interested in that guy, are you?" Darius asked suddenly,

The question took her by surprise.

"Like you said, what right do you have to be concerned about who I'm interested in?" She maintained her forward gaze.

"None." Darius heaved a sigh. "But that doesn't mean I'm not concerned about you, Audra. I want the best for you. I always have."

"And who made you the determiner of what's best for me?" She glanced at him briefly before returning her eyes to the road. "Tripp is a perfectly nice guy, from a perfectly nice family. He's a fourth-generation rancher, and his parents recently turned the business over to him."

"So he's wealthy and from a *good*—" he used air quotes "—family. Does that mean he can't be a creep? In my experience, that's the dude with the murder room in his basement."

"You have experience with that, do you?" She rolled her

eyes as she turned into the Pine Valley community and the guards waved them through the gates. "Well, in my experience, one guy is just as untrustworthy as the next. It's just a matter of playing the odds and hoping you win."

"You deserve better, Audra. Better than Tripp or me." Darius's voice was faint. Almost as if he'd said the words to himself and she just happened to overhear them.

"Am I supposed to be flattered that you're so concerned about my well-being that you've appointed yourself the judge of who is good enough for me and who isn't?" Her voice was suddenly tense. She clutched the steering wheel as she swung into the driveway of her rental and parked in the attached garage.

Audra turned off the engine and turned to face him. "If you'd really cared, you would've stuck around. Or at least been honest about why you left."

Darius grimaced. He opened his mouth to speak, then shut it again.

Figures.

"It doesn't really matter now, does it?" It hurt that he wouldn't even put in the effort to make a good excuse. Or, heaven forbid, finally tell her the truth. "Good night, Darius."

She stepped out of the car and shut the door much harder than she'd intended to.

Darius climbed out of the car, too. He removed the blanket from her leather seats and folded it.

"Despite how the day ended, I enjoyed working with you today, Audra."

"Same," she murmured begrudgingly.

He handed the blanket to her. "Thanks for the ride. Good night."

Darius walked out of the garage and across the lawn that separated their driveways.

Audra punched the button and watched as the garage door lowered, her eyes burning with tears.

Lulu opened the door of her hotel room at the Bellamy and looked either way. The hallway was clear of her costars, the camera crew and the numerous people who worked behind the scenes of the show.

She slipped out of the door, closing it behind her and hurrying to the elevator, relieved to make it to the lobby without encountering any of the show's staff.

She headed away from the main entrance, toward an obscure side entrance where her ride service was waiting.

Lulu adjusted her shades and tugged the sloppy beanie hat further down on her head as she slipped into the back seat of the car.

When the car dropped her off at the requested address, she got out, propped her leather backpack on her shoulder and tipped the man generously. When he drove away, she walked a few doors down to her actual destination.

Lulu climbed the stairs to the front door of the brick home painted beige. The fabric awning, shutters and wide front door were dark green, complementing the greenery in the landscaping.

Lulu sucked in a deep breath and rang the doorbell.

The door opened and Kace stood there staring at her. One side of his mouth curled in a sexy grin that made her want to climb him like a five-foot-eleven tree and have her way with him.

"About time you showed up." He swung the door open wider, allowing her to step inside.

"Don't get cocky, cowboy. Just because I'm here, it doesn't mean I'll stay." She stood along the wall, her arms folded as she surveyed the space. She'd been there before, but at the time she'd been too preoccupied with tearing off Kace's clothes to pay attention to the wallpaper and drapes.

"Yes, ma'am." He gave her a sly grin.

"And you did *not* know I'd come here."

He didn't acknowledge her objection. "The lasagna will be done shortly. I was just about to heat up the dinner rolls."

He led her through the house into the formal dining room where he had two places set.

"You *did* expect me." Lulu turned to him in amazement.

"I certainly hoped you'd come." He shrugged, an almost sheepish smile on his handsome face as he raked his hands through his brown mop of curls, still damp from the shower. "Belief can be a powerful thing."

"My grandmother used to say that." She smiled faintly.

"A wise woman," Kace said as he took her backpack and jacket. He placed them in one chair and pulled out another for her.

"I'd prefer to help in the kitchen, if you don't mind." She inhaled the fresh, clean scent of his soap.

He led the way to the kitchen, and they chatted while she cut up vegetables for their salad.

"This is such a beautiful, charming old home." She glanced around the space. "When was it built?"

"Back in 1925. It belonged to my grandparents. My grandmother left it to me. I'm the only child of their only child," he said, "so the competition wasn't very stiff."

She laughed. "Did they do all of this updating to the place, too?"

The house was filled with character and original features like the marble fireplace hearth, hardwood floors and beautiful French doors. But it had lots of modern conveniences, too, like a beautiful kitchen island with seating and stainless steel appliances.

"No, that was all me. I started with the kitchen and I've been doing one room at a time until I'm finished."

"It's beautiful, and it's nothing at all like I would've expected your place to be. But for that matter, you're nothing at all like I would've expected, either."

He slipped one arm around her waist and cradled her cheek with the other hand. "Neither are you, Lulu Shepard." He pressed a soft, sweet kiss to her mouth.

Lulu wrapped her arms around his back, still slightly damp through his soft cotton T-shirt. She lifted onto her toes, trying to close the remaining gap between their heights in her three-inch heels.

There was something in Kace's kiss that sparked a fire within her and sent shivers down her spine. Her body instantly reacted to his touch. Her nipples beaded and she ached for him.

Kace backed her against a wall, his hands roaming over her curves as his kiss grew more demanding. Her heart thumped harder and her pulse raced as his tongue glided against hers and he gripped her bottom, pulling her body tighter against his hardened length.

"I don't think I have to tell you how much I want you," he whispered against her skin as he trailed kisses down her neck.

He grabbed the edge of her short knit dress and inched the hem up over her hips.

Suddenly, the oven's buzzer sounded.

Kace blew out a frustrated breath and pressed another kiss to her lips. "We'll finish this later."

Lulu could only manage a nod. She lowered the hem of her dress, her heart still racing and her chest heaving as she caught her breath.

Kace took the lasagna and rolls out of the oven and took them to the table. She followed with the salad and bottle of wine.

They actually managed to make it through the meal— laughing, chatting and shamelessly flirting—before he took her to bed and made love to her.

They lay together in the dark, her cheek pressed to his chest and her leg entwined with his. She was in heaven. And she'd like nothing better than to lie in his arms all night. But it was late, and she needed to get back to the hotel before someone came looking for her.

Lu lifted her head and placed a kiss on his stubbled chin. "I'd better go."

"Don't leave. Please. Stay." He cradled her cheek.

"You know why I need to leave." She ran her fingers through his soft, damp hair. "The last thing either of us wants is for the cameras to capture my 'walk of shame' in the morning."

"I'm not ashamed of what we have together, Lu. Are you?"

"No, of course not. I just didn't think you wanted everyone to know your business."

"I don't." He shrugged. "But I do want everyone to know you're mine."

Kace raked her hair to one side so he could get a clear view of her face in the light coming from a bedside lamp. He pressed another kiss to her mouth as he glided his hands up her bare back.

"Does that mean you want…are you asking me—"

"I'm completely enamored with you, Lu. I want to be with you. Just you. And the thought of another man touching you this way drives me insane." His intense gaze met hers. "I don't want to creep around town, pretending we can barely stand each other. I want to take you out for a night on the town. Because that's what you deserve."

He kissed her again, and she could swear she was melting into a puddle of goo.

"Why?" She pulled back from his kiss, her eyes searching his. "Why do you want to be with me, Kace?"

His eyes widened, as if he was shocked that she needed to ask. "Because I see you, Lulu. All of you. You're strong and kind and brave. You're compassionate. You've got an incredibly big heart. There's so much more wit and depth than you show people on TV each week. I wish everyone could see you the way I do."

Tears welled in her eyes, her vision blurring. She couldn't stop the tears that rolled down her cheeks. Her heart felt as if it were swelling inside her chest.

Lulu pressed her mouth to his.

For the first time in a long time, she felt truly seen by a man. Kace could see through all the pretense and bullshit. He appreciated and wanted the woman she was when they were alone, and the hot lights and cameras were turned off. Without the makeup and all of the trappings of the *Secret Lives* lifestyle.

He just wanted *her*. And she wanted him, too.

She had no intention of leaving this bed tonight. Maybe ever.

Ten

Darius had spent the entire morning on one video conference or phone call after another. They'd tweaked the fall line, decided on which garments would be worn together and in which colors. Now they were deciding which of the models engaged for the show should wear each outfit.

The doorbell rang and the delivery person handed him the package he knew contained the prototypes of the swimsuits he'd designed for the show.

He tossed the package on his desk and kept working. He was always a little nervous to see his creations come to life for the first time. There was something amazing about holding a garment in his hand that he'd conceived from beginning to end. If it hit the mark, it was an incredible rush. If it didn't, it was a mentally exhausting letdown. Right now, he couldn't afford either. He needed to stay focused on the job at hand.

Two hours later, he and the team had decided which model would wear each look and the order in which the models would appear. They'd given the swimsuit designs tentative placement in the lineup, until he had the chance to examine each garment and determine if they met the Thr3d standards—both functionally and aesthetically.

Shortly after the conference call, his cell phone rang. He didn't recognize the number.

"Hello?"

"Darius, hi. It's Sophie. I got your number from Kellan. I hope you don't mind."

"No, of course not." He looked up from his laptop where he'd been scrolling through a list of potential music for the runway show. "What can I do for you, Sophie?"

"I don't know how long you plan to be in town, so I wanted to squeeze in some time for us to get to know each other."

"Sure," he said absently. "I'd like that, too."

"I'm going horseback riding at my friend's ranch on the edge of town tomorrow afternoon. Have you ever been horseback riding?"

"No, Sophie," he said patiently with a small chuckle. "It's not a popular activity in Central LA, where I grew up."

"Right." Sophie laughed nervously. "Well, I know you've probably been working like crazy. But I was hoping you could spare a couple of hours to go riding with me."

"I don't know, Soph." The nickname came out without thought. It felt natural. "Tomorrow, I'm simulating a run-through of the entire runway show. I'm not sure I'll be done by early afternoon. My team is a couple of hours behind me in LA."

"When we were volunteering on Saturday, you said yourself that everything is pretty much set for the show. That you're just making yourself crazy by going over every single detail again and again," she reminded him.

He had said that. *Note to self: learn to keep your big mouth shut.*

"C'mon, Darius, it'll be fun. I promise," she continued when he didn't respond. "And it'll give you a chance to explore Royal a bit more. You can't spend your entire stay here locked away in that house. Besides, a little fresh air and brisk activity is good for the creative process. It always spurs new ideas for me or helps me find a solution to whatever design issue I'm trying to tackle."

So this is what it's like to have a little sister.

He could just imagine how Sophie had worked the sad voice and big puppy dog eyes when she was a kid. No wonder Kellan said she had him and Vaughn wrapped around her pinkie finger.

"All right, Sophie. You've convinced me." He leaned back in his chair and glided a hand over his stubbly head. He made a mental note to run a razor over it in the morning. "I'll be there. Just text me the time and location."

"I'll send you a text message shortly."

He could practically hear the victory grin in Sophie's voice when they said their goodbyes.

Darius stood and stretched, walking around the desk. He pressed the heel of his palms to his eyes. Honestly, he could probably use the time away from his computer. He was beginning to go cross-eyed and his brain was in a fog.

Perfect time to shift gears.

Darius opened the package with the four swimsuits. He held each garment up to the light and examined it carefully, testing whether the material was opaque enough. Then he took each individual suit and stretched the material in all four directions.

Everything looks good.

He heard a splash and walked over to the window. It was Audra's first swim since their argument.

He was glad she'd resumed her swimming. Audra had been on her high school and college swim teams and she loved the water. She was practically a mermaid. He hated being the reason she stopped doing something she loved so much.

For her, swimming was moving meditation. She worked her problems out as her hands and feet sliced through the water.

Darius couldn't tear himself from the window. He'd always found watching Audra swim hypnotic and calming. In some small way, she was part of his life again. At least for as long as they were both in Royal.

Darius climbed into his newly rented SUV and drove to Magnolia Acres, as Sophie had directed. Apparently, a longtime friend of his siblings' mother owned the ranch, located on the edge of town.

He'd almost canceled their appointment when Sophie mentioned that Dixie Musgraves—the owner of both the ranch and the home Audra was renting—had been her late mother's best friend. Wouldn't the woman resent him—the product of an affair Buckley Blackwood had behind her best friend's back?

Sophie assured Darius that Dixie didn't blame him for their father's indiscretions. None of them did.

He hadn't been completely convinced, but Sophie was persistent. And there was something about her that made him hate the idea of disappointing her.

So here he was.

Darius parked and climbed out of the black luxury SUV. Unsure what constituted appropriate horse-riding gear, he'd worn his broken-in jeans, a plaid shirt layered over a performance T-shirt and a pair of Thr3d hiking boots. It was a beautiful afternoon; sunny and temperate for March.

He approached the open stables, but no one seemed to be around. "Sophie!" he called.

A couple of the horses looked at him, while the rest seemed unimpressed by his arrival. He couldn't help stopping to stare at them. He'd never been this close to a horse before.

They were beautiful, majestic animals. And much larger than he'd imagined. Even at his height of six-two, the horses' heads towered over his.

After fifteen minutes, he checked his watch. It was ten minutes past the time he and Sophie had agreed to meet.

He'd rearranged his day, started early and gotten nearly everything completed before leaving the house just so he could be here. But if Sophie was just blowing him off, there were tons of things he could be doing instead.

"I'm sorry I'm late, but I was out by the creek on the

other end of the ranch doing some sketching and lost track of…" Audra hurried into the stable, breathless, then caught sight of him. "Darius? What are you doing here?"

Strands of her wavy hair clung to her forehead, wet with perspiration. She tucked a few loose strands behind her ear and glanced down at her clothing. Her cheeks turned bright red.

Her light blue shirt was smudged with dirt and there was a smidgen of it on one cheek. Dust and streaks of dirt were on her cropped cargo pants, too. She folded her arms over her chest.

"I'm here to meet my…" His words trailed off quickly and he tugged at the collar of his shirt, allowing cool air inside. "Sophie invited me to go riding. As a way to spark creativity. I've got a problem I've been trying to figure out."

He hated keeping something from Audra again. He kept his words as close to the truth as possible without revealing the nature of his relationship with the Blackwoods.

"That's why she invited me here." Audra narrowed her gaze at him, closing the space between them. "What kind of game are the two of you running?"

Darius folded his arms and studied Audra, who was clearly agitated. "You think I had something to do with this?"

"You keep showing up everywhere I am." She gestured wildly. "How do you explain that?"

"I can't." He shrugged. "But I had no idea you'd be here in Royal. I had no clue you were renting the house next door to the one Miranda provided. I didn't expect to see you at the Texas Cattleman's Club on Saturday, and believe me, I sure as hell didn't expect to see you here." He kept his voice calm.

Audra was a little firecracker who wore her emotions on her sleeve. The most passionate person he'd ever known.

He'd never had a more ardent lover than Audra. She'd ruined him for any woman after her.

"Why should I believe you?" She was asking, her button nose scrunched and her brows furrowed.

"Why would I lie to you about this?"

"Why should you lie to me about *anything*, Darius?" There was hurt in her tone and expression.

"Audra, I'm not lying to you. I really had no idea you'd be here. Trust me, if—"

"How could I possibly trust a man who'd lie about his own parents being dead? Who would do something like that?"

Shit.

His heart thumped in his chest and his pulse raced. "How long have you known?"

"Three years. I read that—"

"Rock magazine article," he finished her statement with a heavy sigh. He wished he could take back that interview. He'd won an award that night, had drunk far too much premium vodka—something he'd stayed away from ever since—and had granted a magazine reporter an impromptu interview.

Darius had said a lot of things he shouldn't have. He'd come off as arrogant and resentful. And he'd talked too honestly about his estranged relationship with his mother and stepfather.

He'd felt awful when he'd read the magazine article. Though he hadn't spoken with his parents much prior to the publication of the article, he'd called to apologize. The upside was that he'd done a better job of staying in contact with them ever since.

He'd call. Briefly inquire after their health. Ask if either of them needed anything. Then he'd tell them that he would get out to see them whenever he could.

Only he never did.

As long as his parents weren't willing to reveal the name of his biological father, he hadn't been able to get over his resentment.

"Audra, I'm sorry. I didn't try to deceive you. I just—"

"You just what, Darius? Explain why'd you'd lie to me about something like that. What kind of sick person—"

"I didn't intend to lie to you, Audra. You asked about my parents, and I told you they were no longer in my life." He shrugged. "A week later I heard you telling a friend my parents were dead. I was going to correct you, but then… I didn't. Because at that time, they were as good as dead to me. I was bitter and angry, and I didn't want anything to do with them." He shrugged. "So rather than creating an embarrassing situation for both of us, I allowed the misunderstanding to stand. It was wrong of me. I realized that rather quickly. But I didn't know how to fix it. If I told you the truth—"

"I'd think you were an ass. Which you are. What could your parents have possibly done to make you so angry with them?"

He opened his mouth to speak, but she cut him off with the wave of her hand.

"Never mind. It doesn't even matter. Anyone who could lie to the person they claimed to love about something like that…" Her voice broke. "I was foolish to believe you ever loved me."

"No, that isn't true." His heart thumped and his pulse raced. He didn't blame Audra for thinking badly of him. He'd been a jerk for the way he'd ended things between them and a liar for allowing her to believe his parents were dead. Still, he couldn't abide her doubting he'd ever really loved her.

"How could you possibly think that I didn't love you?" Darius stepped closer and lightly gripped her shoulders. His eyes searched hers. "You meant everything to me,

Audra. Walking away from you was the hardest thing I've ever done."

"Then why'd you do it? If you loved me so much, why'd you walk away?" Her voice trembled and the corners of her eyes were wet with tears.

He dropped his gaze from hers momentarily before forcing his eyes to meet hers again.

"Is it really that hard for you to understand why, Audra?" He dropped his hands from her shoulders. "You're a diamond heiress. The princess of a political dynasty. Your family has more money than God. And I was this poor, scholarship student whose mother tanked her acting career with booze and pills. Not the kind of thing a conservative senator who runs on a family values platform wants for his daughter."

Darius ran a hand over his head, the skin damp with sweat, despite the cool temperature. Revealing the ugly truth that he'd been a coward left him drained.

He'd ended it because he'd known it would only be a matter of time before Audra would move on. She'd eventually find someone who fit into her world and could give her the life she deserved.

He'd wanted to spare them both the pain of getting in any deeper. And he'd thought it would hurt less if he'd ended things on his terms, rather than waiting for the other shoe to fall. That it would lessen the inevitable sting of rejection he knew all too well.

He'd been wrong.

"I never treated you differently, Darius. The money never mattered to me."

"It *did* matter," he countered. "After I insisted on paying for our dates, you didn't want to go to your favorite restaurants anymore. You'd pass on trips with your friends."

"I was being considerate. If you hadn't been so bullheaded, I could've just paid for both of us. I had plenty, and I didn't mind sharing."

"I didn't want you to feel like I was using you."

"Nobody thought that."

"Your friends certainly did."

Her eyes widened, as if she was mortified by his statement, but she didn't deny it. "They told you that?"

"Not in those exact words. But I got the point, just the same." The muscles in his shoulders tensed as he'd recalled the painful memories. "Jessica told me about all of the trips and events you'd skipped because of me. The ones I didn't know about. And your friend Jason wondered aloud how long you planned to 'slum it.'" Darius leaned against one of the empty stalls. "He said it was practically a rich kid rite of passage and that you had a thing for lost causes."

"And you took their word for it? Without even asking me?" she demanded, her voice trembling.

"Not at first. But then I realized that they were right. Eventually, you'd want a man with wealth, power and an upstanding family name. I had none of those, and nothing to give you except for what felt, at the time, like one hell of a long shot. You deserved better than that."

"So is that when you first appointed yourself arbiter of What Audra Deserves?" Her expression was a mixture of sadness, anger and disappointment. "Who your parents are and the number of zeroes in your bank account was never an issue for me, Darius."

"No?" He folded his arms, peering at her intensely.

"How could you even ask me that?"

"Because you never introduced me to your parents when they came to visit you on campus. You never so much as hinted that you wanted me to meet them."

The pain of that long-ago realization still hurt.

"I never… I mean, I didn't…" she stammered.

"You wanted to have this conversation, Audra. So let's

have it. You were embarrassed to introduce me to your parents because you knew they'd never approve of you dating me."

"That isn't true. I…" Audra suddenly looked deflated. "I mean…yes, I knew they would think I wasn't being sensible about my future and what was best for the family." She sighed. "I can't even tell you how many times I've heard that line."

"It's okay, babe." He didn't want to hurt her more than he already had. "I understand. Family is a complicated thing. No one knows that more than me. But that's why I walked away. In the end, it was inevitable."

"No, you're wrong." She met his gaze. "I might've been hesitant to tell my parents that I was head over heels for someone they wouldn't have chosen for me. But I *was* going to tell them. I loved you, Darius. I would've done anything for you. I thought you felt the same."

"I did. Audra, I've never loved anyone as much as I loved you."

"But not enough to share your reservations with me. Or enough to tell me the truth about your parents. Not enough to—"

Darius cradled her face and lowered his mouth to hers, silencing her with a kiss. He savored the lips he'd been longing to kiss since he'd set eyes on them in that diner. They were as soft and sweet as he remembered. Flavored by the lip gloss she wore.

Audra tensed in his arms initially, surprised by his sudden action. Though she couldn't have been much more surprised than he was.

He honestly hadn't intended to kiss her. He'd just needed to convince her that what he'd felt for her was real, regardless of what else she might think of him.

Audra tipped her head back, her mouth parting as she wrapped her arms around him.

Darius pressed a hand to her back as his tongue glided against hers and the smooth, round, steel barbell that pierced it. A jolt of desire ran through his body at the sensation. She clutched at the back of his shirt, erasing the sliver of space between their bodies. And he soon lost himself in the warmth of her embrace, the hunger in her kiss.

He'd missed everything about this woman.

The feel of her. The taste of her. The way she'd made him feel.

Darius was relieved by her reaction. If she'd given the slightest indication the kiss was unwanted, he would've apologized for reading her wrong and never laid a hand on her again. But instead of withdrawing, Audra curled deeper into him. She welcomed his kiss with a sweet little murmur, as if she couldn't get enough. The vibration of that carnal sound sent a shiver down his spine, his body responding to hers.

He teetered backward, his back pressed against the post behind him. She moved closer, eliminating the space created by the shift in his position.

Darius glided a hand beneath her shirt. His fingertips caressed the soft, smooth skin on her back. His other hand inched downward, resting just short of the curvy ass that left him mesmerized every time she walked away from him. Her figure was a little fuller now than it had been five years ago. But the additional weight suited her, having settled in all the right places.

He kissed her harder. Deeper. Both of them were breathing heavily, but too consumed with the passion rising between them to stop.

Audra's hands glided up his chest and she fumbled with the buttons on his shirt. She slipped one button through its snug hole. Then another. And another.

His mind raced, and his heart thumped wildly. The sound of his own heartbeat filled his ears.

He wanted her. *Desperately.*

Darius ached to examine every inch of her fuller frame. To feel her body beneath his. To relive the indescribable pleasure of being inside her. But he'd imagined it too long to settle for a quick roll in the literal hay with Mr. Ed and his friends watching.

"Audra, I—" He stopped suddenly.

Was that the sound of tires on gravel?

"What is it?" Audra frowned, her breathing ragged.

"I think someone is coming." He loosened his grip on her.

"Oh." She stepped beyond his reach, smoothing her hair back and rubbing at the stray gloss around her lips.

Lip gloss. Shit.

He rubbed at his mouth with the back of his hand as Sophie and Nigel strode into the stables hand in hand.

"There you two are. I thought you might've started down the trail without us, since neither of you responded to my text message that we were running late." Sophie's gaze went from Darius to Audra and back again.

He'd left his phone in the truck, not wanting it to get jostled as he rode a horse. And he hadn't felt Audra's phone in any of her pockets as she'd pressed against him.

"Nigel had to handle some last-minute business with the show," Sophie continued, when neither of them spoke. "I hope we haven't inconvenienced either of you too much."

"Actually…" Audra said, "I'm beat. I've been out here most of the day. I just want to take a long bath. Maybe turn in early tonight."

"Of course. I'm sorry we kept you waiting." Sophie's brows furrowed and she glanced between them again, as if trying to determine if something had gone wrong. "Rain check?"

"Absolutely." Audra smiled at Sophie. The two women hugged. "Goodbye, Nigel." She nodded at the man, but then barely cast a glance in Darius's direction as she called out, "Goodbye, Darius."

Audra was gone before he could blink.

"Sorry we interrupted," Sophie said, breaking into his thoughts.

"Interrupted?" It was best to plead ignorance.

Sophie exchanged a knowing look with her fiancé, then gestured to her face. "You have her lip gloss all over your mouth."

Darius scrubbed at his mouth and the area surrounding it with the back of his hand again. This time harder.

He was glad Sophie didn't ask what had happened between him and Audra. Though his lip gloss–stained lips told the story well enough.

"Now it's time for your first riding lesson." His sister grinned. "I'll show you how to strap on a saddle."

Darius followed Sophie to one of the stalls, which housed a majestic horse with a shiny black coat. He listened as Sophie schooled him on the horse he'd be riding and gave him pointers on warming up to the animal.

But he was only thinking of Audra and the bitter words she'd flung at him prior to their kiss.

If you loved me so much, why'd you walk away?

I loved you, Darius. I would've done anything for you. I thought you felt the same.

The heat and passion between them were as intense as ever. But he'd wounded Audra, and she no longer trusted him. He'd wrecked their relationship, and there was no one but himself to blame.

Eleven

Audra paced just inside the front door of her rental home. She'd kissed Darius in the stables three days ago, and she hadn't seen him since. In fact, she'd gone out of her way to avoid him. That included not swimming for the past three days.

Now she was restless. Partly because her routine had been disrupted. Partly because her daily swims helped her to blow off steam. And partly because she hadn't been able to stop thinking of that kiss.

Darius was such an amazing kisser.

There was something in his kiss that was hungry, yet tender. She never understood how he managed that. She only knew that she'd never had a kiss quite like it. And though her head knew that the last thing she needed was to kiss Darius again, her heart and her body craved it.

Audra dragged a hand through her hair and sighed.

She was being ridiculous. There was no need for her to avoid Darius. They were two reasonable adults whose relationship didn't work out.

Shit happened.

But they could still be cordial. They could see each other around town and maybe even laugh off the kiss.

Audra checked the clock. Sophie was expecting her at the TCC clubhouse in half an hour for more restoration work. She didn't know whether Darius intended to be there, but she wouldn't tiptoe around on eggshells trying to avoid him anymore. So they might as well get the awkward conversation over.

She made her way to his place. Eyes closed briefly, she sucked in a deep breath and rang the bell.

Audra knew he was there, but part of her hoped he wouldn't answer the door. She heard movement inside.

No such luck.

She could see him through the glass pane. He paused momentarily, his eyes widening.

"Audra, hey." He leaned against the doorframe. "What can I do for you?"

"Can we talk?"

"Sure." He gestured for her to come inside. "I'm heading out in a few minutes."

"Going to the TCC clubhouse for volunteer duty? Me, too," she said when he'd nodded in response. "That's why I thought we should talk. If we get paired together again, I don't want things to be weird between us."

He rubbed the sexy scruff on his chin, and she instantly recalled the scrape of his stubbly beard against her skin when they'd kissed.

"I'm glad you came by, Audra. I wanted to apologize. I shouldn't have kissed you. I made an awkward situation unbearable."

"I appreciate the apology, but it isn't necessary. After all, I kissed you back." She shrugged as if it were no big deal, refusing to acknowledge the racing of her pulse. "We got caught up in the moment."

"Yeah, I guess we did."

Heat flared in her chest and her belly tensed as they stared at each other, neither of them speaking. Finally, Darius broke the silence.

"Still, I shouldn't have…and it won't happen again. So there's no need for you to stop using the pool. I screwed things up between us, but I honestly do care for you." He sighed. "I hope that we can be friends."

"I'd like that." She nodded.

Darius checked his watch, then grabbed his keys off the kitchen counter. "It's getting late. We'd better head out."

She couldn't help smiling. Darius hated being late. In fact, he was usually early for everything.

"You know, it's silly for both of us to drive when we're headed to the same place. Why don't I give you a ride to the clubhouse?" Audra tried not to sound eager.

"Or I could give you one. Your driving still makes me a little nervous." He chuckled.

Audra laughed, the tension between them easing slightly. "It isn't my driving that makes you nervous. It's the fact that you aren't in control. Same reason you don't love flying."

"Maybe there's some truth to that." Darius massaged the back of his neck. "But I had to get over it. The flying thing I mean. I had to hop a plane with a moment's notice to meet with investors in the beginning. So I finally read that book you gave me on nervous flyers. It helped. I hardly think about it anymore."

"I'm glad. And I accept your offer. Let me close up the house, then I'll meet you at your SUV."

Darius agreed, his mouth cocked in a wry grin that did things to her.

It's just a ride into town.

They'd be alone in the car together five minutes each way. Ten, tops. She could certainly keep her head, and legs, together that long.

Still, Darius Taylor-Pratt was her personal Kryptonite. She needed to maintain emotional distance from the man. Or else she was going to need to get herself a damned good lead suit.

"Audra, you look rather happy this morning." Sophie grinned as she dispensed coffee into two mugs.

"Good morning, Sophie."

Audra liked Sophie Blackwood. She could imagine them becoming friends. So she didn't want to hurt Sophie's feelings, but they needed to have a serious conversation.

"Could we talk for a sec?" Audra stepped closer and lowered her voice.

"Uh-oh." Sophie put the mugs back on the table. "You're upset about the other day."

"I'm not upset." Audra touched the woman's arm. "I realize that you're happy and in love and you think everyone else should be, too. But Darius and I had our chance. It didn't work out for us. We're both okay with that."

"Are you?" Sophie asked. "I mean, I know it's none of my business, but we couldn't help noticing that your lip gloss was smudged on Darius's face. You two were obviously kissing before we arrived."

Audra's face heated. She cleared her throat. "Darius and I talked this morning. It was a mistake neither of us plans to repeat. I appreciate your concern, but we're both good with things the way they are."

"I hope I haven't caused any problems between you." Sophie sounded incredibly sad.

"Everything is fine. In fact, we rode in together this morning. Just because it made sense," she added.

"All right," Sophie agreed begrudgingly. "No more shenanigans from me. Scout's honor." She touched three fingers to her forehead in a Scout salute.

"Thanks, Sophie. Now tell me where you need me this morning."

"Come with me. I've got just the spot for you."

A slow smile spread across Sophie's face and her brown eyes danced mischievously. Audra groaned quietly. Despite the other woman's promise, something told Audra that her plea to Sophie had fallen on deaf ears.

"Thanks for volunteering again today." Kellan approached as Darius filled his mug with steaming hot coffee.

"No problem. How's your wife?" Darius inquired.

"Mornings are tough for Irina right now. But she's anxious to meet you. She wants me to invite you for dinner one evening."

"Sounds great. Let's shoot for a date after Fashion Week. Right now, even when I'm not working, my brain is running through everything and trying to head off a million ways the show could go wrong."

"Sounds like a lot of pressure." Kellan sipped his coffee.

"It is." Darius added two packets of sugar to his cup. "But I enjoy the entire process. It's just the nature of the business. I'm fortunate to be doing work I love."

"Can't ask for much more than that in life." Kellan set his empty coffee mug with the other dirty ones. "There's one other thing that Sophie and I would like to talk to you about."

"Oh?" Darius sipped his hot coffee. His gut tensed at Kellan's serious tone. "What is it?"

"It's about our father's estate. As you know, the old bastard cut us out of the will and left everything to his ex-wife." Kellan tried to maintain an even temperament, but even without knowing the man well, Darius could tell that he was seething beneath that cool facade.

"Yes. What of it?" Darius hadn't talked about money or the estate with either Sophie or Kellan. He didn't want them thinking he was only after a payday.

"Miranda was married to our father for a short time. The house, the land it sits on, the Blackwood Bank…none of those things should go to her. They should stay in the family." Kellan frowned deeply, and his blue eyes turned stormy. The crinkles around his narrowed gaze, filled with pain, made him look considerably older than he had moments ago. "Sophie, Vaughn and I put up with a lot of shit from our dad over the years. So did our mother. Those holdings are part of our family's legacy. That's why Sophie and I are contesting the will. And we'd like you to join us in the claim against Miranda."

"I see." Darius sipped his coffee. His mind spun as he considered what Kellan was asking of him.

Miranda had made it clear that she had a genuine interest in partnering with his company. If he joined his siblings in contesting the will, he could kiss the deal with Miranda's Goddess brand goodbye.

There was a hell of a lot of money at stake.

According to his personal lawyer, Blackwood's estate was worth hundreds of millions of dollars, even split between the four siblings.

But the deal with Miranda would also be extremely lucrative—not just for him personally, but for his employees and the investors who'd believed in his vision from the start. And creating a line for the Goddess brand could be the springboard that would prompt other companies to collaborate with Thr3d to create their clothing lines, too.

"What's Vaughn's position on this?" Darius asked.

Kellan laughed bitterly. "He wants nothing to do with our father's legacy. If Vaughn up and changed the name of his company from Blackwood Energy to something else completely, I'd hardly be surprised. His position is that Miranda should enjoy whatever portion of the inheritance would've gone to him. Sophie and I, clearly, don't agree."

Darius hated to disappoint his new brother. He liked Kellan and Sophie and relished the kinship he felt with them. But he had an obligation to his business. He'd spent most of his adult life constructing what he hoped would one day be a billion-dollar international brand.

He couldn't allow the warm, fuzzy feelings toward his newfound family to destroy everything he'd built. Not now, when it felt like his goal was in reach.

"Look, Kellan, I appreciate that you and Sophie want me to join in on the claim. That's generous of you, given the circumstances. But the reason I came here was to partner with Miranda and her Goddess brand. If I join you and Sophie in the suit against her—"

"You'll blow the deal." Kellan groaned quietly and shrugged one shoulder. "I get it. You've known us all of two weeks. You've probably been working toward a deal like this for years."

"Exactly. And I'm not saying that I won't do it. Just that I need some time to weigh out the pros and cons. My entire team is depending on me. I can't make a decision on a whim just because I'm incredibly fond of both of you. I hope you understand."

"I do." Kellan nodded. "We'll respect your choice, either way. It doesn't change the fact that you're our brother, and we want you to be part of our lives."

"Thanks." Darius's shoulders relaxed. He really did like both Kellan and Sophie. "Can I get back to you on this in a few weeks?"

"Fine by me. I think Sophie would be okay with it, too." Kellan glanced toward where Sophie was waving the two of them over. "It appears we're being summoned." Kellan nodded toward their sister.

Darius finished his coffee and discarded his cup. As he approached Sophie, there was a mischievous glint in her eyes.

Please, no more of Sophie's unsolicited matchmeddling.

"Good morning, Kellan and Darius. We have new work assignments." Sophie consulted the clipboard in her hand.

"Okay," Darius said cautiously, his belly tensing with the suspicion that his sister was up to something. "Just tell me where you need me."

"We'll be working in the gardens again, but with different partners this time."

"Who am I working with this morning?"

Sophie's grin deepened. "Rafaela Marchesi." She swept her hand in the direction of a beautiful woman, who he'd guess was about ten years his senior. She stood about three inches shy of his height and had cascading waves of thick brown hair.

The woman grinned and her eyes, the color of root beer, danced as she surveyed him. She extended a hand for him to kiss.

He held it in both of his instead. "It's a pleasure to meet you Ms. Marchesi. I look forward to working with you."

"Likewise, Darius." The woman smiled, seemingly amused that he'd politely dodged kissing her hand.

She was statuesque, with her hourglass figure and perfect posture. Her designer skinny jeans clung to her frame and her off-shoulder blouse nicely complemented her shape.

Rafaela slipped her arm through his. "And please, I must insist that you call me Rafaela."

"I will." He nodded. Something about the hungry way in which the woman scanned his frame made him feel naked.

"Audra, there you are." Sophie called to her as she entered the outdoor space.

His gaze met Audra's and then hers zeroed in on the woman's arm wrapped around his. The easy smile on her face turned to a scowl momentarily. But then she forced a smile.

"You haven't lost your partner already, have you?" Sophie teased.

Tripp, the man who'd been so fascinated with Audra the previous week, suddenly appeared. He handed her a bottle of water.

Darius's hands curled into fists at his sides suddenly and his jaw clenched. He shifted his gaze to Sophie, who was smiling like a Cheshire cat.

Well played, Sophie.

"Darius, you must tell me all about your company. Sophie tells me that you're a designer and that you'll be doing a show at LA Fashion Week. How fabulous," Rafaela was saying as she led him to the far side of the garden. "Of course, you must know that before I joined the cast of *Secret Lives*, I was a model myself."

Rafaela is a member of the Secret Lives *cast?*

"No, I wasn't aware." He really needed to catch an episode or two of the show, if for no other reason than to be able to identify any other cast members he might run into around town. "But it doesn't surprise me."

Her smile widened, as her grip on his bicep tightened. "You're a very handsome man, Darius. Have you ever been married?"

He sucked in a deep breath and sighed.

It's going to be an incredibly long day.

Twelve

Audra worked with Tripp to replant new bushes. Her new partner was handsome, to say the least. But he was also well aware of it. Yet, despite his cocky, flirtatious, uninhibited nature, Tripp was funny. They'd spent a good portion of the afternoon laughing.

The two of them had been teamed up with his sister, Tessa, and her husband, Ryan Bateman. They were an adorable couple. Down-to-earth, sweet and funny. The three of them had kept Audra in stitches with their antics. When she learned Ryan had lived next door to Tripp and Tessa's family and the three of them had been friends practically since infancy, she wasn't surprised. Their love and friendship was evident, especially in their teasing banter.

It only made sense that Ryan and Tessa had eventually fallen for each other. She envied their love. It was apparent that their relationship had been built on friendship first.

Audra was not quite thirty, but in recent years, more and more of her friends and cousins were getting married. She'd started to think more about settling down and raising a family of her own.

She glanced over at Darius, who was working with former model Rafaela Marchesi. The woman touched Darius every chance she got, and she drank in his physique like it was a thousand-dollar bottle of champagne and someone else was paying the tab.

Of course, Rafaela had five ex-husbands and was a star on the *Secret Lives of NYC Ex-Wives* reality show filming in town. So someone else undoubtedly *was* paying the tab. The way she looked at Darius, Rafaela was evidently cruising for her sixth husband and considered Darius a good prospect.

"Audra." Tripp touched her shoulder and she nearly jumped out of her skin. "Sorry, I didn't mean to startle you, but I called you several times and you didn't hear me. They're about to serve lunch."

"Sorry. I was lost in thought." Her cheeks heated under the knowing grins of Tessa and Ryan. Tripp seemed far less amused. "You don't need to wait for me. I'm just going to finish planting this last bush, then I'll be right in."

"We'll catch up to you guys," Tripp told his sister and his brother-in-law as everyone else in the yard, including Darius and Rafaela headed inside. "Save us a place."

Ryan nodded, then slipped his arm around Tessa and headed toward the building.

Tripp helped her set the last bush into the ground and then filled the hole with dirt. Then she watered it.

"Thanks for waiting for me, Tripp." Audra removed her gloves and slid her sunglasses on top of her head. "But you didn't need to. You're probably starving."

"After all of the work we did this morning, I'll bet you are, too." He removed his own gloves and put them with their tools. They both headed inside. "So, that Darius guy... how long ago did you two break up?"

She tensed a little. It was no secret that she and Darius had been a couple. Sophie had told Tripp and the others as much when they'd volunteered last week. Still, it felt odd to talk to Tripp about it. Especially when she was having a myriad of conflicting feelings about Darius.

"Five years," she said finally. "Sometimes it feels like it was a lifetime ago. Other times—"

"It feels like it was just yesterday?" His light brown eyes twinkled in the sun. "I've been there before. Must've been weird for you, running into him here after all this time."

"It was. It is," she stammered. "But I think we've come to an understanding."

"Is that why you've been staring at Rafaela all morning like you're ready to drag her all over the yard by her extensions?"

"I was *not* looking at her that way," Audra protested. When he stared at her incredulously, she sighed. "Okay, so maybe I was. It wasn't intentional."

Or maybe I don't have things worked out as well as I thought.

"I know you didn't ask for my advice, and if you don't want it, feel free to tell me to shut the hell up." He stopped, just before they stepped inside the building.

Audra studied Tripp's face. She barely knew him. Why should she care that he'd noticed her staring flaming daggers at Rafaela Marchesi? And who cared about his advice on the subject?

Evidently, she did.

"Okay, Wise One." She folded her arms and tipped her chin. "What say you?"

A wide grin spread across his handsome face. "Be honest with the guy and with yourself. Whatever it is you're feeling, just…feel it. Don't pretend the feelings aren't there. Wade through them, rather than trying to find a way around them. That'll only get you stuck in the quicksand. If you don't tackle your emotions head-on, they'll sabotage future relationships."

"Wow. That was remarkably insightful." She narrowed her gaze at him. "I wasn't expecting that."

"I am so misunderstood and underappreciated, I might add." He laughed, the sound filling the courtyard. "I happen to be a font of fantastic relationship advice. I just haven't worked out the whole applying-it-to-myself thing, yet."

"Yeah, I get that." Audra couldn't help laughing, too. "I

guess I'm surprised because…" She shrugged, her words trailing off. "I don't know."

"Because I'm obviously attracted to you. So you didn't expect me to do something as selfless as suggest you be honest about your feelings for your old flame?" Tripp folded his arms.

"Something like that."

"Then let me set your mind at ease. I'm not being self-less. I'd love to spend time one-on-one with you, Audra. But if we ever do, I don't want that guy lingering in your head," he said with a self-assured smirk.

"You know, Tripp Noble, you're much deeper than you let on." Audra smiled. "And thank you for the excellent advice."

"That must net me a hug or something." He opened his arms wide.

Audra laughed and hugged Tripp before they headed inside to wash their hands and join the others for lunch.

Tripp was right. Her declaration earlier that everything was fine between her and Darius was complete and utter bullshit. She had a ton of feelings for Darius that she still hadn't worked out. Things she still wanted to say to him.

Maybe the reason she'd been unable to make a deeper connection with Cash was because she still hadn't worked out her feelings about Darius.

She'd been lodged in quicksand for the past five years, just as Tripp had indicated.

Audra wasn't sure how or when, but now that she knew what needed to be done, she had every intention of work-ing out the doubts and lingering emotions that had plagued her since her and Darius's sudden breakup.

Whatever the results of their conversation, at least she'd finally be able to move on.

At the end of the day, Audra, Tripp, Tessa and Ryan cleaned up their space and returned the tools they'd been using. Audra had put away a small load of tools when Darius approached.

"Hey, Audra, I wondered if you still planned to ride home with me?" he asked tentatively.

"Of course. Why wouldn't I? Or do you have plans with Rafaela now?" Her gut suddenly twisted at the thought. "If so, I'm sure I can find a ride with someone else."

"No, I don't have plans with Rafaela." He lowered his head and whispered conspiratorially, "And don't say her name too many times, or I have a sneaking suspicion she'll suddenly appear."

"Who is she, Beetlejuice?" She couldn't help giggling.

"Don't know, and I don't want to find out." He chuckled.

"All I'm saying is, you don't have to try so hard to get rid of me." Audra forced a smile. "If your plans have changed, I understand."

"I asked because I thought maybe *your* plans had changed." He rubbed the back of his neck.

"Why?" She fell in line beside him as he walked back toward the clubhouse.

He hesitated before responding. "I wasn't spying on you or anything, but I saw you hug Tripp."

It was petty, but she felt a slight sense of satisfaction that Darius felt a twinge of jealousy, too. "I was thanking him. He helped me out with something."

"Oh. Well, I just need to talk to a couple of people before we leave." He checked his watch. "Meet you at the door in ten?"

She nodded as she watched him walk away, spending a little more time admiring his ass than she should have.

"Seems that absence does indeed make the heart grow fonder." Sophie approached out of nowhere, startling Audra.

"Sophie!" Audra dragged a hand over her head. "You scared me to death."

"Guess you didn't hear me calling you because you were

too busy studying Darius's derriere." Sophie grinned mischievously. "The man you supposedly have zero interest in."

"Doesn't mean my eyes don't work." Audra glanced longingly in Darius's direction one more moment before turning to face Sophie's incredulous stare. "Fine, maybe I do still have feelings for him. That doesn't mean we're right for each other."

"Relationships are scary, I get it." Sophie's expression softened. "But there's only one way to find out if there's something there. And avoiding each other isn't it."

"I know," Audra said quietly. She turned to face Sophie head-on. "And I'm going to talk to Darius, but I don't need your push or pull to do it."

"Yes, ma'am." Sophie smiled. "Think I need to apologize to Darius for putting Rafaela Marchesi on his trail?"

They both laughed.

"No, he'll be fine. We both will. No matter what happens."

"I know. I guess I just want everyone to be as happy and in love as Nigel and I are." Sophie beamed. "By the way, the final design for our rings is so beautiful. It was the perfect compromise. I can't thank you enough for coming here and designing them."

"My pleasure." Audra squeezed Sophie's hand. "My team has been working hard on your custom pieces. In a few days, I'll return to Dallas to pick up your rings. Hopefully, all of your bridal party jewelry will be completed by then. Once you've approved all of the pieces, I'll head back to Dallas."

"That's wonderful!" Sophie clapped her hands excitedly, but then her expression suddenly changed. "Wait, you aren't staying for the wedding?"

"I don't typically attend my client's weddings, Sophie. This entire experience is far different than anything I've done before."

"Then why not make another exception? Stay for the wedding." Sophie's eyes pleaded. "Besides, I don't just think of you as my jewelry designer. Since you've been here, you've become a friend."

Audra was touched by the woman's words. "I feel the same."

"Then stay, please. You've already leased Dixie's place for the rest of the month. Might as well enjoy it."

"It is a beautiful town, and everyone here is so nice," Audra had to admit. "A girl could become accustomed to this."

Sophie's eyes danced. "Then why don't you make Royal your new home?"

"What?" Audra laughed. "I said I liked it here, Sophie. I didn't say I was ready to relocate."

"Why not?" Sophie asked matter-of-factly. "We're a stone's throw from Dallas, so it would be easy enough to access your shop. Besides, you already said you like it here more than Dallas. And everyone around here really likes you."

"And being here has been great. But moving here? I don't know about that."

"Well, it's not like you have to decide today," the younger woman said. "But if you did, there would be a whole lot of us ready to welcome you."

"It means the world to me that you want me here. And if I ever do decide to pull up stakes, I promise to give Royal serious consideration."

"That's all I ask." Sophie seemed pleased with her answer. She nodded toward the door. "Your chariot awaits."

Darius looked handsome, if a little tired, as he stood by the front door, patiently waiting for her.

They chatted cordially about their day during the short ride home. It was over before she could blink.

She was dirty and tired, and she needed a bath and a

nap. But when Darius turned off the engine, she honestly wasn't ready to end their time together. She'd forgotten how much she enjoyed just being with him. There'd always been something so calming about his presence. It balanced out her high-intensity personality.

"How are the runway show plans coming?" she asked, needing a reason to spend just a few minutes more in his company.

"Everything is going according to plan so far, despite four last-minute additions that I'm hoping will be show-stoppers."

"That's a bold move," she said. "What did you add to the show, if you don't mind me asking?"

"I don't." His gaze lingered on hers for a moment and it warmed something deep inside her chest. "But I'd rather show you. Come in for an early nightcap?"

"I'd love to, but I'm filthy and tired." She forced a laugh, fighting back the sadness she felt at turning down his offer. Talking to Darius about his upcoming show over a glass of wine sounded like a lovely way to spend the evening. And a great opportunity to finish the conversation they'd begun in the stables. This time, hopefully, there would be no tongue involved.

"I'm heading straight for the shower, too. But I'd love to show you what you inspired me to add to the show."

"Me?"

"Yes, you, Audra." He chuckled. "Don't act so surprised. I'm sure I'm not the first man you've inspired, and I won't likely be the last."

"I'm intrigued," she said finally. "If I don't pass out from sheer exhaustion after my shower, I'll drop by."

"Perfect." The glint of victory was in his dark eyes. He knew her well enough to know her curiosity would get the better of her. "I have a few bottles chilling in the wine fridge, and I'll leave the patio door unlocked."

They parted ways, and Audra headed straight for the laundry. She peeled off the layers of filthy clothing and dropped them into the washing machine. Then she got into the steaming hot shower. Audra hummed softly, as the hot water cascaded over her. Her skin tingled with excitement in anticipation of spending more time with Darius.

Thirteen

Audra slipped on a simple denim shift minidress. It was adorable but also sexy without looking as if she was trying too hard.

She pulled her still-damp, wavy hair into a high ponytail, slipped on a pair of sandals with a low heel and applied her lip gloss.

Audra opened the iron gate that separated their backyards. It was strange to make her way directly toward the house, since she usually made a point of not glancing in that direction on her way to the pool.

The lights were on in the family room and in the space she knew to be the office. Despite her efforts not to, she'd sometimes caught a glimpse of him working there.

Audra inhaled deeply, then knocked on the patio door's metal frame.

No answer.

She slid the door open and stepped inside.

"Darius?"

She called him twice more. Still, no answer.

Audra ventured in the direction of his office. The door was open, and the light was on, so she stepped inside.

The space was neat and organized. His laptop was on the desk, closed. Two dry-erase boards and a large corkboard dominated the walls. She approached the corkboard where four swimsuits were pinned. Audra didn't touch them, fearful the entire board would fall. She shifted her attention to the sketches posted. Two male figures and two female figures wore the designs pinned on the board. She studied the female figures.

There wasn't a ton of detail. Just enough that the woman felt familiar.

"Audra." Darius stood beside her. "I didn't hear you come in."

"I knocked, and I called you when I stepped inside, but you didn't respond." She turned to face him. "I hope it's okay that I let myself in."

"Of course. I got a late start on that shower. My assistant called with a few questions."

"This late in the day on a Saturday?"

"It's not as late there, but yeah, she's about as obsessive as I am." He chuckled. "It's why we work so well together. Besides, I give each employee a stake in the company. I find it makes them more invested in the outcomes."

"So Thr3d is a privately owned company?"

"It is. And I'll keep it that way for as long as it makes sense." He stepped farther inside the room. The scent of his shower gel tickled her nostrils.

Audra turned back toward the board with the sketches. "That's me, isn't it?"

"Sometimes, when my brain felt all tied in knots, I'd watch you swim," he admitted, not responding to her question directly. "There's something soothing about how gracefully your arms and legs cut through the water. And then one day I got the idea to create a few swimwear pieces for the lineup."

"I didn't think Thr3d carried swimwear."

"We haven't. At least, not until now. And maybe we never will." He shrugged. "Depends on how they're received."

"You started these designs from scratch since you arrived?" She looked back at him.

"I did. It was a risky move, but your passion for swimming…it motivated me. I couldn't let the idea alone until I saw it through."

"Your team must've really loved that," Audra teased.

He grinned. "I've undoubtedly been called some very unsavory names behind my back these past couple of weeks. But now everyone is pleased with the way things turned out."

"May I?" She indicated the one-piece swimming suit.

"Please." He unpinned the garment and handed it to Audra. "Since you were the inspiration for the piece, I'd love to get your honest, unfiltered opinion."

"Have you ever known me to offer any other kind?"

"No." Darius chuckled, rubbing his chin.

The sensation of his scruff sensitizing her flesh in the barn that day ghosted over her skin, and she shivered.

"Your candidness is one of the things I appreciate most about you," he said.

"Then why didn't you give me the same courtesy? Didn't you think I deserved that much?" The words escaped her mouth before she could reel them back in.

Audra wanted to finish their conversation. She really did. But she'd hoped to at least get a glass of wine out of the deal first. Perhaps that would've taken the edge off of her tone. It was an honest question. She wasn't looking for confrontation.

Darius sat on the edge of a black filing cabinet, suddenly seeming to need more space between them. His eyes were filled with regret and perhaps shame.

"It's like I told you at the stables. The lie about my parents—it began as a misunderstanding and then…it sort of became my shield." He shrugged. "Suddenly, my ugly, messy history had been erased, and I didn't need to talk about it. I was happier with you than I'd been in a long time. I didn't want to ruin it."

"And if we'd stayed together…would you have just gone on lying to me?"

"No, of course not. But I was afraid that once you knew the truth, it'd be over between us."

"I would've been hurt, naturally. But if you'd just been honest with me…" Audra shook her head, the words dying on her lips.

What good will it do either of us to rehash the past?

She stood in front of Darius. "I didn't come here to argue. But for the past five years, I've been pretending I'm fine. Telling myself it was all just water under the bridge. But that isn't true. I loved you, Darius. When you suddenly declared that we were over, with no real explanation, it felt as if our relationship never mattered to you. Like *I* never mattered to you. That's what I've struggled to get past. How could I have been so wrong?"

Unshed tears stung her eyes and clouded her vision. She turned away from him, but he grasped her wrist.

"You weren't wrong, Audra." His voice was a rough whisper as he tugged her toward him, forcing her to meet his gaze. He placed her hand over his heart. "I loved you so much. But I'd had so much rejection in my life. I couldn't bear the thought of being rejected by the person I loved most."

Audra swallowed hard and wet her lips. Her chest heaved with shallow breaths. "I understand now why you believed I would've done that. I'd always given in to my parents' wishes. But I'd decided that I wasn't going to give you up. I was going to tell them about us, I swear. I just needed time."

"I believe you, sweetheart." His eyes didn't leave hers. "I screwed up. I should've told you how I—"

Audra pressed her lips to his. She didn't want contrition, she wanted *this*. His mouth on hers as her trembling hands cradled his face.

Darius slipped his arms around her waist, pulling her closer, so that she stood between his legs. He pressed his large hands to her back as he kissed her. His strong hands glided down and cupped her bottom, pulling her flush against him. Erasing the space between them.

Audra tugged the hem of his shirt up, pressing her fingers to his bare back. She glided her hands over the muscles beneath his skin. Relished the terrain that was familiar, and yet much different than before.

Darius broke their kiss, just long enough to help her tug his shirt over his head and toss it onto the floor.

"Someone has been working out." She squeezed his biceps before kissing him again.

"Had to do something with all of that frustration," he muttered, between kisses to her neck and shoulder.

"Funny, I did just the opposite. I ate my feelings. Thus the additional pounds." She'd gained nearly ten pounds in that first year. They'd been joined by another ten over the course of the next four years, though the swimming kept the weight gain gradual.

"I liked your body just fine before. But I'm mesmerized by it now." He kissed his way down her chest, unbuttoning the three buttons on the placard of the dress and giving himself better access.

He kissed the top of one breast as he tugged the collar of the dress to one side, exposing more of her shoulder.

Audra's heart was racing. There was a dull, steady pulse between her thighs. Like a heartbeat. Her beaded nipples tingled with anticipation.

As much as she already missed his lips on hers, she eagerly anticipated the sensation of him taking one of her painfully hard nipples into his mouth. Thoughts of all the other ways he could use that amazing mouth made her head spin.

She pulled just out of his grip. For a moment, he seemed panicked, as if he was worried he'd upset her. Or maybe he thought she'd changed her mind. But instead, she gripped the bottom of the dress and pulled it up over her hips.

Darius put his hands over hers, halting her progress. His breathing was ragged.

"Audra, are you sure this is what you want?" His warm breath tickled her skin as his lips grazed her ear.

It was good they hadn't had any wine yet. Neither of them would have reason to doubt her decision.

Audra nodded. "Yes. Take me to bed, Darius. Now. Please."

For an instant, she regretted adding the little plea at the end. She wouldn't grovel before the man who'd lied to and rejected her. But as she stared into his eyes, it was clear she was the one who had complete control.

Audra had always loved the way Darius looked at her. Especially when they'd made love. He'd regarded her as if there wasn't anything in the world that he wanted more. She felt that now: desired, appreciated. A reflection of just how intensely she wanted him, too.

He helped her yank the fabric over her head and toss it onto the floor. Darius studied her, as she stood there in a black lace bra and cheeky little black lace boy shorts that provided plenty of coverage from the front but left very little to the imagination from the back.

From the tenting of the front panel of his athletic shorts, he obviously enjoyed the view.

He stood and opened his hand, extending it to her.

Audra placed her hand in his, willing the trembling in her limbs and the butterflies in her belly to stop.

Darius took her to the master bedroom on the other side of the house and laid her on the bed. He stripped off his shorts, revealing a pair of stretch boxers with Dolce & Gabbana printed on the waistband.

He crawled onto the bed, hovering over her. He pressed one kiss to her lips and then another. And another.

Sliding the band from her ponytail, he sifted his fingers through her hair as he kissed her, his tongue seeking hers and licking at the barbell piercing. His thick, hard erection pressed against her thigh.

She wanted him. More than she wanted anything else in that moment. She wouldn't let herself think beyond that. Otherwise, she'd begin to question herself. To question him. But right now, she didn't want to think. She only wanted to feel.

Darius flipped onto his back, pulling her on top of him without breaking their kiss. His hands glided up and down her back. He gripped her bottom, pulling her against his hardened shaft.

She sucked in a deep breath at the delicious sensation of his steely length pressed against her heated, sensitive flesh—the feeling so much more intense now than before. There was a fluttering low in her belly and electricity zipped along her spine.

Audra whimpered, the sound lost in their increasingly fervent kiss.

"You have no idea how badly I want you." He pushed aside the curtain of dark brown hair that blocked his view of her face. "I haven't been able to stop thinking about you since—"

"The diner?" She hadn't been able to stop thinking of him since then, either.

"No matter how hard I try to push you out of my head... you're always there."

Audra felt that way, too. Since long before they'd crossed paths at that diner.

She'd smiled and gone on with her life for the past five years. Started her dream business. Found success. Tried to find love again. But inside, she'd been splintered and falling apart, trying to hide the devastation.

Whatever it is you're feeling, just...feel it. Don't pretend the feelings aren't there.

Audra pressed her mouth to his again and kissed him. She was done talking.

Darius unfastened her bra and slipped it from her shoulders. Then he rolled her onto her back and trailed kisses down her chest. He took one beaded tip into his warm mouth, sucking it, then teasing it with his tongue as she squirmed beneath him.

He slowly kissed his way down her belly, flicking the dangling, diamond butterfly belly ring with his tongue. The pulsing between her thighs beat like a drum.

Darius tugged the lacy material down her thighs and tossed it onto the floor. When he spread her with his thumbs and tasted her there, she gasped at the intense pleasure. Audra dug her heels into the mattress, her hips straining toward his mouth.

A silent plea for more.

Legs trembling and heart racing, her belly flipped as she careened closer and closer to the edge. She'd forgotten how deeply committed the man was to cunnilingus. He went for it without hesitation.

Every. Fucking. Time.

He never dialed it in. Instead, he got off on it as much as she did. Like there was nothing more important in his world than bringing her to ecstasy.

"OhmygodOhmygodOhmygod… YES!"

Fireworks exploded behind her tightly closed eyelids. She dug her heels in, trying to get a reprieve from the pleasure rocketing through her body. Her legs quivered as she arched her back. She was breathless and dizzy.

"That's my girl." Darius pressed soft, warm kisses to her inner thigh. Then he trailed them up her body. He kissed her shoulder and her neck, then whispered in her ear, "There is something so goddamn gratifying about that rapturous expression on your face when you're right there on the brink."

Audra felt giddy, then emotional, then a little angry.

She'd been his. She'd dreamed of someday being his wife, of sharing this passion and chemistry and affection for the rest of their lives. But he'd destroyed everything they'd built because he hadn't trusted her with his truth. Hadn't had enough faith in her to believe that she'd choose him.

"What's wrong, babe?" Darius furrowed his brows as he studied her face. He seemed to sense the sudden tension in her body.

"Nothing," Audra whispered.

Talking about it right now would only fuel the hurt and anger that simmered beneath the surface.

She kissed his mouth, tangy with a hint of her own essence. Cradling his cheek, she glided her pierced tongue against his.

Darius slipped his fingers into her hair, angling her head to deepen their kiss until they were both breathless. His thick, hard shaft teased her entrance.

He rolled off her suddenly, then returned from the bathroom with a strip of condoms. He ripped one open and sheathed himself.

Something in his ravenous gaze made her heart expand. She remembered the first time he looked at her that way. It was the night he'd first told her he loved her.

Darius gripped the base of his length and eased himself inside her, evoking a quiet gasp from her.

The connection between them was deeply satisfying. She'd craved his touch, his kiss. He pressed his mouth to hers, as he inched his way inside of her, stretching her body as it welcomed his again.

Audra sucked in a deep breath when he hit bottom. The friction of his body grinding against the already sensitive bundle of nerves brought her closer to the edge with every thrust until she shattered, clutching his strong biceps and calling his name.

He kissed her neck, his strokes harder and faster. His

harsh whisper warmed her cheek. "God, I've missed you, Audra."

Her eyes suddenly burned with tears.

Darius tensed, then trembled. He fell onto his back beside her, both of them breathing heavily.

Neither of them spoke, and the awkward silence between them amplified every other sound. The tick of the wall clock. The roar of a passing motorcycle. The quiet whir of the warm air blowing through an overhead vent. The pounding of her own pulse.

Audra silently wiped away the tears that streaked her flaming cheeks.

She was beyond embarrassed.

Crying during sex? Really?

She'd never done that before. Not ever. No matter how great the sex was. And she knew better than to fall for the sweet nothings a man whispered while on the verge. In that moment of orgasm-induced, temporary insanity, he'd promise you the world.

No one should be held to the things they uttered on the verge of carnal bliss.

So why had she been so touched by Darius's simple admission?

Audra discreetly wiped away the warm tears that leaked from the corners of her eyes as the truth hit her.

She'd been moved by Darius's words because he'd expressed exactly what she was feeling.

She'd missed him, too. In a way she hadn't missed any other man. Because she'd loved him like she'd loved no other.

No matter how much she tried to deny it, the truth was she still loved Darius. And she wanted him in her life.

The man you want isn't necessarily the man you need, Audra.

Her mother's words echoed in her head. She'd always

trotted out that phrase whenever Audra was interested in someone who didn't quite fit her mother's plans for her. Which was why she'd hesitated to introduce her parents to Darius back then.

But maybe her mother was right.

She wanted Darius, but she needed a partner she could count on. Someone who trusted her implicitly. But there was something Darius was hiding from her still. She'd sensed it that day at the diner. And she sensed it now.

She'd given in to desire. Given him her body. Taken his. But she would never again give her heart to a man who couldn't be trusted with it.

Fourteen

Darius's heart thudded in his chest, his breathing labored as he came down from the incredible high of being with Audra again.

Making love to her was even better than he remembered. So much so that he'd told her how much he'd missed her.

Every word he'd spoken was true. He just hadn't intended to say them. Especially not in the heat of passion.

He'd seen the glint of tears in her eyes. Was it because she believed him or because she didn't?

Either way, things now felt awkward between them. Both of them likely embarrassed by their outbursts of emotion.

Darius rolled onto his side. He pressed a soft kiss to her lips and stroked her cheek. "You were incredible, Audra."

She glided her fingertips down his side. "So were you."

Darius kissed her again and excused himself. In the restroom, he splashed cold water on his face.

Just take it easy. Everything will be fine.

Who was he kidding? Everything was *not* fine. He'd finally cleared the air with Audra about what had happened back then. But now here he was forced to keep another truth from her.

He couldn't even consider getting serious with Audra until he could tell her everything. Why he'd really been summoned to Royal. What his connection was to the Blackwoods. But he couldn't do that until he'd talked to his mother and stepfather.

He'd fly home today to talk to them, if that were possible. But they were still on the twenty-one-day tour of Europe they'd always dreamed about. They wouldn't be back until after his show.

When he returned to the bedroom, Audra was gone, and the bedroom door was open. He put on his boxers and trekked through the house to find her in the office. She was in her panties and bra, bending to retrieve the dress they'd discarded there earlier.

"You're not leaving, are you?" He leaned against the doorframe.

"It's late, and we've both had a really long day." She sunk her teeth gently into her lower lip when her gaze dropped below his waist momentarily. Her cheeks flushed and she redirected her gaze, as if she hadn't seen him in a lot less moments before. "Besides, you probably have an early morning planned."

Darius looped an arm around her waist. He tipped her chin so her eyes met his. "Stay. Please."

Her breath hitched at his soft plea. "I shouldn't. It'd be weird."

"Only if we allow it to be." He shrugged. "Besides, you promised to model those swimsuits for me."

She laughed nervously, leaning into him rather than pulling away. "I believe what I promised was an honest opinion."

"How can you do that if you don't try it on?"

"I suppose you're right. And a promise is a promise."

She laid the dress across a chair and grabbed the one-piece swimming suit.

"The deconstructed one-shoulder design is gorgeous. It's both modest and sexy with all of this sheer detailing." She held it up to the light. "And the solid fabric isn't so thin that it's transparent." Audra turned the suit around, laying it across his desk. She trailed her fingers over the back. "Premium fabric, well made, thoughtfully designed, and it's my favorite color."

"Eggplant," he chimed in, chuckling when they said it simultaneously. He shrugged at her look of surprise. "What?

How could I forget that? I've never met another person whose favorite color was eggplant."

Audra fought back the smile that lit her eyes. She checked the label inside. "Did you really order this in my size? How'd you know?"

"I am a clothing designer," he reminded her. "I've gotten pretty good at guesstimating a woman's measurements. I'll grab a bottle of wine while you try the suit on. Red or white?"

"White." The tension seemed to melt from her shoulders. She no longer seemed anxious to leave.

Darius leaned in and kissed her cheek. "Be right back."

He found his shorts and shirt and got dressed before returning to the kitchen to throw together a quick charcuterie and cheese tray. He opened a bottle of chardonnay and grabbed two wineglasses, slipping the stems into the designated notches on the board.

When he returned to the office, Audra spun slowly, giving him a good look at the suit from all sides.

"What do you think?" She beamed, one fist propped on her hip.

"Wow." He set the tray down and rubbed his chin as he assessed the fit of the suit. "You look incredible, Audra. Even more so than I imagined when I designed it for you."

She cocked her head. "You designed the suit for me?"

Suddenly, he couldn't seem to keep his mouth shut. "I designed it with your body type in mind."

"In my favorite color and size." She approached him with an incredulous grin that made her eyes twinkle.

"Wine?" He handed her a glass, then took a seat in front of the desk, not responding to her implication.

Audra flashed a teasing smile, then sipped her wine. Setting her glass down, she plucked a few kalamata olives and a square of French Gruyère cheese from the tray. She popped them in her mouth, then strode around the room in the suit.

She turned to look down at the back of the suit, her body slightly twisted. "I like the way this one provides full coverage in the back." She bent over and touched her toes, her dark brown hair falling forward.

Yep. Definitely a fan of that new, curvier ass.

God bless every pint of ice cream, donut, cookie and latte that had contributed to it over the past five years.

Darius adjusted himself in the chair and crossed one ankle over his opposite knee.

"And I love that it stays put. It doesn't ride up when you bend or stretch." Audra ran her fingers through her hair and grabbed a couple of red grapes from the tray. "Should I try on the bikini now?"

God, yes.

"If you wouldn't mind," he said nonchalantly, without looking up from the tray where he was spreading chèvre on a cracker and topping it with prosciutto.

Audra left the room with the bikini in her hand.

He'd just seen every inch of her, up close and personal. Yet he was practically hyperventilating at the thought of seeing her in that bikini.

He was a complete goner.

Audra returned in a few minutes, wearing the two-piece garment. He nearly choked on his prosciutto and cracker.

She patted his back and handed him his glass of wine as he coughed and sputtered.

Smooth, playa. Really smooth.

"Are you all right?" She stood over him, her warm brown eyes assessing him as she tried to hold back a grin.

"Fine." He drank more wine. "Promise."

Audra strutted to the middle of the room and turned slowly so he could see the bikini from every angle. "That reaction… I'm not sure if that means I look really bad in the suit or—"

"You look amazing. Trust me." He walked toward her but stopped a few feet shy. Arms folded, he propped his chin on his fist and studied the fit of the suit and the give of the fabric as she moved. "How do you feel in it?"

"I really like this one, too," she said. "It says it's the same size, but it fits more snugly. It doesn't have full coverage in the back, like the first one did. But it doesn't show so much skin that I feel self-conscious."

"May I?" He reached toward her.

"After what happened earlier?" Audra's cheeks flushed. "I should think so."

"It's become habit, I suppose. I always ask permission if I need to touch one of the models." He adjusted the band just below her bust. "Do the ties feel secure?" He rested his fingertips on her waistline, just above the ties at her hips.

Audra stared at him for a moment, her gaze heated. She looped her arms around his neck and lifted onto her toes.

"Why don't we find out?" she asked in a soft, husky voice, moments before his mouth crashed against hers.

Darius pressed one hand flat to her back, the other gripped the firm, round globes that had sent his pulse racing.

He kissed her hungrily. As if they hadn't made love less than an hour ago. In response, she clutched his shirt, pulling him closer. Seemingly as desperate for the connection as he was.

Darius lifted her, his hands planted firmly on her bottom. Audra wrapped her legs around him.

They both groaned a little at the sensation of his hardened length surging against the warm space between her thighs.

Darius took a few steps backward until his calves hit the sofa behind him. He sank down with Audra straddling his lap. She dug her knees into the sofa on either side of him, as she worked her hips, sending a jolt of sensation up his spine and making his heart thump against his chest.

Darius tugged on the ribbon at the back of the bikini top, then loosened the ribbon at the back of her neck. Audra yanked the untethered material from between their bodies and dropped it onto the floor.

He kissed her hard, his pulse racing and his head spinning. Audra was the only woman who'd ever made him feel such a crazed desperation to kiss her. To touch her. To make love to her. As if nothing else mattered.

Audra grasped the bottom of his shirt and tugged it over his head. When she'd discarded the garment, Darius took her in his arms again.

He loved the feel of her naked breasts against his chest. He trailed his fingertips down her back with a light, feather touch, then gripped her hips as she moved against him, increasing the friction against her clit through the thin garments they wore.

Finally, he couldn't take another moment of the heat and desire building between them. He needed to be inside this incredible woman again.

He loosened the bow on each hip until the bikini bottom fell open. Audra shifted her weight to her knees, allowing him to lift his hips and slide his shorts and boxers off. He retrieved one of the condoms from the pocket of his shorts, where he'd, thankfully, had the presence of mind to stash them when he'd gotten dressed.

Darius ripped open the foil packet and sheathed himself. He grabbed the base of his length and pressed it against her slick opening, his other hand resting on her hip.

Audra's lashes fluttered as she slowly lowered herself onto him. Their bodies fit together as if the past five years apart had never existed.

She whimpered with pleasure, her head lolling to one

side. He swept her hair off her neck and shoulder and planted kisses there. Then he placed his hands on her bottom, guiding her up and down his shaft.

Audra was getting closer. Her whimpers came louder and faster as their hips slammed together. She dug her fingers into his shoulders, her cries growing louder.

"Fuck, Audra." His voice trembled, his arousal building. "You feel so fucking good. I need you to come for me, baby. Because I don't know how much longer I can hold on."

Her eyes drifted shut and she slipped a hand between them, her fingers moving over her clit. Her movements, slow and deliberate at first, became quicker and more determined.

He'd always loved her uninhibited nature. She wasn't ashamed to ask for or take whatever she needed.

It was one of the sexiest things about her.

He tightened his grip on her hips as he glided her up and down on his painfully hard shaft. Her breathing was quick and shallow. Her whimpers loud and breathy. Finally, her body tensed, the muscles inside her quivering as she called out his name.

Darius laid her on the couch, his hips thrusting hard and fast and the pressure building until he shuddered, cursing and moaning, as he found his own release.

He kissed her, his heart racing as he tried to catch his breath.

"Don't go, Audra." Darius couldn't bear the thought of her leaving. He craved the warmth and comfort of falling asleep with her in his arms. The joy of waking to her lovely face and sweet smile. "Stay. Please."

She stroked his cheek and nodded. Her kiss-swollen lips quirked in a faint smile that made his heart feel full and reminded him of all the reasons he'd fallen in love with her back then.

The reasons he was falling for her all over again.

* * *

Later, they sat in bed drinking wine and nibbling from the charcuterie tray. He was glad she'd accepted his invitation to stay.

"Well, we know the bikini is easy to get in and out of." Her mouth curved in a mischievous grin. "I'll have to swim in it to see if it stays on as well as it comes off."

Darius chuckled, then pressed a kiss to her lips. "If you could swim in both suits, that'd be great. I'd love to see how they hold up to chlorine and a hand wash."

"Sure." She swiped some aged Gouda and a few grapes from the tray, nibbling on them. An uncomfortable silence settled over them again.

Darius set his wineglass down and turned to her. "Audra, we should probably talk about what's happened between us tonight."

"I disagree." She tucked some of her wavy hair behind her ear. "I don't mean never," she clarified. "I just don't think either of us is prepared to have this discussion right now, while our emotions are still high." She plucked another grape from the tray and chewed thoughtfully. "We should process what's happened and how we feel about it. So neither of us makes any promises we aren't prepared to keep."

Her voice was calm, her reasoning cerebral and dispassionate. The very opposite of the woman who'd clawed her way up his body not an hour before.

"Are you sure that's what you want, Audra?" He threaded their fingers.

"Of course." She pressed her lips into a smile and nodded once. "We're both really involved in our work right now. I'm racing to make sure all of Sophie and Nigel's pieces are completed on time and to their satisfaction. You've got the biggest event of your career coming up in less than a week. I don't want this to become a distraction…for either of us."

"Okay." Darius kissed her hand, his eyes not leaving hers. "Then we'll revisit this conversation—"

"After LA Fashion Week and Sophie and Nigel's wedding." She shrugged. "That's just a few weeks. If this is really something worth exploring, a few weeks of contemplation won't hurt."

"Right," Darius agreed with more conviction than he felt. He snatched a few grapes from the tray. "In the meantime, maybe you'll let me take you out to dinner in town."

"As your friend and neighbor?" she asked, her eyes searching his.

"As the woman I'm dating…or whatever this is that we're doing." He pressed a lingering kiss to her mouth.

"Dare, I don't know if it's wise for us to take this beyond these walls."

He was surprised that she used the nickname she'd always called him. It didn't even seem like a conscious decision. Just something that had slipped out. But that didn't soften the impact of her words.

They were five years older, both successful entrepreneurs. Yet, their relationship had regressed. Now she wasn't just hiding him from her disapproving parents. She wanted him to be her dirty little secret.

"We should decide on our next steps, based purely on what we want," she continued. "The fewer people involved in that conversation, the better."

"You mean Sophie." Darius swept back the hair that fell over one eye when she nodded and tucked it behind her ear. He kissed her. "If you really want to hide out here in my bed, I think I could be okay with that. For now."

"Oh, you're taking me out all right, big shot." She stroked his stubbled chin. "But for now, if anyone asks, we're just friends. Deal?"

"Deal." He moved the tray onto the floor. Then he pulled her closer and kissed her.

Audra wasn't prepared to decide whether this was a meaningless fling or destiny. He could pretend that was fine by him. But he was clear on how he felt.

He'd made a colossally boneheaded mistake when he'd walked away from her, and he'd been given a second chance. He wouldn't blow it.

Besides, two weeks would give him time to tell his parents that he now knew Buckley Blackwood was his father. So when he and Audra finally talked, he could tell her everything.

Lies and half-truths would never come between them again.

Fifteen

Audra had spent most of the past three days either in bed with Darius or working quietly beside him in his office or by the pool.

He'd taken her out to dinner nearly every night. They'd gone to the Glass House—an upscale farm-to-table restaurant, and the Silver Saddle—a bar and tapas restaurant. Both were located in the Bellamy, Royal's five-star resort, inspired by the lavish Biltmore estate in Asheville, North Carolina.

They'd also shared a casual meal at the place that had first brought them together: Royal Diner.

But with just a few days left to prepare for the runway show, Darius needed to get back to California to be onsite. He'd made love to her that morning, kissed her goodbye then left her naked and sated in his bed.

Audra slept in an extra hour, then climbed out of bed and put on the Thr3d bikini that Darius had designed just for her. He'd had a second made more precisely to her measurements than the first. It fit perfectly. She went to the kitchen to grab a glass of juice before her morning swim when she saw Darius's thoughtful gift.

There was a gorgeous bouquet of two dozen red roses in a clear glass vase with a lovely note that made her smile. Another two dozen pink roses were on the coffee table in the family room with another sweet note apologizing for not being able to be there. Later, when she went to the bathroom to grab a towel, she discovered another two dozen roses, only these were white. The card read: *Can't wait to see you again. So come join me. If you do, I have a special surprise for you.*

Audra couldn't help the grin that spread from ear to ear. She regarded herself in the bathroom mirror. She looked like a giddy schoolgirl who'd fallen head over heels in love.

And maybe she had. Because Audra couldn't imagine going back to life without him.

But even if she could get over their past and her nagging suspicions that there was something he wasn't telling her, there were additional obstacles they'd need to address.

The Audra Lee Covington brand headquarters was in Dallas. Thr3d was based in Los Angeles. And they were both obsessed with their businesses. Could they make time for a long-distance relationship once they'd returned to their everyday lives? Was that what either of them wanted?

Then there were her parents.

Darius hadn't been wrong believing that her parents would've disapproved of their relationship. He wasn't from a wealthy, powerful or political family. None of that had mattered to her then. Nor did it matter now. She hoped her parents would be impressed that Darius had built Thr3d from nothing.

If they couldn't respect her choice, it would put a further strain on her relationship with them. But she didn't need their money or their approval. She and her eponymous business could survive without either. Still, she'd be much happier if her parents could accept her relationship with Darius.

"You're getting way ahead of yourself. There is no relationship," she muttered, removing the silk scarf she slept in and smoothing down her hair, pineappled in a wavy ponytail near the front of her head. She released her hair and slipped the tie onto her wrist until she got ready to get into the pool.

Her phone rang and she glanced down at it.

Cash again.

Audra sighed. She realized that Cash's pride was

wounded when she'd broken things off with him. But she'd done so as kindly as possible. They'd known each other for so long, and their families were close. She hadn't wanted to hurt him or create tension between their parents.

Cash was a good guy. He cared about the community and championed a number of worthy causes. She respected him, and she believed he'd someday accomplish great things. But she just didn't love him in that way, and she realized now that she never would.

But Cash was obviously still determined to win her back.

That was why she'd eagerly accepted Sophie and Nigel's proposal to spend time in Royal. And she was glad she had. It'd given her a chance to clear her head. Reminded her of what a healthy, happy relationship looked like. And maybe, just maybe, she would get her happily-ever-after with Darius, after all.

Audra had been on the phone all day. She'd fielded calls from her design team, last-minute requests from clothing designers showing at LA Fashion Week, and an actress and her musician husband who wanted to borrow pieces for a movie premiere.

She was physically and mentally exhausted. And famished.

Audra was back at her own rental home, and she'd worked through lunch to take a call with a West Coast designer.

She made herself a grilled cheese sandwich on artisan bread with smoked provolone, prosciutto, caramelized onions and heirloom tomatoes. Then she dove back into working on the engagement ring and wedding band designs for another couple.

Her phone rang again.

It was Sophie. Audra sighed. She adored Sophie and Nigel, but if Sophie made one more change or special request for their rings or custom bridal party gifts, Audra was going to scream.

"Hey, Sophie. What's up?"

"Audra, I'm glad I caught you. The *Secret Lives* ladies invited me to join them for a girls' night out before the wedding. I've invited a few friends. You should join us."

"I don't know, Sophie," Audra studied the ring design on her tablet. She wasn't satisfied with it. "I'll probably be working late."

"You and Darius are workaholics. You can't work around the clock. Besides, taking a little break will give you a fresh perspective. I do it all the time."

Audra's mouth twisted as she studied the design. Sophie was right, she needed to step away from it for a few hours and come back with fresh eyes.

"This isn't another setup, is it?" Audra paced the floor. "If so, hard pass."

"It isn't. I promise. It'll just be me, the girls, a couple of cameras and a few million viewers." Sophie laughed. "Free publicity for my brand and yours. Are you really going to say no to that?"

She has a point. "Where?"

"The Glass House. Have you been there?"

Audra glanced at the three vases overflowing with roses that she'd brought back to her place, thinking of the dinner she and Darius had there a couple nights before. "Yes."

"Perfect. Then you know where it is. Get dolled up and meet us there at seven thirty. My friends are a hoot. This is going to be tons of fun, I promise."

Audra agreed and ended the call with Sophie.

A girls' night out might be nice. Most of her friends lived in New York or LA, so she hadn't had many girls' nights since moving to Dallas. She'd focused on work and growing the Audra Lee Covington brand. She had no regrets about that. Still, it'd been nice spending time with Sophie and Darius in Royal.

It almost felt like she had a social life again.

She'd gone to plenty of functions while she and Cash dated, but they were usually stuffy fund-raisers at country clubs and the homes of wealthy donors. Not the kind of place where she could cut loose and be herself.

Audra turned off her tablet and went to the closet to find something to wear. She was actually looking forward to a night out with Sophie and her friends.

Audra stepped out of her convertible and into the lobby of the Glass House.

"Audra, I'm glad you made it," Sophie practically squealed. "You already know Tessa Bateman and Milan Valez. Meet the rest of my friends."

Sophie introduced her to Shelby Mackenzie; Sophie's new sister-in-law, Irina Blackwood, who was expecting; Rachel Galloway; Lydia Harris, whose husband, James, was the current president of the Texas Cattleman's Club; Alexis Slade-Clayton; and Dixie Musgraves, who owned both her rental home and the ranch where she and Darius had kissed.

Then there were the *Secret Lives* ladies: Rafaela Marchesi, Lulu Shepard, Seraphina Martinez, who was engaged to a local man and would be leaving the show at the end of the season, and Zooey Kostas. Miranda Dupree Blackwood—Sophie's ex-stepmother, to whom her father had left his fortune—was notably absent.

"A few others might join us later, but the majority of us are here. We're just waiting for the camera crew to get everything set up in the room," Sophie informed her.

One of the producers of the show announced they were ready, and the hostess asked them to follow her to a private dining room.

Audra froze. She could swear she heard someone call her name. *It can't be.* She turned around.

It definitely was.

"What are you doing in Royal?"

"Looking for you, of course." Her ex, Cash, gave her a bright smile, his hazel eyes twinkling.

Audra looked over at the group of women who were staring in their direction with interest.

"I'll catch up with you shortly," she said with an overly cheerful voice.

She didn't do drama or messiness. As the daughter of a politician, it was something that had been drilled into her head as a little girl.

Smile for the cameras. You can fall apart once you're alone in your room.

With the *Secret Lives* cast and crew onsite, the last thing she needed was for them to get wind of possible drama between the diamond heiress and her ex, the aspiring politician. The headline practically wrote itself.

Out of either concern or curiosity, the women hadn't moved.

"Cash is a family friend. We've known each other since we were five. It's fine, I promise." That seemed to convince them.

Audra turned back to her ex, her smile gone. "Did you follow me here?"

"Yes, but not in a creepy way." He ran a hand through his dark blond hair and chuckled. "I went to the house where you've been staying. You were pulling out of the driveway, so I followed you here."

"How did you know where I'm staying?" She propped a hand on her hip.

"Your mother told me. I was concerned because you haven't been answering my calls."

Audra was going to have to have a talk with her mother.

"Well, as you can see, I'm fine, Cash. You shouldn't have come here. Good night." She turned to walk away.

"Audra, wait. Since I'm here, let me treat you to dinner."

"I already have plans."

"Then I won't keep you long. Maybe we could just have a quick coffee?" Cash smiled in that disarming way he employed with complaining constituents and opposing lawmakers.

Audra sighed. She glanced around the lobby, hoping no one recognized either of them. "Thirty minutes, Cash."

"That's more than enough time to say what I came to say." A broad smile spread across his handsome face, revealing his perfectly white teeth.

"Is everything all right, Audra?" Sophie approached suddenly and slipped her arm through Audra's. She eyed Cash as if she was trying to place his face. "We're starting soon."

"Sophie Blackwood, right?" He grinned.

"That's right." Sophie frowned. "Do we know each other?"

"State Representative Cassius Johannsson." He extended his hand and shook hers. "And sadly, Audra's ex." He kept his tone and expression light.

"Oh." Sophie's gaze shifted from Cash's to hers, then back again. "And how do you know me?"

"I worked with your father in the past." His tone became more solemn. "He was extremely proud of you, Sophie. I'm very sorry for your family's loss. I know your father could be a tough old guy, but we worked on a lot of important projects together. He's done more good than you probably know."

"Thank you, Representative Johannsson." Sophie seemed more perturbed than comforted by the man's words. She raked her fingers through her dark hair. "What brings you to Royal?"

"Call me Cash. All my friends do." He smiled warmly

as he smoothed the lapels of his impeccable navy suit. He nodded toward Audra. "I'm sorry to interfere with your plans for the evening, but I need to speak with Audra for a few minutes. You'll hardly notice she's gone."

"We're just going to have coffee and a quick chat over at the bar," Audra assured her. "Don't wait for me to order, but I'll be there as soon as I can."

Audra forced a smile so her new friend wouldn't worry. Cash was harmless, if overly persistent. It was the politician in him. Win or lose, the campaign was never really over.

Sophie nodded, then turned to leave.

Audra turned to Cash, her arms folded. "Did you really need to tell her we dated?"

"It's true." He shrugged; his eyes suddenly filled with sadness. "And it's certainly not something I'm trying to hide."

He'd loved her, and she'd broken his heart. The least she could do was have a cup of coffee with him and make her intentions clear.

Sixteen

Audra and Cash sat at the bar. She ordered coffee and he ordered braised beef sliders, parmesan vegetable fritters and a Sazerac—his preferred drink.

"You're sure I can't get you a Sex on the Beach?" Cash turned on his stool to face her.

"No, thank you. I'd much rather talk about why you followed me here."

"Isn't it obvious?" He laid a gentle hand on her forearm. "I miss you, Audra."

She didn't respond right away. What could she say that she hadn't said before?

"I know things weren't perfect between us, Audra. Being a public servant is a demanding job. Surely, you understand that. Your father has been an elected official most of your life."

"I do understand. But your career isn't the issue, Cash. I'm fond of you, but I just don't feel the same way about you that you do about me." Audra thanked the bartender when he set her coffee in front of her. She added sugar and cream.

"Maybe not right now, but if you'd only give it a little more time…" He stroked her forearm with his thumb, a soothing technique he'd employed whenever she was upset. "You'd realize how good we are together."

Audra withdrew her arm from his grasp. "We're just not compatible romantically. You're a good man, Cash, but we want very different things from life. Isn't it better that we figured that out now? I want a relationship that makes me happy, and I want the same for you."

She picked up her cup and sipped her coffee.

"Is that what you've found with that Thr3d guy you've been seen all over town with?"

Audra nearly spilled her coffee. She slammed the mug down. It clanked against the saucer.

"You've been following me?"

"I spent the past few hours in town. When I mentioned that we were longtime friends, the locals couldn't wait to tell me about the guy you've been spending so much time with. The guy you're living next door to." He emphasized the last sentence, indicating that he suspected there was something going on between her and Darius.

She had no wish to deny it. Nor would she apologize for being a grown-ass, unattached woman living her best life. But she'd been the one who'd insisted on keeping their relationship secret.

If anyone asks, we're just friends.

But there were no restrictions on sharing their past. "We dated in grad school. But renting homes next door to each other in Royal is purely coincidence, as crazy as it might seem."

It was the truth, and yet it sounded impossible, even to her.

"Either way, it's none of your business. Nor is it anyone else's," she added, in case he planned to run back to her mother with news of her suspected fling.

"Our relationship ended less than three months ago, Audra. I'm worried this guy is taking advantage of you at a vulnerable point in your life."

"I broke it off with you, remember?"

"I know, but..." He gripped his glass. "I assumed this was a phase you needed to go through. That you'd eventually realize how well matched we are."

"I don't want to be *well matched*, Cash. I want to be totally, completely, unapologetically in love."

"We were happy together, Audra. And our parents were

happy for us. They've been hoping we'd get together our entire lives."

"But I wasn't happy. Or does that not matter to any of you?"

Cash took a healthy sip of his Sazerac; a sure sign his patience was wearing thin. A tendency he shared with her father.

"How much do you know about this guy, Audra?"

She frowned, her forehead tensing. He'd hit a nerve. And from the calculating expression on his face, Cash knew it, too.

"I know enough. So stop prying. What I do and whom I do it with is none of your affair. Nor is it my parents'."

"We're concerned. That's all."

"I thank you for your concern. But go home. I'm fine, and I'll deal with my parents tomorrow."

"Don't be so hard on them." He tapped a finger on the bar. "They're just trying to protect you."

She'd had about enough of his condescension.

"I love my parents, but I'm tired of everything I do being weighed by its political merits first. The schools I attended, whether or not I pledged a sorority and which one. What career I chose. I've had enough of it. And I've had enough of this."

She sat taller, steeling her spine as she fixed her gaze on his. "It's over, Cash. I'd like to believe we can still be friends, but I have nothing more to offer you."

"Audra, you don't mean that."

"Yes, I do." She placed a hand over his on the bar. As angry as she was with Cash, she didn't relish hurting him.

"Don't you want to be with someone who truly adores you? Because, as your friend, that's what I want for you. It's what you deserve. But I can't give that to you."

He looked as if she'd cleaved his heart with an arrow. "You said I wasn't romantic enough. So I thought I'd come down here and surprise you. Show you that I can be the man you want."

"You shouldn't have to change who you are, and I'd never expect you to." Audra checked the time on her phone. She leaned in and kissed his cheek. "Goodbye, Cash. Give my regards to your parents and have a safe trip back to Dallas."

Audra walked toward the private room where Sophie and her friends were waiting. She didn't know what would become of the relationship she was forging with Darius. But she knew one thing for sure. She wouldn't settle for a relationship with Cash.

She didn't love him. Not in the way he deserved to be loved. And he certainly wasn't capable of providing her with the passion and companionship she enjoyed with Darius.

Her cheeks tightened in an involuntary smile as she wondered what Darius was doing now.

Before she'd arrived tonight, she hadn't decided whether to accept Darius's invitation to his show. But now she was sure. She was counting the days until they'd be together again.

Seventeen

Darius had been running all day. He was sure he hadn't slept more than three hours a night since he'd returned home. A direct contrast to the sound sleep he'd been getting with Audra in his arms back in Royal.

He was tired, cranky, and now that he thought of it, he was hungry.

"Did I eat today?" he asked his assistant, Anastasia Winters.

"Not unless you're counting that gum you've been chewing for the past hour." She pushed up the cuff of her sweater revealing one of two elaborate tattoo sleeves. This one dominated by vibrant greens, blues and aqua.

"Have *you* eaten?" he asked.

She gave him an even dirtier look.

"God, I'm sorry." He stood, rubbing a hand over his head. "I vowed to myself that I'd never be that boss. We should get something. Why don't you order in? Your choice."

Anastasia grinned. "Then we're ordering from my favorite steak house. Want your usual?"

"That's fine." He settled back in his chair.

"Sounds like I arrived just in time." Audra was standing in the doorway, patting her stomach. "I'm starving and I could go for a good steak."

"Audra." Darius stood, making his way across the room.

She hadn't responded either way to his invitation to join him in Los Angeles for the show and he'd assumed she hadn't planned to come.

He hugged her tightly, lifting her off her feet. He whispered in her ear, "This is an amazing surprise."

She looked incredible in a simple red dress that grazed her thighs, a fitted, waist-length leather jacket and a sexy pair of cutout peep-toe heels.

He could already envision the entire outfit piled on the floor beside his bed. On second thought, the heels would stay on.

Darius put her down, his hand pressed to her cheek. He wanted so badly to kiss her, but they'd agreed to take this slowly and play it cool in public.

Anastasia cleared her throat.

"Oh, I'm sorry. Audra, this is my assistant, Anastasia Winters. Stasia, this is my friend from grad school—"

"You went to grad school with Audra Lee Covington? You never mentioned that. Wow, boss, talk about burying the lede." She stepped forward, wiping her hands on her blue jeans and sifting her fingers through her blond hair streaked with shades of purple, pink and aqua.

Stasia looked starstruck as she extended her hand to Audra. "Hello, Ms. Covington, it's such a pleasure to meet you. Your jewelry designs are absolutely amazing."

"Thank you, Anastasia. Please, call me Audra. And it's a pleasure to meet you, too. I've heard a lot about you. Darius thinks quite highly of you."

"I feel the same. I give him a hard time, but he's an amazing boss and Thr3d is a fantastic company. I'm lucky to work here."

"You're not just saying that because I'm treating you to lunch, are you?" Darius teased.

"You're treating me to lunch because I'm an amazing assistant and you'd be lost without me." Stasia grinned, then studied the two of them for a moment. "You know, I could use some fresh air. I think I'll walk over there and eat. How about I bring something back for the two of you in—" she checked her watch "—about an hour. The menu is in the file in your desk. Just let me know what you want."

"I can wait an hour. How about you, Audra?" Darius asked.

"Sounds good to me." She put her purse down and started to take off her jacket.

Darius slipped it from Audra's shoulders and hung it on a nearby hook. "Perfect. I'll call you in thirty minutes. Be sure to grab the corporate—"

"Credit card?" Stasia waved it in front of him, then slipped it into her back pocket. "I'm on it. I'll be gone for an hour, and I'll make sure everyone else knows not to bother you. I already set your phone to Do Not Disturb." She gave him a knowing look and pulled the door closed. "Goodbye, you two."

"Sorry about that." Darius sat behind his desk. "I never said anything to Stasia about us, I swear."

She stood in front of him. "I'm pretty sure that reception you gave me was what clued her in."

"Maybe I could've dialed back a little," he conceded. "But I showed admirable restraint, given how incredible you look in that dress."

"Do I?" She smoothed the garment down over her hips.

"You do." Darius pulled Audra closer. She pressed her warm lips to his clean-shaven head, then sat on his lap.

There was something comforting about the woman who believed in his dream from the beginning being there on the eve of the biggest moment of his career. Everything seemed to slow down, and for the first time in days, he could catch his breath.

Audra seemed just as happy to see him.

He kissed her, the kiss slowly building in intensity. His fingers dug into the smooth, toasted-brown skin of her thighs and itched to glide beneath the red fabric and bury his fingers in the wet heat between her strong thighs.

Admirable restraint indeed.

Audra pulled away, one hand to his cheek. She smiled. "Good thing I wore the nontransferable lipstick today."

"I guess it is." He kissed her again. "You should've told me you were coming in today. I would've picked you up from the airport. Where's your luggage?"

"Downstairs. I came straight here. I haven't even checked into my hotel yet."

"Don't. Stay at my place. I'll take you out there now."

"All the way out to Pasadena? With traffic it'll take you forever to go all the way out there and come back. I'll take a car service instead."

"Are you sure? I don't mind." For Audra, he'd make the time. The show was just two days away, but his team was more than capable of handling everything. He was a perfectionist, and his obsession with getting every detail right was in overdrive.

She kissed him again, her hand pressed to his chest. "I'm positive." She leaned in and whispered in his ear. "Besides, the sooner you're done here, the sooner I'll see you back at your place."

"I can't disagree with your logic," he said, his voice faint.

He picked up his cell phone and tapped out a message. "There. I just sent my address and the code to get inside the house. Will you at least stay for lunch?"

"Sure, if you have the time."

"Good. I'll call Stas with our lunch orders and then give you a tour of the place."

"Thought you'd never ask." She smiled. "I'd love to see it."

"There's one more thing I want to ask." He hesitated. "I'd love it if you'd model one of the swimsuits in the show."

"On the runway? You can't be serious." She paced the floor beside his desk. "Whatever tall, thin, leggy glamazon you hired to walk the runway in the suit will look far better in it than me."

"I disagree." He stood, too, and wrapped his arms around her waist, stilling her. "You forget that I've already seen you in it. I designed those swimsuits for you, and you looked absolutely stunning in them."

"When do you need an answer?"

"By tomorrow at five."

She stroked his cheek. "Let me think about it. I'll let you know by then."

They called their lunch orders in to Stasia, and he showed her the fall lineup. After lunch, he gave her a tour of Thr3d's headquarters. Then he ordered a car service to take her to his house in Pasadena.

As he watched her leave, he knew two things.

First, as soon as the show was over, he'd tell his parents that he knew Buckley Blackwood was his biological father.

Second, as soon as his parents knew the truth, he'd tell Audra everything. And he'd introduce Audra to his mother and Will.

Eighteen

Audra tipped the driver and closed the door behind her. She slipped off her heels and padded through the large, beautiful, modern two-story home.

Darius Taylor-Pratt had certainly done well for himself. The home itself was gorgeous, and Audra could tell that it had been professionally decorated.

Every painting, every vase, every little knickknack was simply perfect.

It was the kind of inviting space one would hardly want to leave. And yet Darius had.

He'd been in Royal for several weeks. And she got the feeling that even when he was in LA, he spent most of his time at the office.

Audra took in the open space and light, bright modern decor. Initially, she'd been reluctant to accept Darius's invitation to stay with him. That's why she'd booked a hotel. But now she was glad she was here. It felt good to get to know this part of him.

Earlier, she'd been given a tour of his business and got to meet several of his employees. And now she was getting to see the space he called home.

She felt closer to him. As if she had gotten a few more of the missing puzzle pieces that comprised the complicated man she was falling for all over again.

She walked through the house and accessed the back patio. The outdoor space was lovely, and the pool was much bigger than the one at his rental in Royal.

She couldn't wait to hop in later. But for now, she needed a quick nap before heading out to her first client meeting.

Many of her clients lived in LA. Actors, pop stars, athletes, corporate heiresses, socialites, fashion designers and more. She spent a lot of time in LA icing the biggest names on the red carpet—even if their jewelry pieces were loaned, rather than purchased.

Establishing boutiques in Los Angeles and New York, where the bulk of her clients resided, was the next step in her ten-year business plan. A flagship boutique in Los Angeles or New York would expedite the growth of the Audra Lee Covington brand.

She hoped to squeeze in a few real estate appointments to test out the feasibility of buying space here. Maybe after the runway show, Darius would be willing to accompany her.

Audra made her way to the master bedroom, slipped out of the dress Darius had loved so much and crawled under the covers that still smelled like him.

Darius dragged himself into the house well after nine that evening. The downstairs space was dark except for the glow of the candles on the kitchen counter and on the dining room table.

The scent of the candles wafted through the space along with the savory scent of food. There were bags from one of his favorite restaurants in the trash.

She'd ordered dinner for them and he'd missed it.

They'd been running a mock runway show, still trying to iron out the run of show and the music selections. He'd let time get away from him. By the time he'd thought to call Audra, he hadn't gotten an answer.

"Audra," he called up the stairs. "Are you here?"

He went up the stairs and followed the sound of splashing water. He leaned against the doorframe and grinned. "There you are, beautiful. I'm sorry I missed dinner."

Audra was soaking in a tub filled with bubbles. A glorious, sweet scent filled the room.

"I understand how it is being a creative." She shrugged. "I'm just glad you made it home… I mean, to your home… when you did." Her cheeks flushed, as if she'd been embarrassed by saying *home*, as if they lived there together.

But it had given him a sense of warmth and comfort. Made him entertain the idea of coming home to Audra every day.

She sat up, the water sloshing. "I hope you don't mind that I used your tub."

"Not at all," he stepped inside the room and sat on the edge of the large garden tub. "I hardly use it. I'm more of a shower guy."

"Then you should join me." She grinned. "You've had a long, hard day. I'm sure you could use a relaxing soak."

She had a point; besides, he could hardly resist her tempting offer, especially when she batted those beautiful brown eyes.

Darius stripped down and slipped into the tub behind her, wrapping her in his arms.

The warm water soothed his tired body and having her slick skin pressed to his was like a balm that calmed all the disquieting thoughts in his mind.

He relaxed against the back of the tub. His eyes drifted shut as he leaned his head against the wall.

"This *is* relaxing. I should do this more often."

"You should," she said. "It's a shame to have such a beautiful tub and barely use it. It's practically free therapy."

"Well, when you put it that way, how can I say no?" He kissed the side of her face. "Sorry I'm so late. We were practicing the runway lineup. Time got away from me."

Audra rested her arms atop his. "This is the biggest moment of your career. Of course, you want everything to be perfect. I realized when I came here that you'd be preoccupied with work. That's why I booked client appointments. I only returned a couple of hours ago myself."

"That's great." He was relieved she hadn't been knocking about the house bored while she waited for him. "Who'd you meet with?"

Audra rattled off the list of celebs and society folks and updated him on some of the appointments she had for the rest of the week. Many of them tastemakers and household names.

He squeezed her tight and kissed the side of her cheek. "I'm so incredibly proud of you, Audra. You've done everything you set out to do back when we were in grad school. Celebrities and royalty are beating down your door."

She glanced over her shoulder at him, a wide smile on her face. "Thanks. That means a lot. No one has ever said that to me. My dad was disappointed I didn't want to work for the family diamond business or go into politics. And my mother would be happier if I settled down with the 'right' man—" she used air quotes "—and became a society wife. But what I've done is nothing compared to what you've accomplished. You built Thr3d from nothing."

"Don't ever underestimate what you've accomplished, Audra. You followed your dream, despite the pressure from your parents to conform to their expectations. And you're incredibly talented. There's a reason A-listers are beating down your door."

She settled back against his chest. "Who knew that when we were plotting our dreams out five years ago that we'd both actually achieve them?"

He smiled fondly, recalling those lazy Sunday mornings when they'd sit in bed and plan their futures.

They'd both gotten exactly what they wanted; except he'd always planned that they'd do it together.

"How did your client meetings go?" he asked.

"Everything here went well."

"Did something happen in Royal?"

"I had an unexpected visitor. My ex, Cassius Johannsson. He's a Texas state representative. And our families have been friends for decades. We dated for a while, but I ended things three months ago."

"I see." Darius sucked in a quiet breath. "What did he want?"

"Me." She turned her body to face his and hugged her knees. "He still has it in his head that I'll eventually come back to him."

"And how did you respond?" His heart raced.

"I told him that we're too different. I'm sorry my leaving hurt him, but it was the right thing for both of us." Audra smoothed back her hair. "I told him we could go back to being friends, but that's all I can offer him."

Darius could swear his heart leaped in his chest. Relieved, he pulled her into a passionate kiss.

Maybe Cash really was the better man. Maybe he deserved a woman like Audra more than Darius did. And maybe it made him selfish to want Audra for himself, but he did.

As soon as he could, he'd tell her everything. And this time, he wouldn't walk away.

After their bath, he took her to bed and made love to her. He held her in his arms as they drifted off to sleep after a late dinner and cocktails.

Audra rolled over to face him. She kissed him, then whispered, "I'll do it."

His brain was fuzzy, thanks to the combination of King's Finest bourbon, great sex and the promise of sound sleep.

"Fantastic, babe," he muttered, then added, "What is it that you're going to do?"

"I'll model the one-piece swimsuit in the show."

His brain woke up a little. "Are you sure?"

"My parents will probably freak," she said. "But yes. I want to do this. For you, but also for me."

He pulled her to him and cradled her in his arms. "I'll let

the team know tomorrow. We won't announce that you'll be in the show. Instead, we'll say that we have a special guest appearing."

"Perfect." She seemed relieved.

She was perfect. She was everything he wanted. And he wouldn't blow this chance to have her back in his life again.

He just needed a few more days. Time to get through the show and for his parents to arrive back in town. Then he would confess everything to Audra and tell her he wanted to be with her, and only her.

Nineteen

Darius had been running all day on adrenaline and energy drinks. He was as terrified as he was excited by the fact that the show was beginning in minutes.

"Everyone take their places!" Stasia barked over her headset, and all the models started to line up. A few of them still had a makeup artist or a hairstylist trailing behind them, adding final touches.

Stasia turned to him, cutting off the microphone. "You okay, boss? You look a little green."

"It's just the lighting. I'm fine." He narrowed his gaze at her. "Is the DJ ready to go?"

"Checked with him two minutes ago. He's ready whenever we are." She nodded behind him. "And so is she."

Before he could ask whom, Stasia had cut her microphone back on and was talking to a member of the lighting crew.

He turned in the direction she'd indicated just in time to see Audra.

"You look gorgeous." He leaned in and kissed her cheek, not wanting to ruin her lipstick.

"Thanks." Audra smoothed down the white, silk robe covering the eggplant-colored swimsuit. "How are you?"

"I'm fine." *Why does everyone keep asking that?* He must look as stressed as he felt. "Thanks for doing this. It's going to be an amazing finish to the show. Now you'd better go find your place in line before Stasia blows a gasket." He smiled.

"I will." She walked toward the queue, but then turned back to him. "Just take a deep breath. Everything is going to be fine. The collection is amazing, and buyers are going to be clamoring for it. You've outdone yourself, and I'm incredibly proud of you."

An involuntary smile spread across his face and a sense of calm descended over him. He nodded, thankful Audra was there.

Audra was right. The show had been amazing, and the swimwear had been a big hit, as had she. The crowd went crazy when they discovered that Audra Lee Covington was the special guest, modeling the swimsuit that was the pièce de résistance of the show.

Audra's pep talk had calmed him considerably. But it wasn't until he'd gone out onto the stage to thunderous applause, holding Audra's hand, that he'd taken his first full, deep breath all day.

Now as he stood on one of his favorite rooftop bars in LA, surveying the skyline, he felt amazing. Almost like he was floating.

The rest of the team was scattered throughout the crowded after-party and Audra had gone to talk to a friend.

He glanced over to where she stood among a group of people taking center stage. Her magnificent, one-shoulder, gold lace dress had a dreamy layer of organza over the skirt. A high split over her right leg revealed miles of smooth, creamy brown skin. Her hair was still pulled up in the braided crown she'd worn during the show.

He couldn't wait to get her back home, all to himself.

"We're about to head out." Anastasia approached him, holding the hand of her girlfriend, May Chen. "We're both wiped out and I imagine you are, too."

"I am. I might sleep for two days after this." Darius took a pull of his bourbon, then set his glass down. "It goes without saying that I could never have done this without you. You're incredible." He hugged her. "Thank you for putting up with me."

"Same." She winked. "The show was amazing. We're already getting international orders for the collection. A few buyers want to know if they can order the swimwear for this summer."

It was something they'd anticipated and hoped for. A plan was in place to ensure delivery.

"Great to hear. Now get out of here and get some much-needed rest."

Anastasia and May turned to leave, but then Stasia whispered something to May and walked back to him.

"Look, boss, I can understand why you might not want to tell us how you feel about Audra, but I hope you haven't made the mistake of not telling *her* how you feel." They both glanced over to where Audra had dissolved into laughter.

A slow smile spread across his face. He picked up his glass and finished his bourbon. "Go," he said, one side of his mouth pulled into a smirk.

Stasia grinned. "Good night. See you Monday," she called over her shoulder as she grabbed May's hand and they disappeared into the crowd.

"So…" Audra was standing in front of him. "Are we going to another after-party or do I get to take my man home to bed?"

"Your man, huh?" He set his glass down. His heart beat faster as he took a few steps toward her and took her hands in his. "I like the sound of that."

She leaned toward him, her eyes drifting closed.

"You know there are gossip columnists and paparazzi still hanging around," he whispered, eyeing the crowd for cell phones or cameras pointed in their direction.

"I do, and I don't care." Her eyes were filled with a certainty that made his heart dance. "Now kiss me."

She didn't need to tell him twice.

He cradled her face and closed the space between them, pressing his lips to hers.

He was falling in love with this woman all over again. And he couldn't wait to get her back to his place, strip her of that beautiful gold dress and show her *exactly* how he felt about her.

They'd barely stepped over the threshold in Darius's darkened foyer when Audra grabbed him by the lapels of his tan Tom Ford suit and kissed him.

"Have I told you how dashing you looked tonight?" Audra glided her palms up his crisp, white dress shirt. Then she slipped the jacket from his shoulders and onto a nearby chair in the foyer.

"You did, but I can't say I mind hearing it again." He trailed kisses down her neck. "Nor do I mind restating how stunning you look in that dress. Still, I'd much rather see you out of it."

He fumbled in the limited lighting to find the zipper that started beneath her arm and went down to her waist. He helped her shimmy out of it.

The cool air hit her skin as she stood in the foyer in the La Perla strapless bra and thong she'd purchased earlier that day.

Darius kissed her, his hands gliding down her back and squeezing her naked bottom.

The space between her thighs pulsed and throbbed, and her nipples tightened as the kiss grew more heated.

Audra unbuttoned his shirt and stripped him of it, then fumbled with the brown leather belt at his waist.

She glided down the zipper his hardened length strained against. He stepped out of the pants as they hit the floor.

Neither of them seemed to care about wrinkling the expensive garment.

She slipped her hand beneath the waistband of his underwear and wrapped her fingers around his heated flesh.

She glided her thumb over its damp tip and pumped his length with her closed fist.

He gasped. His breathing became more shallow with each stroke.

As she brought him closer to the edge, his kiss became hungrier. Like he needed it as much as his next breath.

But then he grabbed her wrist and led her up the darkened stairs to his bedroom.

He laid her on the bed, but before he could kiss her again, she pressed a hand to his shoulder, stopping him.

"Dare, I've tried to convince myself that this was just a fling. That I could get involved with you again without it meaning anything." She swallowed hard, her pulse racing. "But that's a lie. The truth is I've fallen faster and harder for you now than I did then and…" Her voice wavered.

Feel whatever it is you feel. Don't try to avoid it.

"I love you, Darius."

It was too much too soon. But it was the truth. And she needed him to understand just how high the stakes were for her.

"Audra, baby…" He sighed quietly. "I love you, too. More than you know. But there are so many things we need to talk about. So many things I need to tell you."

"I know." She cut him off by pressing a thumb to his mouth, then gliding it across his lower lip. "But if it's all the same to you, I'd rather we didn't discuss them tonight. The last few days have been so perfect. Let's not ruin it." She pressed a soft kiss to his lips, then another.

They faced numerous challenges, if they wanted to make a real go at this relationship. Starting with their demanding careers, her family's objections and the logistics of him being in LA while she was in Dallas. And she wasn't ignoring any of that.

But for tonight, it was enough that he loved her, too. And that she'd been brave enough to admit that she loved him.

The rest they'd work out later.

In this moment, all she needed was for the man she loved to take her into his arms and make love to her as if nothing else in the world mattered but the two of them.

Twenty

Darius came out of his walk-in master closet, overflowing with Thr3d sneakers and gear. It was Monday morning. But instead of returning to the office to follow up on the success of the runway show, he'd offered to pick his mother and Will up from the airport.

They'd seemed surprised that he'd offered. Which only exacerbated his guilt about how distant he'd been with them.

He glanced over at his bed where Audra was still sleeping. She'd forgotten to wear her usual silk headscarf and her dark hair was spread out over the silk pillowcase.

The sheet was slung low over her bare back and one leg was tangled in the covers.

He chuckled. Audra was as wild a sleeper as she was a lover.

And he wouldn't change a thing about her.

He only hoped that after he told her the truth about why he'd come to Royal, she'd love him still.

He leaned down and pressed a kiss to the soft skin of her bare back and whispered in her ear. "I have some business to handle before I go into work this morning. But I'll call you as soon as I can."

She murmured something unintelligible, and he couldn't help smiling. He jotted down a note and left it on the table on her side of the bed.

"Darius, sweetie, it's so good to see you." His mother hugged him. Her face had lit up the moment she exited Los Angeles International Airport and saw him leaning against his black Range Rover.

"Hey, Mom." He hugged her back. "How was the trip?"

"Fantastic!" Will grinned, pulling their luggage behind him. "Just wait until I show you all of the pictures." He patted the camera around his neck. "How was your big fashion show?"

"Spectacular." Darius grabbed the luggage from his stepfather.

"Doesn't surprise us one bit." Will's blue eyes sparkled in the sunlight. He patted Darius's shoulder, then raked his fingers through the chin-length gray hair that had fallen into his face. "We've always believed in you, son."

Will had referred to him as *son* his entire life. But once Darius had learned Will wasn't his biological father, he'd cringed inside when the man referred to him that way. It had felt like just another part of their lie.

But it didn't feel that way now. Hearing Will call him *son* warmed his heart.

"Thanks," Darius said finally, unlocking the cargo gate and lifting it. The two of them put the luggage inside the truck.

On the drive to the home he'd purchased for them in Brentwood, he let the two of them chatter on about their three-week excursion. And he politely answered their questions about Thr3d's runway show.

Once he'd gotten them home and lugged their bags inside, he shoved his hand in his pocket and leaned against the wall. "I need to talk to you about something."

His mother nodded sadly as she and Will exchanged looks. "We thought as much."

"Let's have a seat." Will gestured toward the living room where Darius sat in the chair across from his parents. "All right, Darius. What's on your mind, son?"

He sucked in a deep breath. "I know who my biological father is."

"That can't be." His mother's eyes were filled with confusion. Will squeezed her hand and it seemed to calm her.

"I was summoned to Royal, Texas, by Miranda Dupree—Buckley Blackwood's ex-wife. He died a few months ago, and he charged her with finding me and telling me the truth about my paternity."

"That gutless bastard," his mother muttered. Tears filled her eyes and streamed down her cheeks. "All these years, he made us promise never to tell you and then he goes and pulls this stunt on his deathbed. If he wasn't already dead, I'd shoot him myself."

"Liberty, I know you're upset, but it's probably best not to go saying you'd shoot the boy's father," Will said calmly.

"It was a cowardly move," his mother insisted, rising to her feet. "He could've had the decency to warn us he was going to pull this stunt. But as usual, he didn't give a damn about anyone but himself."

"That's not exactly true," Will, ever the voice of reason, countered. "He did provide for the boy. Made sure he was able to go to the best schools and had all of the necessities."

"The necessities a boy needs include the love, support and discipline of his father. Buckley Blackwood never provided any of that, Will. You did."

The truth of his mother's statement hit Darius hard. Will Pratt was a good man. He'd cared for Darius and loved him like he'd been his own flesh and blood. And all Darius had been able to see was that they'd lied to him.

He'd never asked himself why.

"Kellan Blackwood, my half brother, said that Buck may have tied some sort of nondisclosure to his financial support. Is that true?"

"You talked to one of Buck's sons?" His mother stopped pacing and stared at him in disbelief. "I mean, they were willing to talk to you? Despite…" Her words trailed off and she lowered her gaze.

"Despite the fact that you had an affair with their father while he was married to their mother?" He said the words without malice. "Yes. I was surprised about that, too."

His mother sat on the coffee table in front of him and pushed up her sleeves. "I didn't know he was married at the time. Not until afterward."

Darius raised a brow. "You honestly didn't know?"

"I swear to you, sweetheart. I didn't. I know I made a lot of bad choices back then, but believe me, even at my lowest, I thought far too highly of myself to willingly become anyone's side chick."

Now that did sound like his mother. She was in her late fifties and still turning heads.

"It wasn't until I told him I was pregnant that he admitted he was married. He offered…" She lowered her gaze to her clasped hands and sighed. "He knew that if his wife learned he'd fathered a child with someone else, she would've divorced him—and taken him to the cleaners. So when I was insistent that I wanted to raise you, he promised to take care of you financially as long as—"

"As long as you never revealed his identity to me."

"Or to anyone," she confirmed. "But then Will came into our lives when you were still quite young. He adored you, and when we got serious, I insisted on telling Will the truth." She reached back for her husband and he squeezed her hand. "But we've never told another soul…not even you, for fear he'd stop providing support or perhaps even take legal action."

Darius walked over to the window and stared out onto the manicured lawn. So many emotions weighed on his chest, he could barely breathe.

"Sweetheart, please say something." Liberty walked over to him.

"Like what, Ma? What am I supposed to say? That it sucks to know I was Buckley Blackwood's unwanted bastard child? That this explains why I felt like I never really belonged anywhere?"

"How can you say you were unwanted?" She cradled his cheek. "I knew I was risking my career by taking time off to have a baby, especially as a single mother. But I didn't care, because from the moment I learned of you, you were mine, and I loved you more than anything else in the world. And think of Will." She dropped her hand from his cheek as they both turned to look at the man seated behind her. "Sometimes, I think he fell for you before he fell in love with me."

His mother and Will both chuckled.

"He had no obligation to you, Darius. Will *chose* to be your father. He even gave you his name. Does that sound like a man who didn't want you?"

"No." Darius sighed, rubbing his jaw. "It doesn't. And it's something I've been thinking about a lot these past few weeks. When you first told me Will wasn't my biological father, I was furious because a part of me believed that if you'd lied about Will being my dad, maybe you'd lied about my real father not wanting to be part of my life. And when you wouldn't even tell me who he was…" Darius shrugged. "I was bitter, angry and immature, and then I held a grudge against you both. Neither of you deserved that. I'm sorry. I realize now that you were both just trying to do right by me."

His mother hugged him tightly. Her tears wet his shirt. Will came over and hugged them both.

Suddenly, it felt as if he could breathe more easily. He couldn't regain the time they'd lost to his bitter grudge against his parents. The missed birthdays and anniversaries. But he could do right by them both going forward, just as they'd tried to do for him.

"Enough with the hug fest," Darius said, his own vision clouded. "There's a lot I need to catch the two of you up on."

Will grinned. "Let me put on a pot of coffee and you can tell us all about it."

Darius sat with his parents and explained that Buck had left all of his children out of the will, and that Sophie and Kellan had asked them to join them in contesting it. But that it would destroy his chances of working with Miranda's Goddess brand. Then he told them all about Audra and his time with her in Royal.

"I can't wait to meet this young lady." His mother beamed, sipping her coffee.

"And I can't wait for you to meet her," he said.

His phone rang. *Stasia.*

He excused himself to take the call.

Three international buyers wanted to place swimsuit orders if they could get an expedited delivery date.

Darius hadn't planned to go into the office today. Instead, he'd planned to return home and tell Audra everything right away.

But that conversation with Audra would have to wait a few hours longer.

"Sorry, Mom. Sorry, Wi—Dad, but we've got an emergency at the office. But I'll be in touch to make arrangements for you to meet Audra."

Will nodded, his eyes glossy. He'd obviously been moved by Darius calling him Dad for the first time since he'd learned the truth.

He hugged the man who'd taught him how to ride a bike. How to hit a baseball. How to be a responsible, loving man.

Then he went to the Range Rover and headed into the office. As soon as he'd resolved the issue at hand, he'd sit down with Audra and tell her the truth.

Twenty-One

Audra returned to Darius's house after an appointment with a real estate agent. The agent had showed her three available spaces. There was a newly vacant shop in Beverly Hills, a soon-to-be-available boutique at the Beverly Center and an office building in Pasadena that she could remodel to fit her specific needs. The Beverly Hills space had the right address for her upscale jewelry business, but the space in Pasadena was tempting because she could design it any way she wanted. And yes, maybe there was the additional lure of it being close to Darius's house.

She sat down to review her notes on each space, but her phone rang.

Cash.

He hadn't contacted her again since their chat at the Glass House in Royal. And since she'd threatened to never tell her mother anything again if she couldn't keep from blabbing her whereabouts to Cash, she doubted he was in Los Angeles looking for her.

This time, she wasn't going to ignore his call. Nor would she spare his feelings.

"Cash, why are you calling me?"

"You said we were still friends, right?" His voice sounded strange. "So I'm calling you as a friend."

She drew in a deep breath and sighed. "Well, you've caught me at a bad time. I'm working on something right now."

"In Los Angeles?"

Her cheeks flamed with heat. "So what, you're a stalker now, Cash?"

He laughed bitterly. "Hardly. I saw you in the fashion

section of the local paper. I can't imagine your parents are too thrilled about you strutting down the runway in a bathing suit and making out with the designer at a rooftop bar."

"The photos are in the paper back in Dallas?" Now her face and neck really stung with heat.

It was a wonder her mother hadn't already called her in a panic with her usual speech about "behavior befitting a Covington."

"Thank you for the heads-up, Cash. I had no idea about the photos." Audra paced the floor. "I'd better call my mother before she hears it from someone else."

"Of all the women I've known, I always thought you were the one that never judged a man by the size of his bank account."

"I don't." Audra stopped her pacing and frowned. "You've known me most of my life, Cash. So why would you suddenly believe I've changed? I told you that Darius and I have known each other since grad school. Back when he had nothing but a dream and determination."

"So your newfound relationship with the guy has nothing to do with him being on the verge of inheriting millions?"

"What the hell are you talking about?"

"C'mon, Audra. Are you really going to tell me you had no idea that Darius Taylor-Pratt is the long-lost, secret heir of the late Buckley Blackwood? The half brother of your client, Sophie Blackwood?"

"No." Audra shook her head as she dropped into the closest chair, her knees suddenly giving way. "That's not possible. Darius or Sophie…one of them would've told me, if that were true."

"If you honestly didn't know, I guess neither of them is quite the friend you believed them to be," Cash said coolly.

"How sure are you about this?"

"DNA test sure." There was a bitter edge to his voice.

"And how would you know this?" The line went silent. "Cash, how do you know?" she demanded.

"I needed to know who this guy was. That he wasn't some user who'd only come back into your life because he needed something from you," he said. "I was only trying to protect you."

"By snooping into my life and the lives of my friends? I never asked you to do any of that."

"I thought I owed it to your parents to—"

"Oh, I get it. This isn't about me at all. If you can't become his son-in-law, you're going to try to impress my father by 'rescuing' me from a man you believe unworthy of James Covington's daughter."

"I resent the implication that I'm doing this for selfish reasons."

"I resent the fact that you're meddling in my business. I don't need or want your help. If you call me again, I'll tell my father, the police and the local newspapers that you've been stalking me and otherwise showing poor judgment by bribing hospital employees."

It was a guess, but it made sense. Who else could give Cash a peek at the results of a DNA test?

"Audra, I'm sorry for implying that you were after Darius for his family's fortune. But if he really didn't tell you why he came to town…well, it's obvious you can't trust anything this guy says. I don't want to see you get hurt."

"Call me again, Cash, and it'll be the end of your political career. You won't be able to get elected as dog catcher."

Audra ended the call and turned her phone off, dropping it onto the sofa beside her.

He lied to me again?

Her head felt light and there was a knot in her gut. She needed to talk to Darius. But she wanted to look him in the eyes when she did.

Audra wiped angrily at the tears that slid down her cheeks.

She needed a good long swim, a hot bath and a bottle of wine. Then, when Darius got home, the two of them were going to talk.

Darius returned to the house as quickly as he could. When he stepped inside, he was thrilled to see Audra, but she didn't look nearly as happy to see him. She sat at the kitchen island clutching a glass of white wine.

"Audra, sweetheart, is something wrong?" His heart suddenly beat harder.

"Is it true?"

"Is *what* true?"

She put the glass down, staring at him. "Is it true that you're Buckley Blackwood's son? That Sophie Blackwood is your younger sister? That the two of you conspired to get us back together? Was that why she hired me in the first place?"

"No! I mean, yes I am a Blackwood. But I swear to you, the first I learned of it was the day I landed in town. About an hour before you saw me at the diner. That's why I was there eating my comfort meal. I was devastated, confused… I didn't know what to think or if I could trust what I'd been told."

Her eyes were wet with tears. She wiped at them angrily, not allowing the tears to fall.

"So you lied to me. *Again*." Her voice quivered.

The pain in her voice broke his heart. He'd let her down. *Again*.

"I didn't lie to you, Audra. I *did* go to Royal to do business with Miranda. But after I arrived, I learned that her real reason for bringing me there was to tell me that Buckley Blackwood, a man I'd never met, was my biological father."

"So you didn't lie about being a Blackwood the same

way you didn't lie to me about your parents?" she asked incredulously, her arms folded.

"I deserved that." Darius ran a hand over his freshly shaved head and sighed. "But I swear to you, Audra, I planned to tell you everything just as soon as I could."

"When did you know for sure you were Blackwood's son?"

"I got the DNA test results the day we got paired up to volunteer at the TCC clubhouse."

"So you knew before we slept together." The pain in her eyes at the realization broke his heart. Because he'd hurt her again, even if he hadn't meant to.

"I did. But I couldn't say anything. Not until my parents got back in town, and I could talk to them face-to-face. I needed them to hear it from me first. I couldn't let them learn about it in the newspaper or on the cover of some magazine. They've been in Europe for the past three weeks."

She rolled her eyes. "Wow, that's convenient."

"It also happens to be true. I picked them up from the airport and told them this morning. I was going to rush back here to talk to you, but Stasia called me with a crisis at the office. As soon as we resolved it, I came right back here to tell you everything, I swear."

"I honestly don't know what to believe anymore, Darius." Audra hopped down from the bar stool. "Even if all that were true, it doesn't explain Sophie hiring me and pretending she didn't know my ex was her brother. Nor does it explain us ending up renting the houses next door to each other. There are just far too many coincidences here." She turned and walked toward the steps. "I may be gullible, but I'm not stupid."

"Audra!" He followed her up to his bedroom where she'd already pulled out her luggage and started to pack.

"I asked Sophie and Kellan not to tell anyone until I

could tell my parents in person. That's why Sophie didn't tell you we were siblings."

"But she definitely knew. That's why she tried so hard to get us back together."

"Please don't be angry with Sophie. She was only trying to respect my wishes and give me a chance to work all of this out."

Audra picked up the cutout peep-toe heels she'd been wearing when she'd showed up at his office and stuffed them into her suitcase.

"It's been killing me to keep this from you, but I had to protect my parents. I couldn't allow them to be blindsided by this the way they were by that article three years ago."

She continued to pack in silence, her cheeks and forehead flushed.

"Audra, sweetheart, you have to believe me." He lifted her chin gently, but she still wouldn't meet his gaze. "This is what I meant the other day when I said there was a lot we needed to talk about."

"So this is my fault because I didn't want to talk that night?" She pulled out of his grasp, suddenly indignant.

"No, of course not. How could you have known…" He rubbed the back of his neck, the realization suddenly dawning on him. "Wait…how *did* you know?"

"My ex called me this morning to accuse me of choosing you over him because you're a Blackwood." She held up a hand. "And yes, I'm pretty sure he did something either illegal or just plain shady as fuck to find out. But the point is, once again you've made a complete fool out of me, Darius. Because I believed in you. And I love you. But I don't know which is worse. That I'm not sure if I can trust you or that I *know* you don't trust me."

Her words hit him like a punch to the gut.

"Audra, it isn't that I didn't trust you. It just didn't feel right to tell anyone else until I'd talked to my parents. I owed them that much. I know you probably don't understand that—"

"No, I don't." Audra's voice trembled. She swiped a finger beneath her eye, then resumed her packing.

Darius sat on the edge of the bed they'd made love in, been so happy in, less than twelve hours ago.

"What can I do to prove that I'm telling you the absolute truth? I'll do anything, Audra." He grasped her hand. "Because I do love you. And there's no one in the world I'd rather be with."

She didn't look at him, but she didn't withdraw her hand from his grasp.

"I need some time to sort this all out. I'm sure you can understand that." She wouldn't look at him.

"Of course." He released her hand reluctantly. "But don't leave. You have client appointments booked all this week. You stay here. I'll go to a hotel, or maybe I'll crash at my parents' place."

"I'm not going to run you out of your own house."

"I want you to stay. Please. Just give me a few minutes to throw a bag together and I'll leave."

Darius grabbed the go-bag he kept in his closet and added a few more items. When he returned to the bedroom, Audra was still standing there, her arms wrapped around her middle.

"Thank you for giving me space." Her voice trembled, and she cast her gaze in the opposite direction. As if glancing at his face was too painful.

"For you, Audra? Anything." He hiked the bag on his shoulder. "I'll call in a few days. Call me, if you're ready to talk before then." He leaned in and kissed her cheek, then headed for the door.

She sank onto the bed, as if exhausted by the entire ordeal.

"Audra." He turned back to her briefly. "I really am

sorry. I keep finding new and inventive ways to sabotage the thing I want most in the world. To be with you."

Darius got in the Range Rover and drove to his parents' house in Brentwood.

The thing he'd feared so, five years ago, had finally happened; Audra was rejecting him. And he deserved it.

Twenty-Two

Audra padded down the stairs in her bare feet. Given the circumstances, it was strange to be at Darius's house. But Darius had been adamant that she should stay. She was grateful for the offer, given her state of mind.

Audra called in a delivery order from her favorite Asian fusion restaurant in LA. While she was waiting, there was another call she needed to make.

The conversation had been stewing in her brain for the past eighteen hours.

She selected the number from her contacts list. A part of her hoped no one would answer.

"Hey, Audra! Are you still in LA?" a cheery voice greeted her.

"Yes, or didn't your brother tell you?" Audra tried not to sound snappy. After all, Sophie Blackwood was still a client.

"Kellan?" There was wariness in Sophie's voice. A sense that the jig was up.

"No." The word came out as a crisp, complete sentence. "Darius. Darius is your brother, isn't he?"

Sophie hesitated before answering. "Did Darius tell you that?"

"No. My ex did. Which made me feel pretty stupid since you both claim to be my friends." Audra paced the floor. "Darius gave me his excuses. Now I'd like to know why *you* didn't tell me that the ex I just happened to run into at Royal Diner was your long-lost brother."

Sophie sighed. "Darius didn't want anyone to know before he told his parents. And he didn't want his paternity to become a lurid headline that would steal the thunder from Thr3d's runway show. Besides, it wasn't my story to tell. So when Darius said he wasn't ready to divulge that information to the world…we respected his wishes," Sophie said contritely.

Audra could understand Darius's reasoning. It was considerate of him to deliver the news to his parents in person. A juicy tabloid headline about Blackwood's secret love child would definitely have overshadowed the positive press Thr3d was getting after their successful runway show. So at least their stories aligned.

But did he really equate her with the general public, not to be trusted with the information? The fact that he hadn't trusted her hurt even more.

"And Darius and I ending up in Royal simultaneously, renting houses next door to each other? That couldn't possibly be a coincidence." Audra plopped down in a chair in the family room off the kitchen. "Darius obviously put you up to this."

Sophie hesitated again. "Yes and no."

"What exactly does that mean?" Audra's patience was wearing thin.

"It means Darius had nothing to do with it."

"But you did?"

"Yes." Sophie sighed. "After we learned about Darius being our brother, I looked into him. I went through his social media accounts as far back as I could go. That led me to you. That's when I realized who you were and that the two of you were once together."

"So Darius didn't ask you to hire me?"

"No. I hadn't met him yet, and he still had no clue he was a Blackwood then. But when I learned his story, I felt bad about everything he'd been through. I wanted to do something for him. So I commissioned you to make our wedding rings and wedding party gifts. And I invited you to stay in town hoping—"

"That Darius and I would run into each other. God, Sophie. Life isn't like *The Parent Trap*. You can't trick people into getting back together."

"Well…it kind of worked, didn't it?"

"No, it most certainly did not." Audra's face got hot. She walked over to the patio door overlooking the pool. "At least, not now that I know you manufactured the entire thing. I do not like being manipulated. Putting us next door to each other and then telling me to use his swimming pool? That was incredibly shady."

"That's just the thing, I didn't realize he was in town until you told me. And I certainly had no idea Miranda had put him up at the house next door to the one you were renting. But when I learned that you two were staying next door to each other… Well, you really couldn't ask for a bigger sign, could you?"

"You just said you invited me to stay in town so Darius and I could meet. If you didn't arrange his arrival, how'd you plan to get the two of us together?" Audra asked, still dubious of Sophie's claims.

"I was going to reach out and ask him to spend a week in town leading up to my wedding. I figured you'd still be here, too. I planned to place you two together at the prewedding festivities."

Audra sank her teeth into her lower lip, trying to decide whether or not to believe her.

"And all that talk about us being friends…that was part of your plan, too?" she asked finally.

"No, of course not. I genuinely like you, Audra. It didn't take long for me to see why my brother adores you."

"Did Darius talk to you about me?"

"Never. But he didn't need to. Anyone who's seen you two together can see just how much he adores you and how into him you are. When you said you were going to LA for his show, I was thrilled. And then when I saw that photo in the paper of you two kissing—"

"You saw it, too?"

"I did." There was a giddy grin in Sophie's voice. "And I couldn't have been happier for both of you."

Audra sighed. "Thank you for your honesty, Sophie. I'll see you back in Royal in a few days. I have a few more things to handle here in LA."

"So you'll still be at the wedding?" The joy in Sophie's voice was evident.

"A promise is a promise," Audra muttered. "I might not appreciate your matchmaking scheme, but I don't doubt your heart was in the right place. Speaking of the wedding, will everything be ready at the clubhouse in time?"

"Everything is ready, but I had another idea. My mom and dad are gone, but I thought that if I could have the wedding at Blackwood Hollow, then at least I'd have the memories of my parents surrounding me. Sounds corny, right?"

"No, Sophie. That sounds lovely."

"I've been trying to get up the nerve to ask Miranda, since she owns the estate now."

"Nigel knows her pretty well, doesn't he? If he thinks she'd be open to the idea, then you should at least try. Give Miranda a chance. Maybe she'll surprise you."

The doorbell rang, and Audra said her goodbyes. When she opened the door, a scruffy older man with chin-length gray hair and sparkling blue eyes stood at the door, holding her delivery bag. Something about him looked incredibly familiar, though she couldn't place him.

Not surprising. Half of the people in LA were current, former or aspiring actors.

She held up the tip, taking the bag from him.

The man released the bag but waved off the tip. He jerked a thumb over his shoulder. "I already tipped the guy, though not nearly as generously as you were going to," he said.

"If you're not the delivery guy…" Audra took a few steps back, her eyes scanning the space for anything she could use as a weapon. "Who the hell are you?"

"Guess that wasn't the best introduction." He chuckled good-naturedly and extended his hand. "Hello, Audra. I'm William Pratt, Darius's stepfather."

Now she remembered where she'd seen the man's face. There were photos of Darius's mother and stepfather in his guestroom and one in his office.

She shook the man's hand. "Good to meet you, Mr. Pratt. But if you know who I am, then you probably know Darius isn't here and why. So how can I help you?"

"May I come in?" The two men might not be related by blood, but it was obvious where Darius had gotten his charm.

She let him in, taking the food to the kitchen and washing her hands. She set out two place settings. "I hope you like Asian fusion because I got carried away and ordered too much."

"I'll try anything once." He shrugged.

Audra divided the food on their plates, giving him a small portion to sample. She climbed onto a stool and opened her chopsticks.

"So why was it that you wanted to see me, Mr. Pratt?"

"Call me, Will, please." He studied the small portions of braised pork, thinly sliced, marinated Angus beef and ground chicken as if he wasn't sure which would be the least offensive to his taste buds.

"May I suggest you start with the marinated beef?" She held back a grin. "It's particularly good with the rice."

He nodded his thanks and tried a bite. Then he smiled. "Not bad."

"Did Darius send you here?" She picked up some of the braised pork with her chopsticks.

"No, and I'll likely have quite a bit of explaining to do once he finds out." The man's eyes crinkled with a small smile. "But he was just so down about what happened between you. I just couldn't sit by and not do anything. Figured talking to you was at least worth a try."

Audra studied the man as he tried the braised pork. He seemed genuine, and he obviously cared very much for Darius.

She put her chopsticks down and sat up tall in her seat as she faced the man.

"All right, Mr. Pratt—"

"Will."

"All right, Will. What is it that you came to say in Darius's defense?"

The man put his fork down and wiped his mouth and scraggly beard with one of the white napkins. He turned toward her.

"I came to remind you of what you probably already know. Darius has made some mistakes, but he's a good man."

"How can you say that when he walked away from you two, just like he walked away from me back in grad school?"

"Even when he was angry with his mother and me, he still took care of us. Bought us a home the moment he could afford to. Sends us money every month to supplement our incomes. And as for you, Audra, I suspect he never stopped thinking of you. Never stopped rehashing the horrible mistake he made in walking away from you because he was afraid you'd eventually turn your back on him."

"I would never have done that."

"I think he knows that now," the man said kindly.

"He still obviously doesn't trust me, or he wouldn't have

believed that I'd leak the info to the media." It hurt her just to say the words.

"I don't suspect he believed that of you at all. But it's a sensitive subject, and I think he felt guilty about talking to anyone about it while his mother and I were still in the dark. I suspect that had a lot to do with the guilt he felt over that magazine article that came out a few years ago."

"You're a thoughtful man, Will Pratt. Darius is lucky to have you as a father."

"Thank you, Audra." A wide grin spread across the man's face. "Before I go, there's one more thing I want you to know."

"Yes?" She picked up her chopsticks again.

"My son loves you very much. I know he's made some flubs where we're both concerned. But the rejection and betrayal he felt when he learned I wasn't his biological father…it hit him hard and he's been struggling ever since. If you can find it in your heart to give him another chance, I know he's worth it."

Will thanked her for the meal and left.

Audra closed the door behind him and sighed.

She loved Darius. But that wasn't enough if he didn't trust her and if she couldn't trust him.

One thing she realized for sure; she needed the time and space to figure this out for herself. And she couldn't do that here, in the house where everything reminded her of Darius. After her meal, Audra rescheduled her remaining client meetings and booked herself a flight for Dallas.

She needed the comfort of home.

Twenty-Three

Darius stared at the note in his hand, studying the perfect penmanship. Aesthetically, it was beautiful. Almost worthy of being framed and hung on the wall. But its contents were devastating.

Audra had returned to Dallas, declaring that she needed the time and space to think. She'd asked him to allow her that.

So that was what he was doing. It'd been a week since she'd left that note on his nightstand after sending him a text message to say he could come back to his house because she was already on a plane heading home.

Stasia walked into his office and he dropped the note, shifting a blue file folder on top of it.

Her attention went directly to the corner of the note, which peeked out from beneath the file folder.

He obviously wasn't fooling her.

She closed the door behind her and sank into one of the chairs on the opposite side of his desk. "I'm really sorry, Darius. Audra obviously means a lot to you."

"Thanks," he muttered, not looking up. He'd given Stasia the basics on what had happened between him and Audra when she'd persisted in asking.

Mostly so she'd stop. And so she'd understand if he was a bit short with everyone.

"Look, I know she asked for space, and I'm glad you're respecting her request. But you should let her know how deeply you care for her. Before she ends up hooking up with some other guy, like her shady ex, the tattler. What if they make a connection? Are you gonna wait until she's walking up to the altar with this guy before you speak up? Or maybe you plan to wait until her first baby shower or—"

"All right, Stasia." He held up a hand.

It tore a hole in his heart to think of Audra getting with some other guy, like that low-life, politician ex who'd obviously used sleazy tactics to delve into his past.

"You've made your point. But if she doesn't want to talk to me, what am I supposed to do? I don't know if you've heard the news, but creepy dudes who can't take no for an answer are definitely out for the foreseeable future. So I don't want to be that guy."

"There is a delicate line to walk," she acknowledged. "So I'm certainly not encouraging you to harass her like her jerk ex-boyfriend. But you can't just sit here and do nothing. Send her an email. Leave a voice message. Send her something through snail mail. Hell, hire a skywriter or the Goodyear blimp, if you have to. Just don't let this phenomenal, brilliant, amazing woman go without a fight. I definitely wouldn't. You don't think I snagged a woman as gorgeous as May by sitting up in my office and wallowing in my feelings for a week, do you?"

"I thought May asked you out." He folded his arms.

"Totally not the point." She leveled a finger at him.

"What is the point, Stasia?" He shuffled some papers, busily.

She got up from her chair, taking the hint. "The point is don't compound your past mistakes with an even bigger one. If you let Audra walk away again, we both know you'll never forgive yourself." She frowned, fiddling with one of the two cotton candy–colored braids her hair was divided into. "Oh, and Miranda Dupree called before you arrived. She asked if you'll be in Royal again soon because she has some designs she'd like to show you. She said no tricks this time. She emailed a few preliminary sketches to prove it. I forwarded them to you."

"Do me a favor, Stas. Get Miranda on the phone. Before I agree to anything, she and I need to talk, so that we're not wasting each other's time."

"I'll buzz you as soon as I get her on the line." Anastasia left his office and closed the door, putting Miranda through a minute later.

"Didn't trust me not to pull any more shenanigans?" Miranda asked, teasingly. "The invitation is straightforward this time. I already sent proof."

"Thank you for that," Darius said. "But that isn't why I called. I've decided that if Sophie and Kellan move forward with contesting the estate, I'm going to join them. So if that's a deal-breaker for you—"

"I honestly think that Buck would be happy to know that the three of you banded together." There was a hint of laughter in her voice. "And no, I'm not offended by your decision. I would do the same thing in your place. As for this, it's business. I was already on board with this collaboration, but after seeing your fall collection, especially the rollout of the swimwear, I have no doubt that Thr3d is who we want to partner with on this project."

He breathed out a quiet sigh of relief.

"Thank you for understanding my position, Miranda. I have a few things to wrap up here in LA, but I can be back in Royal by the day after tomorrow. Let's say we'll meet on Thursday at 1 p.m.?"

Miranda agreed to the time and he forwarded the info to Stasia, advising her that he'd be working from his satellite office in Royal for the next week or so.

First, he'd settle this deal with Goddess. Then, if he hadn't heard from Audra, he'd take Stasia's advice, even if he had to send his message via carrier pigeon.

"This preliminary meeting has gone far better than I expected." Miranda scanned the design options Darius had brought as part of Thr3d's collaboration proposal. "I don't know how I'm going to narrow it down to just fifteen pieces."

"I'm glad you're pleased." Darius sat in the same chair he'd occupied the first day he'd come to Royal. The day he'd discovered that he was Buckley Blackwood's son. "I'm particularly glad that you like our interpretation of your preliminary sketches."

"They're amazing." Miranda picked up one of the legging tracksuit designs his team had reimagined. "I honestly couldn't be more thrilled. So if Thr3d is ready to move forward on this, Goddess is, too. We'll let the lawyers hash out the details of the contract."

Darius agreed and they exchanged their lawyers' business cards.

Miranda picked up the house phone and took a call. She hung up the phone after very few words.

"We have a guest I think you'll be interested in seeing. Your sister, Sophie."

"How did she know I was in town?" he asked.

"She probably doesn't. She's here to see me." Miranda sat on the front edge of the desk.

"Darius, hey." Sophie stepped into the office and gave him a big smile. She hugged him warmly before turning to her former stepmother. "Miranda, thank you for seeing me on such short notice."

"We're all done, so I'll head out and give you two privacy," Darius said.

"Actually, I'd prefer that you stay." Sophie leaned in and whispered, "I could use the moral support."

"Sure." He gave her an encouraging smile and returned to his seat. Sophie sat beside him.

"As you know, Miranda, I'm getting married soon. Lately, I've been thinking that I'd really like to have the wedding here at Blackwood Hollow. Both of my parents are gone, but if we could have the wedding here, at least I'll be surrounded by the happy memories I have of them. I realize this is very last minute, and it would be an inconvenience for you, but if—"

"Of course you can have the wedding here, Sophie," Miranda interrupted Sophie's nervous babbling. "I think that's a wonderful idea. Your father would've loved it."

Sophie looked shocked. "Oh, well…thank you, Miranda. That means a lot to Nigel and me. I know it'll mean a lot to Kellan and Vaughn, too."

"My pleasure. Please let me know if I can help with the arrangements in any way." Miranda walked around the desk and sat behind it again.

Sophie and Darius stood and turned to leave, but then Sophie turned back, reluctantly.

"One more thing."

"Yes?" Miranda smiled at her brightly.

"You're welcome to attend."

"Oh. Well, thank you, Sophie." Miranda tucked strands of her fiery red hair behind one ear. Her blue eyes suddenly looked misty. "I'd like that very much."

As Sophie and Darius headed to their cars, Darius nudged her with his elbow. "That wasn't so difficult, now, was it?"

"Thankfully." She sighed. "Lately, I seem to muck up even the simplest things. You and Audra found your way to each other with minimal interference from me. And then she figured out that I'd meddled in your affairs and…" Sophie shook her head and sighed. "Darius, I'm so sorry about making trouble between you and Audra. I messed everything up."

Darius hugged his sister. "It's not your fault, Soph. It's mine. And I have to find a way to fix this."

"You two are perfect for each other. I hope you can work things out."

"Me, too." He squeezed her shoulder, then headed toward his rental.

"Wait, Darius, how long will you be in town?"

"A week, maybe."

"Perfect. I'd like to give you an official welcome celebration. Maybe this Saturday at seven at my place?"

He was going to decline. But Sophie was being thoughtful and welcoming. He should embrace it.

Wasn't that what he'd always wanted?

"Sounds great, Sophie. I'll see you then."

"And you're welcome to bring along a plus-one." A broad smile animated her brown eyes.

Darius got inside his rental SUV and sucked in a deep breath.

It'd been a good day so far. Miranda was moving forward with their deal and had granted Sophie's wedding venue request. Maybe this was the day to reach out to Audra.

Darius returned to his rental home and stood at the window overlooking the pool. He dialed Audra's number. It went immediately to voice mail.

"Hey, Audra. I realize you asked for time and space, and I respect that. But I wanted to tell you again how sorry I am about the mistakes I made then and now." His heart pounded in his chest, and his throat suddenly felt dry. "I'm standing in the rental house in Royal, looking at the pool, thinking of the first day I saw you there. I couldn't believe I'd been given a second chance to make things right with you. And I still managed to screw things up."

Darius swallowed hard, wondering how much longer he had before the call would cut off.

Quit babbling, and just say it.

"I miss you, Audra. And I love you. More than anything. I can't imagine the rest of my life without you in it."

His chest felt tight and it was harder to breathe. He was

going to hang up. But there was something else he needed to say.

"One more thing. Sophie's having a little get-together this Saturday at seven to officially welcome me to town and to the family. I understand if you'd rather not attend, but nothing would make me happier than if you could be there. Take care of yourself, Audra."

Darius set the phone on the counter, hoping she'd call him right away. But she didn't. Not that day or the next.

He'd blown it with Audra, and Stasia was right. For that, he'd never forgive himself.

Twenty-Four

Audra inhaled a deep breath and stepped out of her car. She'd been to Sophie and Nigel's place several times. But this trip was notably different.

Her belly did flips, and her legs felt like Jell-O. She couldn't remember the last time she'd been this nervous.

When she stepped inside, Tessa's face was the first one she recognized.

"Audra, I didn't realize you were in town." Tessa leaned in and hugged her. "Everyone will be thrilled to see you."

"I hope so." Audra forced a smile.

"I know so." Tessa squeezed her hand and grabbed a glass of champagne from a passing tray. She handed the flute to Audra, as if she sensed that she needed it.

She thanked Tessa and gulped some of the bubbly liquid. It tickled her nose.

"Audra! It's great to see you." Lulu Shepard leaned in and surprised Audra with a hug.

The woman was practically beaming as Kace wrapped his arm around her waist, tucking her close to his side.

Look who's not being so mysterious about his feelings anymore.

Kace smiled at her warmly. "Good to have you back in Royal, Audra."

He quickly returned his attention to Lulu. A giddy, love-struck gaze softened his usually serious expression.

They were an adorable couple, and Audra was truly happy for them.

The clinking of a spoon against a glass drew the crowd's attention to where the Blackwood family stood with Darius at the center.

"Vaughn sends his apologies that he couldn't be here with us," Kellan said, a glass of champagne in his hand. "But for everyone who doesn't know, Darius Taylor-Pratt is our brother. Sophie, Nigel, Irina and I just wanted to formally introduce him to you as such and say welcome to our crazy family." Kellan slipped an arm around the waist of his expectant bride. With her strawberry blond hair, dark green eyes and porcelain features, Irina practically glowed.

"To Darius." Kellan held up his glass and everyone followed suit, clinking their glasses with their neighbors and then sipping their champagne.

Audra strained her neck to see Darius through the house full of people, most of whom she recognized from volunteering at the TCC clubhouse. He seemed reluctant to have all of the attention on himself, as he had been during the end of Thr3d's runway show. But he also seemed quietly content to be accepted by this new community and by the siblings he'd never known.

"Thank you, Kellan, Sophie, Nigel and Irina for welcoming me to the Blackwood family." Darius smiled affectionately at his siblings and their partners. "You've been nothing but supportive. Words simply can't convey just how much I appreciate you."

Darius turned his attention to the crowd gathered in front of him. "Thank you all for coming tonight, and for your warm welcome and the sense of community you've extended to me. I look forward to spending a lot more time here in Royal and getting to know you all." He nodded his thanks in response to the enthusiastic applause.

Darius's eyes scanned the space. His eyes lit up when they met hers.

Her belly fluttered and her pulse raced. She offered a small, inconspicuous wave, and her mouth quirked in an involuntary smile.

His smile widened and he whispered something to Sophie, who cast a glance in her direction and pressed a hand to her chest. She waved at Audra, her eyes dancing with joy.

Darius made a beeline through the crowd. "Audra, I'm so glad you're here." He hugged her as if he had no intentions of letting her go. "When you didn't respond to my message—"

"I missed you, too," Audra blurted the words out. She'd listened to the voice message from Darius at least a dozen times. Reluctantly, she pulled back from his embrace so she could meet his gaze. "I know this isn't the time or place, but we need to talk."

Darius led Audra by the hand down a dimly lit hall and into Sophie's office. He switched on the light. And they settled onto the small sofa.

He turned his body toward hers and held her hands in his. "Okay, Audra, I'm ready to hear whatever it is you came to say."

"But this party is for you. Won't Sophie and the others be looking for you?"

"Nothing matters more to me right now than you. My sister will understand." His expression was a mixture of hope and apprehension. "So first, let me assure you that everything I said in that voice mail, I meant. I love you, Audra." He pressed a light kiss to the back of her hand. "I'm sorry I couldn't tell you everything from the start. I really wanted to."

"I believe you." She squeezed his hand. "I understand why you felt you couldn't tell me in the beginning. But I do wish you'd told me before LA."

"So do I. This past week without you…" There was pain in his voice. "I was afraid I'd lost you forever. I've never been more miserable in my life."

"Me, too." She swallowed hard and freed one hand to tuck her hair behind her ear. "I want this to work, Darius. I really do. But I need to know you trust me. *Fully.* The same way you'd want me to trust you. We're either full partners in this relationship or there isn't one."

"I do trust you, Audra. You're the only woman I want in my life." Darius kissed her palm and her belly fluttered. "Forgive me?"

"Yes," she whispered the word as he planted a soft kiss on her wrist and then trailed a string of them up her arm. She pulled away from him and tried to clear her head. Darius needed to understand that she meant what she was about to say. She poked a finger in his chest. "But no more secrets."

"Promise." He nodded solemnly, then captured her mouth in a kiss that was sweet and tentative. But it quickly became intense. Hungry and feverish. Filled with longing, want and desperation.

Audra ached to crawl onto his lap and straddle him, deepening their kiss. But they were likely already the talk of the party. She pressed the heel of her hand against his chest, tearing her mouth from his.

"We'd better get back out there before your little sister comes looking for us." She kissed him once more before climbing to her feet. "But there's one more thing. My parents will be in LA in a few weeks, and I want them to meet you."

He stood, too, looping his arms around her waist. "And what if they don't approve?"

She shrugged. "I *want* them to like you. But I don't *need* them to. Who I love is my choice, not theirs."

He nodded, one edge of his mouth curled with satisfaction at her response. "I'd be honored to meet them," he said. "And you've already met my dad. So my mom's a little jealous. She insisted that I bring you by for dinner the next time you're in LA."

"I can't wait to meet her." Audra grinned.

"We're going straight to the meet-the-parents stage." Darius smiled broadly. "Guess that means this is serious."

"I've never been more serious about anything in my life." The truth of the admission was both terrifying and thrilling.

"Good." He grinned. "I know we still have to work out the logistics. But I'm more than willing to compromise."

"Speaking of logistics…there's something I haven't had a chance to tell you. I leased a shop on Rodeo Drive while I was in Los Angeles." She giggled in response to his look of disbelief. "It was the right decision for my brand. A move I've been contemplating for at least two years. But the bonus is that there's this amazing guy I've fallen for, and he just happens to live in LA."

"Congratulations, Audra. That's fantastic news." Darius hugged her again. "But this won't be a one-sided compromise. I'll be spending a lot more time here in Texas, getting to know the family I've inherited and reacquainting myself with the woman I haven't been able to get out of my head for the past five years."

She beamed, her heart bursting with love and a deep sense of joy. Tears clouded her vision.

"One more thing, beautiful." He brushed the dampness from her cheek with his thumb. "I miss everything about us. Talking to you all night. Falling asleep with you in my arms. Your face being the first one I see each morning. Our early breakfasts and late dinners together. Bubble bath therapy and the tranquility of watching you swim laps in my pool."

The words coming from Darius's mouth were rushed. He paused, inhaling deeply.

"I know we're both busy trying to build empires—" his lips curved in a nervous smile "—but I want to spend every available moment with you. So…what I'm trying to say is… I love you, Audra, and I'd love it if you'd move in with me."

"In LA?" She'd hoped he'd offer but hadn't wanted to push.

"And here in Royal. Or maybe your place in Dallas?" He nuzzled her cheek. "No pressure, if you feel we're moving too fast."

"No, we're not moving too fast." Audra shook her head, without an ounce of doubt. "We're moving five years too slow. And I can't wait to make up for lost time." Her mouth stretched in a playful grin. "Besides, I *really* like that pool."

Darius laughed, the tension in his expression easing. His eyes were filled with emotion as he leaned in and pressed his warm, open mouth to hers and tunneled his fingers into her hair as he angled her face. Audra tipped her head back and clutched his shirt, eager for more of his kiss.

So maybe the party would have to wait a while longer.

* * * * *

HEARTBREAKER

JOANNE ROCK

For all my readers going through a hard time, here's hoping this story lifts your spirit.

One

Gage Striker hadn't been in the same room as Elena Rollins in six years. They'd never spoken after their breakup. Never texted. Never called.

And yet, the exact moment his former lover crossed the threshold of his remote Montana home, crashing his private party, he knew. He sensed her nearness like a breath on the back of his neck—a prickling awareness that set every nerve ending on alert.

How had she gained admittance? He'd hired a security team to prevent just such intrusions. Heads would roll for the oversight, given how many celebrity guests were under his roof at his Mesa Falls Ranch home tonight— guests who rightly expected their privacy to be protected. In the meantime, he needed to contain the problem. Just as soon as he located her.

Gage stood in the massive foyer with his friend and
Mesa Falls co-owner Weston Rivera. The DJ was playing a pop song in the great room behind them and a
handful of people were dancing. Just then, a commo-
tion erupted near the front door as one of the evening's
more prominent celebrities strolled in with her entourage. Social media star Chiara Campagna caused quite
a stir with her sleek dark hair and wide dark eyes, but
Gage's attention passed over her quickly.

Elena was his real concern.

Guests poured from the great room into the foyer,
phones recording Chiara's entrance as she accepted a
magnolia flower from a greeter. It amazed him how
much attention she attracted, especially among the
handful of Hollywood elite who'd been invited to this
evening's party, a PR effort to raise awareness about
the ranch's environmental initiatives.

And to provide cover for the fact that all six of the
owners of Mesa Falls Ranch were scheduled to fly in for
a meeting this weekend. They were in crisis mode. The
tabloids had been far too interested in the ranch ever
since the actress Tabitha Barnes used their holiday gala
as a platform to make explosive allegations about one
of Mesa Falls' former guests. Gage kept waiting for the
spotlight to fade and the public to move on to the next
scandal, but tabloid reporters had started showing up
to chase the story once they discovered how much time
Alonzo Salazar had spent at the ranch before his death.

Much to Gage's personal frustration, Elena had recently embarked on a new career in entertainment journalism. He had a strong suspicion she'd taken the job
only when she'd seen a chance for payback given the

way they'd parted. With all the gossip Elena Rollins could have covered closer to her Southern California home, of course she'd post a photo of her plane ticket to Missoula, Montana, on her social media account with a provocative caption about hunting down answers.

He'd known all week she was coming for him.

With an effort, Gage returned his attention to his business partner, and the coolly poised blonde at his side. The woman didn't look familiar, but it was clear by the way Weston curled a possessive arm around her waist that she was someone special to him.

"This is more than we planned for, mate," Gage observed as he took a rough head count of the crowd in the foyer. "We need better security." Then, forcing a more pleasant note into his voice, he peered down at Weston's guest. "I'm Gage, by the way."

"April Stephens," the woman replied, her blue eyes darting around the room and up to the cathedral ceiling where hidden lights cast a warm glow on the partygoers. "And thank you for inviting me. Your home is beautiful."

"Thank you." He had helped design the modern take on a lodge-style home, but he hadn't spent much time on-site since his business interests kept him on the move. At fourteen thousand square feet, the property was made for entertaining more than anything. "I know this isn't everyone's idea of a party, though, love. Come back in the summer when we can kick our shoes off, barbecue some ribs and throw horseshoes by the pool. That's more my speed."

He'd never bought into his parents' belief that appearances were everything. He might have been born with the proverbial silver spoon, but he'd chucked it aside as soon as he realized how much baggage came with it. Now, he had his own wealth. Made his own rules. Funny how he still ended up throwing parties for the overprivileged. At least he called the shots these days.

Weston leaned forward to address Gage. "I need all the help I can get convincing April to spend more time here."

Intriguing that Weston would make his interest in the woman so clear. Gage had known Weston since boarding school days and he couldn't recall a single female in all that time whom his footloose, mountaineering friend had gone out of his way to impress.

Gage nodded, respecting Weston's wishes even though he couldn't imagine diving into relationship waters again. He returned his attention to his friend's date.

"Definitely come back and spend some time with us when there's not so much hype." He snapped his fingers suddenly, remembering why he should know the woman. "April. You're the financial forensics investigator. How's your case going?"

So this was the woman who'd been hired by Alonzo Salazar's son to trace his mysterious finances. Gage's former mentor had recently been unmasked as the man behind a Hollywood tell-all book that had caused Tabitha Barnes and her family a world of trouble.

"It's closed," she assured him. "I've tracked enough of Alonzo's earnings to satisfy my client, so I'm officially finished with my work at Mesa Falls. I'll be flying back to Denver tomorrow."

Gage nodded, realizing she wasn't going to offer any

specifics. He would ask Devon Salazar for an update on the case in the morning since her findings could very well turn media scrutiny in another direction. Away from the ranch.

The encouraging thought immediately faded, however, as he felt the hairs at his shirt collar stand on end. The hum of awareness grew to a buzzing sensation until he had no choice but to turn around.

And came face-to-face with his former lover.

Elena Rollins stepped toward him, swathed in strapless crimson silk and velvet. Her dark hair was half pinned up and half trailing down her back, a few glossy curls spilling over one bare shoulder. Even now, six years later, she took his breath away as fast as a punch to his chest. For a single devastating instant, he thought the smile curving her red lips was for him.

Then, she opened her arms wide.

"April!" Elena greeted Weston Rivera's date warmly, wrapping her in a one-armed embrace like they were old friends.

Only then did Gage notice how Elena gripped her phone in her other hand, holding it out at arm's length to record everything. Was it a live video? Anger surged through him at the same time he wondered how in the hell she knew April Stephens.

"Smile for my followers," Elena instructed her friend as the two women eased apart. She lifted her cell to get both of them in the shot.

April hesitated, clearly confused about being in the spotlight.

"Were you unaware of Elena's day job?" Gage asked April as he plucked the device from Elena's red talons and dropped it in the pocket of his tuxedo jacket. "She's now a professional menace."

Elena rounded on him, pinning him with her dark eyes. They stood deadlocked in fuming silence. Weston might have said something to him—Gage couldn't be sure—before Weston and April headed off. Now it was Gage and his ex, surrounded by at least twenty-five other guests still filming Chiara Campagna's every movement on their phones.

"That belongs to me," Elena sniped, tipping her chin at him. "You have no right to take it."

"You have no right to be here, but I see you didn't let that stop you from finagling your way onto the property."

She glared at him, dark eyes narrowing. "My video is probably still recording. Maybe you should return my phone before you cause a scene that will bring you bad press."

Extending a palm, she waited for him to hand it over.

"If you have a problem with me, why don't you tell it to the security team you tricked into admitting you tonight?" He pointed toward the door where two bodyguards in gray suits were stationed on either side of the entrance. "You're trespassing."

The crush of people in the foyer began to ease as Chiara Campagna's entourage made their way into the great room, pausing just inside the open double doors to take a few photos with her friends. At least there would be less of an audience for whatever antics Elena had in mind.

"Is that a dare, Gage?" Her voice hit a husky note, no doubt carefully calibrated to distract a man.

It damn well wasn't going to work on him.

"I'm giving you a choice," he clarified, unwilling to give her the public showdown she so clearly wanted to record and share with her followers. "You can speak with me privately about whatever it is you're doing in my house, or you can let my team escort you off the premises right now. Either way, I can promise you there won't be any cameras involved."

"How positively boring." She gave him a tight smile and a theatrical sigh before folding her arms across her chest. "Maybe using cameras could spice things up a bit."

She gave him a once-over with her dark gaze.

He reminded himself that if she got under his skin, she won. But he couldn't deny a momentary impulse to kiss her senseless for trying to play him.

"What will it be, Elena?" he pressed, keeping his voice even. "Talk or walk?"

"Very well." She gestured with her hands, holding them up in a sign of surrender. "Spirit me away to your lair, Gage, and do with me what you will." She tipped her head to one side, a thoughtful expression stealing across her face. "Oh, wait a minute." She bit her lip and shook her head. "You don't indulge your bad-boy side anymore, do you? Your father saw to that a long time ago, paying off all the questionable influences to leave his precious heir alone."

The seductive, playful note in her voice was gone, a cold chill stealing into her gaze.

He'd known she had an ax to grind with him after the way his father had bribed her to get out of his life.

He hadn't realized how hard she'd come out swinging.

* * *

Elena followed Gage through his massive home on unsteady legs.

At well over six feet tall, he cut an imposing figure. His build was as formidable as ever, broad chest and muscular arms filling out his tuxedo. As she walked behind him, she could appreciate the way those broad shoulders narrowed to his waist, how his dark hair brushed the collar of his jacket. She caught a glimpse of the tattoos on his forearms just beneath his shirt cuffs. She used to love tracing the intricate colorful patterns there, asking him the stories behind each. And he would tell her, spinning tales of his past in the New Zealand accent that was an aphrodisiac to her. Or maybe it was just Gage—pure and simple. He could have spoken with a Southern drawl or a Boston accent, and she probably would have thought it the sexiest thing she'd ever heard.

He had affected her that way at one time.

She hadn't been prepared for how seeing him would affect her now. Six years had passed since their relationship ended in an icy goodbye, with Gage believing his father's story that she'd allowed herself to be paid off in order to leave Gage alone. She'd been so angry at his automatic condemnation that she hadn't bothered to correct him. If he thought that poorly of her character, then he'd never really known her at all, and couldn't have possibly loved her.

So she'd told herself that their split was a good thing. An eye-opening moment about someone she'd cared for deeply. She'd even been married since then, a colossal flop of an endeavor that had left her broke and humiliated. Her cooking-show-host husband had taken up with his assistant while Elena was out of town at a conference. She'd become a divorce cliché before she'd turned thirty.

Sadly, even her husband's infidelity hadn't left her as unsettled as seeing Gage tonight. Which spoke volumes about her poor decision in marrying Tomas in the first place.

She thrust those thoughts from her mind as Gage led her from the party to a quiet corner at the opposite end of the house. The sound of music faded as they entered a gray stone corridor illuminated by recessed lights in the pale wood ceiling. The building materials were sleek and expensive looking, the walls mostly unadorned. Even the floors were free of rugs; her high heels echoed in the wide hallway.

They soon arrived in a sitting room with a gray stone fireplace. Or maybe it was an office. She realized the mammoth glass-topped table with steel legs was actually a desk. There was a deep leather couch tucked against one wall and a television screen mounted on the one opposite.

The surroundings were as cold and unwelcoming as her host.

Gage closed the double doors behind them and then turned to face her. The room was soundproof; you'd never know a noisy party was taking place in another section of the house.

"Do you care to tell me what you're doing here?" he asked her now, his brown eyes unreadable as he studied her by the light of two ultramodern chandeliers with sleek white glass spokes. "Or would you like me to get you a drink first?"

The angles of his face were more prominent than she remembered, from the square jaw and high cheekbones to the slash of his widow's peak. His face was shadowed with a few days' growth of neatly groomed beard. He went to a built-in gray cabinet beneath the television screen, raising the wooden lid to reveal a wet bar. There was a small selection of the best whiskeys the world had to offer, cut crystal glasses stacked to one side.

"I've had a challenging year, but I haven't resorted to bourbon yet." She didn't tend to drink hard liquor after seeing what alcohol had done to her mother. "But please, help yourself if you like."

While he poured from the only decanted bottle, Elena had a vivid memory of what Gage's preferred bourbon tasted like on his tongue when he kissed her. The memory—so sudden and visceral it shocked her— sent an unwelcome flash of heat through her. Her skin tightened uncomfortably, and she fought the urge to pace away from him.

To find some breathing room on the other side of this hard-surfaced echo chamber that passed as living space in Gage's world.

But she couldn't afford to give away how much his nearness rattled her.

"On second thought," she mused aloud, thinking this man and the memories he evoked posed a more immediate threat to her mental well-being than any spirit, "maybe a small taste couldn't hurt."

He glanced her way, but she didn't allow herself to meet his eyes. She pretended a sudden interest in the flames of the fireplace while she tried to pull herself together.

She heard an ice cube clink in a glass. The splash of liquid as he poured her drink. The soft thud of the cabinet lid being shut.

"Here you go." Gage's voice sounded over her left shoulder. "I added ice to yours to mellow it a bit. Would you like a seat?"

"No, thank you." She accepted the glass he handed her, careful to avoid brushing his fingers with hers. She remembered all too well how his touch had affected her. "There's no need to pretend this is a social visit."

She crossed one arm over her midsection and lifted the glass to her nose, swirling the drink as she inhaled the fragrance of toasted vanilla and charred oak.

Neither of which quite captured her memory of the taste on Gage's tongue when they kissed.

"I won't lose sight of that anytime soon," he assured her, gesturing toward the couch. "Sit."

Unwilling to argue, she moved to the far end of the sofa and settled herself on a cushion. He joined her there, leaving a few feet between them. Settling his drink on the window ledge that butted up against the sofa back, he shifted sideways to face her. She did the same.

"Care to tell me why you're here?" he asked, easing a finger beneath his bow tie to loosen it a fraction.

She remembered how much he disliked formal attire, even though his family's living in the public eye had called for it. Then, when they'd been dating, he'd been building his portfolio as a venture capitalist, a role that often put him in business attire. And while these days his tremendous success and wealth surely allowed him to wear whatever he felt like, he was still frequently photographed in bespoke suits.

Not that she went out of her way to find out what he was doing. Given his success in Silicon Valley, his name periodically cropped up at the Hollywood parties she used to attend with Tomas.

And damn, but her memories had sent her thoughts on a wild ride. She refocused on his question.

"Based on the way you labeled me a professional menace, I'm fairly certain you already know why I'm here." She'd been sure to fill her social media with posts about her trip to Montana so that Gage would hear of her impending arrival one way or another. "As an entertainment reporter, I saw an opportunity to unearth a story that readers want right now."

"Since when do you work for the tabloids?"

She shrugged away the pain that came with thinking about that. "Since my faithless ex-husband tied up our assets with frivolous litigation in an effort to make my life miserable. I took a job that would net me enough quick cash to live on until things are settled."

That narrative didn't begin to cover the financial and emotional hardship of her contentious divorce. She'd made the mistake of thinking Tomas would behave like a grown-up and had moved out of the house immediately. Afterward, she'd discovered what a disadvantage it put her at to vacate their shared residence. She'd just wanted him to sign the paperwork and sever their ties. Only later did she realize how shortsighted she'd been to trust that Tomas would be fair.

"I'm sorry to hear about the divorce." The empathy in Gage's voice was real enough. His gaze flicked over her as he took a sip of his drink and returned the glass to the window ledge. Then his tone changed. "But there are only a million ways for one of the sharpest women I know to make a living. Why choose to upend other people's lives to make a buck?"

"I won't thank you for a backhanded compliment intended to make me feel guilty about my job." Why she took it was none of his business. Although if ever there was a time in her life for work that allowed her an outlet for her disillusionment and bitterness, this was it. "For what it's worth, I like to seek out targets for my work that deserve public censure."

"You can't possibly be suggesting that I fall into that category," he replied, displeasure in his voice.

Gage Striker was a man who'd never known a moment's doubt. A man who wouldn't know how it felt to have the world think the worst of him. To have to fight for respectability.

She skirted around his comment, not ready to cross swords with him directly.

Yet.

"I was thinking more of Alonzo Salazar, whose tell-all book ruined lives. The man profited from real people's heartbreak." She shifted on the leather sofa to face Gage more directly and to retrieve her drink. The silk of her dress's skirt swished against her calves, the velvet ruffle at the hem trailing over her foot as she crossed her legs.

Gage followed her movements with his gaze, making her far too aware of herself.

Of him.

"And yet it just so happens that pursuing the Alonzo

Salazar story brought you to my doorstep." He lowered his voice as he leaned closer. "That feels a little too convenient to be coincidence, doesn't it?"

To put off answering, she sipped the bourbon, letting the flavors play over her tongue. A hint of caramel. A touch of smoke as she swallowed.

And then, there it was. The afterburn in her throat with a hint of cherry. The scent of leather. The flavor of the last kiss she remembered sharing with Gage.

"It's decidedly inconvenient for me." She resisted the urge to plant the cool glass against her forehead, as her skin warmed at his nearness and the memories of his mouth on hers. "My work here would be much easier if we didn't have such an…acrimonious history."

"Acrimonious," he repeated. "Is that what we're calling it?"

"I wouldn't say we're friends. Would you?" She set the drink aside, knowing better than to play with fire.

"Far from it," he agreed easily. "Which is the real reason you're here, Elena, no matter what you say."

Her heart sped faster at the confrontational note in his tone. A part of her had always regretted not telling him exactly what she thought of him before she left.

"And what reason is that, Gage, since you apparently know me so well?"

She could swear she saw the flames from the fireplace reflected in his dark gaze. It must be that, and not a wicked light in his eyes.

"We both know you're here for revenge."

Two

Gage wondered how she could possibly look him in the eye and claim otherwise.

She sat beside him in his study in her bloodred dress, glossy tendrils of hair winding around her shoulders like Medusa's serpents. It was all an enticing distraction from the threat she posed. To his name, his reputation and everything he'd worked hard to build at Mesa Falls Ranch.

"Revenge for what, exactly?" she asked finally, recrossing her legs in the opposite direction, causing the long slit in her dress to part and expose her lean calves. Velvet ribbons from her high-heeled shoes wound around her lower legs, their soft bows drawing his gaze to her feet, where red-painted toenails peeped from supple leather.

She was a breathtaking woman, even when she didn't

dress to turn heads. Tonight, he couldn't look away from her if he tried. And damn it, he needed to try harder.

"For your wounded pride. For the slight from my family when my father bribed you to leave me. You were livid with him." And she hadn't even blinked when he'd asked her if she'd accepted the payment. Her affirmation—the defiant lift of her chin—had iced all the feelings he'd had for her. "With me."

He'd never understood how she could have transferred so much anger to him when she was the one who'd sold out what they had. Later, it occurred to him that his father might have filled her head with lies about Gage not wanting her in his life. But by then, she was long gone and none of it mattered.

She'd moved half a world away, returning to Southern California, where they'd first met, while he remained in New Zealand to help his father campaign for a parliament seat and a more prominent position in his party. For Gage's father, politics had been a paramount concern his whole life, an important way to maintain Striker family interests. Sadly, now that Gage's fortune outstripped his father's several times over, his relationship with his dad seemed even more tenuous.

"It's been six years since we ended things," she reminded him, glancing down at her fingernails as if the discussion bored her. "I moved on. Married someone else."

"And look how well that worked out for you."

The beat of silence afterward told him the barb had hit the mark. It also made him realize how damned petty that had been. Her gaze flicked up to his, her expression tinged with a hint of pain before the walls went back up again.

"I agree that was a foolish move." Her easy response surprised him as she leaned back deeper into the couch cushions, relaxing her rigid posture a fraction. "But my point is that I certainly wouldn't hatch a revenge scheme after all this time."

"I have no business commenting on your marriage." He squeezed the bridge of his nose, the tension in his head a sign that she was getting under his skin. "My apologies."

She inclined her head, gracious as a queen. "And I'm sorry for sneaking into the party under another woman's name. But given our history, I didn't feel comfortable requesting an invitation."

He couldn't help a wry laugh as he forced himself to gaze into the fireplace flames instead of at the woman on the couch beside him. "Probably because I would have never granted you one. You have to know that it's my job to protect the privacy of my guests. Which means no tabloid reporters."

"Nevertheless, I need to have my phone back." She shifted beside him, running her palm over the expanse between them and drawing his focus to her left hand that bore no ring. Not even a lingering tan line. "My followers will think something happened to me after my video cut off in the middle."

"Then they seriously underestimate your resourcefulness." They'd met the year before he'd taken his first company public. Back then, the tech start-up offering network privacy tools had been the sole focus of his life. Elena had been working for a rival firm, and she'd quit her job because she believed in his product more.

She'd shown up in his office to tell him so, offering her services as an influencer to a younger demographic. At the time, she'd had a homegrown following for her beauty and fashion tips, and he hadn't understood how that could help him. She'd single-handedly taught him the value of never underestimating a target market, making a clever video that brought him fifty thousand converts to his network security product overnight. He'd given her a percentage and a job. In the end, he'd lost more than a woman he loved when they parted. He'd lost a hell of a team member since she'd handed in her resignation the same day they broke up.

"Then what will it take to recover my device?" she pressed, a hint of agitation creeping into her tone. "Let's open the negotiations so we don't take up any more of each other's time."

She reached for the bourbon on the rocks he'd poured her, and then, as if thinking the better of it, she returned her hand to her lap.

"For starters, be honest with me about what you're doing in Montana." He rose from the couch and returned to the wet bar, pouring her a glass of ice water. Delivering it to her, he noticed how carefully she took it from him. Somehow, the absence of contact only ratcheted up the awareness between them as he reclaimed his seat.

"Thank you." She took a long sip before setting the glass beside the first one. A hint of lipstick on the crystal distracted him for a moment. "And I was honest with you. I'm going to get answers about Alonzo Salazar's ill-gotten gains and where the proceeds from his book went. I'm not leaving the ranch until I either find out or have a solid lead that points somewhere else."

Gage already knew from his exchange with the investigator April Stephens that she'd found answers to that same question. But he wasn't going to point Elena in her direction since he didn't want to aid her in her quest.

Alonzo's secrets were tied up with his own. His former mentor had been privy to the nuances of a boarding school tragedy that involved all six of the ranch's owners, something they'd taken pains to put behind them for good. So his primary objective was to keep Alonzo's past on lockdown. For starters, he sure as hell wasn't letting the woman seated beside him anywhere near April Stephens tonight. Thankfully, the investigator would be leaving Mesa Falls Ranch in the morning.

"So you're just here for a story," he concluded, willing to capitalize on their past affair to maneuver her if it came down to that. He happened to know her very, very well. "Not out of any desire to see me again."

He could tell he caught her off guard by the slightest hint of her shoulders straightening. Was it in awareness of him? Or was she just squaring up for the next round of battle?

"You're safe with me, Gage. I promised your father you would be, after all."

They settled back into sparring roles, and if he were being honest, he was more comfortable seeing her as the enemy than a woman out of options after a well-publicized divorce. It spoke volumes about her financial position—and, perhaps, her personal confidence—that she was selling stories to the tabloids. The Elena he'd known had been a fierce businesswoman.

"And you're not seeking some sort of misguided revenge." He stated it as fact, wanting clarification on that point.

Or perhaps he just needed to rile her.

A light trill of laughter bubbled up from her throat. Rising from the couch, she paced closer to the fireplace, peering back over one shoulder at him. "I'd have to feel something for you if I wanted revenge, Gage."

She said it so coolly, he almost believed her. But at the last moment, a hint of something else flitted through her gaze. The look was fleeting, but it had been there before she quickly turned away. In that moment, he'd glimpsed something more than cool detachment.

Getting to his feet, he closed the distance between them to join her beside the sleek stone hearth. Eyes locked on her subtle curves as she stared down into the flames, he remembered a thousand other times he'd touched her. Tasted her. Made her moan with pleasure.

The past simmered around him, hotter than any blaze.

"I don't believe you."

Gage's words, spoken while he stood far too close to her, stopped her short.

Her breath caught. Her pulse stuttered for a protracted moment.

Thankfully, her back was to him. So she closed her eyes and steeled herself against the tingling in her nerve endings that reminded her of how hot they'd burned together, once upon a time. That hint of bourbon she'd sipped danced in her veins, seeming to warm her everywhere.

But she wasn't here to play games with him. And she couldn't afford to let her guard down for a single second. She needed this story to shore up her finances. If she happened to inconvenience Gage Striker in the process, all the better. Revenge? She preferred to view it as a reminder to him that a Striker couldn't pay his way out of all life's inconveniences.

"It hardly matters whether you believe me or not." She shrugged and traced a pattern in the dark gray stone of the fireplace surround with her finger—anything to delay facing him.

"You feel something for me." That voice, pitched so low for her ears alone, was like a fingernail stroke down her spine. "It's probably nothing good, but I am one hundred percent confident you aren't indifferent."

He'd dropped the gauntlet, and they both knew it.

The silence between them stretched. She'd tried acting once, when she'd first fled her father's run-down desert shack for Los Angeles at seventeen. She hadn't been any good at it then, either, but she'd never had as much motivation as she did right now. Taking a deep breath, she spun on her heel to look Gage in the eye.

"Sorry to disappoint you." She flipped a few curls over her shoulder. "But I'm in Montana for work, not to rehash a long-dead past. So if we're done here, I'll see myself out."

She sidled past him, but at the last moment, his palm landed lightly on her elbow.

"Wait." His touch fell away, quickly breaking their connection.

Because he didn't care to make contact with the woman who'd betrayed him? Or because he felt the same jolt of attraction she felt?

She stopped and turned back around to face him.

"You really plan to stay in town to chase this story?" His voice had lost some of its antagonistic edge.

"I'm not going anywhere until I have answers." She would be in Mesa Falls for as long as she could afford it, anyway. Rooms at the main lodge weren't cheap, but she didn't think Gage would ban her from the ranch property altogether given how hard his PR team had worked to bring the place into the public eye. She didn't think he'd risk the potential bad press.

He gave a decisive nod. "Then stay with me."

She blinked, certain she'd misheard. "Excuse me?"

"If you are that indifferent to me, it should hardly be a problem to stay under the same roof while you re-search your piece," he told her mildly, heading back to the couch to retrieve their drinks. He drained the rest of his bourbon and then returned with her water.

"So you can keep an eye on me while I'm here? Make sure I don't find the answers I seek?" She clutched the glass, savoring its coolness against her palm while she struggled to keep her edge. She had no illusions he was opening his home to her out of the goodness of his heart. "I don't think so."

"Why waste your mental energy figuring out how to sneak into my home when you could have full access?" he asked, his tone deceptively reasonable.

"Why not just kick me out, the way you threatened to upstairs?" She didn't trust the offer. Couldn't trust him.

"While I don't mind negative publicity for myself,

I'd rather not stir it up for Mesa Falls." He paced past her toward the huge table that seemed to function as a desk. Withdrawing her phone from the pocket of his tuxedo jacket, he laid it on the glass-topped surface. "So I'd rather not resort to removing you from the property altogether. But to answer your earlier question, I would find it convenient to have some awareness of your movements while you're in town."

Her gaze had dropped to her phone, but his words made her attention snap back to him. "So you admit you want to keep tabs on me?"

"You're hardly making your movements secret when you're posting them online," he scoffed. "But yes. Having you under my roof will help me stay informed so I don't have to check my social media accounts."

He had a point. She'd be deceiving herself if she thought he was going to ignore her presence in town altogether now that she'd made it clear she wanted answers about Alonzo Salazar.

"For that matter," he continued, perhaps sensing her indecision, "you'd have access to me twenty-four/seven."

"For what purpose?" she asked coolly, not appreciating the implication that she might desire such access.

Gage shrugged. "You tell me. I assumed you might have questions about the ranch. Moving forward, I've committed to spending more time on-site to ensure the ranch's mission is fulfilled."

"Are you saying you'd be willing to answer my questions?" she pressed, draining her drink and trying not to think about what it would be like to move into Gage's home for days.

Or weeks.

Her stomach knotted. His easy dismissal of what they'd shared six years ago had hurt her deeply. For the first time, she debated the wisdom of coming to Montana and reopening that old wound.

"I can't promise that. I'm simply offering you the opportunity to ask." He moved toward her again, plucking her empty glass from her fingers and setting it aside on the fireplace mantel. "Put your money where your mouth is, Elena. If you're not out for revenge, and you don't feel a damned thing about me, then work on your story from my home, where you won't have to sneak around my security. And yes, I get to pretend I at least have a chance to influence your work."

She longed to refuse. To walk away from him and the deal with the devil he was offering.

But he'd effectively called her bluff. And bottom line, she couldn't afford to turn him down. Smoothing a nonexistent wrinkle from her velvet-and-satin gown, she told herself it was a welcome opportunity. A chance to learn insider details about Alonzo Salazar's life and legacy.

"I've heard more gracious invitations," she said finally. "But I'm hardly in a position to be choosy."

He gave a satisfied nod.

"Excellent. Are you staying in the lodge? I'll send someone over to retrieve your things." Gage pulled his own phone from his pocket and began tapping out a message.

"Right now?" She thought about what her hotel room looked like, her meager possessions offering a far more realistic portrait of her desperate finances than the beautiful gown she'd finagled from a local vendor for the event at almost no cost to her.

"I'm sure you're in a hurry to begin pursuing your story." He pocketed the device again. "Didn't you tell me your followers deserve answers?"

She began to see how neatly he'd maneuvered her into doing what he wanted. But what were his real motives? "I hope that doesn't mean I've effectively become your prisoner in this remote home."

"An intriguing idea, but no." The curve of his lips didn't seem quite like a smile. Wolfish anticipation, maybe. "You can, of course, come and go as you please. Although running from me at first opportunity hardly seems like the action of a woman who's indifferent." A note of challenge hung in his voice.

"I only meant that I'd like to retrieve my own things from the lodge." She wasn't sure how much of her life she could hide from Gage if he decided he wanted answers of his own. But she definitely didn't want him to know the extent of her financial hardship.

"And miss the rest of the party you took pains to crash?" He shook his head and moved closer to her. "The evening has only just begun. Enjoy yourself here, and your bags will be in your suite by the time you're ready to retire for the night."

He extended his arm to her, as if he were courting her and not taunting her. Tempting her. Teasing her.

He'd said he didn't believe that she was indifferent to him, and clearly, he still didn't.

She suspected Gage would do everything in his power to prove her a liar on that count. But then, given how quickly he'd believed the worst of her, what was one more black mark against her name?

She'd wheedled her way into his home. Now it was up to her to make the most of the opportunity. So she slid her hand around his forearm, wordlessly accepting his invitation.

His dark eyes met hers and she felt that crackle of electricity between them again. She flicked her gaze away, her darting glance landing on her smartphone.

"My camera—" she began.

"—is off-limits for the rest of the party." He laid a hand over hers where it rested on his arm. "It will be safe here when you return to your suite tonight."

Confused, she peered around the office.

"My suite?"

"This will be your sitting area while you're staying with me. Your bedroom is through there." He pointed to double doors behind the massive desk.

"I see you have plenty of room for me," she noted drily. She'd understood that Gage had achieved new heights of wealth in recent years, but seeing the way he lived firsthand was still eye-opening.

"I do, indeed." He squeezed her hand lightly before letting go and leading her out of the suite and back toward the party. "You'll hardly know we're sharing the same roof again."

Based on the way her pulse quickened when he was near, she seriously doubted it.

Three

Later that evening, Elena went into the kitchen and helped herself to a plate of fruit before declaring the night a total bust. Becoming an invited guest at Gage's soiree tonight had done little to help Elena's story.

Of course, the fact that Gage had attached himself to her for most of the party surely had something to do with it. Sighing with frustration, she drizzled a yogurt dip over her pile of strawberries and pineapple slices. No matter what he said to the contrary, he planned to be her watchdog more than her host.

Which would be easier to deal with, frankly, if his nearness didn't affect her so much. As it stood, her thoughts scattered like dandelion fluff on a spring breeze whenever he was close.

She scooped up some raspberries from a chilled dish

on one of the kitchen islands and dumped them on her china plate next to a few wedges of cheese and some baguette slices. She'd given up searching the party for April Stephens, the woman she'd met at their shared dress fitting earlier in the day. April had seemed like a promising lead for more information about the Mesa Falls Ranch owners since she, too, was in Montana to investigate the finances of Alonzo Salazar.

But by all accounts, the woman had left the party alone shortly after Gage had pulled Elena aside to speak to her. As for the other ranch owners, she'd spotted Weston Rivera drinking by himself in a back den, and his brother, Miles, in a heated conversation with Desmond Pierce out by the pool in the backyard. But they'd both stopped talking as soon as she'd stepped outside, making it impossible for her to overhear anything.

And Gage, the only other owner on-site tonight, was never far from Elena's side. Even now, he entered the kitchen moments behind her, balancing a trio of half-empty champagne flutes in one hand.

With his bow tie long gone, he looked deliciously disheveled. The top button of his tuxedo shirt was undone, and his five o'clock shadow had been darkening steadily as the evening wore on. She noticed that other women's eyes followed him when he walked past. It provided some small comfort that she wasn't the only person captivated by his dark good looks and athletic physique.

But she knew better than to get involved. Again.

"The catering staff not only serves the food, they provide cleanup afterward," she noted, nodding to his handful of crystal stemware. "That's what you pay them for."

"Thank you, Elena, for the entertaining tips. But when one is trapped in a room where the conversation has turned to which lipstick is the longest-wearing, the urge to escape by any means becomes overwhelming." Setting the glasses in the sink, he joined her at the kitchen island. "May I join you?"

He was already helping himself to half a baguette, not bothering with a plate. She hid a smile. His father might have poured a lot of time and money into cultivating an heir with posh manners and social savvy, but Gage had resisted at least some of the efforts to tame him.

"Only if we can talk about something besides makeup." She found a napkin and retrieved her glass of water to bring with her. "I've had all the party small talk I can bear, too."

It frustrated her that she'd learned so little about the Mesa Falls Ranch owners or Alonzo Salazar this evening. But maybe she could still learn something from her host.

The crowd had thinned out considerably. The only guests still dancing in the great room were younger members of the celebrity entourages. It looked like one of the pop singers was deep in conversation with a European model Elena had spoken to only briefly. The party guests weren't the kinds of people Gage had normally chosen to surround himself with, but then, the evening had been carefully planned by the ranch's public relations staff to showcase Mesa Falls for young influencers who might bring more attention to the ranch's environmental initiatives.

She admired the intent, even if the crowd was far

different from what she was used to. They all seemed so damned young.

"Let's sit at the breakfast bar." He nodded toward the coffee station near the back windows overlooking the darkened pool area outside. "That way I can keep an eye on things until these people run out of gas."

Elena slid into the cushioned wraparound bench that surrounded the table on three sides. Even though it was close to the kitchen, the spot was quiet since the catering staff was based in a mobile food preparation truck outside.

Gage slid in to sit near her, closer than she'd expected him to. To converse? Or to prove his point about her not being indifferent? Glancing over at him, she had to concede that she couldn't read the nuances of his expression anymore. Or perhaps he'd cultivated a greater skill in keeping his thoughts to himself since she'd known him. No doubt that was a formidable asset in his business dealings.

"So how long are you in town for?" she asked as she unfolded a linen napkin and laid it over her lap. She might as well dig for answers from the only Mesa Falls Ranch owner she knew personally. "You mentioned staying in Montana beyond tonight, but the last I knew your full-time residence was in Palo Alto."

He'd only just purchased that property when she'd met him. They'd talked about moving in together before things fell apart on the ill-fated trip to New Zealand to meet his family.

"It has been my home base ever since I purchased it." He tore the baguette in half and offered her a piece, but she shook her head. "But Weston is looking for someone else to oversee the ranch full-time."

Sitting so close to him called forth old memories. His aftershave was the same; since they'd broken up, the scent had sometimes tempted her in her dreams.

Dropping a few raspberries into her chilled water, she tried to refocus on their conversation, needing to learn what she could from him.

"Is Weston leaving the group?" she asked, mentally reviewing what she knew about the six partners. Weston Rivera was the younger of the Rivera brothers, both of whom owned a stake in the ranch. Weston had diverse investments around the country—mostly in fast-growth start-ups that had made him a very rich man. Miles Rivera ran their family's ranch in the foothills of the Sierra Nevada Mountains in central California.

"No. But now that we're beginning to attract tabloid attention—" he paused to give her a meaningful look "—Weston doesn't want to be solely responsible for overseeing the security and privacy of the guests."

Either that, or he wanted help ensuring the ranch owners' secrets were kept on lockdown. She was willing to bet the latter.

"So you're moving here more permanently?" She couldn't envision Gage retreating from the world in this remote corner of western Montana.

He might not have gone into politics like his father wanted, and he definitely didn't fit the same spit-shined image his father projected, but he had inherited his family's comfort in social situations. More than that, he was good with people, and seemed to enjoy working in team settings, not on isolated ranches.

"For now, yes." He stabbed a fat strawberry with his dessert fork. "We'll see how the year unfolds with all the media interest in Alonzo."

She sipped her water and watched the antics in the great room as two young men held a dance-off for the enjoyment of the six or seven ladies draped on Gage's leather sofas. Suit jackets discarded, the men spun on the toes of their slick dress shoes and performed hip swivels that had the women cheering and whistling.

The DJ seemed oblivious, spinning records and nodding to herself as she cued one song after another. One of her headphones had slipped off her ear.

"If you keep hosting house parties like this one, your time in town won't be boring," Elena observed lightly, amazed at the agility of the dancers.

Gage looked into the great room and shook his head. "I'm not sure living room dance battles are going to provide much entertainment. Besides, I like ranch life. Don't forget, I grew up on a cattle station before my father turned his attention to politics."

In fact, that detail of his past had slipped her mind. But now it all came back to her. They'd made plans to see the cattle station on her trip to New Zealand with him. But before they could, his father had intervened to confront Elena about her relationship with Gage. She'd flown home early. Alone.

She was still lost in thought when the DJ finished her set. A woman Elena guessed was part of the ranch's PR staff arrived in the great room to urge the last of the guests into the swag room, enticing them with the promise of luxe goods and a fitting for a custom Stetson. The great room suddenly went quiet, as the group shuffled out, drinks in hand.

"What about you?" Gage asked, as she realized they were now alone. "How will you fare in the remote mountains, far from LA life?"

Awareness drifted around her like smoke, clinging to her skin. And yet, remembering how things had ended between them, she forced herself back down to earth. The pain of losing him had led her to a rebound marriage that nearly destroyed her life. She couldn't give Gage any sway over her again.

"In light of my legal battles with my ex, taking some time to clear my head and commune with nature will be a good thing."

Gage made himself a stack of cheese slices and crackers, building his next bite with architectural care that relayed how hard he was working not to show his feelings, too. "I'm having a tough time envisioning you communing with nature."

"I may not have grown up on a cattle station, but I spent my youth in the California desert, sleeping under the stars as often as I slept under a roof. It was remote in its own way." She let herself smile at the good memories. It had taken years of therapy for her to tease out the happy times among the sad and scary ones with her alcoholic mother, but Elena made an effort now. "I hope to explore all that the ranch has to offer."

She'd tried on a lot of hats since running away from home at seventeen. She'd been a beauty influencer with her online makeup tutorials and endorsements that had helped finance college courses. A businesswoman in the years Gage had known her. Then, after that, a supportive wife to her husband's career. None of those things had worked out for her.

She wasn't sure where to turn next, but she knew for sure running hadn't done her one bit of good. She was done being reactive. Over the years, she'd let her family dictate her choices. Then Gage's overbearing father. Then her husband. Now, she was taking her life into her own hands.

For good.

Gage led Elena through his now quiet house half an hour later, not sure what to make of the changes he saw in her.

She wasn't the same woman he'd dated six years ago. But just because he could no longer see her fiercely competitive side didn't mean it wasn't there. No matter how she downplayed her presence in Montana, he couldn't shake the sense that she was here to right an old wrong. To make him pay for not standing up to his father on her behalf.

And yet, what had she expected when she'd completely hidden her past from him? He'd been blindsided by the revelation that her father was a wanted man. That she'd spent much of her teens on the run from the law with him. That her mother was an alcoholic with a violent streak that had landed both parents in jail more than once. Not that any of that reflected on Elena in the least. But it had hurt that she hadn't confided any of it, leaving him to find out from his father's private investigator. Her lack of trust showed how little she thought of him.

Now, she was back. And he didn't know what to think about it other than her presence was still more intoxicating than any bourbon. Even walking four feet behind him, Elena's draw was magnetic, pulling him inexorably backward.

"Thanks for showing me the way," she said as they returned to the living area outside her bedroom, the same spot where they'd spoken earlier in the evening. She retrieved her smartphone that he'd left there.

The velvet flounce hem of her dress swished softly as she moved. He hadn't realized how his ears had been attuned to that sound all evening until it stopped in the quiet stillness of the room.

Grinding his teeth as he tried not to think of her legs beneath the fabric, Gage reached for the double doors into the bedroom and swung them wide. "Your things from the guest lodge are already here, and there are towels in the bathroom."

He nodded with satisfaction to see the bouquet of bear grass on the bedside table. The pretty native wildflowers were protected in many areas, but the Mesa Falls ranching practices had brought the flowers back in abundance on the ranch. His staff had done well prepping her room on such short notice.

And he wasn't going to think too hard about why he wanted to please a woman who'd tricked his security to get through his front door. He hoped he was only giving her a peace offering so she'd be less likely to backstab him with a tabloid hit piece.

"How beautiful," she murmured, brushing past him and bending over to sniff the white-and-yellow bouquet on her way to the bed. "Thank you, Gage."

If the warmth in her voice hadn't undone him, the sight of her beside the king-size bed would have. She was already reaching for the jeweled clip that held half of her hair up, taking the curls down for the night.

He watched, speechless, as the silky mass tumbled free. Curls danced and sprang around her shoulders as she moved. He knew he should say good-night and retreat. Leave her to get ready for bed.

But his mind had already supplied an alternate ending to the evening. One that included him stepping behind her to lower the zipper on her long, strapless gown. Letting the fabric fall away from her curves so he could touch her everywhere. And finding out if sex between them was still every bit as explosive as it had been six years ago. The connection between them had been so strong; the feelings held him hostage, preventing him from finding a long-term relationship after Elena. Everyone else came up short.

"You're welcome." He edged the words over a throat gone dry, still willing his feet to move. "If there's anything else you need…"

Help with a zipper. A neck massage. Multiple orgasms. He could think of so many things.

"I'm all set." She set her phone and the hair clip on the nightstand beside the flowers. "I appreciate you letting me stay."

He questioned the wisdom of that decision now, realizing how thoroughly she could distract him. How easy it would be for her to slide past his defenses and learn everything about the Mesa Falls Ranch owners that he needed to keep private.

With an effort, he reminded himself where his loyalties lay.

"It's no trouble." He saw it as his duty, actually. He

was moving to Montana to keep the past on lockdown. To do that, he'd need to keep an eye on Elena Rollins. "And I'll ask one of the ranch hands to bring over an extra utility vehicle for you tomorrow so you can start exploring the place."

"Thank you." A warm light touched her gaze for a moment—a hint of genuine pleasure.

"I'll clear my schedule for the afternoon to accompany you." Somehow, some way, he needed to rein in his attraction to her before then.

He hoped like hell that it was tough tonight only because he was tired. But he suspected that was a whole lot of wishful thinking.

Her smile faded and he could see her defenses falling into place as he tried to shore up his own.

"In that case, I'll see you then." She gave a regal nod, all but dismissing him. "Sleep well, Gage."

Wheeling around to leave, to put as much space between them as possible before he did something he would regret, he already knew he wouldn't have a moment of sleep that wasn't filled with red-hot dreams of her.

Four

Shortly before noon the next day, Elena caught herself checking her watch again and cursed.

Curled up in the window seat of the spacious bedroom, she adjusted a gray cashmere throw over her legs and told herself to stop thinking about her upcoming appointment to explore the ranch with Gage. The man had dominated her thoughts this morning when she was supposed to be compiling notes for her lawyer to answer her ex-husband's latest bogus claim about their supposed "shared debt." But time and time again, while she was compiling digital copies of her old credit card statements from the months before she and Tomas split, her thoughts veered to the powerful man determined to play host to her this week.

Fluffing a silk pillow behind her back, Elena forced

herself to relax. She glanced out the window with its glorious view of the Bitterroot Mountains, still capped with snow even though signs of spring were everywhere else. She had to admit she felt insanely comfortable in Gage's home—on a surface level at least. It wasn't surprising, considering the Egyptian cotton sheets, thick Turkish bath towels and fresh flowers on her nightstand. She hadn't been surrounded by this much luxury since the time she'd visited Gage's family in New Zealand. And despite some vivid dreams of Gage the night before, she'd had the best night's sleep she could remember in ages.

Even in the brief, happy first year of her marriage to Tomas when they'd both been doing well in their careers, her focus had been saving money for the bigger home he hoped to purchase for the family he supposedly wanted. So she'd never indulged in the kinds of high-end touches that graced every corner of Gage's place.

She clicked the Send button, emailing her attorney proof that she hadn't been the one to run up the debt Tomas now wanted her to share responsibility for. It didn't matter that they'd been divorced for months now, he still found ways to violate the terms of the arrangement, or to claim she had, all of which cost them both a fortune in legal fees. Between that nonsense and his live-in lover stationing herself in Elena's former home day and night to make sure Elena never removed so much as a dish towel, her frustration level with the whole process was through the roof.

No sooner had the email sent than her phone lit up with a text from Gage.

The fields are still muddy. I have outerwear for you so you don't ruin your clothes. I'm at your door.

She lightly swiped her thumb over the words while they sank in. Holding on to her enmity wasn't as easy when he did thoughtful things. It made her remember the past she'd shared with him before things fell apart. Before he'd revealed his judgmental side.

Casting aside the cashmere throw, Elena padded in stocking feet across the dense Persian rug and through the sitting room to the outer double doors. She opened them to find her host dressed in a taupe riding jacket trimmed with dark brown leather at the collar. From his jeans and boots to the wide, camel-colored Stetson on his head, Gage Striker fit the role of an American cowboy with enticing ease.

All the more reason she needed to remember they weren't friends and she wasn't here as his pampered guest, no matter how much she enjoyed the beautiful accommodations. She needed to keep some barriers firmly in place.

"Good morning. I come bearing gifts." He held out a heavy denim jacket with a shearling collar for her. A box with the name of a saddlery shop sat at his feet. "Are you still game for seeing the ranch?" His gaze roamed over her yoga pants and slouchy sweater.

"I'll be honest. I spent half the morning thinking about how to give you the slip." She took the coat, not surprised to see the designer label, and the tag that indicated the garment was the perfect size for her. She didn't waste any time before she reset her defenses.

"I'm not sure I should let you buy me off, Gage. Don't journalists frown on bribes?"

He stiffened a moment before recovering himself, no doubt remembering a bribe of another sort—the one his father had offered for her to leave the Striker family in peace. Regret mingled with old anger.

"Real journalists, yes." Retrieving the boot box, he stepped inside the sitting room. "Scandalmongers, however, accept them gladly. Especially the ones who didn't think to pack the right shoes for a Montana spring."

Still clutching the coat, she followed him to the couch, curious in spite of herself. "Is your staff already spying on me? My shoe collection isn't really anyone else's business."

"No one is spying," he assured her, removing his hat before dropping onto the leather seat beside her. "But I did make an educated guess that you left most of your boots at home based on the size of your suitcase when I happened to see it last night." He toed the box closer to her. "Come on and open this. Tell me how I did choosing something for a renowned style influencer. Will the boots work? Or will you hashtag them 'never in a million years'?"

Her defenses were harder to maintain when he was being charming. Her influencer status had dropped off significantly in the last years she'd been focused on her marriage, but she was trying to be a social media presence again. Picking up the box, she set it on her lap and pulled the top off. The scent of leather wafted up as she peeled aside the sheet of crisp tissue paper to reveal a pair of high-cut black riding boots with a distinctive blue cuff.

"They're gorgeous," she breathed reverently, running a hand over the sumptuous leather. "Now I can go riding, too."

"That was my thinking." He nodded, seeming satisfied as she unzipped the first boot. "You said you were interested in communing with nature while you're in Montana. The boots will help."

She was surprised he'd keyed in on that comment from the night before. She'd forgotten that he was a keen listener and observer.

While she slid her foot into the first boot, Gage was already prepping the second for her. "You're being suspiciously accommodating today," she observed as she slipped on the next one and zipped it up. Standing, she reached for the coat he'd given her, only to have him beat her to it. "It makes me wonder about your motives."

Rising, he held out an arm of the coat for her. Chivalrous. Thoughtful.

Sexy.

"The sooner I show you around the ranch, and give you opportunities to find your story," he said as he helped her into the other sleeve, "the faster you'll learn there's nothing here that will help you in your quest for answers about Alonzo."

He skillfully shifted her hair to one side before he slid the coat into place. For the space of a moment, his hands rested on her shoulders before sliding away again, the touch awakening an awareness of him she didn't want to feel today. Even now, after he retrieved his hat and was escorting her toward the door, her body hummed from that brief contact.

"So all this thoughtfulness is self-serving?" she retorted, desperate to rally her absent defenses as she charged ahead of him. But she still felt hurt all the same.

"Elena." Her name, softly spoken, stopped her. Or maybe it was the unexpected tenderness in his tone when he said it.

Whatever it was, she turned around and locked eyes with him.

"We broke each other's hearts once, but it was a long time ago." His dark eyes seemed to see right through her, past any lame attempt to keep him at arm's length, right down to where she kept all her real feelings. "I don't think we need to keep operating like we're mortal enemies because of a long-ago breakup, do you?"

It was a skillful maneuver, putting her in a position where she would only seem childish and petulant if she kept needling him.

"Maybe I can rein it in," she offered, her gaze sliding away from his. "At least long enough for the tour. Why don't we talk about your former mentor instead? You can tell me all about Alonzo Salazar, a man who truly took scandalmongering to a whole new height."

Gage managed to put off the conversation long enough to get the ranch tour under way. They were in a high-performance utility vehicle that seated two. He'd taken his time snapping the windscreen into place and helping her buckle into the open-air seat, all the while planning his strategy for addressing her question about Alonzo.

Once they were cruising along the dirt path that ran

along the Kootenai Creek that fed into the Bitterroot River, Elena gripped the roll bar and pinned him with a frank gaze.

"For a man who offered me full-time access to ask questions, you're noticeably silent on the subject of Alonzo," she observed lightly. She reached to tighten the pink scarf she'd wrapped around her hair, trying to stop the dark strands from whipping in the breeze.

The windscreen helped, but it wasn't the same as riding in a car. They bounced over a rocky hill and he turned sharply to follow the creek bed.

"I said you could ask questions. I didn't guarantee I'd answer." He slowed down to point out an osprey that had been startled from its perch. The huge bird emitted a series of high-pitched whistles as it circled. "It's been my instinct to keep my personal affairs private for as long as I've been in the public eye, so I have to make a concerted effort to be more forthcoming with you."

"You're weighing how much you can share with me." She distilled his answer to the basic point even as her eyes followed the osprey until it settled in a nearby ponderosa pine. "Why don't I help you out by telling you what I already know?"

She turned expectant eyes his way, and he had the impression—not for the first time—that Elena was in a constant state of wariness with him. He understood it, given how they'd broken up. But it meant he had to be far more watchful of her, unsure when her sharp tongue would strike next.

"Fair enough," he agreed, giving the vehicle more gas to take them up a ridge.

"No one knew Alonzo Salazar—a retired English

teacher from the prestigious Dowdon School—was the man behind the tell-all book *Hollywood Newlyweds*, which he wrote as A. J. Sorenson, until he was publicly unmasked at the publicity event held here last Christmas." Elena pulled her phone from her jacket and snapped a selfie, no doubt collecting images for the day's social media feed. "The disclosure was all the more shocking because it was made by Tabitha Barnes, the actress whose real-life affair was exposed in the book. After it came out, her powerful director husband divorced her. He also severed his relationship with the girl he'd believed to be his daughter because as the book revealed, she was fathered by another man."

Considering what that girl must have gone through as a teenager—being abandoned and locked out of her childhood home by the man she'd thought was her father—was enough to make anyone think Alonzo was a dirtball. But Gage had known Alonzo well enough to believe the guy had some kind of compelling reason for what he'd done.

"Right. But just to be clear, I didn't know anything about Alonzo's secret pen name until that night." He still didn't know how Alonzo had managed to keep the secret his whole life, especially when Tabitha Barnes had threatened to sue the publisher. But the truth hadn't come out until months after his death. "Neither did any of the other ranch owners. Neither did his own sons."

As they reached the top of the ridge that offered a spectacular view of the river valley below, Gage parked the vehicle at the edge of a clearing and switched off the engine.

Elena unfastened her seat belt and turned more fully toward him. They sat in the open air, birds calling and the creek babbling below them.

"Supposing that's true—and I'm not convinced it is—why haven't you or any of the other ranch owners released a statement condemning his actions?" She tilted her head and gave him a questioning look. Her long dark hair spilled over her shoulder with the movement, reminding him how much he'd dreamed about running his fingers through all those silky waves. "You all were Alonzo's students at the Dowdon School. I know from our past conversations that he was a mentor to you and your friends, so I'm aware that you respect him. But it can't be good for the ranch to be associated with that kind of scandal. Why protect him?"

His publicity coordinator had posed the same question. But when Gage had met with Weston, Miles and Desmond before the party last night, they'd agreed the less said the better. Yet, he needed a different strategy with Elena. He had to keep her close, to buy himself time to figure out why Alonzo had written a book that had torn apart lives. Devon Salazar hadn't returned his calls yet today, but maybe Alonzo's son would share April Stephens's findings.

"Keep in mind that he wrote the book as fiction, and changed all the names, so I don't believe it was his intention to hurt anyone with it." Gage tipped back the brim of his hat to feel the sun on his face, breathing in the spring air to help cool the desire for Elena that was never far from the surface. "Remember the book was out for over a year before some Hollywood gossip columnist got a hold of it and decided to make a game out of matching up the characters to real people. That's when the fascination with the story began on a large scale, not because Alonzo billed it as anything true-to-life."

"I'll definitely revisit that." She nodded thoughtfully, her gaze flicking back to his. "I'd forgotten about that. I think the media frenzy took hold around the time we were dating."

The months they'd been so wrapped up in each other that they hadn't done much of anything else but talk, touch and make love.

"No wonder it didn't make an impression with us back then." He couldn't imagine how she'd left a relationship as intense as theirs only to turn right around and marry someone else. He'd been hurt by that all over again, thinking right up until he'd seen the engagement announcement that she would change her mind.

"No wonder." A ghost of a smile, fleeting and faint, chased over her features. "So you and your partners have decided to withhold judgment until you know more. But what happens when Devon Salazar's financial forensics investigator reveals where Alonzo was funneling profits from the story? No matter what his original intentions, you have to admit it doesn't look good for him to pocket the royalties and essentially profit off someone else's heartache."

Gage hadn't realized how thoroughly Elena had done her homework, but clearly she knew about April Stephens and her visit to Mesa Falls Ranch.

"My guess is that he didn't personally profit, which is why I'm not jumping on the bandwagon to condemn the guy." He shrugged his shoulders, ready to move on. "And you shouldn't either until you know more."

"You're really going to try to pretend you're as in the dark as I am about this?" she pushed.

"I know more than you only because I considered Alonzo a friend, and I know his character. He wasn't a good dad to his sons, but I like to think he tried to make up for that by being a father figure to my friends and me." Rolling his shoulders, Gage reached for the key in the ignition to start the vehicle. "And on that note, let's move on."

"Wait." She laid her hand on his, halting him before he could turn the engine over. "Why not tell me the good things about him, then? How did you and the other owners end up as lifelong friends with a teacher from your boarding school?"

Her touch short-circuited his brain, preventing him from answering even if he'd wanted to. Which he most definitely did not. Instead, he captured her hand in his, holding it.

"Can we have a conversation, not an interrogation?" he asked, running his thumb over the backs of her knuckles for a moment, savoring the feel of her skin. "Maybe save some of your questions for dinner tonight?"

She shook her head as she withdrew her fingers. "I don't have the luxury of pursuing answers at my leisure, Gage. This is my job, and I don't get paid until I have a story."

He noticed she didn't address the dinner invitation. Because she didn't want to spend more time with him? Or because she suspected it would lead them to act on the heat sparking between them?

"That seems like a mercenary approach." He would be meeting with the other ranch owners later. Even if he couldn't reach Devon Salazar before then, he'd at least be able to talk to Wes to see if he'd gleaned anything from April about her investigation. The two of them had obviously hit it off. "You'll notice I'm not talking to anyone else from the tabloids, so it's not like anyone will beat you to the story."

"What if you don't have the answers I need?" she asked, her words trailing off as a herd of bighorn sheep stepped into view just below the ridge. "Oh wow," she breathed reverently, all her focus on three ewes at the head of the group. "What are they?"

"Bighorn sheep." He glanced sideways at her. "You've never seen one before?"

"Never. Although I might have seen little ones without the heavy horns and thought they were goats." She started recording a video on her phone. The screen showed the animals up close.

He pointed to the ewes at the head of the group. "They'd be some big goats," he teased, liking the smile that curved her lips in response.

She'd been stunning the night before in her vibrant crimson dress, but he was even more captivated by her now, her skin free of any makeup, her mouth a soft shade of rosy pink. One dark curl teased across her cheek in the breeze while the tail of her scarf flapped close to his cheek as he leaned closer to watch with her.

He breathed in her clean scent, remembering the way she used to dot lavender essential oil behind each ear instead of perfume. And, as if that one small reminiscence had been the dam holding back all the rest, memories rushed at him like a rogue wave. Sitting behind her in a tub full of rose petals and washing her hair. Driving up the Pacific Coast Highway with her in the passenger seat of his BMW Z8 roadster, the sounds of Big Sur mingling with her laughter. Undressing her in the private elevator on the way up to their penthouse suite in Seattle on a business trip.

"But I'm no wildlife expert," she exclaimed, snapping him out of his reverie. "How would I know?"

She tapped the screen to stop recording, then turned to catch him staring.

For a moment, the past and present blurred. Maybe it was because he wished he still had the right to wrap her in his arms and taste her. Tempt her into forgetting everything else but how good he could make her feel.

Her breath caught before she spoke.

"Whatever you're thinking," she said with a husky note in her voice until she cleared her throat and started again, "is a mistake."

The determination in her tone helped redirect his brain. Straightening in his seat, he nodded.

"Should we get out and walk around? Stretch our legs?" he offered, not sure there was enough fresh air in the Bitterroot Range to help him keep his thoughts off Elena's lips.

But he'd damned well try.

He'd shouldered the burden of being the point man at Mesa Falls to give Weston a break from a job he'd done so well for years. He couldn't spill all of the owners' secrets to the first reporter who showed up. Even if this particular reporter was causing heat to creep up his spine and flare along his shoulders.

"Sure." She unlatched the simple door that was more like a roll bar, and stepped outside before he could offer her his hand. "It will help me break in the new boots."

Fixing his attention on her legs was almost as dangerous as thinking about the past they'd shared. Both fueled flames he wasn't sure how to tamp down. Cursing himself for the lack of focus, he emerged from the vehicle and met her behind it, pointing to a trail that led down to the creek.

"Let's go this way." He wrenched off his jacket and tossed it in the cargo bed along with his Stetson. "It's warming up," he noted, tugging his long sleeves higher.

Elena's gaze dropped to his forearms, and he remembered her fascination with his tattoos. Seeing the way her dark eyes wandered over him, he vowed to send a generous bonus to the guy back home in New Zealand who'd done the distinctive work.

Because yeah, it was a blissful relief to know he wasn't the only one battling an attraction.

"Can I ask you something?" When she looked into his eyes, her expression was thoughtful. Curious.

"As long as it's not about Alonzo—"

She was already shaking her head. "We never spoke after the day I flew home alone from New Zealand. But I've always wondered about something."

He tensed, guessing he wouldn't like whatever came next. So much for thinking she might be feeling the old attraction, too. "That was the second-worst day of my life," he admitted, already raw from battling the draw of this woman. "I don't remember it that well."

But she kept going, her chin tilting up as she met his

gaze. "When your father told you to break things off with me because my family would be an embarrassment to the Strikers, did you even consider asking me about it first?"

Five

Elena's defensiveness was ratcheting up in equal measure to her attraction.

The sight of those tattoos crawling up Gage's forearms had given her vivid memories of times his arms had been pinned to the bed on either side of her, muscles flexing while he moved over her. She'd been moments away from swooning on the spot. So she'd reached for the verbal sword and shield to hang on to the old sense of betrayal. She wasn't proud of herself for the predictable antics, but she was too susceptible to Gage's brand of sex appeal.

"My father confronted you before he shared his findings with me," Gage reminded her quietly, peering out over the herd of sheep still emerging from the pine grove before he brushed past her to keep walking. "I had zero time to process anything he said about you before he finished with his coup de grâce—that you'd already accepted his bribe to remove yourself from my life."

She wanted to believe that she heard a hint of regret in his voice. Over losing her? Or over the fact that she'd hidden her past for the entire duration of their relationship?

Probably the latter, she thought as she hurried to keep up with him. She might not have accepted the payoff, but she was hardly blameless in the breakup. She'd started packing her things before she'd even talked to Gage. It was interesting to realize she'd been that defensive even then—already protecting herself from getting dumped by being the one to walk away first.

"I was furious with him," she admitted, pulling out her phone to snap some more photos of the sharp cliffs jutting up from the creek bed. She appreciated having something to do with her nervous energy during an awkward conversation. "I felt embarrassed, too, that I'd been waiting for the perfect moment to tell you about my family and in doing that, I'd lost the chance to share that story in a less damning light."

She switched over to video mode and filmed another minute of the sheep making their way down to the creek bed, hoping she could find a way to make the nature footage fun for her followers. She was losing her edge in a competitive digital marketplace. One more thing her divorce had cost her since she could no longer afford to attend the kinds of parties and events that people loved to see in her feed.

"Your father was on the run from the law. Is there a way to put a good face on that?" Gage moved farther down the hill leading to the creek, his long strides making it easy for him to cover a lot of ground.

At least the cheerful chirp of birds all around them helped her to detach from the frustration that normally came from discussing her father.

"Of course not. He's a thief, and he should have turned himself in long ago." She hadn't seen her dad since she'd left home at seventeen bound for LA, but she'd always imagined him living in Mexico now, freed from the burden of raising a daughter. "At the time, he convinced me that he couldn't possibly do that—turn himself in—because my mother had left us, and there would be no one to look after me if he went to prison."

"Or so he said." Gage kept trekking down the slope, winding around boulders and trees. As Elena followed, the sound of rushing water grew louder. "But was your welfare really his top priority if he's still running from justice over a decade later?"

"Of course not. But when I was fifteen and still living at home, I will confess I was rooting for him to elude the cops every time we had a close call. If he'd gone to jail, I would have been in the foster system."

"But instead of telling me that, you decided to take the cash my father offered you." He shook his head, obviously still thinking the worst of her.

And didn't that remind her exactly why she'd chosen to leave him in the first place?

"You made it clear what you thought about me," she retorted, anger coursing through her. "There was no way we could have stayed together after that."

Her boot heel skidded on dead leaves, and she stuck a hand out to grab Gage's shoulder.

With lightning-fast reflexes, he reached back to steady her, his hands bracketing her waist. Her heart pounded from his touch. His sudden nearness. All that delectable maleness reminding her that she'd deliberately married someone who didn't make her insides melt, hoping she'd be safe from the rush of strong emotions that made her feel unstable. Unpredictable.

"Are you okay?" He stood too close, fixing her with his gaze, his strong hands lingering on her.

She remained very still, not sure if she was more worried that he wouldn't let go of her—or that he would. Because he was in front of her on the downward incline, his eyes were almost level with hers. He was close enough she could see the fine scar above one eyebrow that she knew was from a hiking accident long ago. She'd kissed that place before, and demanded to know the story.

Too many memories.

"Fine." She forced the words past her lips, her throat dry as she tried to hold on to the anger she'd been feeling just a moment before. "I just wasn't looking where I was going."

His fingers fell away from her, but he didn't step back. For a moment, he seemed to take her measure.

"We're almost there, anyway. I thought you might like to see this." He nodded to his left, where a deer path seemed to lead down a steeper ledge. "Will you take my hand for about ten more steps?"

She wondered why he bothered when he thought so little of her.

He held out an upturned palm, letting her choose. It made her think of how prickly she'd become since their breakup. Not just with him, but probably even with Tomas. She hadn't always been that way—ready to lash out at any moment.

As much as she wanted to protect herself from hurt, she refused to be the kind of person who assumed the worst about everyone. Wordlessly, she laid her palm on his and wrapped her fingers around the back of his hand.

He tightened his grip, leading her down the short embankment to a place where the copse of pine trees opened up, revealing a new view of the creek. Water sluiced down a rocky incline so fast a mist rose above the falls. Glossy dark boulders jutted from either side. The sound of the surge filled the clearing.

"It's so pretty." She still held his hand, remembering the last time they'd stood on an embankment overlooking crashing water. "Montana's answer to Big Sur."

His gaze flicked away from the view and over to her, the shared memory hanging between them. They'd been so incandescently happy that trip up the Pacific Coast Highway, drunk on new love and letting it carry them away. How naive she'd been to think that could last.

She would bet his thoughts were veering down that same dark path, because his expression clouded. He gave a clipped nod of acknowledgment before he turned around to retrace their steps.

"I have a meeting with the other owners this afternoon," he said as he started up the steep path, tugging her with him. "We should get back."

Retracing her steps up the cliff path beside him, Elena told herself to count it as a victory that she'd weathered the afternoon without letting the old heat between them burn her. But seeing how much the memories affected him, too, didn't feel like a win. Hollowness yawned inside her. She wanted answers to the Alonzo mystery soon so she could leave Montana—and Gage— behind her for good.

Gage half expected Elena to follow him into the private library outside his home office, where he was holding the owners' meeting. She'd made no secret of being in town only for her story.

But she was nowhere in sight as he keyed in the code for the door, a security necessity given his work in investment banking and his access to extremely sensitive financial information. Could Elena be rethinking her decision to stay here with him? Their walk back from the waterfall had been silent and awkward, as though their shared past was riding shotgun in the utility vehicle with them on the way home.

She'd made it clear she wouldn't revisit that time any more than he wanted to. Yet no matter how much they pummeled back the past, it seemed determined to weigh into every conversation. Her casual mention of that day at Big Sur shouldn't have the power to set fire to his nerve endings, but he'd still ended up standing under a freezing-cold shower stream as soon as they'd returned from the tour.

"Wait up, Gage. Right behind you," a familiar male voice called to him before he could pull the door shut.

Peering back, he saw Desmond Pierce charging down the hall toward him, his tie a little askew, but other than that still looking like Mr. Hollywood with his crisp white dress shirt and no hair out of place. His aviator shades glinted under the hallway lights.

"Hiding a hangover under the shades?" Gage asked as he held the door.

"Hardly," Desmond answered drily, pulling off the sunglasses and tucking them into his breast pocket. "Night in and night out, I get to see the way my guests let alcohol make their decisions on the casino floor. I'm probably the soberest guy you know." He paused in the threshold to keep the door open. "Miles is right behind me. He's talking to your security guard in the foyer. Smart move keeping the bodyguards here through the weekend with all the celebrity guests coming and going."

Desmond owned and operated a handful of casino resorts, spending most of his time at his first operation on Lake Tahoe, close to where two other Mesa Falls Ranch owners lived—Jonah Norlander and Alec Jacobsen—both of whom were MIA this weekend.

"What about Weston?" Gage pressed the button to partially open the blinds.

"He texted Miles on our way over here." Desmond took care of switching on the gas fireplace. "Wes climbed Trapper Peak this morning to follow April Stephens, and things must have gone well because now they're in a cabin together somewhere on the mountain."

Gage swore at the same time Miles, Weston's older brother, came into view at the end of the corridor. Phone in hand, Miles jabbed at the screen while he walked.

"Wes can't make it," Miles announced, a hint of disdain in his voice. "He's in love."

"You make it sound like a communicable disease."

Gage waved him into the room and allowed the door to shut behind them before he rearmed the lock.

"The end result is the same," Miles muttered, jamming his phone back into his jacket pocket. "Wes is quarantined for the day and can't be with us."

Miles ran the Rivera Ranch on the California side of the Sierra Nevada Mountains, a huge spread that had once been a point of contention between the brothers. Because Weston and his father had been at loggerheads since Wes was a kid, Miles had been given responsibility for the whole thing. While that sucked for Wes, Gage always figured it hurt Miles more to bear that family responsibility alone when he could have had help. Gage knew how it felt to carry the weight of expectation that came with being an heir. He'd never wanted it.

"That's not a bad thing," Desmond pointed out, already seated in one of four leather barrel chairs positioned around a cushioned ottoman. "We could use an in with April Stephens considering she was hired to track Alonzo's money."

Miles stopped by the wet bar and helped himself to a glass of Gage's bourbon before taking the chair across from Desmond. "If Weston has learned her secrets, though, he hasn't shared them with me."

"She reports to Devon Salazar," Gage reminded them, retrieving the bourbon decanter along with a couple of glasses and a tray. He set all of it down on the ottoman in the middle of the chairs. "We don't have to ask Weston to betray her confidence when we can go straight to Alonzo's son. We might not trust Devon, but he owes us the truth since he kicked off this whole investigation by turning to us for answers."

"So we wait?" Desmond asked, not hiding his discontent with the plan. "That doesn't seem like a wise course of action when we have a tabloid reporter on-site actively trying to shake loose whatever she can about Alonzo."

The other men both looked expectantly at Gage.

He took his time pouring his drink before settling into his chair, the scents of leather, oak and old books providing none of the usual comfort.

"I'm taking care of that," he assured them before he took a sip. "I spent all afternoon with her, keeping her distracted."

He'd distracted himself quite a bit along the way, too, his thoughts alternating between highlights from their past and how much he still wanted her. Recalling the bribe she'd accepted from his father had reminded him he couldn't act on it.

"Why not entice her to write something else?" Miles suggested, scowling into the flames of the gas fireplace. "A tabloid reporter must have more lucrative options for stories than Alonzo. There are enough celebrities still on-site—"

Desmond snapped his fingers.

"Introduce her to Chiara Campagna," he suggested, sitting up straighter in his chair. "Give the tabloid reporter a behind-the-scenes opportunity with one of the world's most sought-after personalities."

Miles scoffed. "Chiara Campagna is famous for nothing."

"There's just one problem. I don't know Chiara," Gage reminded them, wondering if there was a chance Elena would consider it if he offered her access.

"She was here last night for a reason." Desmond pulled out his phone. "She's good friends with Jonah's wife, Astrid."

Jonah had married his college sweetheart, a Finnish supermodel, and the couple had bought a place on Lake Tahoe near Desmond's casino resort. Jonah was the only one of the ranch's owners to tie the knot so far, maintaining a reasonably normal life in spite of the tragedy that had marked their boarding school days. When their mutual friend Zach Eldridge had cliff-jumped to his death during a horseback riding trip, their lives had changed forever. Thanks to Gage's powerful father, the story had been kept out of the papers so it wouldn't reflect negatively on Zach's surviving classmates, but it haunted them anyway. Gage had been particularly troubled; thanks to his father's interference, Zach had never been properly mourned by the school. Gage's father didn't want the good Striker name associated with a death some viewed as a suicide.

Alonzo Salazar had been their class adviser at the time and had helped them weather the aftermath. For Gage, that had meant Alonzo convincing him to stay in school when he'd been determined to quit to spite his dad.

"How does that help us?" Miles asked while Desmond kept typing away.

"Jonah told me Chiara plans to spend a few days with Astrid after leaving Mesa Falls. Gage can take the reporter to Jonah's place in Tahoe for a couple of days so Astrid can introduce her to Chiara. It's win-win. This will get the reporter off ranch property and hand her a story that will net her a bigger payout. With any luck,

she'll go back to LA afterward and forget all about us."
Desmond spelled out his plan without ever glancing up
from his phone. He obviously wasn't concerned that the
last thing Gage needed was to spend more time in close
proximity to his ex.

"I need to be here," he insisted, figuring that was
an argument his friends could appreciate. "We decided
I'm the new point man on-site now that Weston's distracted. I can't just take off the day after I dig into the
new role."

"Managing a persistent reporter is more important
than being at Mesa Falls," Miles countered, draining
his drink and setting the glass on the tray. "I can stay
until you get back."

Desmond swung to look at Miles at the same time
Gage did, mirroring his surprise.

"What about Rivera Ranch?" Gage asked, knowing
he wasn't getting out of this assignment if Miles was
ready to abandon his own spread for the sake of managing Mesa Falls for a few days.

"I hire good people so I don't have to be there every
second." He shot to his feet, looking uncomfortable
with the topic and ready to change it. "Are we sure Astrid will share her pseudocelebrity friend long enough
to give Elena an interview?"

Gage hid an amused smile at Miles's obvious distaste for the new breed of fame. He hadn't been a be-
liever either, until Elena had personally demonstrated
the power of social media influence. He understood the
sway people like her—and, on a bigger scale, Chiara
Campagna—could have in the court of public opinion.

Desmond held up his phone. "Astrid already said it's

no problem. Chiara is going to visit their new baby, so Gage, you can meet her, too."

"There's a baby." Gage hadn't meant to say it out loud, but he'd forgotten all about the fact that Jonah was a new father. "Has anyone else seen it?"

"*It* is a her," Desmond clarified. "Her name is Katja, and Jonah is over the moon about her. You should have gone to see them already."

"What have you got against babies?" Miles asked, looking slightly more cheerful now that Gage was in the hot seat.

"Nothing." He rose to his feet and finished his bourbon. "It's just one more thing Zach will never have. And I know we try not to talk about him or about how much what happened sucks, but there's something about these life milestones that brings it back, you know?"

Neither of them answered because of course they knew. The ticking of the grandfather clock seemed to increase in volume, filling the room.

When the silence stretched out, Gage set his glass on the fireplace mantel. "It's a good plan to distract Elena," he said finally, hoping he could convince her. "I'll touch base with Astrid before we go, but as soon as she confirms Chiara will grant an interview, I'll call for a pilot."

Desmond nodded. "You're welcome to stay at the casino if you'd rather not stay at Jonah's. I'll make sure there's a suite available."

"Thank you." Gage suspected he'd need that kind of distance. For him, Jonah's happiness as a father would be a vivid reminder of the life and opportunities Zach would never have. "I appreciate that."

Of course, staying in a suite with Elena would present problems of another kind. But he'd gladly face the fireworks he felt whenever she was around rather than think about all the ways he'd failed his old friend.

Chiara Campagna sat in her makeup chair, getting ready for tonight's appearance at a Hollywood premiere and reflecting on her upcoming trip. She'd just returned from Montana and now looked forward to the time in Lake Tahoe to see her friend Astrid. Chiara could count on one hand the people who had elevated her social media status to the precarious heights it had reached two years ago, and former supermodel Astrid Norlander was one of them.

Chiara scrolled through her social media feeds while her makeup artist added jewels along her temple to match her sequined dress. She was looking for mentions of Elena Rollins, the woman Astrid had texted her about, asking Chiara if she'd meet her. Chiara recognized the woman's face; if she remembered correctly, she was a beauty influencer who'd let her profile go quiet during a brief marriage to a well-known cooking show host. A mistake Chiara didn't plan to make; she would never give up her job for the sake of supporting someone else's. She'd come a long way from her hopes of a career as a mixed-media artist, leaving behind her dream of large-scale collage installations and working with found objects to create beauty. But at least she had discovered another way to use her creative skills, honing an online presence.

"Can you tilt your chin up?" the makeup artist asked,

changing his brush for a wedge-shaped sponge. "I'm going to highlight the cheekbones a little more."

Chiara tapped off her phone screen and obediently moved her head right and left. She was already planning her time in Tahoe. She would bill it as a girls' retreat weekend and maybe invite a couple of others to fill out the photos she would post. She'd bring lots of outdoor gear and do some things outside. Work-wise, she'd be fine.

But Astrid had mentioned that Gage Striker would be there with Elena, putting two of the Mesa Falls Ranch owners in her path again. And while Chiara adored Astrid, she had a long-standing grievance with the men of Mesa Falls. They'd all been friends with Zach Eldridge, a boy she'd loved and lost when she was fifteen and he was sixteen. She thought she might be one of the few people in the world who knew that Zach had been on a horseback riding trip with those friends when he died. Gage Striker's powerful father had taken pains to cover up his son's connection to the death but Chiara had still managed to find out the truth.

Chiara would never forget how she'd snuck onto the Dowdon campus to find out what had really happened to Zach, a friend who'd loved art as passionately as she did. She'd confronted Gage and Miles separately, asking them for the truth, and they'd both given her canned responses that sounded rehearsed. She'd cried. Begged. Completely embarrassed herself for love of Zach, desperate to understand what had really gone wrong that terrible week.

She knew Zach had been upset about something. He

hadn't been himself at the last school art show, a coed event between her all-girls institution and Dowdon.

Yet when she'd seen Zach's friends at Gage's house, neither of them appeared to recognize her as Kara Marsh, the girl she'd been before she adopted her social media persona. Perhaps that was just as well, as it meant they wouldn't be on their guard around her. Because with Alonzo Salazar in the news since Christmastime, and his connection to his former students becoming a point of public interest, Chiara sensed that answers about what really happened to Zach were finally simmering close to the surface. She owed it to her friend to make sure his story was told at last, no matter whom it might hurt.

Six

Elena needed a reprieve from all the feelings stirred up by being with Gage. But when she sat down to her laptop to work the evening after they'd toured the ranch together, her inbox exploded with bad news.

Emails from the bank, emails from creditors, emails from her work popped up one after another. As she scrolled through them all at the massive desk in her sitting room, she realized that her financial situation had turned dire. The woman who was subletting her apartment had given Elena a bad check, and that had made one of Elena's checks for her utilities bounce, too. The news seemed no better on the work front with two tabloid outlets both asking her when she'd have a story on Alonzo. She felt confident that her angle could warrant a bidding war for the piece, but since she had zero to offer them yet, she had no hope for seeing her next paycheck anytime soon.

Worse, her subscriber and follower numbers had taken another downturn, meaning her social media channels were going to be less attractive outlets for advertisers. And while she didn't object to returning to the business world and the kind of job she used to have with one of Gage's companies, she also knew that her value as an employee had gone down, too. What good was a social media expert without the following to back her up?

Staring into the flames blazing inside the sleek stone fireplace, Elena's head throbbed with the new layers of stress. It all served to remind her she should have been more aggressive in her divorce. Taking the high road had not only left her with less access to the marital assets, but being parted from her physical things also robbed her of a surface level of comfort.

A soft rap on the door startled her from the regrets that tormented her and served no purpose.

"Yes?" She swiped a hand across her eyes and blinked. She needed to pull herself together. She couldn't change the past...with her ex or with Gage.

"It's Gage." His deep voice slid straight past her defenses, conjuring up old confidences and quiet conversations. "Can I talk to you for a minute?"

Closing her laptop, she exhaled hard before shoving to her feet.

"Sure," she called, hoping to keep her tone light. Breezy. Like her world wasn't collapsing in on itself. "Come on in."

The door opened and Gage stepped inside, pulling

all her focus to his broad shoulders in a steel-gray dress shirt. The fabric skimmed taut muscles, tapering down to the hem, which was untucked from his black trousers. With the sleeves rolled to the middle of his forearms, dark webs of tattoos were left exposed. It took her a moment to drag her gaze from them up to his face. His brown eyes roamed over her; he was studying her as thoroughly as she'd studied him.

Awareness flared to life again, the response more immediate each time she saw him. She stood in front of the big desk, keeping several feet between her and Gage. She wore a long cashmere cardigan over a pink silk T-shirt and matching lounge pants, but she wouldn't have minded a few more layers when her body responded so thoroughly to this man.

"I'm sorry to disturb you." His attention lingered on her face as he moved deeper into the room. "Is everything all right?"

"Absolutely," she lied, unwilling to show vulnerability, especially to this man. "Just going over some of my research on Alonzo."

She played the card most certain to get him to back off.

"In that case, I won't keep you for long." He paused near the fireplace, folded his arms and tilted a shoulder against the dark stone wall. "But I thought I'd mention a potential professional opportunity for you."

Frowning, she couldn't guess what that meant.

"I'm sure you're not here to offer me a job." She pivoted to face him, but stayed by the desk, knowing it was wisest not to stand too close to him when he looked good enough to taste and she was feeling adrift.

"No." His smile seemed more wary than amused. "But I have business to take care of with Jonah Norlander, one of the other ranch owners who is married to—"

"The whole planet knows he married Astrid Koskinen, the former supermodel." Elena's curiosity spiked, and she was grateful for the distraction from the sex appeal of the hot investment banker standing in front of her. "They just had their first child together."

"Correct." Gage nodded. "And apparently Astrid has a close friendship with Chiara Campagna."

"She does." Elena had been studying the new landscape of beauty and fashion influencers in her quest to recharge her social media presence, and was fully aware of the currency Chiara commanded right now. "I would have tried to speak to her last night, but she had left the party by the time you and I finished our talk. She's already back in LA, and I saw on her feed she's attending a Hollywood premiere tonight."

Gage's dark eyebrows lifted, and he straightened from where he'd been leaning against the fireplace. "In that case, maybe you'll be interested in what I have to offer. Chiara is going to be in Tahoe visiting with Astrid this week at the same time I'll be working with Jonah. If you go as my guest, you'd have an opportunity to interview Chiara."

His offer stunned her, and quite frankly, couldn't have come at a better time. But the thrill of what that could mean for her was quickly tempered by suspicion.

"How do you know she'd let me interview her?"

Gage shrugged, the gray cotton of his shirt hugging tighter along one shoulder. "You're a convincing woman, and you'll be meeting Chiara in the home of a friend she trusts. Why wouldn't she give you an interview?"

"Her time is worth a fortune, that's why. She won't just give it away to someone like me, unless…" Her suspicion grew stronger as she recalled how little Gage followed fashion and beauty. It didn't add up that he would tout this meeting as a professional opportunity for her unless he had a very specific reason. "She's doing a personal favor for the Mesa Falls Ranch owners."

He wandered closer to the desk, one hand shoved in his pocket. "Far more likely she'll be there to see Astrid's new baby, but make of it what you will." He skimmed a palm along the glass-topped desk before lifting his gaze to hers. "You told me you're following the Alonzo Salazar story for the paycheck, so I thought maybe the chance to speak with Chiara in that kind of setting would be enticing."

Chiara Campagna was social media gold right now. If Elena could capitalize on that, she would still have a piece that tabloids would vie for, and the payout would probably be even higher than the story she'd wanted about Alonzo.

"What's the catch?" she pressed, certain this opportunity hadn't landed in her lap by coincidence.

A scowl furrowed his brow. "I guess the catch is that you'd have to report on someone who is in the public eye by choice, unlike Alonzo, who never pursued fame and avoided it by writing a work of fiction under an assumed name." He gestured toward her closed laptop on the desk. "But if you'd rather keep searching for dirt about my former mentor, be my guest."

He shifted on his feet as if he was going to leave.

"Wait." Her hand darted out to rest on his forearm before she'd had a chance to think about the wisdom of touching him.

He stilled under her touch, and her heartbeat quickened at his sudden nearness.

For one breathless moment, their eyes met, and there was a world of possibility between them. She resisted an insane urge to stroke her fingers along his skin, forcing herself to let go.

"It's an offer I can't refuse," she admitted, needing this chance he'd given her not only to pay her rent, but to end the hardscrabble months she'd struggled through ever since her divorce. "If you're willing to take me to Tahoe with you, I'd be grateful for the introduction to Chiara."

She hadn't realized until that moment how tense he'd been, but now she could see the lines of his shoulders relax as he nodded.

"Good." He checked his watch, his forearm flexing under the charcoal-colored leather strap. "You'll have time to pack in the morning. I hope to leave by noon tomorrow."

"I'll be ready," she assured him, relaxing a fraction now that they were in agreement about something. "How long will we be in Tahoe?"

"Three days should be sufficient for me." He was close now, near enough for her to catch the scent of his aftershave. "Will that give you enough time?"

She breathed deeply, letting the hint of cedarwood tantalize her senses. She wanted to tell herself that she felt drawn to him only because they'd shared a sensual connection and a romantic history, but she knew there was more at work between them than that. It didn't help that she'd been feeling vulnerable tonight, and Gage had appeared at her door with a chance for her to reclaim some financial independence.

The gift may have been dropped into her lap in an effort to distract her from pursuing the mystery of Alonzo Salazar, but it was still a gift. And she was grateful.

"Three days is fine," she answered, suspecting the hardest part about the trip would be avoiding the draw of the man beside her.

"Excellent." He gave a clipped nod. "I'll let the pilot know there will be two of us for the flight. We'll head over to the airstrip at noon."

"Thank you." She hugged her arms around herself, mostly to ensure she didn't do something unwise like reach out and touch him again. The memory of his skin under her fingertips burned in her brain. "I appreciate the invitation, Gage."

His name sounded intimate on her lips. Maybe because it was late, and they were alone. Maybe because a bed waited in the next room.

His attention dipped to her lips for an instant and her mouth went dry. It seemed like forever since they'd kissed, and yet she remembered with perfect clarity how he'd savored her lips with infinite tenderness. Devoured her with all the hunger and urgency of taut, fiery need.

But before the moment could spin out of control, he took a step back.

"It's no problem." He shoved his hands in his pants pockets. "I'd better let you get some sleep."

"Good night." She pushed the words past her chalk-dry throat, her body mourning the loss of his nearness even as her brain applauded the boundaries.

He was already stalking toward the door, his footsteps sure and quick. Running from the same seductive thoughts plaguing her? She couldn't be sure, but she knew that three days in Tahoe together were certain to push the issue.

But perhaps between his business, her interview with Chiara and visiting his friends with a new baby, they would be too busy to indulge in the desire that smoldered between them. She'd just have to make sure they were alone together as little as possible. Because she already knew that underneath all that red-hot attraction, there wasn't enough trust to hold them together.

Gage had done his level best to distract himself with business obligations during the two-hour flight to Tahoe. After how close he'd come to kissing Elena the night before—an impulse he felt every time he was around her—he'd been determined to lose himself in work for the course of the trip.

Things had started off well enough, with each of them taking seats on opposite sides of the aircraft. Wearing a tailored jacket and matching skirt in deep emerald, with her mass of dark hair piled on her head, she looked every inch the businesswoman he remembered. He'd assumed she'd been working for the past hour.

But something in her tone distracted him as she spoke to a friend on a video call. She sounded upset.

Glancing up from his tablet, he saw her seated at the built-in workstation in the front of the plane, her laptop open while she engaged in an animated dialogue with a woman he didn't recognize. Up until now, Elena had kept her head down and her eyes on her work, seemingly as committed to ignoring the sparks jumping between them as he was.

Yet how could he pretend not to hear her when her stream of agitated whispers indicated she was obviously distressed?

She peered back over her shoulder, catching him staring. Any guilt he might have experienced at not giving her more privacy was immediately negated by the sight of her red-rimmed eyes.

He unfastened his seat belt but by the time he made it to her, she was already stabbing the button to disconnect the call, her screen going black.

"Is everything all right?" He wanted to touch her, to offer what comfort he could, but he also didn't want to overstep those prickly defenses of hers. "Can I get you anything?"

"No. Thank you." She blinked fast, tugging tissues from a slim, sapphire-colored bag. "I'm fine."

"Elena." He lowered himself to kneel in front of her, needing to see her face. "You're obviously not fine. What's wrong?"

She squeezed the bridge of her nose for a moment, then patted her eyes with the tissue, seeming to pull her emotions back under control. "That was a friend of mine from LA." She stuffed the tissue back in her bag. "She'd offered to help me retrieve a few things from the home I once shared with Tomas, but apparently his new fiancée refused to allow her inside to collect them." Elena looked like she'd been about to say more on the subject, but stopped herself. "It's nothing that plenty of other people haven't been through when they split up. I don't know why I let it get to me."

"These items are legally yours?" he asked, recalling she'd been separated for a year. At her nod, he asked, "Wasn't that all spelled out in the paperwork?"

Sighing, she seemed to surrender to the topic she clearly hadn't wished to discuss.

"Yes, but I kept waiting for a good time to return to the house, trying to avoid his fiancée."

"I remember hearing he proposed to his assistant on his cooking show," Gage said drily, hating the guy on Elena's behalf. "Sounded like a ratings ploy to me. But you have a legal right to your possessions, Elena. There's no need to be diplomatic with people who are denying your rights."

The aircraft hit a pocket of turbulence, forcing Gage to grip the arms of her chair to steady himself.

"I realize that. I just really didn't want to play out that whole drama of confronting the woman who wormed her way into my life, pretending to be my friend right up until the weekend she slept with my husband." She gasped as they bounced through another air pocket, her fingers covering his briefly where they rested on the arms of her chair. Her gaze flicked to his before she took hold of her seat cushion instead. "It's so trite. So not what I imagined for myself. And I kept thinking Tomas would man up and send me my things, but now I think he's just dragging his feet in the hope I'll forget about it. His new fiancée is spiteful and—sadly—my size."

She shook her head, obviously frustrated, a dark curl sliding loose from her topknot. The strand caught her eyelashes, and Gage couldn't suppress the urge to peel it gently away from her eyes. Her glossy hair gleamed under the soft cabin lights, the strands smooth against his finger as he let them coil back into place alongside her ear.

"So your friend was denied entrance to your former marital home to retrieve your possessions?" He wanted to be sure he had his facts straight, already seeing a way to be of assistance.

Because it bugged the hell out of him to think Elena had been going without personal effects for months in an effort to be reasonable. He'd understood her financial position had taken a hit in the split from her ex, but given her drive and resourcefulness, he'd assumed she would bounce back. It hadn't made sense to him that she'd arrived in Montana with little luggage and few clothes when she had once been a successful lifestyle blogger. When they'd been together, her closets were full; she'd never lacked for fashion samples from all the big designers.

Now? She hadn't even brought boots to the mountains for the weekend. Whether she admitted it or not, Gage suspected she was struggling.

"Yes." Elena confirmed his understanding of what had happened, sounding more resolved and less upset now that she'd had a few minutes to settle down. "Which only confirms for me that it's long past time to go over to the house and deal with the situation personally. No more deceiving myself things will work out for the best."

Gage studied her, curious about this side of Elena that he hadn't seen when they'd been dating. She'd always been so sure of herself. So fiercely committed to whatever path she chose.

He realized he'd probably been watching her for too long, his body too close to hers. His hands were still braced on the armrests of her seat. The scent of the perfume she favored—something tinged with lavender—teased his nose. And damn, but this was not the time to touch her.

"Do you need anything in the meantime?" he asked, wanting to help ease the burden of her months of frustration. To say nothing of the heartache that must have come before it. "Is there anything I can do to make things easier for you until you return to Los Angeles?"

"No. Thank you." She made a point of peering out the window off to one side, as if she wasn't ready to accept any favors from him. "I really appreciate you bringing me with you today. That's plenty."

She might not be looking at him, but he could sense her awareness of him in the way she gripped the seat cushion more tightly.

He would let it go for now.

Easing away from her, he took the seat closest to Elena as the pilot descended toward the northwestern edge of Lake Tahoe. Gage would contact a friend in security to ensure Elena's things were retrieved at a time when her ex-husband was present. For that matter, Gage had seen the name of the friend who'd attempted to help her today on Elena's tablet before she ended the call. He could solicit input from her to be certain they collected what belonged to Elena—quickly, legally and without having Elena inconvenienced another minute.

He liked the idea of doing this small thing for her,

even if he hadn't forgiven the way she'd allowed his father to buy her off. There was blame to go around for their unhappy split, and Gage had never felt right about bringing Elena to New Zealand in the first place when he'd known the way his father liked meddling in his life. How might things have been different between Elena and Gage if she'd come around to telling him about her past on her own, instead of having the details thrust into the spotlight by his father?

There was no way to know, of course. Elena had to live with the consequences of her actions in their breakup. But with this one simple act, helping Elena out, Gage could rest easier knowing he'd tried to atone for his role in the split.

Too bad it wouldn't come close to fulfilling his need to kiss her. Touch her. Make her forget that bastard of an ex-husband of hers had ever existed.

Seven

Three hours later, Elena sat ensconced in comfort inside Jonah and Astrid Norlander's mountainside mansion overlooking Lake Tahoe, the hospitality of her hosts almost making her forget what a frustrating day it had been up until then.

"Would you like to sit outside while we wait for Chiara?" Astrid asked her, pointing through the wall of windows toward the huge deck with deep couches built around a fireplace table that was already lit. A long, lithe Finnish beauty, the former supermodel had ethereal blue eyes and platinum shoulder-length hair. She wore not one smidge of makeup that Elena could see, and she was still so striking that it was difficult not to stare. "There are patio heaters and blankets, but with the sun on us, I think we'll be warm enough without them."

Even the woman's accent was gorgeous. She went to the kitchen and added a couple of orange slices to her seltzer water, then padded to the back door and slid into a pair of fur-lined clogs.

"Sure, I'd love to join you outside." Elena rose and picked up her white wine spritzer from the table. It was a light drink, the type she didn't mind sipping to be social. "The guys look fairly absorbed in their game."

Jonah and Gage sat at the bar between the kitchen and great room, their eyes on a flat-screen above the fireplace, where coverage of college basketball was in full swing.

"They both went to UCLA as undergrads," Astrid reminded her, pushing the sliding glass door open. "I think Gage timed his flight to make sure he was here for the game."

Elena smiled, recalling sitting courtside a few times with Gage while they'd dated. Back then, when he was working almost all the time, she had enjoyed seeing him relax for a couple of hours. "That wouldn't surprise me in the least," she said, stepping through the oversize glass door before Astrid slid it back into place.

"Your suit is gorgeous, by the way," Astrid observed, stroking her fingers over the fabric of the sleeve in a friendly way. "Is the designer anyone I know?"

"It's one I made, actually." Flattered, Elena took a moment to enjoy the compliment, glancing down at the angled cuffs and buttons she'd found in salvage shops three years ago.

"Wow." Astrid's gaze zeroed in on the boning around the corset-style waist. "There are so many unique details. You're incredibly talented."

Elena searched the woman's face, wondering at first if she was just making polite conversation, but seeing genuine interest in her eyes, she explained, "When I blogged more regularly, I made some pieces that I wanted to wear and couldn't find. I did a few social media stories about the process of picking fabrics and finding a tailor for sewing samples."

The reminder of the hard work she'd done to build her blog and connect with followers made her regret slowing down when she'd married. Why had she turned her full attention to supporting Tomas in his work instead of being loyal to the people who had been loyal to her? Why hadn't she found a healthy balance between Tomas's career and her own?

"You are very talented," Astrid repeated, underscoring the words by pointing with her index finger. "Wait." She froze, turning her head toward the house. "Did you hear the baby cry?"

Astrid pulled her phone from her pocket and checked the nursery monitor feed that she'd already viewed a handful of times since Elena and Gage arrived. Katja had been sleeping the entire time.

"Is she okay?" Elena asked as she moved to the sleek steel-and-wood railing surrounding the deck. The springtime air was cool, and there was still snow on the mountaintops, but the sun felt warm on her face and the breeze was scented with green and growing things.

"She's fine." Astrid laid the phone on the marble tabletop surrounding the row of flames that shot up in the center. "But I just buzzed Chiara in at the front gate. Do you mind if I go greet her and then I'll come right back? I can't wait to introduce the two of you."

"Of course." Elena walked the dark wood planks of the raised deck as Astrid disappeared inside the house.

Elena's gaze lingered on the wall of windows, and she caught sight of Gage for a moment. He met her gaze, and perhaps because he noticed she was alone, he stepped outside a second later. He'd worn a black suit over a gray-and-white-striped T-shirt for their visit. The cotton shirt stretched smoothly across his chest in a way that called to her fingers to touch. Beyond the obvious attraction, there was also a new level of appreciation for how he'd treated her today. She'd felt so defeated when she struck out with her latest attempt to retrieve her possessions from her former home. Her friend Zoe had been upset by the hostility she'd experienced from the moment Tomas's new fiancée opened the front door. And worst of all, Elena had been so frustrated herself that she'd nearly broken down in tears in front of Gage.

Thankfully, he'd been extremely kind about it, listening to her concerns, not judging, and allowing her to move past the anger to focus on their trip.

"How are you doing?" he asked, concern in his dark eyes as he closed the distance between them. "Can I get you something else to drink besides the wine?"

She appreciated his thoughtfulness since he knew she imbibed very little—the bourbon that first night at his house being a notable exception. But there had been extenuating circumstances.

"It's mostly club soda. But thank you." She felt at a loss for how to navigate her new relationship with him. Between his kindness on the flight to Tahoe and the way he'd set up an interview with a woman who could single-handedly reignite Elena's lapsed social media presence, she could no longer pretend that Gage was her enemy. "Astrid went to greet Chiara, by the way. Thank you again for setting up the meeting."

Turning to look out over the mountains, she sipped her drink, grateful for the cooling effect of the chilled wine and soda. With Gage standing so close to her, she definitely wouldn't be needing the patio heater to keep warm. His shoulder brushed hers and a thrill chased up her spine.

"Good. We'll stay long enough for you to obtain what you need, see the baby and then return to the casino residence." They'd dropped their bags at the posh four-bedroom house earlier before continuing to Jonah's in a rented Land Rover. Desmond Pierce owned the casino and was letting them stay there for free.

Gage leaned closer to speak in a tone meant just for her, even though they were alone on the patio. "You can give me the high sign when you're ready to leave."

"What's the high sign?" she pressed, hearing Astrid's voice inside the great room, and guessing her hostess was returning.

"Whatever you want." He kept his dark eyes fixed on her in a way that made her heart beat faster. "A wink, maybe." He lifted his attention to her updo. "Or you could let your hair down." His focus shifted back to her eyes. "I'd definitely notice that."

With an effort, she restrained a shiver at the thoughts those words ignited. "That would be a bad idea, as I'm sure you already know."

Behind them, she heard the sliding door open. The noise of the game on the TV and the voices from the house grew louder.

"Then I'll have to settle for a long, smoldering look," he told her softly, still speaking for her ears alone. "Once I see that, I'll have you out the door in no time."

She wanted to tell herself he was just teasing. Just trying to rile her. But his lingering attention suggested otherwise in the moment before he pivoted to greet Chiara Campagna.

Elena did the same, forcing herself to flip the switch into professional mode. Still, the breathless anticipation of their flirtation didn't fade.

Not when Gage excused himself to return to the house and give Elena space for her interview. And not when she delved into a conversation with one of her generation's most sought-after beauty and fashion icons. But no matter how often she found her thoughts straying to Gage Striker, Elena refused to consider the scenarios he'd painted in her mind as anything more than outrageous fantasies that had no place in her real life.

Seated in one of the paired leather recliners in Jonah's great room, Gage peered out the wall of windows. Chiara Campagna was lifting her phone to take a photo of herself with Elena.

He could only see Elena's face in profile, so it was difficult to read her mood. He knew he'd caught her off guard when he'd voiced his desire for her, but it wasn't as if she'd been unaware of it. They'd been sidestepping it since their first meeting at Mesa Falls, circling and taking each other's measure after all this time. By now, he'd seen enough to know he wanted her as much as ever, no matter how things had ended between them before.

He refused to pretend otherwise.

"She's still there," Jonah observed drily from his seat beside Gage, his voice even louder than the TV's impressive surround-sound audio. "You've checked out your date at least five times since we sat down."

Caught.

"She's been an unexpected complication at Mesa Falls," Gage explained, forcing his attention back to the game even as Jonah stabbed the remote to lower the television volume. "I didn't anticipate having to take a role on-site in Montana, and I sure as hell didn't expect to have to confront my ex in the process."

He'd known Jonah since they were thirteen, meeting him the same way he'd met the other owners of Mesa Falls Ranch: as suite mates at Dowdon. There'd been four of them in a room at the end of the hall, and three in the room across from them. Seven friends. Six who graduated. The six who remained now owned and operated the ranch together as a way to honor the life of the one they'd lost.

Jonah made a dismissive sound. Dressed in a weathered college T-shirt in honor of the game they watched, he didn't look much different from how he had in their school days, except his dark blond hair was cut shorter and he had some kind of verse in Finnish tattooed around both biceps. "With the way you two look at each other, she won't be an ex for long."

"Old flames die hard. Or so the saying goes." Gage retrieved his craft beer from the table between their chairs and tipped the bottle to his lips, wishing he could quench his thirst for Elena as simply.

Jonah sat forward in his recliner so his leather loafers were back on the floor. "You're not concerned about

starting a relationship with someone who's actively trying to put Alonzo's name back in the public eye?"

"Who said anything about a relationship?" Gage re-
sented the question. It was as if he was betraying the
memory of a guy who'd helped them through the aftermath of a hellish trauma. "I've got no choice but to keep
an eye on the situation. I need to stick close to her, and
I can't pretend the attraction doesn't exist."

"Call it what you will," Jonah conceded. "But Elena
Rollins means trouble for the ranch. You know that as
well as I do."

"That's why we're redirecting her with the Chiara
interview today," Gage reminded him, refusing to feel
guilty about distracting her with this trip since the re-
sulting story would further her prospects far more than
anything she might learn about Alonzo Salazar. It ben-
efited them both. "I'm taking what precautions I can,
but I can't prevent her from finding out the truth about
Alonzo if she's determined to dig."

"If only we knew the truth as well, maybe we could
prepare for the consequences." Jonah's final words were
drowned out by the sudden wail of an infant from somewhere deeper in the house. Unbelievably, the guy broke
into a broad grin. "Duty calls. Excuse me."

Gage watched as he wound through the house to
the main staircase and took the polished steps two at a
time, his hand running along the mahogany banister. A
moment later, Astrid appeared in the doorway from the
outdoor patio, hurrying through the great room with a
quick wave to Gage before she followed her husband
up the stairs.

The sight of their commitment to their new child

reminded Gage of the hopes he'd once harbored for his future with Elena. There'd been a time they'd discussed their dream home, designing and decorating it over shared meals or in stolen conversations between business meetings. They'd even talked about having a family together.

They'd spoken about most everything, it seemed, except her past. Instead, she'd allowed it to blindside him, unwilling to give him any time to process it before she boarded a jet and took it right out of his life. Now, he knew better than to expect more from her. They could have a physical relationship instead. Straightforward. No strings.

His thoughts were interrupted by the sound of the patio doors opening again. Chiara and Elena entered the great room. Chiara was showing Elena a photo on her phone. He caught the end of a conversation about dyeing techniques for silk kimonos.

Elena's gaze flicked to his, the eye contact as tantalizing as any touch after their exchange on the deck earlier. He liked thinking he'd invaded her thoughts as surely as she dominated his.

"Gage, will you take a photo of us by the fireplace?" Chiara asked suddenly, passing him her phone. "I took some of us outside, but I need to be sure I have some images of Elena's suit."

"Of course." He was surprised the woman remembered him by name from the party the other night since they hadn't been formally introduced. But he was glad to see Chiara seemed as enthused about the meeting with Elena as Elena had been about interviewing her. "It's a beautiful jacket," he remarked as he adjusted the focus.

Of course he'd noticed Elena's stunning emerald-colored skirt and jacket, even though he'd been determined to focus on his work and not her during their trip here. But that plan had fallen by the wayside, and now that he'd allowed himself to consider the possibility of being with her again, he couldn't peel his eyes off her.

The double-breasted blazer was sewn with corset details, making the fabric hug her narrow waist. Even viewing her through the phone's camera, Elena set him on fire. He clicked a few shots and then passed the device back to its owner.

Chiara reached for it, then pocketed it in the long white cardigan she wore with brown suede pants and silver pumps. "But did you know that Elena designed it herself? I'm so impressed with everything from the fabric choice to the clever boning sewn into the seams."

Gage hadn't known that. New facets of this woman kept cropping up, making him wonder how well he'd ever known her.

Something he was determined to change, if only to anticipate her next move.

Before he could respond, their hosts called them from the stairs.

"Friends, we'd like to introduce you to someone." Jonah stood beside his wife, who cradled a pink blanket in her arms. The smallest hint of an infant's face was visible from Gage's vantage point.

What struck him most was how damned happy Jonah appeared. His eyes filled with paternal pride as he gazed down at his daughter in his wife's arms. Though Gage hadn't thought about marriage in six years, he could still understand the appeal as long as you were with someone you trusted implicitly. And how often did that happen in life?

The women rushed to surround Astrid, cooing over the baby and admiring everything about her. Gage moved more slowly, clapping Jonah on the back when he got to him.

"Congratulations, man. I'm so happy for you."

"Thank you." He lowered his voice for Gage's ears only. "I'm still scared out of my mind I'll screw up something. But apparently, from what I hear from other parents, that feeling doesn't go away for at least eighteen more years."

Gage's father hadn't invested that much concern in Gage's upbringing, shipping him off to the United States for school to ensure his antics—youthful attempts to capture his dad's attention—didn't taint the family reputation. Alonzo Salazar had been more like a father to Gage than the man who'd sired him.

"The fact that you worry about being a good parent says a whole hell of a lot about the job you're already doing," Gage assured him as he watched Astrid pass the pink bundle to Elena.

Something about seeing her hold the little girl, an expression of tender fascination on her face, felt like a sucker punch to Gage. A reminder of the chance for the family they'd never gotten.

Still, he couldn't have looked away if he tried. Transfixed, he was still watching her fifteen minutes later when Astrid and Jonah disappeared into the kitchen to oversee preparations for the evening meal. Chiara followed them, leaving Gage alone with Elena in the front room near the foyer.

"Would you like to hold her?" Elena asked, approaching him with Katja in her arms. "You have a lot more experience with children than I do given all those cousins who have kids."

And in a flash he was transported to that time he'd taken her to New Zealand to meet most of his relatives at a family party. It had been a huge deal for him, introducing her to everyone. His mother had insisted on holding a big reception on his father's estate, inviting half the country.

He reached to take the baby from Elena, his arm brushing her breast in a purely accidental way. Awareness of her exploded. Bending closer to speak into her ear, he said, "I hope you're contemplating giving me that high sign sooner rather than later."

Elena quickly stepped back once she'd safely passed him the infant. "You speak as if I would be green-lighting a whole lot more than an exit strategy, but I haven't given you any cause to think I'm foolish enough to get close to you again, Gage."

"Foolish or not, you can't deny there's a strong sense of unfinished business between us." He tucked the pink blanket around the little girl's foot, keeping her wrapped up tight. Her blue eyes were open, her focus vague. She smelled like baby shampoo.

And she seemed a whole lot happier for his attention than Elena, who paced in front of the windows overlooking the horseshoe-shaped driveway.

"Perhaps. But I promised your father I'd leave you alone," she reminded him, falling back on that old rift between them and using it to keep a wedge there. "I can't go back on my word."

"That didn't concern you when you snuck past my security to get into my house, so I can't imagine you're all that worried about what Nigel Striker thinks about you now." He found himself parrying her maneuvers, and forced himself to stop. "But if going back on your agreement concerns you, I'll repay the old man as a way to buy you out of the deal."

That stopped her pacing.

She stared at him from across the living room, her jaw dropping in disbelief.

"You can't be serious." She shook her head, as if trying to convince herself she'd heard correctly.

"On the contrary, I couldn't be more sincere, Elena. I've already wasted too much time trying to ignore an attraction that refuses to die. I'm done deceiving myself that this thing between us will end up any way but in flames." He moved toward her, his boots echoing on the polished marble. "I think, in your heart of hearts, you know that, too."

"Leave my heart out of it," she warned him, dark eyes narrowing.

He didn't stop until he was standing much too close to her, the only barrier between them a contented baby.

"As you wish." He nodded, agreeing to her terms. "But I'll take all the rest of you just as soon as you're ready to give it."

She was still staring at him in a wordless standoff when Astrid called them into the dining room for the meal. Gage already knew the food wasn't going to do anything to take the edge off the real hunger.

Eight

Back in the Land Rover after dinner, Elena buckled her seat belt for the short drive to where they were staying. The day had been more fun than work, even though she'd signed on for an interview with Chiara Campagna. As it turned out, Astrid and Chiara were not only smart, creative women with tons of knowledge about fashion, they were also a blast to be around. The evening had gone better than Elena could have hoped.

The only moments that had given her pause involved Gage making his renewed interest in her known. Because although she'd felt the sparks fly between them from the moment he'd filched her phone at the party the other night, she had thought he was firmly opposed to reigniting the flame. Now, she knew otherwise, and she wasn't sure what to do about that.

She'd been floored when he'd offered to repay his father for the bribe he'd offered her. It made her regret that she'd never come clean about that. In the past, she'd told herself that it wouldn't matter to Gage that she hadn't accepted the money because Gage had been so quick to believe the worst of her anyway. But this week had forced her to rethink that perspective—a viewpoint she'd formed in the heat of anger and hurt. In truth, she'd been quick to believe the worst of him, too, and the realization was more than a little uncomfortable.

"Did you get everything you needed from Chiara tonight?" Gage asked as he pulled the SUV out onto the main road. Keeping one hand on the wheel, he changed the screen on his dashboard map for directions to the casino. "Or will the two of you be getting together again?"

Elena peered across the dark interior of the vehicle. With shadows playing across his face, his bone structure was all the more defined, the shadow of bristle along his jaw sending her into a tantalizing daydream about kissing him there.

Clearly, her body was rebelling against her for all the times she'd put up barriers between them. She tried to remember his question.

"While I definitely have enough to run a series of spotlights on her and her work, *she* asked *me* if we could get together again this week," she answered finally. After two years of focusing on the social media for her ex-husband's cooking show, Elena had been floundering to get her own voice back for her own brand. But tonight had reminded her how much she had enjoyed what she did. How much she had to offer her followers.

"It seemed like you two hit it off." Gage nodded, sounding satisfied. "Good for you."

His obvious pleasure in her success confused her, after they'd been at odds so often this week. That dynamic anchored her, helping her to stay strong against his undeniable appeal. But he'd shifted the playing field on her tonight and she didn't know what that meant for where things would go next. She wasn't ready to jump back into a relationship. Even a hot, passionate fling.

No matter how fun that might be.

To distract herself, she turned on her phone and idly opened her most active social media platform.

And nearly had a heart attack. Gasping, she fumbled her phone.

"What's wrong?" Gage asked. "Should I pull over?"

"No. Sorry. Nothing's wrong." She stared in disbelief at her number of followers, refreshing the page to see if there'd been a mistake. "My following has more than quadrupled in size tonight."

"What did you post?" he asked, brows furrowing.

"Absolutely nothing." She clicked open her mentions and found the posts from Chiara and Astrid. "But your friends posted about my suit. I can't believe this."

There were more comments than she could ever hope to reply to personally. In the course of one evening, her social capital had grown to more impressive proportions than ever, even bigger than when her blog had been at its most successful.

"I'm glad to hear it." He steered the SUV away from the lake, into the hills overlooking the water. "With the boost in followers, will your piece on Chiara fetch a higher price?"

The evening had quickly grown cold after the sunset, and now she was grateful for the vehicle's heated seats keeping her warm. Her gaze roamed over Gage, his nearness sending another jolt of heat through her.

"Definitely. It also takes the pressure off to lock in a quick sale for the interview since the increased reach expands my options for revenue streams." She couldn't begin to quantify what a gift this meeting had been for her, but her brain worked overtime strategizing her next move to solidify the growth.

Besides, thinking about business helped keep her thoughts off the upcoming night with Gage as he turned into the driveway of the four-bedroom vacation home perched above the lake. She should address his proposition. Make it clear that indulging in the attraction wasn't a good idea, even if thoughts of him dominated far too much of her brain space lately.

The dense stand of pine trees all around the house kept it hidden from view of the main casino building nearby, giving them the illusion of total privacy. Gage had told her Desmond managed nine other residences in addition to the main resort. While the high-roller suites were glitzy and modern, the villas were positioned as elegant mountain retreats.

Gage thumbed the remote door opener for the two-bay garage tucked under one side of the house. Light flooded from the space, spilling out onto the stone driveway. The garage was vacant except for a couple of kayaks stowed on one wall rack, and two bikes on another.

Elena was about to tuck her phone back into her purse when a new message caught her eye, this one from

Zoe, her friend in California who'd attempted to collect her things from Tomas's house that morning. Unable to ignore Zoe, who'd been even more distressed than her about not making it past Tomas's fiancée, Elena clicked open the message while Gage shut off the vehicle and came around to her side of the Land Rover.

He opened her door and offered his hand, the simple courtesy reminding her she was being rude to keep checking her phone.

"My apologies." Bracing herself for the thrill of his touch before taking his hand, she gripped her phone in the other. "I just saw a text from my friend in Los Angeles and I wanted to thank her for her efforts to obtain my things from my old house, even though her mission wasn't a success this morning."

"Of course." Gage's touch didn't linger once she was on her feet, and Elena couldn't deny that she missed it. "It's been a long day, and I'm sure you've got a lot on your mind."

Perhaps she should be relieved that Gage wasn't pressing the issue of taking their relationship further this evening. Especially when he'd already done her a tremendous kindness in that valuable introduction. No doubt, her feelings were a confusing knot. His willingness to give her space was welcome, and yet she thought about his touch whenever she wasn't actively experiencing it.

That didn't bode well for maintaining her boundaries.

He held the door to the house for her and they went inside, passing through a mudroom before entering the kitchen. They'd been in the house only briefly earlier, mostly focused on stowing their bags. Now, Elena took in the gourmet kitchen with top-of-the-line appliances and custom maple cabinetry. Industrial-looking pendant lamps went well with the French country decor, the contrast of antique and modern style giving the room character. Red accents in the leather bar stools and the knobs on the Wolf range broke up the natural tones of the tan granite and ivory-colored travertine floor.

"Your friend Desmond maintains a beautiful property," she observed, stepping out of her shoes to pad barefoot toward the countertop. The granite was spotless, and there was a hint of lemon cleaner in the air. It was so different from the crappy temporary apartments she'd bounced around in as a kid.

"He does. And his advice was instrumental as we began accepting guests at Mesa Falls Ranch when we expanded it from a working ranch to a luxury retreat." Gage eased out of his jacket and tossed it over a bar stool before turning back to the cabinets, opening and closing a couple. "Can I get you something warm to drink to take the chill off before bed? There are a few flavors of tea."

While it might be tempting to escape to her bedroom and avoid the inevitable draw of being around him, Elena knew hiding from the attraction wasn't going to make it disappear.

"Tea would be nice. Thank you." She dragged one of the leather bar stools away from the counter and slid onto the seat. She placed her phone facedown on the granite, waiting to read Zoe's note until she retired. Right now, she owed Gage her full attention.

Somehow, she needed to address the proposition he'd

made earlier in the evening. She wouldn't sleep with his suggestive proposal left open-ended, clinging to the corners of her mind. Tempting her.

She stared at him as he pulled mugs and a basket of teas from a cupboard, mesmerized by the tattoos visible on his forearm. Or maybe it was the whole man who mesmerized her.

Just watching him walk toward her sent a shiver down her spine.

"So what did your friend in LA have to say?" he asked, setting the basket of teas near her before he tapped the back of her phone with his finger. "Feel free to reply to her if you want. It will take the water a few minutes to boil anyway, and I should shoot Desmond a note to thank him for the accommodations."

"I haven't read her text yet," she replied automatically, even though she reeled from the ping-pong of her thoughts as they veered from steamy to practical and back again. She flipped over her phone to read Zoe's text, trying not to think about Gage's nearness.

Or those long, smoldering looks he'd shared with her.

Still, it took several moments for her mind to refocus on Zoe's message, the words swimming in front of her eyes. Finally, they came into focus, even though they made no sense.

I have your things! All your things, Elena! The pictures and mementos, the kitchenware, the clothes and the shoes.

"I don't understand," she murmured, clicking on the image attached to the note that showed Zoe's smiling face as she hugged a box containing one of Elena's vintage designer handbags. Only then did the reality of Zoe's words start to sink home. Behind Zoe, Elena could see rolling racks full of clothes. "How did she retrieve my things?"

"Is everything all right?" Gage asked, setting his own phone back on the counter before returning to the kettle and filling two mugs with hot water.

"I'm not sure," she explained distractedly, returning to her friend's original message to try to focus on the rest.

The security team your friend sent worked like magic. I didn't have to say a word! Tomas's fiancée ended up leaving the house. Tomas spent whole time apologizing while I went through your list. Security guys had your moped and bike delivered, too. Your doorman put in your storage unit.

This message required reading twice, but she had an excellent idea of the identity of the mystery "friend" who'd sent a security team with Zoe. The only friend who had witnessed her near meltdown when Zoe failed the first time.

"Gage." She realized her fingers were trembling when she set down the phone, her emotions all over the place. "Did you help orchestrate the retrieval of my things from my old home?"

"Absolutely." He carried over the steaming ceramic mugs, setting them on either side of the basket of teas. "I have zero remorse for interfering, and I'd do it all over again."

He met her gaze steadily before he chose a tea and added it to his cup.

He must have contacted Zoe without her knowing. Hired the security people and put her in touch with them, coordinating all of it while he was on the road. With the resources at his disposal, it wouldn't have been *difficult*, but it had surely inconvenienced him. And it must have cost far more than she could ever afford to repay.

Gratitude filled her along with tenderness for this man who'd done so much to help her today. She'd been determined to keep her boundaries in place with him, to deny herself the hot attraction that pulled her toward him whenever he was near. But with this one act of kindness, he'd stripped away her last defense.

She was more than grateful. She was touched.

"Thank you." She wasn't sure she had appreciated how fully the burden of Tomas's games had weighed her down until this moment, when she felt lighter, freer than she had in years. "Truly, I can't thank you enough for making that happen."

Gage slid the basket closer to her, as if to redirect the conversation toward something more concrete. "It was really no trouble, and I'm happy to help."

The part about it being no trouble had to be a massive understatement. She wasn't sure exactly what drove him to orchestrate the task, but she knew for certain that she wouldn't have all her worldly possessions back under her own control if it hadn't been for Gage.

The many feelings she'd been suppressing for him these last few days returned in full force, and then multiplied. The attraction flared hotter until it was impossible to ignore.

Impossible to deny.

So this time, when she met his eyes over the steaming cups, she didn't bother giving him any long, smoldering looks. Instead, she rose from the leather bar stool and rounded the island to stand on the same side of the counter as him. She was done denying that she wanted him.

Later, she'd figure out how to handle the aftermath of giving in to this attraction. For now, she planned to give herself to the moment. Without hesitation, she levered up on her toes and kissed him.

Gage tried like hell to remind himself that gratitude wasn't the same thing as passion.

But having Elena's slender arms twine around his neck, her sweet curves pressed against him and her lips teasing over his, made it damned near impossible to distinguish the difference. For a moment, he allowed himself to breathe in the hint of lavender fragrance on her skin; he wanted to lick every inch of her to find the source. He savored the silken brush of her mouth despite the need to deepen the kiss and tangle his tongue with hers.

All of which meant he was breathing like he'd run a marathon by the time she eased back to study him with her dark eyes.

"You're holding back on me?" she asked, pursing her lips as she tipped her head sideways to look at him. "After all those seductive words in stolen moments at Jonah's house?"

This. Woman.

She seemed to have an IV right into his bloodstream and could heat it up at will.

"After the way things ended last time, I think we need to be very, very clear about what we're getting into before we let passion burn away all of our best intentions." He ached to touch her. To peel away every last stitch of clothing and run his fingertips over her bare skin.

He wanted to see her shiver with pleasure. Give her goose bumps. Watch her come undone from nothing more than his touch, his breath on her most sensitive places.

"Then I will make what I want very, very clear." She mimicked his cadence, reaching up to unfasten the clasp that held her long dark hair in an updo. She opened it, the waves tumbling down her back. "I don't want this night to end any other way but with us in bed, and I trust you, Gage Striker, to make sure that happens."

Wordless, he could only stare for a moment while she held the jeweled combs between her fingers, then let them fall to the countertop. He hadn't thought this would happen tonight. But he'd be damned if he would argue when Elena looked at him with fire in her eyes and in her words.

He'd fallen hard for that strength and passion. Seeing it resurrected now shredded any last restraint.

"Count on me," he vowed to himself more than her.

Spearing his fingers into that long, lush mane, he cupped her head and drew her close for the kiss he wanted. Slow, deep, thorough.

He licked his way inside her mouth, tilting her head

for full access. The soft, needy sounds she made kept him there for a long time, until her knees seemed to give way and she sank more heavily against him. Still, he didn't break the kiss he'd waited forever to taste. He stroked an experimental touch down her throat, pausing to circle the hollow at its base.

She reared back to look at him, her pupils dilated, her eyes passion-dazed. "I will combust out of these clothes if we wait any longer to get naked."

"We can't have that." He kissed his way along her collarbone while his fingers worked the buttons on her suit, unfastening each one until the jacket opened to her narrow waist. Her camisole was next.

The sight of her pale breasts straining the navy blue lace of her bra cups made his mouth water. He spanned her waist with his hands, skimming up her ribs to mold his palms against the swell of her enticing curves. When he tipped a bra strap off her shoulder with one finger, he watched the lace cup roll down to free an enticing taut nipple. He bent to capture it between his lips, drawing on her while she arched toward him, her hands roaming over his chest, down to his waist and underneath his T-shirt.

She wriggled closer, her nails lightly scoring his abs as he turned his attention to the other breast.

Her efforts to undress him slowed as her breath came faster. He helped her by dragging his shirt up and off, leaving it on a bar stool before he turned her in the direction of his bedroom.

"Come with me, sweetheart." He hadn't meant to take things so far in the kitchen. By now, his whole body was on fire.

"That's the plan." She stripped off the lace bra as she walked, letting it fall on a hall table outside his suite. "Now that I've committed to this conflagration, I'm requesting as many orgasms as you deem manageable."

Stepping deeper into his bedroom, she sent him a saucy look over her shoulder, that dark tangle of hair nearly brushing her waist.

"You'll have to beg me for mercy." He toed the door shut behind them, his eyes on Elena as she eased down the zipper on the back of her pencil skirt.

He couldn't lose his pants fast enough—but left on his boxers—before he reached for her skirt. He wanted to feel the way the fabric slid down those memorable hips.

Wrapping an arm around her waist, he drew her back against him, watching her in the silver-framed mirror above the mahogany chest. Her head lolled back against his shoulder while he touched her, tracing the scalloped edge of her blue lace panties. He kissed her hair, his eyes never leaving her reflection, visible thanks to the light of a desk lamp in the sitting area behind them. She trembled against him.

"I've missed you." He spoke into her ear, knowing from her flushed cheeks she was already close to the first orgasm. He remembered she was exquisitely sensitive. "I've missed this."

He meant the passion between them, but he cupped her sex as he said it. She shivered hard, and her nipples beaded.

"Please, Gage," she murmured softly, her hips swaying in a way that threatened his restraint.

He obliged her by skimming aside the panties. Finding the tight bud between her legs. Circling the slick heat.

She went still, her lips parting. She reached back to grip his thigh, her fingers clenching tight until the sweet, convulsive shudders began. Seeing her come apart filled him with hunger, even as a new, fierce protectiveness surged.

When the shudders subsided, she turned into him and he lifted her in his arms, carrying her to the king-size bed. Raking back the white duvet, he settled her in the middle of the mattress before he went to get condoms from his toiletry bag.

He returned to the bed to find her propped against the gray leather headboard, hugging a white pillow to her chest as she watched him come toward her. As he set the condoms on the nightstand, she tossed aside the pillow and dragged him down beside her, her arms locked around his neck.

She was so damned sexy.

With an effort, he managed to strip off his boxers. She arched up off the bed to kiss her way around his chest, interspersing gentle bites while he rolled a condom into place.

Levered above her, he positioned himself between her thighs, and their gazes locked. He caressed her cheek before running his thumb along her lower lip. Then, finally, he eased inside her. Inch by incredible inch, he lost himself in Elena.

Wrapping her legs around him, she anchored her ankles behind his hips. They moved together with the rhythm of two people who've memorized one another's bodies. They started slowly at first, and then picked up the pace, revisiting all the touches that drove one another wild.

For a while, she wanted to be on top, teasing him with her long hair by dragging it across his sensitized skin. Later, she rolled underneath him so she could trace the patterns of his tattoos with her fingers. The movements were intensely seductive and familiar at the same time, calling down memories he wasn't ready for.

In the end, he held her questing fingers captive, pinning them to the pillow on either side of her head to focus solely on the moment. She gave herself to that plan, rolling her hips in time with his thrusts, intensifying every movement. Once he was close to completion, he bent to lave one nipple, tugging it in his mouth until he felt her tense. Letting go, he thrust deep. Hard.

They came together in a rush of sensation. He lost track of everything but how she made him feel. Mindless with pleasure. Whole.

Once he recovered himself enough to move off her, Gage knew that last feeling was a problem. He couldn't rely on Elena to make him feel fulfilled. This relationship wasn't about that, and he'd be wise not to mix up the past and the present.

Still, it was impossible not to hold her tight for long afterward. He told himself it was because he wanted to be ready for the next round of orgasms he had every intention of giving her.

But he feared he knew better.

Nine

Elena awoke to warm sunlight on her face, her body pleasantly aching and thoroughly sated. Memories of the evening before swirled through her mind, from the first kiss in the kitchen to a late-night refrigerator raid and lovemaking in front of the fireplace.

Now, reaching for Gage, she felt empty air on his side of the bed. And flowers? Wrenching her eyes open, Elena discovered a pool of pink rose petals on Gage's pillow, trailing to the floor of the suite. There was also a note on the resort's stationery propped against the fluffy down, two words written in a sure, masculine hand.

Join me.

The rose petals led out the door.

Anticipation hummed warm in her veins even though they'd rolled in these very sheets together just a couple of hours ago. What was it about this man that captivated her so thoroughly? Sliding from the covers, she set her feet on the floor and padded to the bathroom to brush her teeth. Afterward, she found one of Gage's clean T-shirts folded neatly in the top drawer of a bureau, and slipped it on.

She hoped things wouldn't turn awkward between them now that the sun had risen. But she knew inevitably they would because she hadn't told him the truth about what had happened between them six years ago when they broke up. Trust hadn't come easily for either of them then, and it wouldn't return now in light of the way they'd treated each other—red-hot encounters notwithstanding.

For just a little while longer, though, she would live in the moment. Take all the joy she could from this time together.

Grabbing one of the resort robes from a hook in the bathroom, Elena slid it over Gage's shirt and followed the trail of pink petals out of the master suite. She wound an elastic around her hair and scooped up a handful of the rose remnants from the hardwood, bringing them to her nose for a sniff. Her mother had taught her that—take time to smell the roses. She didn't have many good memories of her mom, but it helped to hug close the ones that weren't tainted by her parents' drinking. Fighting. When her mom abandoned the family, it had eliminated the arguments that too often turned to violence, but the hole she left behind had been too big to fill no matter what Elena tried to put there. Work. Ambition. Relationships.

It was simpler to just smell the roses and savor

the present, especially since Elena couldn't change the past. Hiding it hadn't worked with Gage's family. And altering herself to fit into Tomas's life had been foolish.

From now on, she was embracing the journey that had made her the woman she was today. As she made her way through the family room, she saw that the petal path led through the double doors leading out to a patio overlooking the lake. She stepped outside to find a bubbling hot tub steaming white puffs into the cool mountain air.

Gage sprawled in the far corner, his arms spread wide along the edges of the tub, ropes of muscle drawing her eye, the black ink of his tattoos shiny and wet. Her personal Poseidon.

"Good morning, lovely." His New Zealand accent wrapped around her ears, the words as unhurried as his gaze. "I thought you might like a soak to start the day. The view isn't bad, either."

He nodded toward the lake visible through the trees, the mountains in the distance still capped with snow even though spring buds were visible on nearby branches. But she preferred the view of Gage's naked chest rising from the water.

"As it happens, I might have a few muscles that would benefit from the pulsating jets." She slid off the robe, setting it on the wooden bench that wrapped two sides of the tub. She reached for the hem of the T-shirt, then hesitated. "What would you rate the level of privacy out here?" She peered around.

Gage's pupils darkened with satisfying speed. "Maybe for my sanity you should keep the T-shirt on."

"As you wish." Elena stepped over the edge of the partially sunken tub, then tucked the end of her ponytail through the elastic to keep her hair out of the water before she sank into one of the seats. "How did you sleep?"

"Did we sleep?" He reached for a towel at the edge of the tub and dried his hands before grabbing his phone. "Let me just send a text for room service to set up breakfast while we're out here."

Elena waited, appreciating Gage's thoughtful efficiency. But as she took in the luxury of their surroundings, she realized the sharp contrast in their lifestyles. She knew that Gage's level of wealth was even more staggering than when they'd dated before. More daunting. A private jet brought him where he wanted to go. Catered meals appeared with a text. Expensive vehicles and exotic vacation destinations were the norm while Elena had worked her way up from virtually nothing. People like Gage's parents would always view her past as a liability, an unfair burden for their son. And although she liked her life just fine, she would always be an outsider in Gage's privileged world.

Tipping her head back to breathe in the mountain air, she closed her eyes and soaked up the sensations of the jets against her shoulders. Bubbles burst at the surface, spraying her face with a light mist. Birds called to one another in the nearby trees, a boat motor sounding in the lake below. The hot tub water sloshed side to side as she heard Gage settle deeper into the spa a moment before his palms landed on her waist through the wet shirt, his fingers wrapping around her hip.

She didn't open her eyes, simply feeling him come

closer as he repositioned himself next to her. His thigh brushed hers and her body stirred, still hungry for him.

"How do you want to spend your day?" He spoke into her ear, the sound giving her shivers before he kissed her neck. "Keeping in mind I want to spoil you."

The temptation to lose herself in his touch nearly overwhelmed her. But how long could they indulge this attraction before they addressed the inevitable problems that came with it?

Starting with the fact that she'd let him believe she'd accepted his father's bribe all those years ago. The thought felt like a bucket of cold water despite the heat of the spa tub.

"We should probably talk first." Sitting up straighter, Elena opened her eyes. "Last night happened so fast."

Easing back, Gage looked wary. Water droplets clung to the bristles along his jaw. "What's there to discuss? Last night was a gift. Today can be, too, if we let it."

The temptation to defer an unhappy conversation was strong, but she'd gone that route before and lived to regret it.

She swiped away a damp strand of hair that came loose from her elastic.

"Six years ago, I let myself get caught up in the idea of living in the moment so much that I never acknowledged my past." She hadn't wanted to taint Gage's opinion of her, so she'd kept it to herself that her father was a wanted man. "And when you finally learned the truth about my family, you didn't learn it from me. I'm not making that mistake again."

The warmth in Gage's dark eyes cooled, his expression growing distant as he leaned back against the hot tub wall. His gaze turned assessing.

"Meaning you're keeping more secrets from me?" he asked.

Guilt stung. She didn't know how else to broach the subject, so without preamble, she admitted, "I never took the bribe your father offered me."

His dark eyebrows lifted in surprise for a moment, then swooped low in a scowl. "What are you talking about?"

"That day in New Zealand with your family," she began slowly, remembering the waves of pain she'd felt from Nigel Striker's cruel words, followed by Gage's automatic assumptions regarding her character. "I was devastated by your father's dismissal of me from your life when I believed…" She'd thought Gage had brought her home to propose. The turn things had taken had been so far off course from what she'd envisioned she hadn't weathered the storm well at all. "When I'd thought things were going so well between us."

"You weren't the only one devastated, Elena." The flash of pain she saw in his eyes was all too real, and it hurt to know that she could have lessened that ache if she'd reacted differently. "My father was merciless in characterizing you as secretive and deceptive about your past. But none of it would have mattered if you hadn't jumped at the chance to take a lucrative detour out of my life."

Had she always known that? Had she subconsciously sabotaged things between them even more than Nigel Striker tried to do? The humming of the hot tub motor seemed to grow louder in her ears, or maybe it was the buzzing of a guilty conscience.

"I didn't take the bribe, Gage. I ripped up the check and threw it at his retreating back." She sat forward on the hot tub bench seat, not feeling at all relaxed despite the rush of the jets on her shoulders.

Gage shook his head in disbelief. "You led me to think you took it."

She bit her lip. "You immediately assumed I had."

"So you lied to me?"

She closed her eyes for a moment, regretting her temper as the buzzing in her ears grew louder. *Yes.*

"I was hurt and angry," she explained. "And I figured you'd learn the truth eventually—"

"Six years later?" There was no way to miss the growing anger—and yes, disillusionment—in his voice. "When it doesn't matter anymore? After you *married* someone else?"

The buzzing sound almost drowned out Gage's words, and Elena turned to see a four-wheeler bump over a ridge and onto the lawn from the tree line.

With a curse of frustration, Gage was on his feet instantly, grabbing a towel and wrapping it around himself as the rider came into view. Desmond Pierce had sharp, aristocratic features like she envisioned on a Mediterranean prince. As he rolled to a stop near the edge of the deck, Elena could see his cool gray eyes as he met Gage's stare.

"What's wrong?" Gage asked, still dripping wet as he tied the towel around his waist and stepped up onto the deck.

Desmond's eyes shifted to her briefly before they moved back to Gage.

"News from Weston. We need to meet this afternoon if you can be at the casino by midday. I've been trying to reach you all morning." Then the man turned to her once more, his posture relaxing somewhat now that his important news was, apparently, delivered. "Sorry to interrupt your morning. I don't think we've been formally introduced. I'm Desmond Pierce."

"Elena Rollins," she said, frustrated and relieved all at once to have her conversation with Gage end abruptly. She knew his ranch partners would take precedence over her, especially in light of what she'd just confessed to him. "And I'll go get dressed so the two of you can speak privately."

She was about to stand up, awkwardly reaching for the robe since she wore nothing beneath Gage's T-shirt, but Gage already had a towel outstretched for her.

"We'll continue our conversation later," Gage spoke to her in low tones, his voice warm against her neck as he draped the towel around her.

"I'm not sure there's much more to say." They'd both made mistakes that had led them to this point. There was no going back to change them now. "I'd be more interested to hear what Desmond has to share with you. I'll bet anything it has to do with Alonzo Salazar."

Gage didn't bother to deny it. He retrieved her robe before setting it on her shoulders.

"Lucky for you," he said as his hands lingered on her upper arms, bringing memories of their night together flaming from her mind through her body, "you have a whole new story to cover that will be far more lucrative than whatever you might dig up on my former mentor." He gave her a meaningful squeeze, eyes flaming with heat, then opened the French doors leading back into the house for her. "I'll finish up as soon as I can here."

Closing the door behind her, Elena didn't linger in the great room. She darted past the breakfast area where the catering staff were arranging the table for their meal, then took refuge in a hot shower to try to figure out what to do next.

She wanted to accept Gage's olive branch—the Chiara Campagna introduction—and forget about Alonzo Salazar. Except what if Gage's former mentor was the same caliber of father figure as Gage's actual dad? What if Alonzo had been a man without scruples, driven to achieve his own ends no matter the cost?

It bugged her to think of letting a man like that get away with bending the world to his will. But for today— for Gage—she'd call Chiara and see about setting up another meeting instead. Maybe focusing on her career and her future would help her to forget about the knot of emotions she felt for Gage.

Ruminating over the view of Lake Tahoe out the window of her luxury hotel suite, Chiara Campagna hurried to pick up the call when she spotted Elena Rollins's number on her caller ID.

"Hello, Elena," she answered, needing to make the woman feel at ease with her. "I hope we're going to hang out today while we're both still in Tahoe."

She regretted manipulating someone as genuinely nice as Elena seemed, but she couldn't afford to lose this chance to find out what information Elena had gathered for her story on Alonzo Salazar and how the Mesa Falls Ranch owners were involved. Those six men knew more about Zach's death than they admitted, and Chiara would never get to the bottom of it without stirring the pot.

Starting with Elena.

"As a matter of fact, I'm free for a few hours. Gage is meeting with Jonah and Desmond Pierce at the casino this afternoon, so I thought I'd see if you and Astrid wanted to see the sights."

"Astrid sounded wiped out when I talked to her this morning." She stretched the truth a bit, but she didn't want to share Elena with Astrid, especially when she needed to pump Elena for information about the Mesa Falls owners. Even though Astrid's husband was one of the owners, too, Chiara had never gotten the impression Jonah had been as close with Zach as Gage Striker. They'd been roommates at school.

"Why don't you and I meet at the casino for drinks?" That would put them in close proximity to where the secretive ranch owners would be getting together.

"You don't get swarmed by fans at places like that?" Elena asked curiously.

"I'll have my secretary call ahead to make sure we have some space to ourselves." Ideally, somewhere close to the meeting among Gage, Jonah and Desmond. She didn't have a plan for crashing it, but being nearby like that might yield an opportunity to find out more.

"Sounds good," Elena said warmly. "I'm so grateful for the help you've already given me, Chiara. I don't know how I can repay you."

Chiara had seen the way Elena's followers jumped

after her posts the day before. Ideally, Elena's gratitude would make it tough for her to turn Chiara down when she asked for some favors in return.

"It's my pleasure to tout talented friends," she told her honestly, typing a list of questions she wanted answered about Gage's partners. "Although I assure you, the big following comes with as many heartaches as joys."

Not that anyone ever believed her about that. But as far as she was concerned, the view from the top of the social media world was a study in terror. The only direction to go was down. For Chiara, the question every day became, would she fall fast in a stomach-churning nosedive? Or would her decline be a slow and steady destruction of everything she'd earned these last few years?

If her time as reigning social media queen was coming to an end, it was all the more reason to hasten her search for answers about Zach. Whatever power she possessed, she was going to leverage it for the sake of the truth.

"That's the story of my life, Chiara," Elena admitted drily. "Just when the joys become their most wonderful, heartache kicks in. I'm still glad for the boost."

"It's no trouble at all." Chiara was already calculating how fast she could get out the door so she'd be there during the owners' meeting. "I can meet you at the casino anytime after noon. We can hit the shops and talk over lunch."

"I'll message you when I'm there," Elena promised before disconnecting the call.

Rushing to dress, Chiara dictated a few more questions into her phone, including what role Gage Striker's father might have played in making sure Zach's death wasn't reported in school for months afterward.

She chose a couture pantsuit for spring that a designer had sent her the week before, slipping into the champagne-colored fabric while she texted her hairdresser to fix her blowout. Another perk in her life she didn't feel worthy of.

It was probably an unhealthy sign that she couldn't simply enjoy life as a macro-influencer, raking in big checks for sponsored content and personal appearances. Instead, she lived with constant imposter syndrome, and a nearly crippling fear that she'd make the wrong choice about what to allow on her feed, wondering if the next sponsored post she agreed to share would label her as a sellout to the world.

Her therapist told her survivor guilt was common in people who'd lost a loved one. Especially when the loved one was someone like Zachary Eldridge, a boy who'd been on track to be a phenomenal artist. His work and friendship had given her all her best ideas for what would one day become her celebrated social media feed—touted as creative and artistic, appealing to multiple sensibilities. Without him, she felt like a fraud.

Sometimes she hoped for her downfall to come sooner rather than later. Because maybe then, when she wasn't on top of the world, she wouldn't battle the sensation that she didn't belong there every single day.

Gage paced the high-roller suite in Desmond's casino. He knew whatever Weston Rivera had reported to Desmond, the news was important if it warranted a meeting. He'd been the first to arrive, and one of the resort's support staff was still in the suite to ensure the hookups were live for a video conference with Miles, Weston and Alec, the partners who couldn't attend in person.

Pausing by the billiard table in the middle of the suite, Gage rolled the cue ball back and forth between his palms. The lake glittered bright blue outside the floor-to-ceiling windows, while indoors the fire in a smooth stone hearth warmed the room. A wooden bar cart had been rolled in from the wine cellar containing a few select bottles and—thankfully—Gage's preferred bourbon.

He poured himself a glass, trying not to think about Elena's news this morning.

She hadn't taken the bribe.

He knew in his gut as soon as she'd said it that it was the truth. He should have known it—if not at the time, when he'd assumed the worst of her, then shortly afterward when she'd left in a fury. It turned out she hadn't been furious with his father for offering to pay her off to make her leave Gage's life. She'd been livid with Gage for believing she could be bought.

Tipping back the measure of aged Kentucky bourbon, he set the stopper back in the decanter and turned away from the bar in time to see Jonah and Desmond enter together. Desmond thanked the AV staff member before dismissing her.

"What gives?" Gage barked more sharply than he'd intended.

Jonah shook his head. "Dude, I've got the newborn.

If anyone should be tired and out of sorts about the snap meeting, it ought to be me."

"Right. Sorry, mate." Gage had been in the middle of the most significant conversation of his life when he'd been interrupted, but he didn't mention that now. He'd have to figure out how to proceed with Elena later, once he knew what was so all-fired important to get everyone together now.

Desmond switched on his laptop and brought online a specially made ninety-inch television screen over the fireplace. The screen divided into three windows, one for each of the other owners. Miles arrived first, with Alec and Weston flickering into view shortly afterward.

"Looks like we're all here," Weston observed, kicking things off while Gage and Jonah took seats on a leather sofa by the fireplace. "I've gotten Devon Salazar's permission to share this information, which came from April's investigation of the money trail for Alonzo's book. She discovered the majority of the income has gone toward the support and education of a thirteen-year-old named Matthew Cruz."

Jonah coughed on the sip of coffee he'd just taken. Gage felt his jaw drop. Alonzo was supporting a kid?

"Is there any reason to believe it's Alonzo's son?" Desmond asked. "Did Devon run DNA?"

"Matthew Cruz looks nothing like any of the Salazars." Weston glanced down at his own laptop as he spoke, and with a keystroke, he shared a photo of a lean, gap-toothed preteen. With dark blond hair and gray eyes, he bore no resemblance to Alonzo, or his sons Marcus and Devon, who owned Salazar Media and had worked with the ranch on branding and promotion.

"If the kid is thirteen years old, it means he was conceived during the worst year of our lives," Alec observed, leaning closer to his computer screen, maybe scrutinizing the photo. It made his face loom large on the television screen. "The boy looks most like Jonah."

Jonah shook his head, his expression thunderous. "Don't even go there. I'm still reeling that Alonzo did all this without breathing a word to any of us. Besides, you know damned well if the kid was any of ours, Alonzo would have kicked our asses if we weren't accountable."

"Why would Alonzo take financial responsibility for anyone that wasn't a blood relative?" Gage asked, trying to make sense of a day that had taken a fast downward spiral after beginning with a trail of rose petals.

"First, we make sure it's not a blood relative," Weston chimed in again, apparently knowing more about the case because things had worked out well between him and the financial forensics investigator. "Devon is going to reach out to Matthew's guardian and see if she'll agree to paternity testing."

"Who's the guardian?" Desmond asked, one shoulder tipped against the stone wall near the fireplace. It was barely past noon and the casino owner was already dressed in an impeccable custom suit.

Weston clicked another button and a new face appeared on the screen where Weston had been a moment ago. "This is Nicole Cruz. She worked briefly at the ranch under the alias Nicole Smith, but she was fired suddenly by a supervisor who said it was performance-related. When I tried to follow up on that incident, I discovered the supervisor quit the next day and didn't leave a forwarding address."

"Which means the supervisor could have been lying. Or someone at the ranch applied pressure for Nicole to leave," Miles pointed out. The two brothers frequently didn't see eye to eye. "Is Nicole the mother?"

"According to her, no," Weston replied. "When she introduced herself to April several weeks ago, she claimed Matthew is her sister's son, and that her sister died suddenly without naming the father. So far, we don't have a photo of the mother since Nicole and Matthew disappeared after Nicole was fired from her job at Mesa Falls."

"So we hire someone to track the kid and his guardian using a last known address," Gage suggested, already itching to start piecing the puzzle together before someone else did. Someone like Elena. Could he trust her to be honest with him about her next move? Despite their night together, he couldn't be sure. "Or are the Salazar heirs already doing that?"

"At the very least," Miles added, "we need to ask around Mesa Falls to figure out who knew her. I'm ready to take some time away from Rivera Ranch, Gage, if you want me to come help out at Mesa Falls."

Gage wondered who was the most surprised by that comment. Weston reared back from his screen like someone had just shoved him. Jonah coughed through another sip of coffee. Desmond made a long, low whistle.

Miles swore and shifted in his seat, the Sierra Nevada Mountains visible out the window of his ranch office behind him. "Every one of you takes time off.

I've earned it. Besides, I'm going to ask the Mesa Falls foreman for some recommendations to bring sustainable ranching practices to Rivera Ranch."

One of the reasons they'd founded Mesa Falls was to highlight more green practices in raising cattle, and the experiment had turned Mesa Falls into a successful showplace.

Gage was the first to recover from his surprise since Miles had already indicated to him that he'd be willing to cover for Gage this week. "I'd appreciate the help for as long as you care to stay. Elena Rollins should be leaving Montana soon and won't be doing a story about Alonzo."

Even as he said it, he realized how much he didn't want her to leave, no matter how upset he'd been by her revelation in the hot tub this morning. Something incredible had happened between them last night, and he wasn't ready to turn his back on it just because she'd shaken his whole view of their past together. They'd been too quick to call it quits the first time. What if they kept things simple this time? Instead of worrying about how they would fit—or not fit—into one another's lives, they could simply spend night after scorching night in one another's arms and not worry about the future.

He hadn't realized how fully he'd lost the thread of the meeting conversation until Desmond said his name.

"Gage? You still with us?"

Damn it.

"Sorry." He wasn't used to being distracted. Especially not by a woman. In his work, he normally juggled ten different tasks at a time. But the lack of trust and honesty between him and Elena burned raw. "Just thinking about how quickly I can tie up loose ends here and be back at Mesa Falls."

Jonah gave him a sympathetic glance as he leaned deeper into the sofa. "We're on to party planning. Miles suggested we host another celebrity shindig on-site and release a statement offering our own narrative about Alonzo. Maybe if we share a story of our own for where the money went, the public interest will die down."

"You mean we lie?" Gage couldn't imagine his friends would sink so low.

"Of course not," Miles was quick to clarify. "Alonzo funneled some of the profits from his book to building infrastructure in poor neighborhoods in cities around the world. We have photos and concrete evidence of those travels, right, Wes?"

"We do," Weston confirmed, clicking more keys before a picture of an old-fashioned bulletin board covered with photographs held up with thumbtacks appeared on his screen. The shots showed Alonzo in foreign countries around the world, posed with volunteer groups in front of a variety of building projects.

"So we have a party," Gage agreed, wondering if he had ever felt in less of a party mode in his life, "and reveal Alonzo's secret life as a philanthropist."

Desmond straightened from his spot near the fireplace. "Do you think Elena will take up the cause? Be the vehicle for the story we want to circulate about Alonzo?"

Gage's gut knotted at the thought of asking her to use her newfound social media cache to share a story that he knew wasn't the full truth. He refused to lie to her after the way he and his father had treated her six years ago.

"I'll see what I can do," he said, unwilling to promise anything.

Especially when feeding Elena a story like that meant she'd be all the more likely to leave Montana—and Gage—for good.

Ten

While she waited for a boutique owner to finish her conversation with Chiara in the casino resort shops, Elena glanced up at the door of the high-roller suite in the second-floor gallery, where Gage was in a meeting.

What had been so important to tear him away from their conversation this morning? He'd closed himself in the den of their suite after Desmond's arrival, not reappearing until it was time to leave for his meeting. She wasn't necessarily hurt by his lack of communication. She understood business didn't stop just because she'd revealed a long-held secret to Gage. But she couldn't deny she was curious to pick up where they left off, to see if her revelation changed anything in their relationship.

Chiara's voice interrupted her thoughts. "Elena, will you hop in a photo with Mimi so I can tag you both and help her find you in case she wants to place a future order for your designs?"

Shaking off the romantic preoccupation with Gage, Elena hurried over, amazed at how Chiara's hustle never took a day off. While Elena had been daydreaming about Gage, Chiara had been talking up Elena's potential future business. Both Astrid and Chiara had insisted she had a real talent for fashion.

"Of course." Elena posed with the woman, one of the boutique's mannequins between them, while Chiara took several photos. "You have a beautiful store. Thank you so much the tour."

After shaking hands with the owner, Chiara and Elena left the store and returned to the shops that fanned out around a courtyard fountain. The water bubbled and splashed from the mouth of a sea dragon before falling into a marble pool at its base.

Again, Elena glanced up at the second-floor gallery toward the high-roller suite, but the door remained closed. She noticed Chiara followed her gaze.

"Astrid made it sound like the Mesa Falls owners were meeting for supersecret reasons." Chiara's green eyes sparkled with mischief, like they shared a secret of their own. "Have you made any progress cracking the code of silence from them about Alonzo Salazar?"

Caught off guard by the question since Chiara was close with Astrid, Elena took a moment to consider her response while a group of young tourists photographed the sea dragon.

"Honestly, I'm backing off the story." She hadn't consciously made the decision until that moment, thinking she'd wait to see how things played out with Chiara. "I was convinced that Salazar had greedy ulterior motives for writing his book when I first started digging, but now I'm not so sure that was the case."

"Really?" Chiara turned her face away from the tourists' cameras, then leaned closer to Elena, green eyes wide. "Do tell."

Her obvious interest gave Elena pause. She wasn't entirely sure why, but she hadn't survived her teens with a drunken nomad for a father by ignoring her instincts. So she spoke more cautiously than she might have otherwise.

"The Mesa Falls owners all trust Salazar. And that says a lot to me." She peered up toward the meeting place again and spied Jonah emerging with Desmond Pierce. "They must be finished now."

"You know they all attended a boarding school where Alonzo was a teacher, right?" Chiara asked, her gaze narrowing as a tall man dressed like a casino employee approached Desmond Pierce and seemed to receive instructions. "I attended a girls' school nearby, but none of them remember me."

Elena did a double take as the words sank in. "You knew them from their school days? Does Astrid know?"

"I mentioned it to her once, but I'm not sure if she remembers. But it's not as surprising as it sounds that none of the owners remember me. I was just plain old Kara Marsh back then—tall and gawky and a long way from being comfortable in my own skin."

As much as Elena longed to find Gage upstairs and pull him into a quiet corner to finish their earlier conversation, she couldn't deny a strong curiosity about

Chiara's tie to Gage and his friends. A tie he apparently didn't know about.

"You changed your name?" Elena wondered how many of her followers knew about this.

"No. I simply use Chiara like a stage name. When I started out, it made it easier to have some separation between my professional world and my personal life." Chiara pointed toward the stairs. "Shall we go up? I'm sure you're eager to see Gage."

Was she that obvious? But as much as she'd thought about him all day, she also feared she was getting in over her head with him. His reaction to her news this morning had been difficult to read. Instead, she delayed a bit longer, asking Chiara another question.

"Doesn't it bother you that they don't remember you?" she pressed, not moving toward the steps.

The sound of the fountain splashing filled the air. A group of young women wearing T-shirts printed with "Bridesmaid" in frilly font giggled as they passed Elena, fruity drinks in hand.

"Not really. I don't want to be Chiara Campagna forever," she mused wistfully, gazing down at a wristwatch with a huge yellow diamond in its face. "But if you change your mind about looking into Alonzo Salazar's connection to the ranch owners, I'd be game to develop an angle with you."

Stunned by the turn the conversation had taken, Elena followed her new friend up the steps to the gallery, where Chiara greeted Jonah. Why would Chiara take an interest in dredging up a past the Mesa Falls Ranch owners clearly wanted to keep quiet? The woman's words stirred Elena's curiosity, making her won-

der if she'd allowed Gage to lure her away from the
Alonzo Salazar scoop too easily. She needed to see
him. Speak to him.

Elena lingered a moment with Chiara to say hello to
Jonah, then excused herself to peer into the suite where
the owner meeting had taken place.

Gage sat with his back to her on a huge, curved
leather sofa, a fitted black jacket drawing attention to
his broad shoulders. He was tapping away on his phone.
There was an artful arrangement of birds of paradise
on the glass-topped table in front of him, and a fire
burned in the sleek, modern hearth. A massive flat-
screen television was mounted over the fireplace, but
the display was dark. On either side of the fireplace,
windows overlooked Lake Tahoe, the clear sky making
the water look impossibly blue.

A moment of nervous anticipation threaded through
her at the sight of Gage. Attraction, uncertainty and a
whole lot of other emotions she didn't bother to unpack
all clamored for her attention.

"Gage?" she called to him and he spun around immediately.

"Elena." His shoulders relaxed a fraction. He remained unsmiling, yet somehow seemed relieved to
see her.

Or maybe that was wishful thinking.

"Am I interrupting you?" She hugged her handmade
hobo bag more tightly to her side, the fake jewels from
repurposed old necklaces digging into her forearm
where she pinned the purse to her body. "I met Chiara
downstairs a couple of hours ago to share ideas about
a potential new business venture."

She was still in a daze that one of the world's most famous faces was interested in helping her move into the fashion world, potentially developing an experimental line of her own as a guest appearance for another brand.

Elena had never visualized something like that for herself, but she would be crazy not to pursue the opportunity while she had it. Although something made her uneasy about the woman's second proposition, suggesting she would support Elena if she wanted to write a piece on Alonzo Salazar despite her growing feelings for Gage.

"I'm glad you're here." Standing, Gage tucked his phone in his jacket pocket and strode toward her, his dark eyes making her melt inside even though she couldn't quite read his expression. "I owed you my undivided attention this morning. My apologies for the interruption."

Her body hummed everywhere as he approached, something that always happened around this man, but the effects were more pronounced after the vivid reminder of what it was like to be with him the night before.

"You're a busy man." Her thoughts traveled back in time to their first encounter. "I understood that from the moment we met, considering how long it took to get a meeting with you."

"These days, I clear my schedule for you." His gaze tracked over her. "How about we have dinner at the resort tonight and we'll pick up where we left off in the hot tub?"

Her pulse thrummed faster, awareness surging through her bloodstream.

"I look forward to it," she confessed, needing to clear the air about their past once and for all.

And once that was done—like it or not—she needed to confront Gage about the mysterious Alonzo Salazar. Because whether or not she shared her findings about the author with the public, she was beginning to suspect the man was the key to a larger story that Gage was keeping hidden from her.

Gage couldn't take his eyes off Elena.

He watched her swirl her dessert fork through the meringue on her fruit-covered *boccone dolce*, her one-shoulder evening dress shimmering in the candlelight. The champagne-colored tulle hugged her curves and turned other men's heads.

The casino's Italian-inspired restaurant was decorated like a Florentine palazzo, with white moldings around the ceilings, neoclassical paintings and elaborate chandeliers. The walls were covered in frescoes between the windows overlooking Lake Tahoe. They sat at a pedestal table on a raised dais encircled by pillars. White curtains were strategically draped throughout, giving them a modicum of privacy within the small dining room.

Throughout the meal, he'd bided his time, not wanting to ambush her with questions about her revelation this morning. So he'd asked her about plans for merging her growing social media platform with her new interest in pursuing fashion more seriously. He'd offered to invest in her next venture, but she'd declined before steering the subject back to him and his movement away from investment banking to pursue his personal investments. Now, he guided things back to her.

"We never spoke about your family when we dated," he reminded her as he dug into his hazelnut torte. In retrospect, while he'd been content to accept her at face value, he'd done them both a disservice by not being more curious about what made her tick. "But I wondered—after learning about your unconventional upbringing—how you managed to catapult yourself to the level of business savvy you possessed when I met you."

A waiter refilled their water glasses, and Elena sampled a raspberry before answering. "I was very honest with you about how I started my social media platform. I chronicled my drive to surround myself with beautiful things, from flea market finds to freecycling. Those posts were very popular because there are a lot of struggling people who appreciate the need to create a physically appealing space with truly limited resources."

"And sponsorships for the blog paid for college?" He remembered her telling him that she'd built the platform out of nothing, but at the time, he'd assumed that was euphemistic. Now, knowing she'd run away from home before she was eighteen, patching together waitressing jobs to pay her rent, he had a far greater appreciation for how hard she must have worked.

"Yes. I took online courses at night and worked during the day, massaging the blog on my breaks." She met his gaze over her water glass before taking a sip. "I was driven, yes. But that time in my life didn't feel nearly as difficult as managing my father had been. Once my life was under my own control, a lot of stress went away."

"How so?" He couldn't imagine navigating adult life as a seventeen-year-old being anything but stressful.

His own father might be a manipulative, controlling bastard. Nigel Striker hadn't approved of his friends, and he'd hurt Elena badly. But at least Gage had never had to worry about where his next meal was coming from, whereas Elena had to deal with that kind of poverty.

She stabbed a strawberry with her fork. The pair of violinists who'd been playing throughout the meal shifted from a complicated allegro to a lilting waltz.

"I didn't have to worry about getting kicked out of a house because the rent didn't get paid," Elena explained, dabbing her lips with her napkin. "Or the police carting off my dad and putting me into a foster home. I trusted myself far more than I trusted my father, and that made my life easier."

Gage finished the late-harvest zinfandel the sommelier had recommended with his dessert, realizing that this woman didn't put her faith in anyone lightly after the way she'd been raised. "On that note, Elena, I have to wonder what it will take for you to trust me again after the way I assumed the worst of you six years ago."

"You believe me now?" she asked, lifting an eyebrow. "Because I have a photograph of the destroyed check somewhere. I thought your father would come clean and tell you the truth one day, but apparently that never happened."

"I don't need photo evidence," he said firmly. "I shouldn't have jumped to that conclusion then, either. And there will come a time of reckoning between my father and me, but right now, I'm going to deal with the PR crisis the ranch is facing first."

"Fair enough," she agreed, pushing aside her half-eaten dessert plate as she studied him across the table. "But if you're asking about how I might trust you again, I think a place to start might be with some honest answers about Alonzo Salazar."

Wariness surged at the reminder of her reason for coming to Montana in the first place.

"Because your followers deserve the truth?" he asked, unable to suppress the trace of bitterness in his voice.

"No." Her dark eyes never wavered from his. "Because I do."

Gage recognized the line she'd drawn in the sand. If he wanted to move forward with their relationship, he needed to share something of himself. They'd dodged the difficult parts when they'd dated six years ago, and that had resulted in a bond that broke when they encountered the first major obstacle.

Now? He wasn't sure he was ready for the kind of relationship they'd been building toward back then. The aftermath when it ended had been painful for them both, and being with Elena would mean a permanent rift between him and his family. He'd dodged that kind of break his whole life, hoping that it wouldn't come to that since it would make things painful for his mother and his sisters.

But he didn't have to decide the future right now. He only had to decide that he wanted Elena for one more night.

And from that perspective, his choice was simple.

Gritting his teeth, he told the most painful truth of his life in the sparest of words.

"Alonzo Salazar was a mentor to me and all the Mesa Falls partners. And he was there for us after one of our friends jumped to his death in an accident that every damned one of us feels responsible for."

Elena felt Gage's hurt in those terse words.

Shock delayed her response, and in that stunned silence, their waiter had returned, effectively shutting down the talk. Gage signed his name on the check and helped her from her chair, no doubt wanting more privacy for a conversation that had moved in a completely unexpected direction. She waited while he settled a long satin trench coat on her shoulders—a gift from Mimi, the boutique owner Elena met today, after Elena had posted a photo of the garment.

Wordlessly, Gage escorted her through the casino to the valet stand out front, where the Land Rover quickly appeared. They made the short drive to the private residence Desmond had offered them for their stay, and once the vehicle was parked inside the garage bay, Gage opened the passenger side door for her.

"I'm so sorry for your loss," she told him quietly, not sure if he'd heard the words back at the restaurant when she'd said the same thing.

He seemed to have retreated from her somehow, but perhaps that was only because they'd been in a public space. Now, she kept hold of his hand, wrapping it between both of her own.

"Thank you. It's nothing I've shared with anyone else in my life." His jaw muscle flexed. "But you wanted to know why I remain loyal to Alonzo, and that time at school with my friends is at the heart of it."

She realized then how little she'd known him six years ago. They'd both coasted along on attraction without digging deeper to see the real people underneath. Was he finally ready to share something about himself?

"I'm surprised a tragedy like that could remain a secret for so long." Especially given the public interest in Alonzo Salazar over the past few months since his authorship of the bestselling novel had been revealed.

"It shouldn't have been such a secret." He gave her fingers a light squeeze before leading her into the house and closing the door behind them. "It's been one of my deepest regrets in life that my father threw his political clout and money around to ensure that the story of Zachary Eldridge's death didn't cast a shadow on us or the Dowdon School, even though all six of the Mesa Falls partners were with him when he died."

The bitterness in his voice was unmistakable.

"What happened?" she asked, letting Gage remove her coat, even as she realized he'd used the task to tuck behind her so his face was hidden from view. And she couldn't blame him. Even hearing about it—about a person she didn't know—chilled her to the core. At least his fingers provided a welcome warmth as they brushed her shoulders.

Gage led her into the sunken great room, switching on the fireplace before pulling her onto the twill sofa cushions with him. He sat forward on the seat, elbows on his knees as he looked into the flames.

"The seven of us were on a horseback riding trip. Our school had stables. We'd taken the horses out longer than we were supposed to—overnight—being rebels and not caring what kind of trouble we got into. Zach had been mysterious all week about some drama in his life, saying he needed us to 'man up' and be there for him."

Elena edged closer, laying her hand on his upper arm. Stroking lightly. "What was the drama?"

"Who knows? We didn't really ask straight-out at first. We just drank stolen hooch and forgot our collective worries, riding deeper and deeper into the mountains until we were mostly lost, but in a good way."

She tried to imagine Gage as a rebellious teenager, before he'd diverted all of that energy into finance. After seeing the posh, fussy home of the Striker family in New Zealand, it was easy to see that his big, expansive personality would have been stifled there. She remembered him saying that his father had sent him to school in the States specifically so Gage wouldn't embarrass their family.

"Did you ever ask? Even when you stopped for the night?"

He shook his head. "I fell asleep because I had too much to drink. I thought most of the other guys did as well, but later I learned Alec, Miles and Zach stayed awake late, talking. Maybe Zach told them more." Gage repositioned the wooden stag statue on the coffee table, tracing the antlers absently. "But the accident didn't happen until the next day."

"Accident?" She zeroed in on the word. When Gage had said before that a friend jumped to his death, she had thought the boy committed suicide. Had she misunderstood?

"Some of the guys wanted to go cliff jumping, but it had rained the night before and the conditions were all wrong for their plans." Gage shook his head, his eyes seemingly fixed on some distant point in the past. "I didn't think they were serious. I thought it was just posturing that would end with all of us getting on the horses and going back to school."

Her stomach knotted; she knew that must not have happened. She tipped her temple to his shoulder for a moment, offering what comfort she could.

"What came next was hotly disputed afterward." Gage moved the stag farther away from him, sliding the wooden creature along the table on its weighted, felt feet. "We all saw counselors in the weeks that followed, thanks to Alonzo's intervention. And the professionals helped us understand that our brains can rewrite traumatic events to make them…bearable."

Elena lifted her head, peering over at him. "What do *you* think happened?" She wound her hand around his upper arm. Squeezed gently.

"I believe Zach jumped. I never viewed it as a suicide because that was just the way the guy was wired—especially that weekend. He pushed boundaries because he said that a good thrill 'fed his art.'" Gage shrugged and drummed his fingers once on the coffee table. "He liked to live on the edge. But after one jump, he never resurfaced."

A pit opened in her stomach.

"Did anyone go in after him?" She hugged closer to Gage, rubbing her cheek against his shoulder. Comforting and taking comfort at the same time.

"Every damned one of us." His dark eyes flared with

something like defensiveness. "Weston was the only one to jump, which could have killed him, too. The rest of us went down to the rocks below and slid in the water that way. We searched until we could barely breathe, knowing all the while we were too late."

"I'm so, so sorry." She couldn't imagine the trauma of an experience like that for sixteen-year-old kids.

"My father showed his true colors in the aftermath, threatening to pull his support of a new library if the school didn't handle the press releases about the death the way he wanted." Gage closed his eyes for a moment. When he reopened them, there was a flinty determination in his gaze. "Our names were never mentioned in connection to the accident, nor was the school's. But while Nigel Striker was being a first-class selfish bastard, Alonzo Salazar did everything humanly possible to help us weather the loss of a friend."

The fierce loyalty of the Mesa Falls Ranch owners toward the *Hollywood Newlyweds* author began to make sense. No matter what Alonzo might have done after the boys went on to graduate, he'd been a friend and mentor to them through unimaginable pain after the death of their friend.

"No wonder you're protective of his legacy," she observed softly, shifting positions to stroke a hand along Gage's back. She felt the ripples of tension relax under her fingertips.

"He might not have been much of a parent to his own sons, but he was the best teacher imaginable to a bunch of kids hanging on to their sanity by the skin of their teeth. He found local jobs for the ones who needed physical activity, and he found causes for the ones who needed something to shout about. Wes ended up as a lifeguard, where he found his passion for saving people." Gage turned toward her, cupping her cheek in his palm. "For me, Alonzo knew that I'd been interested in investing after I did well on a project where we invested in an imaginary company. So Alonzo signed me up for an electronic trading account and put a few hundred bucks in it. Said I could lose it if I wanted, but if I made money, he wanted ten percent of everything."

"Really?" She hadn't expected that. She plugged in what she'd learned about Alonzo with this new glimpse of Gage's past. "Didn't he teach English classes?"

She tipped her cheek more firmly into Gage's hand, drinking in the feel of his caress. Craving more. Sensing that he needed the physical connection, too.

"Yes, but our school had a lot of curriculum overlap. He was friends with the business teacher and knew about the project." Gage lifted a dark eyebrow. "Good thing for me, I guess. I made both of us a tidy sum that year, and I became obsessed with investing."

"What about your friends—" she started to ask, but Gage laid a finger over her lips.

"I think I've had all the sharing I can handle for one night." The serious look in his eyes told her how much the conversation had cost him. But he didn't remove his finger from her lips, and his focus slowly lowered there. "I need to think about something else...or better yet, not think at all."

Elena's breathing quickened. Heat flared along with keen awareness of that sensual touch. His finger shifted slowly, back and forth, along her mouth. Her eyelids fluttered closed as she relished the feel of him there. Anticipating what was to come.

"In that case, let me share something with you," she whispered against the blunt fingertip before nipping it between her teeth.

She opened her eyes to see his pupils widening.

That was all the response she needed. Standing, she reached for the side zipper under one arm of her dress. Lowering it, she let the heavy sequined tulle fall away from her body. The gown pooled at her feet and she stepped out of it along with her metallic leather sandals.

Desire flared in his eyes, the heat of one look burning its way up her legs and over her belly and breasts.

Clad only in her panties and a strapless silk bra the same tan shade as her skin, Elena stepped between his knees.

"I don't know about you…" She skimmed her hands along his broad shoulders, wanting to make him forget everything else but this. Her. "But I've been dreaming about this moment all day."

Eleven

Stepping into his arms felt like coming home.

For a woman who'd never lived in the same place for more than eleven months until after she'd turned eighteen, that sense of homecoming was all the more potent to Elena. She tried not to think about that, not trusting the emotions as Gage's hands wrapped around her hips.

Instead, she lost herself in the warmth of his lips as he brushed a kiss along her ribs. In the huff of his breath along the scalloped lace of her bra. She began unbuttoning his white dress shirt, slipping open one fastening after the next while he skimmed touches up her sides. In the end, he had to help her with his cuff links, but she wrestled the shirt free, baring all that golden muscle to her hungry gaze. Standing, he spun her in his arms so her back was to him before he pulled the pins from her hair, letting the waves fall down her back briefly before he swept it to one side and kissed her neck.

For a moment, their reflection in a wall mirror captivated her. The sight of Gage wrapped around her, his muscles shifting as he caressed her, seemed pulled straight from her fantasies.

She traced a finger through the maze of tattoos on his arms where they banded around her waist, desire heating her from the inside out. His tongue darted beneath her ear, igniting a fresh wave of tingling sensations down her spine.

"Take me," she demanded, reaching up to comb her fingers through his hair. "Please."

She twisted around to face him again, cradling his face and drawing him close to kiss her. He tasted her lips with the skillful finesse of someone who knew his way around her body better than anyone. Better than she did. He wrapped one hand around the length of her hair, tilting her this way and that to give him the best access to her mouth. Her body quivered with pleasure and they weren't even naked.

He lifted her against him with one arm, hauling her close. She helped him by wrapping her legs around his waist and locking her ankles there. With his hands anchored under her thighs, he carried her easily to the bedroom, each stride a delectable torment that brought the hard length of him more fully against her sensitized flesh.

When he set her in the center of the puffy duvet, she unclasped her bra and tossed it aside while he unfastened his belt. His pants. Anticipation coiled inside her until one long, hot look from Gage threatened to send pleasure boiling over.

He hooked a finger in the silk of her thong and drew the fabric slowly down her legs. When they were naked at last, he was about to roll a condom into place when she nudged his hand aside to take over the task. He shuddered with her touch before he stretched out above her.

Breathless, needy, she skated caresses along his arms and chest until he anchored her thigh against his hip and entered her. The shock of sensation buried deep inside her was both sharp and sweet. She held herself still, waiting, adjusting, her fingers twisted in the duvet cover.

When he began to move again, she knew she wouldn't last long. Her gaze shifted to his and she found him looking at her intensely, with a tangle of emotions that confused her as much as her own. Closing her eyes again, she refocused on the physical sensations, feelings that made sense to her.

Gage leaned over her, whispering sweet words in her ear before he fastened a kiss on one taut nipple, drawing on the peak. Elena gasped, her hips bucking.

He drove deeper. Faster. And she was lost.

Her release rolled through her, burning away everything but the sweet fulfillment that came with it. She clung to Gage, hands on his shoulders, moving with him until he couldn't hold back any longer. He came with her, his back arching and his legs tensing. She held him tighter, savoring every moment that was too perfect for words.

When the sensations eased, Gage lay down beside

her, wrapping an arm around her and tucking her under the covers. She waited to catch her breath before she moved closer to kiss his shoulder. His chest.

He stroked her hair and she wondered if he was as reluctant as she was to speak. To shatter the bubble of time where they seemed to understand one another. It was an illusion, she knew, a false sensation perpetuated by all the amazing things they could make one another feel.

Wasn't it?

Not sure she was ready to find out, she tipped her forehead to his chest and felt the beating of his heart instead. Steady. Comforting.

For tonight, she was going to savor that much. The morning was soon enough to wade through the complicated ties that still bound them. She owed him something for turning her life around. It hadn't happened yet, but she could sense her world shifting, surging with new opportunities that hadn't been there before, thanks to him introducing her to Chiara.

Tomorrow would be soon enough to come up with a plan. To thank him and leave him to find someone suitable who would make the Striker family proud.

She just wished the thought of walking away didn't make her chest feel so incredibly hollow inside.

Leaning back into the buttery leather seat of the Learjet, Gage told himself it was a good thing that Elena had agreed to return to Mesa Falls Ranch so readily.

He'd been concerned that she would prefer to stay in Lake Tahoe for the rest of the week, given her new relationship with Chiara Campagna. No doubt Elena would want to explore the business opportunities that the friendship offered, and he certainly couldn't blame her for investigating those possibilities. Yet she'd complied with his wish to fly to Montana today.

He turned to watch her use the photo editing software at the workstation near the front of the aircraft. She'd been manipulating images for the last hour, testing fonts with the graphics and different filters. He recognized some of the garments in the shots—clothes she'd discovered in the casino's boutique or that she'd made herself. There were close-ups of hems and stitches, shoulders and necklines.

To a certain extent, filling her time with work was the norm for Elena Rollins. But Gage couldn't help but wonder if she was busying herself purposely to avoid talking to him. To avoid whatever was happening between them.

He'd sensed her pulling away somehow last night after an incredible sexual encounter. Or had it been the story about his past he'd shared that had left things feeling uneasy between them?

"How's it going?" he asked, unfastening his seat belt to join her at the workstation as the plane began its descent.

Glancing up at his approach, she combed her hair from her face as her brown eyes flicked over him. Memories of her dark hair sliding along his bare skin threatened to derail all his good intentions.

"I'm putting together an inspiration board that can double as creative content on my blog." She leaned back in her chair, her red-tipped fingernail tapping against the mouse, as he took the seat closest to her. "Now that

I won't be selling scandalous news bits to the tabloids, the pressure is on to ensure I can leverage a new revenue stream."

"If you need financial backing, Elena, I can give you extremely favorable terms." He'd barely gotten all the words out when she was already shaking her head.

"Thank you, but no." Shifting in her seat, her calf brushed his for a moment. Quickly, she repositioned herself to avoid further contact. "Too much potential for conflict of interest."

He bit back a retort, knowing the defensiveness he felt had more to do with this damnable sensation he had that she was pulling away from him.

Already.

She'd been back in his life for a handful of days, hardly enough time for them to iron out anything from the past, let alone think about what came next. And there hadn't been nearly enough time for him to enjoy having her back in his bed again.

"You might change your mind about the loan when I tell you I have a big favor to ask of you." He should have brought it up the night before when he'd told her about Zach. But when she'd given him the chance to leave the conversation behind and lose himself in her beautiful body, he'd been powerless to refuse.

"Gage Striker needs a favor from *me*?" She gave a self-deprecating smile. "Do tell."

Frustration knotted in his shoulders.

"I'm not sure why that would surprise you." He didn't understand how or why she'd lost herself in her unsuccessful marriage, but he wouldn't listen to her sell herself short. "You're a smart, enterprising woman on the verge of an exciting new chapter in your life."

For a moment, the only sound was the hum of the engine as the pilot throttled back the speed of the aircraft.

"Thank you." Elena nodded, a single wavy lock slipping in front of her shoulder. Vibrant red cashmere hugged her curves, the V-neck drawing his attention to a silver necklace consisting of her initial beside a diamond-encrusted star. "How can I help?"

"When Desmond called the meeting yesterday, he revealed some startling news about Alonzo's profits from the tell-all book." Since he was done doubting her, he shared the truth without hesitation. "The funds have been supporting a thirteen-year-old boy."

She frowned, sitting up straighter in her seat. "Didn't you say the accident was fourteen years ago?"

"Yes." He suspected his friends had all been awake late into the night trying to piece together that particular puzzle, but Gage felt confident the child didn't belong to Alonzo. DNA testing would prove it soon enough. "And we will continue to investigate that. But since the funds were also financing Alonzo's humanitarian efforts, we wanted to announce that. We hoped a concrete response to the public interest in the story would put an end to the speculation."

"And you're comfortable with only providing half a story?" she asked, crossing her legs in a way that drew his eye to the hem of her black pencil skirt where it grazed her knee.

"I don't think any of us feel compelled to account for every nickel of the guy's money." Gage lifted his attention from her legs, wishing they could have spent this flight in the sleeping suite through the door in the back of the plane. "But I thought I'd give you the right of first refusal for the piece to see if you want to pedal it to whatever outlet you planned to approach when you first came to Montana to explore the issue."

How damned ironic that he'd brought her to Tahoe in the hope of making her lose interest in the Salazar story. Now, he needed a way to entice her to stay in Montana long enough to figure out how to keep her in his life.

She nibbled her lip, a hint of pink gloss disappearing as she did so. "It's not like I'm writing for a venue winning journalism awards," she admitted drily. "I'll do it, but with the understanding that I'll donate my payment to one of Alonzo's humanitarian organizations."

"You would do that?" He hadn't anticipated her generosity, especially when she would need financing to start her next business.

He knew she'd arrived in Mesa Falls with precious little to her name, although perhaps his retrieval of her personal effects from her former home would make things easier for her.

"I won't allow any of your friends to think I was trying to make a buck off a—" her eyes lowered for a moment "—from the hard times you've all been through."

The reminder of Zach always nudged a dark, painful place inside him. Yet somehow, sharing the story with Elena and having her understanding eased a layer of the pain this time.

"Very well. You have my thanks. Our thinking was to offer you the scoop a few hours before we share the details publicly at a party similar to the one that brought you into my home in the first place." He had already sent a memo to the ranch's public relations director. Plans were in place to drop hints that an announcement was forthcoming, ensuring the event was well covered in the media. "We're coordinating a party for next Saturday."

That was over a week away. If he could convince her to stay on at the ranch for that long, Gage hoped it would be enough time to move past whatever barriers Elena was putting up between them.

The aircraft shifted slightly as the landing gear came out with a soft thud that vibrated through his feet. The movement sent her hand darting out to steady herself, her fingers landing on his forearm. The crackle of awareness was there for her, too. He saw it in her eyes before she pulled away.

"Okay." Elena shut her laptop and unplugged the cord, packing up her things for their arrival. "I can use the next week to brainstorm my business plan with Chiara, but I'll remain in Mesa Falls through the party as a way to thank you for the help you've given me this week."

A kind offer, but not at all what he wanted from her.

Gage considered his next move, not wanting to scare her off if she was already planning her life after their affair. He would simply use their remaining time together to remind her how good life could be at his side. For today, he would be grateful for the gift of one more week.

"Thank you." Picking up her hand where it rested on the workstation, he brushed a kiss across the knuckles, inhaling the orange blossom scent of her skin. "I can't deny that I'm looking forward to having you under my roof until then, Elena. I plan to make the most of every day."

* * *

A week later, Elena walked through a fashion studio in New York's Garment District, perusing a breakout Italian designer's new collection for a venerable French fashion house with Astrid and Chiara at her side.

Sample sizes of all the clothes shown in Paris last week hung neatly on rolling racks outlining the big, open space where natural light slanted through huge windows. It was a dream girls' trip, helpfully orchestrated by Gage in his quest to remind her of the perks of continuing their affair. Her stomach knotted at the thought of how much his thoughtfulness swayed her.

But for all the things he'd offered her, never once had he suggested he loved her. Better to enjoy this last hurrah with her friends before she returned to a more down-to-earth life on the West Coast. Alone.

"I can't believe you got us in here, Chiara." Elena sighed wistfully, sliding one hanger farther down the rack to take a better look at a pair of crepe de chine pants with a sexy silhouette that hugged the hips and billowed into a tulle puff midway down the calf. "Let alone that we have a private showing."

Nearby, Astrid squealed over a cashmere sweater dress with cutouts around the waist.

Chiara stood at one of the long windows, gazing down at West Thirty-Eighth Street. "Frankly, it was tougher getting you two to join me than it was to convince Noemi's assistant to let us in here for the day." Chiara fixed Elena with a sidelong stare, her perfectly drawn cat-eye makeup enhancing the sage green of her eyes. "Astrid gets a pass as a new mom, but I'm surprised I had to twist your arm, Elena, when Noemi is actively interested in seeing your drawings."

The invitation from the fashion luminary was both exciting and a little scary, but Elena couldn't pretend fear had anything to do with her reservations about making the trip to New York for the afternoon. She shifted the crepe pants to her left, fingers walking down the remaining hangers on the rolling rack.

"It isn't that I didn't want to be here," she admitted. "But I sense my time is drawing to a close in Mesa Falls and I hesitated to miss a single day with Gage."

The days were fun. The nights were hot enough to fuel a lifetime of sensual fantasies. But she'd indulged that kind of surface relationship with Gage before and knew it wouldn't be enough to keep them together long-term. It had been a careful balance this week to protect her heart and still savor the fun of being with him. She knew even before they'd returned to Mesa Falls that she wanted more from him.

And she felt deserving of more after selling herself short for too long—both with Gage and in the ill-fated marriage that came afterward.

Astrid tugged a silk skirt from the rack, the hand-kerchief hem floating gracefully around her ankles as she held the garment to her waist. "Gage loves you," she informed Elena matter-of-factly. "I'm not sure if he realizes it or not. But I've never seen him look at any-one else the way he looks at you."

The comment felt like a hit to her solar plexus, rob-bing her of breath for a moment and making her see stars behind her eyes as if she was oxygen deprived. Of course, Astrid was only guessing. She couldn't know

Gage's feelings any better than Elena did. Blinking rapidly, she moved to the next rolling rack with new determination to find an outfit for the party the ranch's
publicity department had put together for the following
evening. It wasn't a gala or a fund-raiser, just a private
house party with a DJ and a select guest list including a
handful of Hollywood celebrities, world-class athletes,
a Formula One race car driver and a couple of heavy-
weights from the music industry.

All of whom sounded like safer candidates for her
affection than the man who'd already broken her heart
once, no matter what Astrid believed about the way
Gage looked at her.

"Gage and I have had a long and complicated relationship," Elena explained, unwilling to get drawn into
those old feelings for him even though they'd resurfaced
at an alarming speed during her time with Gage. "But
whatever he might feel for me comes second to his loyalty to his family."

Astrid peered up at her curiously, settling an em-
broidered denim romper back on the rack. "Jonah once
called Nigel Striker a judgmental asshat. I remember
because Jonah gets along with almost everyone."

A sad smile pulled at Elena's lips. Chiara returned to
the rolling rack, her hand moving unerringly to a turquoise-and-green sari-inspired dress. She held it up for
their inspection, a light-as-air coordinating scarf fluttering where it wrapped around the hanger.

"This is you," Chiara announced. "It's a gown to
slay in, and exactly what you need to wear to the house
party."

Elena moved closer, drawn by the featherweight of

the layers printed with swirls of blue and deep purple. The sheer fabric around the shoulders and the effect of the scarf made her think of a butterfly.

"It's beautiful," she murmured, running her hand down the fabric. "The question is, will it be a gown to usher in a new chapter or end one?"

Saying goodbye to Gage wouldn't be easy, but she would fulfill her promise to share the story the ranch owners wanted to spread about Alonzo. After that, she had nothing tying her to Montana. Gage might romance her, but that didn't mean he loved her enough to break with his family to be with her. Nigel Striker had already proved he'd stop at nothing to ensure she stayed far from his son.

"Maybe the party will be a little of both," Chiara informed her, giving her a level look. "But that's okay. There's nothing wrong with walking away from what isn't working so you can move on to new opportunities."

Of course, she was correct. But crazy as it might be, Elena held out a sliver of hope that maybe things would be different this time. Gage had shared a deeply held secret with her. He'd given her a level of trust he'd never bestowed on anyone else. It had to count for something.

Because whether or not Astrid was correct about Gage's feelings for Elena, Elena knew without a doubt about her own emotions where he was concerned. Based on the deep fear in her gut about leaving him after the party, she understood that she'd passed the point of no return.

Somehow, she'd fallen for Gage for a second time.

Twelve

Finishing his meeting with the interior decorator he'd hired as a surprise for Elena, Gage checked in with the contractors who were already tearing out a media room in his home to remake the space into a work studio for her. The construction was moving quickly, and he appreciated the accelerated timetable since he wanted to unveil the new suite to her tonight after the party. She'd known the contractors were on-site at his house all week, but he'd told her they were installing a tasting room in another wing, forestalling more questions about his secret project.

He'd wined and dined Elena all week, hoping to convince her to continue their affair even after she left Montana. When he'd encouraged her to visit New York City with her friends, he'd used the time to take estimates from a handful of highly recommended decorators, finally choosing the guy who'd flown in for today's meeting.

The dude was someone familiar with Elena's blog, and he'd insisted she should be brought in on the decor before they went any further in planning. Gage had appreciated the decorator pushing back on his plans since he had raised a valid point. Elena's future as a designer seemed more and more probable. She'd surely want to weigh in on fabrics and colors for the "home within a home" Gage hoped to create for her. Surely if she had her own retreat space at his house on the ranch in Mesa Falls, and at his place in Silicon Valley, she would be enticed to visit both spots with him as often as possible. She would see that she was the only woman he wanted in his life.

Now that he'd seen how rootless she'd been as a kid, how much her father had dragged her from town to town hiding from the cops and battling his own demons, Gage hoped she'd understand the significance of what he was trying to offer her. A place she could always call home.

Stepping out of the studio, where new windows were being installed to increase the natural light, Gage thanked the head contractor and walked around the exterior of the house to make sure the work crew were being respectful of the grass and gardens. He needed to dress for the evening's event, the party where the owners would share the news about Alonzo Salazar's humanitarian efforts as a way to end the public interest in his story. The PR staff had chosen Miles Rivera's residence as the site for the get-together, hoping to maintain the security of the celebrity guests more easily in a private venue.

Satisfied with the work crew's use of a side lawn to park their trucks, Gage rounded the front of the house and pulled out his phone to let Elena know he would be ready in half an hour for the party.

Only to have a woman's familiar voice stop him cold. "Gage?"

He stopped. Confounded.

Because there, in his front entryway, stood his smiling mother and expressionless father. A designer suitcase rested between them. A liveried chauffeur wheeled a second piece of matching luggage from the back of a luxury SUV idling quietly in the driveway.

His parents looked older than when he'd seen them last. Not just because they were a little grayer. A network of worry lines crawled across each of their faces. The reality of the changes in them brought home to Gage how many years it had been since he'd seen them in person. Guilt pinched at his chest.

"Mom?" Gage stared at her in shock, wondering what on earth they were doing in the States and on his doorstep, tonight of all nights. "What's going on?"

"We're here for the party, Gage," she announced, her pink traveling suit and lightweight trench coat neatly pressed as if she'd journeyed from across town rather than across the globe. She appeared tentative for a moment, perhaps unsure of her welcome. Then she stepped forward to hold out her arms to him.

Regret burned that he'd made his mother doubt his affection for her. No matter what had transpired between him and his father, he didn't blame her for it.

Gage embraced her, pressing a kiss to her cheek as the scent of lemon verbena drifted from her, punching him in the gut with nostalgia despite his strained relationship with his parents.

"I don't understand why you'd come all this way to attend tonight's event." He addressed his father as he stepped back, knowing his parents' presence could send Elena running if he didn't handle the situation carefully. "The event is a publicity function for Mesa Falls Ranch."

A venture they'd never supported since it involved his friends from school, friends who'd been a source of aggravation for Nigel Striker more than once.

His father inclined his head a fraction. His gray suit lapel was decorated with a pin of the New Zealand flag. "Yes. A publicity function carefully calibrated to suggest a revelation about the ranch's tie to Alonzo Salazar." He spoke the name with obvious distaste. "A man I would have hoped you'd have erased all connection to long before now."

Frustration simmered, and Gage felt the painful tension in his temples. Behind them, his housekeeper was already opening the door to usher in Gage's mother. The driver brought the bags inside.

Foreboding loomed like a thundercloud, smothering him with the sense of inevitability. Tonight was going to be a disaster if he didn't get a handle on this unexpected visit fast. The last thing he needed was his father upsetting Elena after how hard Gage had worked this week to make tonight special.

"That's my business, not yours," Gage reminded his father, knowing he'd need to hang on to his patience with both hands if he wanted the evening with Elena to unfold the way he'd hoped. He'd invested too much time in his plans to have his father spoil them now. "And tonight's party is a private affair, but I'd be happy to meet with you tomorrow morning once you've both had a chance to recover from your trip."

New Zealand was nineteen hours ahead of mountain time in the United States. They had to be exhausted. He gestured to his housekeeper to prepare a guest room for them.

"We spent last night in Los Angeles," his mother assured him, sliding a coaxing hand around Gage's arm as she lowered her head to speak softly to him. "We've had plenty of time to acclimate. We're only in town for a couple of days, Gage. Attending the party will give us an opportunity to catch up."

Had his father urged her to guilt Gage into letting them attend? Suspicion mounted along with his irritation. He didn't have time for a big confrontation right now when the driver was due to deliver him and Elena to Miles's house in—he checked his watch—fifteen minutes.

What if Elena was ready early? She could make an appearance in the foyer at any moment. He needed to get his parents out of there.

"Nevertheless—" Gage freed himself from his mother's coercive hold "—we'll have to speak tomorrow. My housekeeper, Mrs. Merchant, will show you to your rooms."

Gage was unconcerned about how his father interpreted his limited hospitality, but his conscience niggled at leaving his mom standing in the hallway with her bags for the staff to oversee. In the end, he had no choice. He headed down the hall toward the back of the house, where he still had just enough time to change.

He'd almost reached the door to his suite when his father's cold voice echoed along the corridor, raking along Gage's last nerve.

"Elena Rollins. What in bloody hell are you doing here?"

The moment seemed surreal enough that Elena briefly hoped she was just having a nightmare.

When she'd arrived in the foyer to ask Gage's housekeeper to snap a few photos for her blog before the party, Elena came face-to-face with the harsh, disapproving man who still occasionally haunted her dreams. Nigel Striker, the man who'd attempted to buy her off and then failed to tell his son for years that she hadn't taken the bribe, was now blocking her path to the living room. He loomed almost as large as Gage, although his shoulders were more stooped now and his gray hair had thinned.

Nigel glared at Elena, while his wife—almost a decade younger than him, but looking equally world-weary at the moment—hurried closer to them.

"Nigel, please. We're Gage's guests," Rosalie Striker murmured, her eyes lingering on Elena briefly before returning to her intractable mate. "Let them get to their party and you can speak to Gage tomorrow."

Something about the woman's intervention freed Elena from the paralysis that seeing Nigel had induced. She wouldn't be intimidated by this man, even if he'd been needlessly cruel to her six years ago. Nigel Striker had simply exploited the weakness that had always existed in her relationship with Gage—the lack of deeper understanding and core trust.

"What am *I* doing here?" she parroted, minus the expletive. "I'm doing a favor for your son, who asked me to attend an event with him this evening."

Anger and an old resentment balled in her stomach. And as Gage entered the foyer from the opposite corridor, seeing him did little to ease those feelings, even if his expression registered concern for her.

Pivoting on her heel, she retreated down the hallway, charging back the way she'd come. She heard quiet, furious voices behind her, but she wasn't even mildly compelled to glance backward.

Gage had asked her to share a story about Alonzo that would feed some of the public fascination with him, and she had. More media outlets would pick it up tonight after the announcement at Miles Rivera's party. Gage had wanted her to attend the event with him, but as far as she was concerned, that part of the deal was off the table now that his parents were under his roof.

"Elena. Wait," Gage called to her as she reached the door to her suite.

The door to the same room where they'd hashed through the logistics of her visit just two weeks ago.

She paused with one hand on the knob, wishing she could scavenge a fraction of all that defensiveness she'd felt around him then. She'd come to this house ready to do battle with him, to take the story she wanted and— yes—maybe have a little revenge for how he'd treated her six years ago.

Now that she'd seen another side of him, a facet of his

kindness and a hint of the difficult journey he'd taken to be a different man from his father, Elena didn't have the heart to do battle with him the same way.

"I'm leaving," she told him quietly, forcing herself to meet his dark eyes. "I've filed the story you asked me to with *The Hollywood Metro*. I'll forward the check to your publicity director so she can give the proceeds to one of Alonzo's preferred charities. But I'm done here."

"No." He opened the door for her, apparently waiting for her to step inside. "Please, Elena. You can't go without giving me a chance to explain."

His gaze roamed over her, and she felt self-conscious in the turquoise-and-green gown that had made her feel so beautiful just half an hour earlier when she'd dressed for the evening with care. The fluttery fabric had matched her light, airy hopefulness. Now, the frothy material reminded her how foolish she'd been to hope for more from a man who still wanted—deserved—closeness with his family.

"You don't need to explain anything, Gage." She cut him short, fearing if they talked much longer she would humiliate herself by bursting into tears. She didn't move to enter the room. She felt so fragile at the moment she feared she might break if she took a single misstep. "Your parents are in town to see you, not me. And I'm not going to add fuel to the fire by remaining here when you and your dad already have a strained relationship."

"I'm not interested in repairing a relationship with my father after the way he's treated you." His words were softly spoken, but the fury behind them was still apparent. He stood just inches from her, still waiting for her to enter the office outside the bedroom he'd given her for her stay.

A visit that had come to an end, as much as she wished otherwise. She couldn't afford to ignore how this would inevitably turn out. Heartbreak delayed would only be heartbreak doubled.

"And what about your mother? Your sisters?" she prodded, trying to help him see the facts he'd been ignoring. "How happy are you going to be alienating your whole family for my sake? They're your flesh and blood, Gage. I'm just the woman sharing your bed temporarily."

"I want you in my life for more than that," he shot back, emotion flaring in his eyes.

Anger? Passion? She couldn't be sure. Her own emotions were so mixed up where he was concerned, she didn't have the clear-eyed judgment necessary to try to interpret his. She felt weary.

"For how long?" she asked, making one last effort to help him see that they were wrong for each other. To think otherwise had been delusional. "Right now, we have great chemistry. But will that still be there three years from now after you've cut yourself off from your family in order to be with me? Or will you wish you'd found someone that your family could embrace instead of someone they're determined to hate?"

"I don't need their approval, Elena." His tone was resolute. Final. "What my father wants doesn't mean a damned thing to me."

She'd like to think things could be simpler, but she couldn't help but remember her own father. No matter his shortcomings, she still wished she could have found a way to have him in her life. To fix the rifts between them so she still had someone she could call family.

"I understand that, Gage," she said sadly. "And what you want doesn't mean a damned thing to him, either. Which makes you far more alike than you realize."

That, at least, seemed to sink home. Some of the determined fire faded from his eyes.

"You really mean that?" he asked, his jaw jutting forward. "You can just walk away thinking I'm as unbending as my old man and I'll only get tired of you anyway?"

It would be different if he loved her. But he'd never said anything to give her that impression, and she refused to put her heart on the line for him a second time. Whatever feelings she'd developed for him again would remain her secret.

Her private heartbreak.

Gage reached for her, but she backed up a step, afraid that the attraction would make her lose sight of reason. Again.

"Why would I believe otherwise?" She stepped into the office outside her bedroom, ready to change out of her party clothes and forget this night ever happened. "I'm going to pack now, Gage. I'll get a flight back home as soon as I can."

His nod was jerky. Abrupt. And it was the only hint that he might be hurting, too.

"I need to put in an appearance at the party," he said finally. "If you leave before I return, would you consider taking a look at the room renovation before you go?"

She couldn't imagine why he would ask her such a thing. Why he would care about her opinion?

"I'd prefer not to run the risk of stumbling into your father." She had no desire to cross swords with Nigel Striker. Especially when Gage could obtain design advice from dozens of other people. "Good night, Gage."

Closing the door between them, Elena told herself it would be the last time she'd ever have to face that level of pain. And she prayed that was true, because one drop more and she would be destroyed. This was almost too much to bear. She'd encouraged him to maintain his ties with his family, but in doing so, she'd cost herself the closest relationship she'd ever had with someone. Because no matter that she'd married Tomas at a sad point in her life, Gage Striker had always held her heart.

Thirteen

Where the hell are you?

Gage read one text while five more rolled in, his phone blowing up with notifications from his friends as the evening wore on. He'd changed into his tux for Miles's party, but hadn't called for his car in case there was a chance he could figure out a way to keep Elena from leaving.

Anger at his father still clouded his head. How could he show up here—tonight—and ruin any chance he might have had with Elena? Again.

Now, Gage sat outside in the dark by the pool, staring up at his own house. The lights were still on in Elena's rooms. They were still on in his parents' suite on the other side of the house, too. The studio his contractors were working on remained dark. It had been foolish of him to ask her to look at it since the space hadn't fully taken shape yet. Without him there to explain what he was doing, she would just think he was putting in a tasting room, like he'd told her several days ago.

Defeat weighed heavy in his chest as he settled deeper into the cushion of the wooden pool lounger.

She was right here in his house, a sexy, beautiful and giving woman he wanted to be with, but he couldn't think of a damned thing to do to make her stay.

When his phone chimed again, he had the urge to chuck it into the pool to stop the buzzing. But seeing the notification from Miles—the host of tonight's shindig and the most levelheaded of the bunch—made him read the message.

How well do you know Chiara Campagna? Found her in my study, and I would swear she was rifling through my notes. Looking for something.

Seriously?

Gage wondered if Miles had been drinking, because it made zero sense that one of the most famous women in the world would want to find out secrets Miles Rivera was keeping. Of all the Mesa Falls partners, Miles would win the award for most apt to do the right thing.

Astrid and Jonah have known her forever. She's cool.

Unconcerned, Gage shot back the text and pocketed his phone. By the time he looked up again, he saw his mother heading his way. No longer wearing her travel suit, she was dressed in a long knit skirt and sweater with a cardigan over the top. He stood out of habit, even though he wasn't sure he wanted to talk to her. His frustration might be with his father, but then again, she hadn't done anything to help defuse the tension earlier.

"Mom, I'm not in the best frame of mind for a conversation. I'm going to have to confront Dad tomorrow, and I want to warn you, I feel certain it won't go well." He figured he might as well give her fair warning.

She settled onto the chaise beside him, her skirt billowing around her, the watery reflection of landscape lights illuminating her face. There was concern in her expression as she looped her arm through his.

"You mean about Elena Rollins refusing his bribe all those years ago?" she asked, picking lint from the arm of her sweater.

"He told you?" It shouldn't surprise him that his mother was party to his dad's deception. And yet it still stung.

"We were never sure what to make of it that you believed she'd taken the money when she hadn't." Rosalie Striker fluffed her dyed brown curls, her hairstyle still exactly the same as the one she'd worn in his youth. "We assumed she wanted you to think she took it. That she used the misunderstanding as a way out of the relationship."

"Only because I was quick to believe the worst of her. Since Dad lied to me." He had to take some ownership for his own actions back then, as did Elena.

Yet he placed the biggest blame firmly in his father's court.

"He did a foolish thing, Gage," his mom admitted,

crossing her ankles. "I hope you won't hold it against him forever. In his own way, he does love you."

And this was how he showed it? Defensiveness ate away at him, especially considering that Elena had just told Gage he wasn't all that different from his old man. Was he that unbending?

"Elena traveled halfway around the world as my guest only to be treated like a viper and asked to leave. Is it any wonder I'm not inclined to roll out the red carpet for Dad when he shows up here?" Gage's attention flicked back to the house, where a light snapped on in the media room he had been remodeling into a studio for Elena.

With no blinds on the new windows the work crew had installed, he could see her inside the house, dressed in jeans and a simple white blouse, pulling a suitcase behind her.

His heart stopped in his chest for a long moment before kicking to life faster.

"I've got to go." Standing, he didn't know what he was going to say to her, but he knew he had to try to find the right words.

Fear of her leaving ate away at his insides.

"Do you love her, son?" His mother's hand circled his as he stood, but her words were what glued his feet in place.

"Love?" Not that it was a foreign concept, per se. But he hadn't thought about it. Or maybe, more truthfully, he'd tried not to think about love and Elena in the same sentence.

Maybe because love hadn't worked out well for him in the past. His relationships with his parents—his father especially—had always been difficult. His closest friendships as a kid had resulted in a loss that left a lifelong wound.

"She's gotten closer to you than any other woman, Gage. Twice." His mother's eyes were wise, her tone gentle as she probed at the edges of his hurt. "Elena Rollins seems too important for you to let her get away."

"I'm going to do my best to make her stay," he assured her, needing to talk to Elena now. Before she got on a plane and never came back.

"You might have to tell her you love her, son." She tipped her cheek to the back of his hand. "Don't keep denying yourself happiness just because Zachary Eldridge didn't have the chance for a long, full life."

When she let go of his hand, it took him a minute to process that he was free to walk away now. Her words looped in his head, making no sense because he'd never thought that way. Never consciously made that sacrifice for the sake of a friend who'd been dead for almost half of Gage's life.

Had he?

Worry fueled his steps as he kept an eye on Elena turning in a slow circle inside the studio space he'd built for her. He feared her leaving, yes. He could admit that. And was it because he loved her?

Gage tried the idea on for size. Found it fit everything he was feeling. Explained everything that had perplexed and infuriated him about his relationship with her over the last couple of weeks.

He loved Elena Rollins. He'd been blind and unbending, but he could fix that. The one constant—the one thing that was never going to change—was how much he loved her.

* * *

Elena might not have realized what she was looking at in the room under construction in the back corner of Gage's mammoth house. Except that the work crew had left a big inspiration board propped up in a corner of the room, with drawings of every architectural element to be incorporated in a design project called "Elena's Studio."

Just seeing the title had made her knees feel a little weak. But then, peering back and forth between the half-finished space and the poster, Elena could see where the ideas on the outline were coming to life in the physical setting. Releasing the handle of her suitcase, she walked across the dark hardwood floor to read the notes under the heading "Window Nook" with a series of photos pinned beside it. The board showed ideas from a built-in chaise surrounded by bookshelves to a candlelit, faux-fur-covered bench with retractable blinds on three sides for privacy. The actual window seat in progress was a bump-out of floor-to-ceiling windows.

In another corner of the room, a raised platform was taking shape and the inspiration board suggested it could have mirrors on three sides for designing clothing on mannequins or doing fittings on real-life models.

Stunned to see the space that propelled her dreams that much closer to reality, Elena was speechless when she heard the door creak open behind her. She knew who would be there: the man who'd created this haven for her by listening to all of her half-formed dreams over the years, then translated them into workable goals for a crew that he'd said was building a wine cellar for him.

"I can't believe you did this." Her hand trembled a

little as she reached out to touch a new window with deep moldings above and below. "It's so much different in here than in the rest of the house."

Gage's home was a modern take on Western design, with natural stone and timber elements in a relentlessly masculine style. Here, the aesthetic was more formal and traditional, with architectural salvage pieces to give the place an older feel.

She glanced back at him, taking in his tuxedo shirt. His jacket was missing, and his bow tie remained undone, as if he'd dressed partway for the event and then reconsidered. He moved deeper into the room, his dress shoes lightly tapping the hardwood.

"I wanted it to look like a New York fashion house. Or a Paris artist's garret. Something that would transport and inspire you to create." He jammed his hands in his pockets, looking thoughtful. "I hired an interior decorator who's a real fan of your blog. But he said we needed to consult you on the design before I did anything else since the style should reflect you."

"You know me well, though. I couldn't have described what I wanted any more perfectly than what you've done here." She pointed to the inspiration board, where all the ideas were laid out with a range of design options for each.

"These are all your ideas, Elena," he said cryptically, his dark eyes moving over the poster. "Six years ago, on that trip up the Pacific Coast Highway, I asked you to tell me what your dream office looked like." He withdrew a hand from his pocket to gesture toward the style specs. "This is what you described."

He couldn't have surprised her more. Turning to face

him, she tried to remember that talk. They'd shared so much about their dreams. The future they both wanted. They just hadn't revealed much about their pasts.

"You kept all of those notes from that conversation?" she marveled.

"I made some notes that night in the hotel and tucked them in a file for one day down the road." His lips curved at one corner. "Believe me, at the time, I didn't think there'd be a six-year delay before I consulted them again."

And yet, he'd kept them.

Her heart melted into a puddle of love for him, and she wondered how she'd ever recover from loving him so much.

Then again, what did it matter if he didn't say the words that she wanted to hear when she had the proof of his feelings in front of her? All around her?

"I can't believe you did all of this in such a short amount of time." She blinked rapidly, daring to look at Gage with new eyes.

With hope.

Wasn't her time with Gage better than any other period in her life?

"It was my pleasure, Elena." He took a step closer to fold her hand in his, his warmth wrapping around her fingers. "I wanted to put everything I had into convincing you to stay with me. To be a part of my life."

She wanted to question him about that, but she sensed he wasn't finished yet, and she didn't want to forestall any insights on this man who confused her even when he made her deliriously happy.

Their conversation echoing slightly in the mostly

empty room, she realized it had been perfectly quiet for a long moment while they collected their thoughts.

"But I've been so busy trying to find tangible ways to make you stay that I may have missed something more obvious." He stared down at their clasped hands, and she could see his jaw flexing as he chewed on a thought she couldn't see.

Hopeful that he was trying to find an answer, pleased to know that making her happy was important to him, Elena lifted his hand and rubbed it against her cheek. The scent of his soap stirred sensual memories, reminding her how much pleasure they could find together. How in sync they were in so many ways outside the bedroom, too.

"It's not as though I haven't been tempted, Gage," she reminded him. "But I think I've wanted something more long-term than you. Knowing that your family doesn't want me in your life is a serious deterrent when my dreams of us have been more…" she pointed to the room around them where pillars and walls had been built to last "…permanent."

"Mine, too," he agreed quickly, unthreading their fingers so he could stroke a hand under her jaw. "I wanted to build this for you. Not just here, but at the Silicon Valley house, too. I've already lined up contractors to remodel a space for you there, as well."

His touch bolstered her as much as his words, the connection between them both physical and something more… But she needed to be sure, for him to be sure.

"Really? What about your family?" she asked, lifting her head up to remind him of that sticky dilemma. "I can't change my past."

"And I'd never want you to," Gage assured her. "My mother already understands that, but I'll have a conversation with my father in the morning. I'm letting him know that while I want them in my life, you come first. And if he wants to be welcome here, he'll find a way to embrace the unique person you are."

She didn't think it would be that simple, but she could live with that if Gage could. "You sound certain."

"I am. Elena, I love you." He caressed her cheek with his fingertips, then combed over the spot with the backs of his knuckles.

She was sure she'd misheard. His touch had distracted her. She went very still. "Excuse me?"

He leaned closer, tipping his forehead to hers. "I love you. I didn't know how much I was denying letting myself feel that way until—" He shook his head. "I'm sorry that I didn't see it before. That I didn't know it six years ago, because it was a mistake to let you go then, too."

She couldn't quite follow all the nuances of what he was saying, but the "I love you" had been as clear and plain as she could ever ask for. It cut through everything else to soothe her heart and assure her this could all work out.

"I love you, too, Gage." She lifted up on her toes to kiss the corner of his lips where he'd been frowning. "It's okay that you didn't know then. As long as you feel sure now."

"Sweetheart, I'm so sure." His New Zealand accent was thick as butter, making her smile even as it tantalized her. "I let my past do a number on me and I knew that was true on a lot of levels, but I didn't realize until just now that I let it rob me of the future I want with you, too."

"How so?" Now that he seemed as relieved as she felt to recognize that what they had was too special to let go, she couldn't help but wonder why he hadn't seen that sooner.

"The role modeling for love in my family—" He shook his head. "Well, you've seen what that looks like. But it didn't matter as a kid once I found friends. Solid, meaningful friendships that were better than any family as far as I was concerned."

Shadows moved through his eyes.

"And then Zach died." She was so grateful he'd shared his past with her, offering her a window of insight she'd been missing six years ago.

"Losing him made it tough for me to let good things into my life. But I know that was wrong of me." He skimmed a touch along her shoulders before tracing the path of her hair down her back. "I should be honoring his memory by living life to the fullest—the way he always did."

"I know what's between us is right." She'd tried loving someone else and the results had been painful for them both.

"I do, too. And I know we'd be damned fools to let go of it again."

"I don't want to be a fool." A laugh bubbled up in her throat, a new happiness crowding her chest. "I feel so lucky to have a second chance."

Hope filled her heart.

"So you will consider a future with me, Elena Rollins?" he asked, wrapping both arms around her and pulling her flush against him. "Will you unpack your suitcase and stay right here? Let me build you a space that's just for you here and in Silicon Valley?" He tilted her face to look deep into her eyes. "Because I want you to always know that whenever you're with me there's a permanent home for you that's just the way you want it."

His words—the sentiment behind them—showed her how thoroughly he understood her. Emotions clogged her throat. "That's a really nice thing to offer a woman who never stayed in one place for more than eleven months until after I turned eighteen."

"You'll always have a home with me." He brushed a kiss over her lips. Soft. Tender.

With the promise of so much more.

* * * * *

COMING SOON!

We really hope you enjoyed reading this book. If you're looking for more romance, be sure to head to the shops when new books are available on

Thursday 6th March

To see which titles are coming soon, please visit

millsandboon.co.uk/nextmonth

MILLS & BOON
MODERN
Power and Passion

Prepare to be swept off your feet by sophisticated, sexy and seductive heroes, in some of the world's most glamourous and romantic locations, where power and passion collide.

MILLS & BOON
HISTORICAL

Awaken the romance of the past

Escape with historical heroes from time gone by. Whether your passion is for wicked Regency Rakes, muscled Viking warriors or rugged Highlanders, indulge your fantasies and awaken the romance of the past.

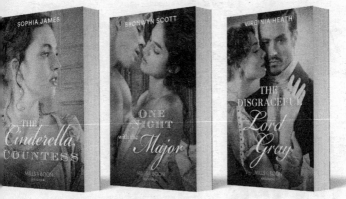

MILLS & BOON

THE HEART OF ROMANCE

A ROMANCE FOR EVERY KIND OF READER

MODERN

Prepare to be swept off your feet by sophisticated, sexy and seductive heroes, in some of the world's most glamourous and romantic locations, where power and passion collide.
8 stories per month.

HISTORICAL

Escape with historical heroes from time gone by. Whether your passion is for wicked Regency Rakes, muscled Vikings or rugged Highlanders, awaken the romance of the past.
6 stories per month.

MEDICAL

Set your pulse racing with dedicated, delectable doctors in the high-pressure world of medicine, where emotions run high and passion, comfort and love are the best medicine.
6 stories per month.

True Love

Celebrate true love with tender stories of heartfelt romance, from the rush of falling in love to the joy a new baby can bring, and focus on the emotional heart of a relationship.
8 stories per month.

Desire

Indulge in secrets and scandal, intense drama and plenty of sizzling hot action with powerful and passionate heroes who have it all: wealth, status, good looks...everything but the right woman.
6 stories per month.

HEROES

Experience all the excitement of a gripping thriller, with an intense romance at its heart. Resourceful, true-to-life women and strong, fearless men face danger and desire - a killer combination!
8 stories per month.

DARE

Sensual love stories featuring smart, sassy heroines you'd want as a best friend, and compelling intense heroes who are worthy of them.
4 stories per month.

To see which titles are coming soon, please visit

millsandboon.co.uk/nextmonth

JOIN US ON SOCIAL MEDIA!

Stay up to date with our latest releases, author
news and gossip, special offers and discounts, and
all the behind-the-scenes action
from Mills & Boon...

 millsandboon

 millsandboonuk

millsandboon

t might just be true love...

LET'S TALK

Romance

For exclusive extracts, competitions
and special offers, find us online:

f facebook.com/millsandboon

🐦 @MillsandBoon

📷 @MillsandBoonUK

Get in touch on 01413 063232

For all the latest titles coming soon, visit
millsandboon.co.uk/nextmonth